Marionette

a novel by
T. B. MARKINSON

COPYRIGHT © 2013 T. B. MARKINSON

Edited by Karin Cox
Cover Design by Erin Dameron-Hill

This book is copyrighted and licensed for your personal enjoyment only. All rights reserved. No part of this publication may be reproduced, stored in a retrieval system, or transmitted in any forms or by any means without the prior permission of the copyright owner. The moral rights of the author have been asserted.

This book is a work of fiction. Names, characters, businesses, places, events, and incidents are the product of the author's imagination or are used fictitiously. Any resemblance to actual persons, living or dead, events, or locales is entirely coincidental.

Chapter One

THE PLAN WAS simple. There were only three steps. Three! And I still fucked up.

Step one: write letter.

Step two: draw bath.

Step three: razor.

I'm not sure how I screwed it all up. What kind of idiot can't follow three simple steps? Maybe there should have been four steps. The fourth would have included time, would have made sure I had enough time for step three to work. I didn't allow enough time. To be honest, I didn't know how long it would take. I still don't. But I learned that it isn't instantaneous.

A gun would have been instantaneous. Jesus! Why didn't I think of that first? That's why men succeed more: they use guns. *Pow!* Sayonara!

I'd had enough time to cut both of my wrists. I thought the razor might hurt, but I don't remember any pain. I remember yelling. I wasn't screaming; Jessica was. She wasn't yelling at me, or maybe she was. I wasn't listening. People say that's one of my biggest problems:

I don't pay attention. In my defense, she wasn't making much sense, so I didn't bother listening. In her defense, if I came home to that, I don't know if I would have been polite and coherent either.

Imagine coming home to find your girlfriend in your bathtub with slit wrists. And I don't even live with her. I have a key to her apartment, but I don't pay the rent or the bills. How rude of me. I didn't account for the untidiness either. It wasn't fair to assume Jess would want to clean up that kind of mess. She did, though. Jess wanted to destroy all of the evidence that I had tried to off myself. I think she did it more for her own peace of mind.

I couldn't implement my plan in my own home. What am I saying? I *didn't* implement my plan. I *failed*.

Failure.

I can add that to my list of accomplishments. It's a growing list. Accomplishment isn't the right word per se, but if all you have are failures to your name, I find it's best to think of them as accomplishments. Probably not the best attitude, but I haven't been in a fabulous frame of mind lately.

People keep telling me I'm too hard on myself. What the fuck do they know? No one knows, not even Jess.

I wouldn't say I'm having a *Bell Jar* moment. Plath was going crazy; I'm not.

Jessica flipped the shit out on me. Who could blame her? I think she feels like a failure too, since she's been trying to help me, and she loves me. Why she does is beyond all comprehension. Sure, sometimes I can be funny. But most of the time, I'm serious. The rest, I'm sad—trapped in my past, reliving the same events over and over in my head.

I know people say they have emotional baggage. Do they know what they're talking about? I have baggage. I'm not bragging about it.

MARIONETTE

I'm just stating the simple truth. I'm an effed-up individual who dwells on the past and tries to numb myself constantly. I don't use drugs, although I'll drink. I just numb myself by disappearing when I'm with people.

Jessica thinks I need to stop my destructive behavior. Sure, sure. I'll just plant my feet firmly on the ground and stop. If only it were that easy. If it were, then I'd do it. At least I *think* I would do it.

I don't mean to knock Jessica. I love her. God, I love her. But I don't know how to explain to her ... how to tell her that I'm broken. Beyond repair. There's not enough glue to put me back together.

Maybe the issue is me. I know that seems obvious. I slit my wrists, after all. No one made me. I did it. But hear me out. Millions of people have difficult lives, yet they still function. Again, I swear this isn't a *Bell Jar* moment. I'm not bonkers. Confused: yes. Scared: check. Angry: most definitely. I spend most of my time annoyed with people. Why do they have to be so fucking stupid?

I like to study history. The history of the little guy. Don't get me wrong, kings, queens, explorers and shit, they're all cool, but I like to see how the little guys make it. How do they survive hardship? Like Elie Wiesel—he survived the Holocaust for Christ's sake, and then he wrote a book about it. I read that book a lot. If he could survive that, why can't I survive my past? Why do I always go back? I didn't live in Auschwitz. My home life sucked. Sucked big time. My parents are horrible people. They do not like me, not one bit. But my home isn't Auschwitz, and my parents are not Nazis. Why can't I be a survivor, be like Elie?

It isn't like I always go back to a particular incident. I'm not a time traveler. (This isn't a *Slaughterhouse-Five* scenario either. I'm not Billy Pilgrim.) I just check out. I don't know where I go, but I'm gone. I'll stop talking—that's another way to become invisible. I might nod my head, act like I'm listening. I'm not. Most people, though, don't really care whether anyone else is listening. Many people don't even notice. They just want to talk. They just want to *feel* as if someone is listening. How many people really care what others think? Not many, from my experience. That's one of the hardest things to live with, feeling alone. Even when I'm with others I feel alone. Even more so. I don't think many people can relate to me. I know I can't relate to them. I feel like I'm on the outside, looking in.

Disappearing all of the time has perpetuated this feeling of being alone. Logically, I should stop disappearing. But my brain doesn't think logically. I'm not sure how it thinks, but I don't feel logical.

I feel ... well, I don't know how I feel. Confused. Scared. Angry. Alone. But now that I think about it, I'm not sure that's true. At times, I'm sure I feel all of those emotions. Other times, I don't feel. Not at all. I don't get it. I wish I could, but I don't.

Explanations—that's what I seek. I've always been one who wonders who, what, and why, which is just another reason I love to study history. Every history test has those "who am I?" questions, and I nail them every time. In fact, I'm a brilliant student. I don't mean to brag. I'm just stating the facts. School and I get along. I have a photographic memory; some think that's cheating, but I can't change it. It's nice if you want good grades.

But when it comes to asking those questions about myself. Who am I? What am I? I can't really answer them. They seem fairly obvious, right? I'm me. I'm a girl. And I'm not one who wants to be a boy, even if I'm in love with a girl. I think people who think that are idiots. Usually, though, they don't see that. I wish idiots would recognize that they're idiots. Life would be so much easier if others said, "Don't bother with me, I'm an idiot."

Marionette

Let's start again, at the beginning. I slit my wrists. My girlfriend came home. She went ape-shit. I got stitches in both arms. I felt a little like Frankenstein—the monster I mean, even if that's not really correct. Everyone thinks the monster's name is Frankenstein, so I'm not about to correct them and tell them it was the doctor's name. My point is that I was patched back together and told to be normal, to be human. Victor Frankenstein, the scientist, didn't try to teach the monster, but at least Jess is trying to teach me how to be normal. How to be human.

I shouldn't scar too much. Oh, there are visible marks that make me self-conscious, but I didn't cut deep enough, which leads some to think I did it for attention. You know what I have to say to that: Fuck off!

I didn't have enough time. It wasn't to get attention. I hate needy people; I'm not one of them. Jess has a doctor friend so I didn't have to go to the hospital for stitches. We both know what would have happened if my parents had found out.

My parents—what can I say about them. Dad is rich, successful, and many people like and respect him. I'm not sure why, because he's a sonofabitch. Mom, well she might be a lunatic—I mean legit crazy. Not born that way, made that way. My twin sister, Abbie, she disappears in different ways. I'm not sure who has the healthier way of disappearing. We aren't close. I wouldn't say we're rivals. We just don't get along. It's like we aren't sisters at all. We're not identical, and since birth we've been moving in different directions. In the fall, she's heading out east for school. I'll be three hours away from home, a little over two hours from Jess.

I don't get along with any of my family. I don't really care to. They aren't nice people. I'm not saying that I'm nice. In fact, I bug the shit out of myself most days, but I hope I'm not like them.

Especially my mom. I hope I'm nothing like her. My father is a controlling asshole. But Mom—she's in a class of her own. Evil. She's evil.

Yes, it's normal for teenagers not to like their parents. To think they don't understand, don't care, and just want to ruin their children's lives. I've seen all the John Hughes movies. I would kill to have parents who are just clueless. Mine aren't clueless—well, maybe about one thing. They don't know I'm gay. They might suspect it, but it's never been confirmed. If they find out, I'll be sent away. Not to a happy place. I'm talking about institutions where they chain you to walls and shock the shit out of you. And not just by what they say. Literally, they shock the shit out of you. Zap! Sometimes people die mysteriously in these joints. Trust me, I know. Don't believe me, ask Alex. Oh wait, she's dead. You can't.

They cannot find out! I don't want to go away—not to that place. They have wanted to do that for a long, long time.

In fact, maybe cutting my wrists wasn't really the beginning at all. Maybe it just leads to the beginning. Did I forget to tell you that I'm seventeen? I always forget my age. I feel so old. I was born in 1974. It's 1992. Ninety-two minus seventy-four makes eighteen. Now you think I'm a liar. But my birthday is late in the year, which is why that's a little confusing. I've always been the baby in my class. Yet, I was always the tallest girl in my class, too. It never made sense to me. I think I was right at the cutoff for waiting another year to start kindergarten. My mom didn't like having me around, so she sent me early. If she had waited, I would have been one of the oldest kids in class; probably still the tallest, though.

I'm a giant compared to my mom. I'm almost six feet. She's barely five. How? Ask Mendel.

Later in the year, I'll be eighteen—an adult.

Marionette

But I've been an adult since I was born. I made a deal with Jess that I would begin therapy when I started college. Like that's going to help. I can't blame Jess. She doesn't know why I did it. I can't tell anyone. And no one would believe me either.

Now that I'm getting ready to "officially" become an adult by graduating high school, Jessica thinks I should get my act together. That's the nice way of saying, "You're effed in the head, pull it together, Paige."

Paige. Paige Alexander, that's my name. I usually don't tell people my last name, though. My dad is well known throughout the West. We live in Colorado, but if you travel through that region, you'll find most know his name.

Jessica says a therapist can help me pull it together. The college I'm attending in the fall has a University Counseling Center. Since I don't want my parents to know, I can't afford a super-expensive therapist. The school's therapist is free for the first five sessions and then fifty bucks a pop after that.

Money isn't an issue for me. Dad puts money into my account each month. My parents' names are on my account, so I live a cash-only existence. Another way to disappear. They can track my ATM withdrawals, but they don't know where I spend my cash. Usually, I don't know either. It's so much easier to spend cash. It's like Monopoly money. One instant, I have a wad of bills, then the next, nada. I wish I had a cool money clip. I should look into getting one. Something that makes me look tough, like a gangster. People don't mess with gangsters.

I'm not a gangster, though. I'm a scrawny white girl. I've been told I'm good looking. I have long legs. People seem to like girls with long, slender legs. I don't. When you aren't coordinated and you have long legs, you fall down a lot. I've broken many bones.

It's taken seventeen years to do all the damage, and now I hope to fix it in one. I promised Jess I'd go to therapy for at least a year. Not sure it'll work, but I made a promise. I'm good with promises. Well, mostly. I recently broke one. To be honest, I was forced to break it. It nearly killed me—literally.

One year.

Jess wanted me to agree to four years—the entire time I'm in school! I didn't want to set that precedent since I plan on going to grad school. I don't want to be in therapy for the next eight to ten years. How depressing would that be? Seriously fucked-up people go to therapy for that long. I'm not fucked up. I just want to control my own fate, not be a puppet for others.

I'm not a sociopath. Wait ... would therapy even help them? Doubt it.

Will the therapist give me one of those personality tests? You know the ones with letters that pinpoint your type. I never know how to answer those questions. Are you organized? Yes ... except when I'm not.

Many have said I'm a "Type A personality." Here are the characteristics:

Ambitious (check!);

Rigidly organized (semi check);

Highly status conscious (my parents force this one on me);

Sensitive (well, that seems unnecessary. Why not just call me a crybaby?);

Cares for other people (yes and no);

Truthful (flat-out no);

Impatient (YES!);

Always trying to help others (in most cases);

MARIONETTE

Takes on more than one can handle (yes, but didn't have a choice);

Wants others to get to the point (well, duh! Who doesn't?);

Obsessed with time management (uh, I mentioned earlier that I failed with time management).

This list doesn't include knowing that I'm always right. It should include that. It should also include knowing that most people are fucking morons. How do they keep surviving and breeding? Also, I think everyone should get out of my way. I like to get from point A to point B fast. I hate pedestrians and drivers who lollygag. If you want to be lookyloos, by all means. Just get the fuck out of my way!

Back to this whole time-management thing. I think I should just get on with it. How long does an introduction need to be anyway? I could have simplified things for you.

I'm seventeen. A girl. I'm going to college in a few months. My whole life is in front of me.

I slit my wrist two days ago.

I'm not insane, but I act like I am.

Why?

Chapter Two

I OPENED THE door to the stairwell. Something about the place screamed: DO NOT ENTER.

For one thing, it smelled like crap. Also, it led to the basement. I've never been fond of basements. The basement is where old people stash all of their junk, which they can't throw out because they're "attached" to it. But it's just crap. Throw it out, fools.

My parents didn't keep anything in their basement. It was spotless. No boxes, toys, photos, furniture, or anything. It was empty. It was like our family didn't have a past at all. Abbie had some childhood photos in her room. I had none. As far as I know, none were taken. Weird, huh? Why would one twin have photos, but not the other? I know I popped out second, but I didn't think second-child syndrome started instantly.

Staring at the stairs that led to the basement, I hesitated. I didn't want to go. I know I made a promise, but shit, people break promises all the time; however, I wasn't one of those people. I sighed and continued my trek down.

On the stairs, I bumped into a woman who looked to be in her twenties. She mumbled, "Excuse me," and then rushed up the stairs. I think she was crying. Great. Just great. They should have a separate entrance and exit, I thought. Not the best planning to have clients see how others looked after their session.

In the hallway, I noticed a sign for the center. In gigantic block lettering it read: UNIVERSITY COUNSELING CENTER. Not only was the lettering huge, it was bright yellow. I was surprised they didn't paint a fucking happy face on it, just to make it more obnoxious. Was yellow lettering supposed to make me feel happy? Calm? Peaceful? It made me angry.

Don't try to influence my feelings. I hate it when people tell me what to think.

An overweight woman sat behind the front desk. She was on the phone. I've mentioned I hate waiting, right? I didn't show any emotion. She smiled at me and held up a finger to let me know she would be right with me.

Annoyed by this, I did my best to look happy. *Think yellow.* I frowned. There, that's my normal look.

Actually, I think my normal look is one of confusion. Whenever I walk into a store, an employee always immediately asks if I'm lost or if I need help. It implies that not only do I look confused, I also look like an imbecile. That makes me mad, so I sometimes overreact and tell the employee to shove it—at least, I do in my head. I'm not an outwardly confrontational person, but if these people could hear my internal dialogue, they would know where to go and exactly what I thought of them. Then they wouldn't give me that silly grin that says, "Everything will be fine. Would you like a lollipop?"

No it won't. Fuck off.

The large woman wore a floral print blouse, a bright scarf, and earrings that dangled down to her shoulders. She also wore a ridiculous amount of eye shadow and liner. Her carefree appearance and bright clothes pissed me off. Why are they forcing it down my throat here?

"Yes, can I help you?"

I wanted to tell her to shove it; instead, I replied, "Yes, ma'am. I'm here to see Liddy Elliot."

She glanced down at the calendar to make sure I wasn't lying. Why someone might lie about having an appointment with a shrink was beyond me, but I guess they do see a lot of crazies.

"Ah, yes, Paige. You're marked down for two." She tapped my name on the appointment book with her pencil.

No shit, Sherlock.

"She's expecting you. So feel free to go into her office. Liddy will be right with you."

I was puzzled. This was my first appointment. Didn't the book scream: newbie! There was a maze of hallways. Was I supposed to know intuitively where I would find her office?

"Can you point me in the right direction? I'm completely turned around down here."

"Tell you what, I'll walk you to her office. Hers is the most difficult to find." She raised her bulk to reveal tailored black slacks and heels. She did have style. I looked down at my jeans and long-sleeved T-shirt, feeling awkward. At least my clothes were clean, albeit slightly wrinkled. Jess bought me an iron a year ago. It's still in the box. It makes a great doorstopper.

As we entered a long hallway, I noticed that most of the offices had the doors shut with signs on them that read: SESSION IN PROGRESS. DO NOT INTERRUPT!

What happened to the perkiness?

"You're really lucky. Liddy is one of our best." The fat woman

Marionette

sounded genuine.

The best, huh. Were they worried I would slit my wrists and spoil their carpet in the front office? That would dash their bubbly message. I smiled at the woman and then looked at the floor.

"Here we are. You can just go in, and Liddy will be right with you."

I stood back and peeked inside the room. How had I ended up here, in some crappy room, hidden away in a basement? Turning to say thank you, I scrutinized the woman who was already scurrying back to her desk to help more crazies.

The hallway was deserted. If I made a break for it, I wouldn't be noticed. Probably not missed either. The first session was free. Maybe I could just convince Jess I was seeing a therapist. Just act happier around her. Think yellow! How hard could that be? And I shouldn't get caught slitting my wrists again, not that she kept any razors or other sharp objects in the apartment anymore. She even got rid of the stapler and three-whole punch. I'm not sure what she thought I planned on doing with those. Can you imagine trying to staple yourself to death? Only a lunatic would attempt that.

I squinted to see further into the room. It was the size of my bathroom. A black and white picture of a mountain being strangled by clouds hung on the wall. Ansel Adams maybe. A calendar featuring Dalmatian puppies decorated the other wall; it was two months behind. There were two chairs and an area rug. How did they find such a minuscule area rug? Maybe it was a bathmat passing as an area rug.

"It's okay. You can go in."

The voice scared the bejesus out of me, and I jumped.

"I'm sorry, I didn't mean to startle you."

I felt ridiculous. I turned to look over my shoulder and saw a beautiful, petite woman. Long blonde hair cascaded down her back. Her soft cobalt eyes and her diminutive mouth both seemed to smile.

"Um … you must be Dr. Elliot." I did my best not to sound like a ninny.

I failed. Add it to my list.

"Yes, I am. And you must be Paige." She reached for my elbow. "Come on, we'll do this together." She guided me into the room and over to a chair, and then she gently shoved me down. For a little gal, she was surprisingly strong and graceful.

She must manhandle a lot of cuckoos.

Liddy walked over to her desk, set her briefcase down, and picked up a notepad and pencil. Looking back at me over her shoulder, she smiled. Her hair covered half of her face. She was doing her best to make things easy for me. It wasn't working. I wish I appreciated the effort, but all I wanted was to bolt from the room.

I scrutinized her again. She had a perfect body. Five feet, five inches would be my guess. With her curves and her sweet scent, she didn't resemble Sigmund Freud at all. I imagined he smelled of sweat, sex, and tobacco. Not sure why, but that's how I imagine him. She smelled like an orange grove on a summer day.

"Do you always study everyone you meet, Paige?" Her smile indicated she was teasing me.

"Nope. Just the ones who are going to put their nose into my business."

She nodded. "I guess we should get down to it then." Her voice was too masculine for someone so feminine and petite.

Sitting down, she said, "As you know, I'm the psychiatrist appointed to you through the university."

Lucky you.

She didn't take the bait, presumably because she couldn't read minds.

"I thought today we would just talk and get to know each other," she said.

"Don't you mean you want to assess the damage?" I tugged on my shirtsleeves to ensure the scars were completely covered.

"That's not exactly what I meant, Paige. I would like to talk so we can find a way to help you."

We? What does she mean we?

"So you want to probe my brain. See what makes me tick. You can probe all you want, but if you even try to make me run through a maze in search of cheese I'm out of here." I tried to laugh but couldn't force it out of my throat.

She looked like she was thinking of what to say next. "Therapy may seem like going through a maze at times, but I don't think the prize will be a piece of cheese."

A prize? Oh boy? This is just as exciting as eating a box of Cracker Jacks. Maybe it will be a plastic ring that pinches my finger. I really like those. Or maybe a fake tattoo; now those are cool. I crossed my legs and arms. Trying to be sassy and in control exhausted me, even if Liddy couldn't hear my efforts.

She tapped her pencil against her notepad, and then continued. "Maybe 'prize' wasn't the right word."

"Are you going to turn me into a freak? Have me shave my head and hand out flowers to people at the airport?" Now *that* would be a nifty reward. Personally, I'd never seen these people at the airport. I remembered seeing them in many of the movies from the eighties. I'd always wondered if they actually existed.

Liddy adjusted herself in her chair and leaned forward, not too close to push the boundary, but too close for my comfort. "No, Paige. Shaving your head would be too easy. I plan to do something much worse to you."

I imagined beads of sweat forming on my brow.

"You might wish, at times, that I would just shave your head and give you a handful of flowers to hand out."

This woman was playing hardball.

Liddy continued to ask me questions and I answered them to the best of my ability. Then she asked one that stood out. "When did you decide to start therapy?"

I didn't decide. It was decided for me. "I promised someone." I looked over her head at the door. It was shut, but not locked. I could still make a break for it. Technically, I had seen a shrink. Promise fulfilled! But Jess still had me on the one-year technicality. Shit!

"Do you want to be here?"

I hesitated. I didn't know the answer. "Can I get back to you on that one?" I bowed my head to avoid eye contact.

"Thank you. I appreciate the honesty. That's a start at least."

What a relief! And here I thought I wasn't impressing her at all. "Are you currently in a relationship?" Her curious eyes screamed, "I want the truth."

"Uh ... do you mean do I have a boyfriend? Nope. No boyfriend." I smiled inwardly at my cleverness.

She continued. "Do you have trouble sleeping?"

I noticed she had a checklist on top of her notepad. Was she literally asking routine questions? Would every session be like this? I bet I could find a book in the library and predict the questions. Sweet! Cheap shrinks are easy to manipulate. I tried to mask my happiness.

"Sometimes," I mumbled.

That was a lie. All of the time. But I couldn't say never. Why would I be in therapy then?

"What activities do you like doing?"

This one confused me. "You mean like reading?" I scratched the top of my head.

She nodded enthusiastically, encouraging me. "Yes. What types of books do you like to read?"

I almost blurted out, *Night*, by Elie Wiesel, but quickly changed my answer to, "Mysteries and such. I like Sue Grafton a lot."

She made a mark on her paper.

"What type of student are you?"

Again I stared blankly. What did she mean? Was she reading the questions wrong from the paper?

"Do you get good grades? Do you have difficulty concentrating in class?" She motioned with her hand implying etcetera.

"Oh." I nodded my head, catching on. "I do okay." Looking at my feet, I determined not to tell her I always got As and that I had a photographic memory. Let her think I was a dunce. The less she knew the better.

"Do you drink or use drugs?" she inquired casually.

Her relaxed tone floored me. Was she trying to trap me? Why would anyone answer truthfully? Was I supposed to say, "Why yes, I'm hardly ever sober. Had four beers on my way here." Did she think asking me in a tone that implied she didn't really care and she was cool, would make me confess all?

"No, of course not." I tried to sound indignant.

Liddy paused, scrutinizing me before jotting something on the check sheet.

"When you are stressed, what helps you relax?"

"I like to take hot baths." It took a lot of control to stifle a laugh.

She didn't react. I wanted to shout, "I can't believe you missed that clue!"

Minutes passed and she apparently finished all the questions.

"Well, I think that is enough for today," Liddy said.

I was dismissed. I felt like a naughty child forced to spend lunchtime in the principal's office. I stood up and headed for the door.

"One last thing, Paige. What's it like carrying the weight of the world on your shoulders?"

I turned and replied, "Why don't you tell me, Doc?"

She laughed, and I bolted.

Chapter Three

I UNLOCKED THE door to my dorm room and sniffed around. I wasn't used to the smell of the past and present occupants of my dormitory. Growing up rich did not prepare me for this stench. How could people live in such filth?

I'd wanted a private room, but my parents refused to fund that expense. They did spring for a room that offered a bathroom accessed by just four girls, instead of a bathroom for an entire floor of girls. I felt that even that was more for show. If their friends found out I was living among the "common folk," people would talk. I appreciated a more private bathroom, but I still had to live with a roommate and two suitemates. Technically, three roommates. Back home, I had an entire wing of the house to myself. I preferred being alone, and my family preferred not being around me; it worked for all of us. No one in my family spent any time with family members. We were all strangers.

Now I was living with someone I'd only met when I carried my first box into the room. I wasn't too impressed by said person; neither was she, I think.

Audrey, my roommate, was out for the moment. I eyed the boxes and clothes tossed indiscriminately around the room. Most of my belongings had been put away. Audrey was rushing the sororities, so she didn't have much time to get organized. From the looks of her boxes, though, she didn't seem to be a tidy person—another aspect that didn't dazzle me.

As she rushed into the room, I could feel her smile before I turned around to say hi. Her chipper "Hello" bothered me. I gave her a cool, "Hello" in reply. Not all of us were shiny happy people. She wore a white tee with a yellow skirt. Fucking yellow!

My roommate was several inches shorter than me. Her chocolate brown eyes always looked troubled, and her mousy brown hair hung down her back in a tangled mess. Did she not own a hairbrush, or was it buried in one of her boxes? What kind of sororities was she rushing? That wasn't my thing, but I can't imagine too many of them were impressed by such a slob.

"Have you met our suitemates yet? They moved in today." Her voice squeaked. Mousy hair and mousy voice. Great, I was living with Minnie Mouse.

"Uh, no, I just got back a few minutes ago." And I wasn't really up for meeting more people today.

"Come on over with me and let's introduce ourselves," chirped Minnie. With a firm grasp on my shirtsleeve, she pulled me through the bathroom door that connected the two rooms. If I'd said no, she probably still would have pulled me the entire way, kicking and screaming. I decided to give in and make a better impression.

I hoped our new neighbors had the foresight to lock their door so we couldn't bust in on them. They didn't.

Minnie crashed through the door and screeched, "Hi!"

One of the fathers in the room slipped with a hammer and

smashed his thumb. Great! This impression was more memorable than if she had dragged me over kicking and screaming.

A giant blonde slowly approached Minnie, leaving a decent amount of space between them as if she thought she might have to make a quick getaway. I know I wanted to.

"Hi. I'm Jenna Parry. You must be our suitemates."

She didn't put her hand out to shake. And I wasn't thrilled about being lumped in with Minnie. Trust me, I'm not the bubbly type.

"Yep, my name is Audrey Andrews and this is—"

"Paige." I had my own voice, and I wanted to put some distance between us.

The other girl stepped forward. Again, she didn't approach too closely. It's funny how much room you can find in a miniature dorm room when you're afraid.

"Hi, I'm Karen Cooper." She moved forward and shook my hand. Then she gingerly reached out to shake Minnie's. Minnie grabbed it and gave it three hard shakes. Jenna still hadn't offered her hand to either of us. I was starting to like Jenna.

The four of us inspected each other. Jenna had light hair, almost white. Her deep azure eyes and naturally bronzed skin told me her hair color wasn't natural. She towered over me. Why wasn't she in any of my classes in grade school so I wouldn't have been the tallest girl and teased constantly? Maybe she was on a basketball scholarship. Karen had curly red hair, and plenty of it, and was stocky, more the soccer type.

Great, I'm living with Minnie and two jocks. What was the point of the personality test I filled out for the university so they could match me up with people I'd get along with? I never said I liked jocks, or happy shit. Why couldn't I have a morose roommate who didn't bother me? Like that girl in *The Breakfast Club*—the depressed one who ate tons of sugar packets. We would have been great roommates. No talking. And I could share a sugar packet or two to keep things friendly.

"When did you move in?" Karen's attempt to start a conversation was valiant. I eyed the bathroom door. I wanted to leave the room and forget all about them.

"Yesterday. Paige had to register for classes today, and I came early to rush." Minnie's words fell out of her mouth so quickly that I couldn't help staring at her lips, wondering how she squeaked so fast.

They didn't seem too surprised that Minnie was the sorority girl type. She had the personality for it, just not the hair. Seriously, what was up with all the tangles?

The four of us stood there, staring. It was excruciating.

Minnie exclaimed, "Have you guys figured out where all of your classes are yet? I never knew this campus was so enormous. I still can't find my chemistry class."

I wanted to ask her if she tried the chemistry building that was right across the street from our dorm, but I didn't.

No one else responded either. Minnie looked at me for help. A few boards came crashing down behind us.

"Do you need any help putting up your lofts? Audrey and I put hers up yesterday and now we're experts." I said.

Minnie smiled at me. The night before, we had been up half the night constructing her fucking loft. I think she learned some new words from me. Minnie, the Catholic, was unfortunate enough to get an atheist as a roommate. Did the university even bother to look at our questionnaires?

"Yes, we could use the help." The answer came from one of the fathers, who was drowning under all of the boards.

A woman put her hand out. "Hi, I'm Karen's mom."

Marionette

"Hi. It's nice to meet you, Mrs. Cooper." We shook hands.

After a quick introduction to the rest of the parents, someone tapped my shoulder. I turned to see Mr. Cooper. "I'm so glad you know how to do this. I've never been very handy." He laughed self-consciously and peeked out of the corner of his eyes at Jenna's father, a manly giant wearing a tool belt.

All of us got to work. It was difficult working in such a confined space with eight people. But I loved that no one spoke, except to say, "Pass the hammer," or "Can you hand me the screwdriver?" Those were the type of conversations I excelled at. Actions, not words. Not one personal detail was exchanged. Not one intimate detail about my life or my family was asked. They knew my first name, and that was all. Once, when applying for college, I thought about changing my last name because it had occasionally appeared in the papers when I was forced to pose for photo ops with my parents. However, I had learned, over the years, that no one really looked at the names under those photos—well, except for the people in the photos.

They might have suspected that I lived with a nut job. But so what, I was fucking surrounded by kooks. How did I get a Mouseketeer as a roommate?

I sighed. It was going to be a long year. Maybe if I got a job I could afford a private room after the first semester. I knew, for a fact, that Abbie had a room to herself. But not me. I had to suffer. I looked at Minnie. She just smiled at me. Jesus! It wasn't fair!

Chapter Four

I SOON LEARNED that I was the shyest person out of the four of us. On many occasions, my three roommates made me uncomfortable by getting undressed in front of me. Growing up, I always had my own room. My sister and I never shared a room, a bathtub, or anything. It was almost like we were raised in separate households. Strangers. I learned to love my isolation.

I think my desire for privacy offended Karen, a free spirit who didn't understand why I was so uptight.

But I was uptight, and I couldn't change that. When I used the bathroom, I locked both doors so no one could barge in on me. The day after meeting Jenna and Karen, I was changing my clothes behind locked doors when Karen shouted that the phone was for me.

I opened the door, shoved the last bit of my shirt into my jeans, and mumbled a thank you.

"Hello?" I said into the receiver.

"How did it go?" My friend Mel always dismissed pleasantries and got right to business.

"Hi, I'm fine. Thanks for asking. How did what go?" I hunched the phone into my shoulder while I pulled my shirt out so I wouldn't look too uptight. Karen looked relieved. Mel, of course, was asking about meeting my therapist, and I didn't want Minnie and group to know about that.

"That good, huh?"

"That about sums it up." I grabbed the phone in my hand again and turned to see a curious audience.

"I really can't talk right now. I wanted to call and check in before you started your classes." Mel sounded tired. She had probably worked ten hours at the mall for the back-to-school crowd.

"Never better."

"It was that bad? Jesus, I'm sorry, but I really have to go. I'll call you later and we'll talk." She rushed through the words.

"Okay. And Mel, tell Wesley I said hi." I hung up. I grinned mischievously, assuming that would get a rise out her. Her boyfriend and I didn't get along, to say the least. I knew she had to get off the phone because Wesley didn't want her talking to me. He despised me, not just because I was gay, but because I was a rich bitch. Two no-nos in his book.

The three stooges stared with their mouths slightly agape. "Are we ready to go?" I asked.

"W-who ... who was that?" stammered Minnie.

"That was my friend Mel."

"Who's Wesley?" she asked.

Oh, so that was it: not only was I living with a Catholic, but with a homophobe. Perfect! Could this living situation improve at all? Stupid questionnaire for roommates. I was utterly convinced they lost mine and just stuck me in this situation.

"Wesley is Mel's boyfriend." I didn't mention that Mel was short for Melanie. Let them sweat it out some. Serves them right for eavesdropping on my phone call. They could have been polite and gone into Karen's and Jenna's room to give me some privacy.

"Anyhoos, are you all ready to go?" I asked.

Jenna started for her room. "Almost." She returned with her keys.

As we left the dorms, I realized that every stereo was blaring. It was the first weekend at college for most of us and classes started on Monday. Obviously, the plan for the weekend was to live it up.

The four of us decided to break in the new town together, which involved going to a fraternity party. I wasn't too keen on the idea, for obvious reasons. However, I never voiced my opinion. I usually kept it pretty quiet that I was dating a woman. My silence on the matter didn't go over all that well with Jess. She was older and was out to everyone, including her work colleagues, friends, family, and the random grocery store clerk. Jess was not shy. I had no desire to let people into my life. It was not that I felt ashamed. I just didn't care enough about people to get close to them. I had few friends in high school and I didn't like my family, so telling them was never an option.

Keeping Jess out of the picture in my college town wouldn't be too difficult. She lived two hours away, and she was four years older. We associated with different groups of people. We decided that when we saw each other, I would head to her town. My parents lived two towns over from Jess. In each city, I lived a different life. At Jess's, I was me. At my parents' place, I was the dutiful daughter. And now, in college, I was the wild college student. Wild, please! But I was a college student, at least.

We arrived at the first frat house after 10 p.m. Music blared, the air was filled with smoke—not just from cigarettes—drunk people lay sprawled in an inch of beer on the ground, and others danced, trying not to spill their beers. No one was older than twenty-five. To the normal college student, this was paradise. Heck, most of the guests weren't of drinking age yet. Throughout my senior year, I heard countless people talk about the allure of college life: beer, parties, sex, independence, and no parents.

But now I was hesitant. I liked the "no parents" part. I liked the freedom part. I just wasn't too keen about the rest. It wasn't that I didn't drink. I drank, but sometimes it made me nervous. I grew up surrounded by alcoholics and drug addicts. I didn't see the appeal of getting wasted all the time. I liked to stay in control. The scene before me was definitely out of control. It made me uncomfortable.

Several frat guys darted towards us as soon as we entered. They wore typical fraternity garb: Ralph Lauren or Eddie Bauer shirts and shorts. Even after the introductions, I didn't remember their names, and I wasn't going to try to find out either. They immediately offered us beer, proving one rumor true: a frattie will give you as much beer as you want in the hopes that it will pay off in the long run. I wasn't falling for it.

It seemed I was alone on this count. One guy said, "What are four beautiful ladies doing in a place like this?"

I rolled my eyes. We'd heard the line before. Hell, it'd been in every girl-chasing college-type movie. No originality at all. Did he think it would work?

Minnie chirped, "Just to have fun."

Seriously, was I doomed to live the next four years in a John Hughes flick? Did no one think for themselves? Did they just spout stuff they saw in movies? Granted, I liked the films. *Breakfast Club, Pretty in Pink, Sixteen Candles*—the list goes on. But they're movies, not guidelines on how to live. Come on, people! Smarten up.

The dude responded, "That's what I like to hear." He had his arm around Minnie's waist already. Shoving a beer into her hand, he whisked her away in a cloud of smoke. I had to give him credit for being fast. I hoped Minnie was just as quick later in the night when it was time to go, but I had my doubts. Maybe she would locate a hole with cheese in it and curl up in it for the night like a good little mousey.

One down, two more to go. It didn't take long. Jenna and Karen found love interests for the night within a few minutes, leaving me alone at a party with hundreds of people. Now that's an impressive feat, but a normal one for me. It's easy to disappear in a crowd.

I stood in a corner, a drink in hand. I wasn't drinking it; it was just for security. If I already had a drink, no guys would approach and ask if I wanted one. My thoughts returned to Liddy and her comment about having the weight of the world on my shoulders. What did she know? How had Jess even convinced me to go to therapy? I was not the opening-up type.

Next time, I just needed to ensure I had more time. Step four, dammit!

I watched a girl across the room who was stumbling drunk. She swatted at an imaginary bug and accidentally whacked her boyfriend in the face. They both giggled hysterically. He was just as drunk, and the two of them toppled over into the inch of beer on the ground. Actually, it was growing, so maybe two inches. Watching them rolling around in the beer—at least I hope it was just beer—made me shudder.

That's when I went back. I no longer saw the drunken college girl. I saw Alex, my best friend. We'd been born three days apart and had grown up together. She lived across the street from us, and right from the start, we were inseparable. I don't have any pictures, but I can remember how beautiful she was. Alex was a knockout. People said we looked alike. But I knew she was more beautiful.

Even when Alex first started to drink, at the age of thirteen, she was still a sweetheart. When she started snorting coke, even that didn't change her heart. It transformed her personality, but not her heart.

It didn't take long for her to become hopelessly hooked. I still remember the night her parents called the cops to force her into rehab. She stood in the middle of the street in a torn T-shirt and jeans and she screamed bloody murder. Two police officers, one man and one woman, tried their best to calm her down. The male police officer seemed reluctant to approach her. Alex's torn shirt exposed the top of one breast. She had started to develop in the fourth grade, and it was easy to mistake her for an adult, which a lot of people did that night. Her body ceased to be a little girl's body far too soon for any child to handle. Grown-ups didn't know what to make of it either. The female cop tried for half an hour, unsuccessfully, to get Alex into the car. The tee kept tearing, and more cleavage fell out. Alex had never liked wearing a bra since she was forced to wear one at such a young age.

No one was outside—odd for a hot summer night—because no one wanted to witness Alex's demise. That was the problem. No one understood her, and no one wanted to be there for her. Even her parents didn't bother leaving their house to help. They had never helped before, so it wasn't surprising to me. The cops kept peering back at Alex's front door. Maybe they were praying one of her parents would help, too.

Alex stood in the street, screaming for me. It had been a scorching July day—the hottest I can remember. Her hair was matted with sweat, her eyes bulged out of her skinny face, and she looked like death. She kept shouting for me. The longer she screamed, the more desperate she became. She started to pull her own hair out. She was in such a rage.

"Why?" she kept screaming. "Why did this happen? Why won't you come? Why?"

My mom wouldn't let me outside to help. Alex wanted me. She wanted me to run away with her. She didn't want to go to some secluded rehabilitation center. Somehow, her parents had scrounged up enough money for a posh facility. They were in over their heads with their house, boat, swimming pool, and two Porsches. It was no secret that they were on the brink of economic ruin.

I fought my mom, kicked and screamed, but she gripped me like I was a ragdoll. She would not let me out of her clutches. Each time I moved forward, she pulled me back, as if I were a marionette on a string.

I can still hear Alex's voice. The desperation. The sadness. The anger. I can still see the tears leaking from her eyes. Venomous tears. The hatred. By the time the cops got her into the back of their vehicle, Alex hated me for not coming. It was the first time I had ever let her down. Turned out to be the last time, as well.

Then, I had hated myself too, for not breaking free. And now, I despised myself even more. I didn't know it then, but that night was a turning point in our lives. Guilt festers inside me. There were times when I felt I could never look in the mirror again—all I saw was Alex. Not me, not Paige—just Alex. Alex's eyes filled with hatred because I didn't go to her when she needed me the most. Smoldering hatred.

She had stared at our front door the entire time she screamed. Could she see my mother holding me back? Did she see how much I struggled to break free? For a brief moment, I thought I'd noticed her locking eyes with my captor. Did she know? Alex's face had hardened and her eyes had blazed with such abhorrence that I had felt my knees give out. Her glare frightened me.

"Why?" she had shouted.

I didn't understand her question at the time. For me, the answer was obvious: she was hooked on drugs and needed help. I didn't know, back then, why she was hooked. If I had paid closer attention to the rambling she had done the day before, I would have put two and two together. I would have fought harder and escaped my mom, the evil bitch.

Then we would have been free. Instead, now we were both trapped. Me in a living body; Alex, in a grave.

"WHY?"

The voice came from behind me. I didn't turn around, trying to figure out whether the person was real or from my imagination. Maybe, if I ignored the question, it didn't matter if it were real or not. I stood frozen. *Why what?*

Someone tapped my shoulder.

Plan A shot, now time for Plan B ... think, Paige.

"Why is the sky blue?" Yes, I admit, that wasn't original. I'm just as bad as the rest of the people at this party. Hackneyed.

"Oh, I don't know. I was never good at science."

I turned and saw a guy holding a beer and swaying in a circle. How he was still standing mystified me. Would he topple over?

"That's okay. I study history." *I study history. Why did I say that?*

"I'm in the businessh program. But I hate mathh," he slurred.

I put my hand on his shoulder to steady him. You might think I was being kind. Maybe I was, but I was more afraid he was going to collapse on top of me. His foul breath invaded my nostrils. Had he just grabbed a fresh beer after puking?

Two more men approached, placed an arm under each of the

drunk's arms, and hotfooted him out of the party.

Again, I was alone. I focused on the partygoers, anything to avoid going back to that night. Fuck, that night tormented me. Alex's eyes, her screaming, and that final look before the cops grabbed her—oh, that final terrifying look. Even now it gives me gooseflesh.

Stop it, Paige!

My roommates stumbled out the back door and discovered me by collapsing on top of me. I struggled to hold all three of them up, but unfortunately, Minnie toppled to the ground. What a shame.

They demanded that we stay at the party. I was the designated driver for the night, and I insisted that we leave. I was victorious.

Minnie and Karen leaned on each other to stagger out to my car. I supported Jenna the entire way, her head resting on top of mine. For someone so slender, she still weighed a ton! I wondered if my muscles would be sore the next day.

Campus police swarmed around our dorm like rattlesnakes—ready to strike at any moment. How was I going to get three extremely inebriated girls up to our room without being noticed?

It didn't help that Minnie and Karen both had the giggles. Putting my finger to my lips to shush them, I motioned for us to take the back stairs. It wasn't a brilliant plan, but it was the only option available.

The first two doors were uneventful, but right when I thought we had made it to our room undetected, two cops popped into sight in our hallway. Just like in the movies.

"Good evening, or shall I say good morning?" said the taller of the two.

"Top of the morning to you." I tried to be cute—sometimes it worked for me.

Karen and Minnie burst into giggles again and Jenna stumbled, almost pulling me down with her. She landed on her ass, propped against her door.

The shorter cop sighed. "How much further do you have to go?"

I pointed to the door Jenna was smashed up against.

The two officers studied all four of us, and then looked at each other. Their haggard faces told me that it had been a long night.

"Take care, girls. And don't forget to drink lots of water."

"Thanks, bye," I said, sure my eyes conveyed my thanks. I yanked Jenna's keys out of her pocket and ushered all three of them inside before the snakes changed their minds.

That night, I lay in bed and listened to Jenna purge her body of the alcohol. Yes, it was going to be a long year. I rolled on my side and pulled my pillow over my head. All I wanted was sleep. Peaceful, dream-free sleep.

CHAPTER FIVE

MONDAY MORNING CAME too fast for all of us. I was the first one up, showered, and off to class. I'd registered late and was stuck with all the early bird classes. Who could speak French at eight in the morning? Maybe the French. I could barely grunt in the morning, let alone conjugate irregular verbs.

The plus side to the crappy schedule was I had my afternoons all to myself. Jess proclaimed cheerily that it gave me time for therapy. Why did she have to throw a wet blanket on everything? However, I was bolstered by the fact that my therapy was only once a week, every Friday afternoon, as a matter of fact. The best way to start any weekend—baring my soul to a complete stranger who fed on the weak like a lion ripping chunks from a dead gazelle. How's that for staying positive.

Mind you, on this particular Monday, I had an appointment with Liddy to get a jumpstart on therapy. Had Jess tipped off Liddy? Had she put a rush order on my happiness? What next? Would Jess start to buy me yellow shirts?

After attending three classes in the morning and listening to introductions about the courses and instructors, I found myself entering the staircase to doom. What a bunch of hypocrites. Mental health professionals spouted that there was no shame in therapy and yet they stuck their offices in the basement. Were they shielding us from the rest of the student populace? Did they think one of us might bite someone, like a rabid dog? Maybe I should stop at the bookstore and purchase a copy of *Cujo*. Get a few pointers.

The cheerful lady was at her desk again. "Hi, Paige. I hope your first day went well. Liddy will be right with you. Go ahead and wait in her office." Words spilled out of her mouth like water bursting through a dam. As soon as she finished, she picked up the ringing phone and said cheerily, "University Counseling Center."

I wasn't happy that she remembered my name; I always tried to remain anonymous. Obviously, I was failing yet again.

It was easier this time to make my way through the maze of hallways to Liddy's office. It was empty, but I went in and sat down. Twice now she'd been late. You'd think therapists would try to avoid being late. They're already dealing with fragile minds, why make them feel unimportant as well? Hypocrites!

"Hello." Her word reached me before I saw her.

"Hello, Dr. Elliot. Hey, you wouldn't happen to know the time by chance?"

She walked to her desk, set her bag down, grabbed a pen and notepad, and responded, "It's a little after two."

"Thanks." I rested my chin on my left hand, revealing my watch.

She shook her head and smiled. "I'm sorry I'm late. I had a hard time getting away from the hospital."

"What happened? Did someone get oatmeal stuck in her hair?" I thought this was clever, for me.

"No. One of my patients tried to commit suicide."

I felt uncomfortable. It wasn't the best start to the session. "Do you deal with a lot of suicidal people?"

"Yes." She studied my face.

I looked down at my shoes.

I remembered the front desk lady saying she was one of their best. Did the perky fat lady see my questionnaire? Is there a law against her snooping? Or did Liddy only see suicidal people? Did the bosses say, "Oh, here's another one who tried to off herself. Give her to Liddy"? Not only did the front desk lady now know my name, but it seemed I had a stigma. I didn't like it one bit.

I examined the wall. "I guess I didn't score that high on the form I had to fill out." Jess had sat next to me while I filled out my forms, to ensure my honesty.

Liddy adjusted her chair and pulled out some papers. "Oh, I wouldn't say that at all. In fact, I would say your score was quite high." She glanced down at the papers. "Question eleven: Have you ever thought about killing yourself? You answered: yes." She peered over the paper and eyeballed me.

I didn't react.

She read, "If yes, when was the last time you thought about taking your life? You answered: yesterday." She set the papers aside. "I'd say you scored a lot of points. Don't you think, Paige?"

I didn't like her approach. I thought she would think me too delicate and would handle me with kid gloves. I was mistaken. Why was she being confrontational? Didn't it worry her? Or did she think I did it for attention?

"I did my best." I took a pen out of my pocket and started to click it.

"It's over 90 degrees outside, and yet you're wearing a long-sleeved shirt. Do you ever push your shirtsleeves up when you're hot?

MARIONETTE

Any reason you don't want to show your forearms?"

I clicked my pen faster and didn't reply.

"I see. Maybe I'm wrong, but it seems to me you should start taking this more seriously."

I stayed quiet, but shamefully tucked my pen back into my pocket, like a good little deranged person.

Liddy's eyes followed my every move. "You don't like talking much, do you?"

"No, ma'am. I don't."

"Do you dislike me or the whole concept?"

"At the moment, I'm not fond of either."

"Why?"

"Don't get me wrong, I think you're nice and all … but I don't like people prying into my life. And you make money from people's suffering. If it wasn't for that, I think we could've been good friends." I smiled bashfully, trying to convey an apology.

"I don't do it for the money, Paige."

"I suppose prostitutes could say the same thing." The words fell out of my mouth before I could stop them.

She contemplated me.

"Are there any subjects you do enjoy talking about?"

I moved my head from side to side. "None come to mind."

At this point, I didn't know why I was wasting my time, not to mention Liddy's. She obviously had patients who needed her. I wondered how the person had tried to commit suicide. Should I probe for pointers? Yet, that person failed too. I already knew how to be unsuccessful.

If it weren't for that promise to Jess, I would have barged out of this office minutes ago. Actually, I never would have been here. I didn't want to find myself. Truth be known, I thought therapy was a huge waste of time, especially for me. I'm not depressed. I'm not crazy. I just want control.

"A lot of people like to talk about themselves." She was fishing.

"I don't find myself all that interesting." I wanted to disappear. To not be noticed by anyone. Ever.

"I do. In fact, I find you fascinating. What do you want to be?"

"You mean, when I grow up?" Wasn't this a question for grade school kids? I rolled my eyes and said, "A writer."

"Now you see, that's interesting. Someone who doesn't like to talk wants to be a writer. That's a conundrum, wouldn't you say?" Her eyes sparkled.

I let out a small chuckle. She relaxed some.

"Why did you come here?"

"I made a promise."

"To whom?"

"That's not important. I made a promise, and I hate breaking promises."

"Did you make this person a promise that you wouldn't try to slit your wrists again?"

I fixed her with a fierce look. *How dare she?*

"I see that struck a nerve." She straightened in her chair.

The two of us scrutinized each other. I'm not sure how long it lasted.

"Oh, look at the time." I motioned to my watch. "Session over."

"How does Friday look for you?"

I sighed. She knew she had me. Why did I say that about promises? I always said too much.

"I'll see you at two." She jotted something down on her notepad. She wasn't looking at me, so I took the opportunity to study her. What a knockout. She still smelled of orange blossoms. Was it wrong to have a crush on your therapist?

As I left the room, she shouted after me, "At two, Paige."

I was miffed. Angry at myself. And at Liddy. And Jess. Why did I have to go through this charade? Why did I have to get caught? How hard is it to kill yourself? For a Type A Personality, this failure was difficult to live with. I hated disappointment. A failure of this enormity was a crushing blow. I would love to try again, just to prove I could do it.

But there *was* that promise. Seriously, though, if I succeeded would it really matter? Now that's a question I would love to discuss in therapy. Unfortunately, I didn't think Liddy would like my approach to the subject. I wasn't positive, but I think she was set on "saving" me. I didn't want saving; I wanted to know how to succeed. Why did everyone have to be so limited in their worldview? The matter revolved around success or failure. There was no reason to bring emotion into it. Let's just say it was cut and dried. Please pardon the pun.

For me, success would mean death. Death meant victory. Control of my life.

CHAPTER SIX

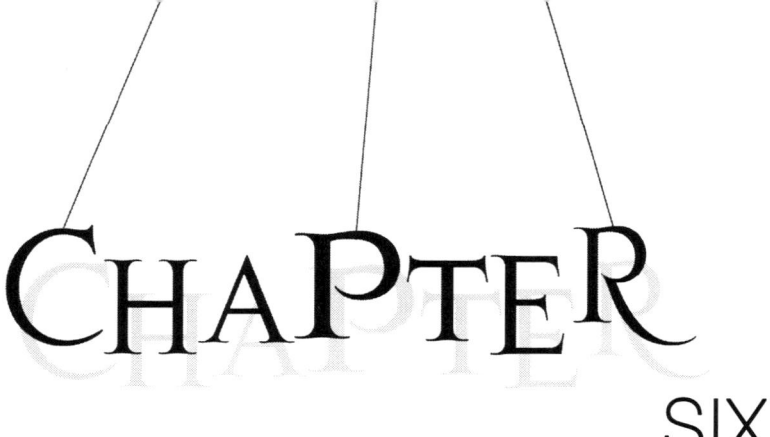

NOT SURPRISINGLY, JENNA and Karen were in my room. Maybe they couldn't get enough of my charming personality or exceptional conversational skills. More than likely, it was because I had a television and they didn't. Not many in the dorm did. Karen was sprawled out on my bed, while Jenna sat in my beanbag. Nothing was sacred in a college dorm room, not even my beanbag.

"Are you ready for dinner?"

I didn't notice Minnie until I heard her squeaky voice. She was tucked away in the corner. I found that odd, since it was her room too. Why did Jenna and Karen claim the supreme seats while Minnie sat meekly in the corner on her desk chair? An uncomfortable desk chair that could have been used in medieval torture rooms.

She continued her chatter. "Jewels and Emily are waiting for us."

"Sorry I'm late ... who's waiting?" I threw my backpack on the floor by my desk. It nearly landed on Jenna's outstretched legs.

"Jewels and Emily—two girls I met during rush. We found out yesterday that we live in the same dorm, so now we can have meals together." She radiated bliss. Minnie turned to Karen and Jenna. "Jewels is the coolest name. Her parents named her that because she is their jewel. Isn't that sweet?"

I wanted to puke, but said, "Oh ... that's nice." I didn't really care, but I was trying to remain civil with the mouse. Do mice have social expectations and rules? "I'm sorry I kept all of you waiting. Give them a call. I need to use the restroom."

While I sat on the toilet, peeing, I heard Karen shout, "So, where were you?"

Really? I had to have the conversation while taking a wee?

I didn't respond. Some of us have manners.

I stepped out of the john—not in a proud way, since how can you walk with dignity after peeing or pooping and knowing three strangers could hear it all?—and stood in front of the bathroom sink. I took extra time washing my hands with scalding hot water.

"Hello to Paige. Where were you?"

I looked at Karen, trying not to blow my top. "Out for a walk."

"For four hours?"

I didn't answer again.

She repeated the question. *I didn't get the memo that my college roommates needed to know my schedule at all times.*

"Yep, for four hours." I dried my hands and asked Minnie if she was ready to go. Karen and Jenna exchanged looks. I felt bad about being rude, but I also felt justified. Why did Karen feel the need to invade my privacy?

Minnie made a beeline for the door. I followed; the other two didn't. I looked back over my shoulder and realized they didn't have any intention of budging. "Aren't you two coming?"

"We already ate, thanks." Jenna finally spoke.

"Oh." Not sure why, but I expected them to leave my room

while Minnie and I were out. I regretted bringing my TV. Big mistake.

Karen shouted for us to have a nice dinner as I shut the door. Didn't she know I was pissed at her? She acted like I hadn't been rude at all. How could she be so oblivious?

Minnie and I stood at the cafeteria entrance, not really speaking. So far, I didn't know how to befriend her. Also, I wasn't too keen on doing so. I had a feeling she felt the same way, but she was trying to make an effort since we had to survive an entire year together. She was the better person, and I let her be.

"H-how are classes going?" she stammered.

"Fine." I shuffled my feet. "Yours?"

"Good ... good."

A few more awkward seconds passed and then Minnie squeaked, "Jewels! Emily! I'm *so* glad to see you."

I was too. Now Minnie had people to talk to. Our brief conversation had drained me entirely.

Minnie made the introductions, and the four of us made our way into the cafeteria. All of us flashed our IDs to get into the food line. Really, who would want to crash a dorm cafeteria for food? I'm sure there were rats in this city that ate better shit than we did. If I could be bothered driving into town, I would have eaten out for each meal.

I ruminated over the thought as I scooped a runny batch of noodles onto my plate and then poured a grotesque-looking Alfredo sauce all over it. Picking up a pair of tongs, I snatched two slices of colorless garlic bread. Next, I hit the salad bar. The lettuce looked wilted and tasteless. Iceberg. Would it kill them to spring for some Romaine? Still, I made a bowl. Balancing pasta, salad, and soda on my tray, I spied Minnie and her friends at a table in the back.

Marionette

Carefully, I guided my way through all of the students and random tables to join my compatriots.

The other three had opted for the fried chicken. They were brave souls. Or stupid. During my first few nights, I would wait in line for the "special" meal of the night. After that, I usually skipped it and went straight for either the pasta or cereal line.

Emily took a bite of her chicken, made a face, and then said, "I'm going to get a bowl of cereal. Does anyone need anything?"

None of us did. She scurried away, happy as a bird. I envied that.

"So, Paige, what's your major?" With effort, Jewels ripped a piece of chicken off a drumstick.

"History." I took a swig of soda, and then remembered I probably should try to carry on the conversation. "What's yours?"

"English, well, actually, creative writing. I want to be a writer. Romance novels. I can just picture myself in a bungalow someplace in the Caribbean, writing my novels by day, sitting on a patio that overlooks the beach. And enjoying the men at night." Her eyes glazed over.

Was all this an act? I stared at her. Was that straight out of one of her novels?

"Oh, that's so cool. What a life that would be," cheeped Minnie.

"What do you want to be, Paige?" probed Jewels.

By this time, Emily had returned and said, "Wait! Let me guess. I love playing this game." She took a drink of her milk. "You want to be an astrologer or an astronomer. Which one studies the stars and planets?" She looked to Jewels and Minnie for the answer.

Jewels declared that astrologers did. No one corrected her. Inwardly, I smiled.

"Good guess, Em. I see where you're going with this, since she always seems lost in her thoughts." Jewels winked at me. How did she figure that out so soon? "But she's studying history. My guess is she wants to teach history."

"Oh, I can totally see that. Right on!" Emily scooped a heap of Cheerios into her mouth.

I didn't bother telling any of them that I wanted to be a writer—not a romance writer, though. I never thought anyone aspired to be a romance writer. I thought that was what happened when writers couldn't write anything else.

I went back. I saw my mother vividly in my mind, yelling at me that writing was a worthless career. I would be a lawyer instead, she bellowed. She had found all of my journals, which I started keeping in elementary school. Early on, one of my teachers encouraged me to write stories. Over the years, I'd written countless stories in my journals. I had shared them with my teacher, who was always supportive of me and encouraged me, even when I was no longer in her class. I always preferred the company of adults. Some would invite me over after school for milk and cookies. I think they knew about my home life. There were no milk and cookies at home. Not that I spoke about it, but it wasn't hard for them to figure it out.

Once, when I was in kindergarten, I had an ear infection. Mom sent me to school anyway. During the morning, my teacher found me crying. The school nurse called my mom and asked for her to come and get me. I sat outside the school waiting for my mom for over three hours. It was a cold day and the wind howled. Each gust of wind screeched through my ear and sent waves of pain up and down my body. When Mom finally arrived, she berated me in front of everyone, calling me a baby and worse things. I can still hear the screeching tires as her car went on two wheels around the roundabout in the parking lot. Even at that age, I knew the roundabout was designed to slow down drivers. Before the car came to a complete stop, she was out of the car, ranting and raving with her hair in a tangle and her nightgown fluttering around her. I didn't want to go home with her, but I had to. Back then, school officials didn't step in too much. Today, that wouldn't fly. Then, everyone looked away, and when they could, they gave me milk and cookies.

When my mother found and read my stories, she blew up. She had a plan before I was old enough to speak: lawyer. Abbie would be a doctor. My mother had always wanted to study either one of those professions, but she never finished college. Abbie was actually pursuing medicine, even though I didn't think she wanted to. My mom is persuasive. Abbie was strong in some areas, but not this one. She had no issues being herself around our parents, but she had no desire to walk away from them and stand on her own two feet. My mother controlled Abbie just like she was a puppet. I always wanted to run away, never wanted to be a part of the family. Abbie rebelled in safe ways, never pushing the boundaries too much so she could stay within the family fold.

Back to my journals: Mom threw them all into the fireplace. She made me watch them burn. I cried, and she backhanded me across the face. That day instilled a burning desire in me. I would become a writer, no matter what. I was either going to write, or I was going to die. I would never become a lawyer. Never! That day, my mom tried to banish who I wanted to be. Since then, I've been trying to reclaim myself.

Yes, I studied history, and my mom thought this was my first step in realizing her dreams. Fuck that. I loved studying history. But if she wanted to think that, she could go for it. I was glad she did. When she realizes I won't pursue law, it will hurt her even more. Let her feel the pain. I rubbed my wrist.

I checked back in on the conversation of my dinner

companions. Jewels was still talking about her writing ambitions. Minnie's eyes had glazed over; ambition was not her forte.

Minnie then butted in and mentioned all of the cute boys in her class. I think she had a boyfriend back home. Oh, I wished his name was Mickey. I could settle for Mick or Mike. Please! Anyhoos, Minnie said having a boyfriend didn't stop her from shopping around. I learned, during their conversation, that all of them had boyfriends back home. When they asked me, I said that I didn't. I wasn't lying; I don't have a boyfriend. Jess is not a boy—so not a lie. But I did have someone.

I forced all of the pasta down and some of the salad. The ranch dressing was rancid. The others grabbed some ice cream, and I thought about it, but I already felt like a slug after eating all of the crappy pasta and gooey sauce.

After dinner, I went back to my room. Minnie joined the other two for a walk, since they all felt guilty about dessert and wanted to walk off the calories. I declined, and Minnie joked that I'd been wandering around for hours earlier. Not entirely true, but I didn't correct her.

Karen and Jenna were still in my room watching a rerun of *Cheers*. At least they liked my favorite show. The two of them talked while I watched. All in all, it wasn't too horrible a night, but I dreaded the next 200 nights. Maybe I should make a countdown, or scratches on the wall to keep track.

When you think about it, dorm life is odd. All of us, from all over, are thrown into one place to eat, sleep, shower, dress, and live. And this was a rite of passage for most American teens, one that you couldn't skip. All freshmen had to live in the dorms for the first year. The only exception was to live at home, which wasn't an option for me.

Marionette

If I could have, I would have attended summer school, but my mother refused. Another thing to be angry about. I had plans. One was to finish college as soon as possible. I knew my parents would cut me off after I graduated. My father had said as much enough times. The sooner, the better. Abbie hoped they would set her up in her profession. And they probably would. She was the "good twin." I hoped they would forget all about me, and vice versa.

It might be a harder task for me—the task of forgetting them. I can still see the reflection of the fire dancing in my mom's eyes as she burned my stories. Did she know she was burning a piece of me? She enjoyed that task more than was necessary. That was when I really started to recognize that my mother was truly insane. There had been signs before, but at that moment, I knew. I didn't want to go crazy. I had to get away from her. It scared me. I heard craziness ran in families. I had to escape before they sucked me into the lunatic realm. There were times I contemplated not going to college at all. Just disappearing. I could live with Jess and get a job. But I feared they would track me down. I would have to move far away. If I could finish college quickly, I'd have a better chance of succeeding. I was taking more credits than all of my roommates. Twenty-one credits. Only ninety-nine more to go. I opened up my French workbook and got to work.

Chapter Seven

WE SAT ACROSS from each other, just staring at each other, not talking. This was a different approach. Not wanting to move, I sat there frozen, like a gazelle hiding from a pack of hyenas. Was Liddy trying to make me feel psychotic?

It was working.

"What are you staring at?" I broke down.

"You. I'm trying to figure you out."

Liddy looked stunning in a pair of jeans and a pink polo sweater. It takes confidence to look amazing in jeans and a sweater. I pushed the thought out of my mind.

"You're creeping me out. What's there to figure out?" I averted my gaze and studied the Dalmatian calendar behind her. It was still two months behind.

"Why do you come here?"

"Didn't we cover this last time? I made a promise."

She cocked her head, scrunched her mouth and examined me.

"Your charming personality," I suggested. Sometimes, humor worked with people.

"I'm going to need more than that." She tapped her pencil against the ubiquitous notepad.

Obviously, humor didn't work with her.

"Have you ever heard the story of the dog who sat on a nail?" I queried.

She shook her head.

"A man goes to his neighbor's house. While talking to his neighbor on the porch, he notices a dog lying on a nail. The guy asks why the dog doesn't move. The neighbor responds by saying that when it hurts enough, he'll move."

Okay, I don't really get the point of this story either, but Jess told it to me days after I tried to off myself, when she was doing her best to assure me that therapy would be great for me. Great! Yeah, I was having a fucking blast so far. Woohoo!

I spied a scuff mark on my shoe and wiped it with my thumb.

Liddy said, "Tell me about your childhood, Paige."

"I was born at a very young age in a small town."

"Why don't we fast forward some?" She smiled. "What was your first bad memory?"

Really? My first bad memory. That seemed like a lame approach. How in the world was Liddy the best? Or should I ask, how awful were the rest?

"I fell off my bike and skinned my knee. It hurt like a sonofabitch."

"Uh-huh, try a different one."

Actually, if she probed that statement further, she may have learned something. No reason to push it, though. How many more sessions did I have to attend to meet my one-year commitment? Forty-nine. Maybe tonight I should come up with forty-nine bogus "bad memories" to share with the inept Liddy. How hard could that be?

"There was the Lego incident. That altered all of our lives, especially mine."

She regarded me for a moment. "I'm going to bite on this one. Tell me about it."

"But you won't bite on the knee story. Your loss." I winked at her.

Liddy hesitated, but she seemed like the type who, once her mind was made up, forged ahead, right or wrong. I wonder what her therapist thought about that.

"The short story: Mom walked through the front room and stepped on a Lego piece. She bent over quickly to remove the offending object from the bottom of her bare foot. Unfortunately, a disc in her back blew when she bent over. More than a decade later, I'm still paying for that incident."

"Was it your Lego piece?" She leaned forward in her chair.

"Yes, but I didn't leave it out."

"Who did?"

"Abbie. My sister."

She leaned back into her seat. "Let me guess, Abbie didn't confess to it."

"You got it, smarty pants." My voice oozed resentment.

"Did you tell them the truth?"

"No. Abbie was always the favorite. I knew no one would believe me."

"What happened after the Lego incident?" Her husky voice startled me.

"I'm not sure I remember it all. I was only six when it happened. I was blamed for ruining the entire family. When the disc exploded, it wrapped around her spinal cord. Doctors couldn't figure out what

MARIONETTE

happened for years. During those years, my mom was bedridden."

"And what happened to you during that time?"

"I grew up fast." I rested my arm on the chair's armrest and cradled my chin with my palm.

"What does that mean?"

"My dad stayed away from home. He said he was too young and busy amassing his fortune to be tied down by an invalid. Abbie disappeared entirely. I really don't have many memories of her during these years. She couldn't handle the sickroom. There was no one else, so I took care of my mom.

"No one bothered to tell me what was going on. I knew my mom was injured. People would ask about her, and I would say that her back didn't work. It was broken. They would give me an odd look. But that wasn't all of it. I never told anyone, but I was convinced that she was dying, and that it was my Lego piece that killed her. I didn't leave it out, but it was still mine." I stood up, and paced in the small room, as if I were a tennis ball bouncing back and forth on a tiny court. Liddy watched me.

"At the time, I didn't realize she was overmedicating. When I'd get home for school, I would always check in on her. She would be in a comatose state, and I couldn't tell if she was breathing. Every day I would venture into her room, inching forward slowly, my heart beating wildly in my throat. I would inch closer to see whether the blanket was moving up and down."

I stopped pacing and leaned against the wall behind Liddy, so she couldn't watch me. She didn't turn around.

"And, boy, did she stink. I think that was one of the reasons Abbie couldn't handle the sickroom. There was a stench all of the time. It could choke a rat. I did my best to keep her showered and stuff, but it was difficult for me. I couldn't carry her to the shower.

"My dad never bothered to hire any nurses. Maybe he hoped she would die, and he wouldn't have to bother with the situation anymore. That's how he views everything: can he profit or should he cut ties? We aren't people. We're things. Commodities. Emotions don't factor into his line of thinking. He's one cold bastard."

Slowly, I dragged myself back to my chair and slumped down. "He likes order and logic. The doctors couldn't find anything wrong with her; ergo, there was nothing wrong with her. He didn't bother to stop and notice the pain she was suffering. Occasionally, he would wander into the room and yell at her to get up. When she didn't budge, he'd leave in exasperation. It's funny; you'd think he was the military type, but he would never survive in the military. He works hard, and he cheats harder. That's how he advanced in this world.

"I don't know how much of this is true, but my mother told me once that he used to pay people to take his tests and complete his assignments in college. I can see him doing that. For him, that would be rational. He wanted to succeed, and in order to do that, he needed help. It wouldn't be cheating; it would be solving a problem, being efficient."

Liddy was still observing me. I felt rather embarrassed to have talked so long. And all of it was true. I had to get better at faking experiences. It all just bubbled out of me. I knew I had rambled. It felt as if I opened my mouth and random memories and thoughts had fallen right out. I couldn't even remember everything that I said.

"Is that when your mother started drinking?"

"No. That didn't start until after her surgery." *How did she know that?* I thought back. *Yes, it was one of the questions on the form I filled out.* "I think she thought everything would go back to normal, but it didn't. She could get out of bed, yes. The pain, though, that never went away. She had good days and bad. I think she started drinking

MARIONETTE

when she realized that nothing would be like it was. Her husband resented her. Abbie abandoned her. She only had me to rely on, and she blamed me for everything. She fucking hated me."

"Why did Abbie abandon her?"

"I never could figure that out. I think she's a lot like my father. Order and logic. All of Abbie's friends had normal parents, so why couldn't she? From an early age, Abbie cared too much about what others thought of her. She had to have the coolest clothes, toys—things. She needed things. Abbie measures her self-worth by them. Having a nutty, smelly mother who was stuck in bed didn't help her fit in. I can remember her friends telling me how sorry they were that Abbie and I lost our mom at such an early age. I didn't say much when they said that, because it confused me. Lost? She wasn't lost—just follow the stench. It was only years later that I realized that lost meant dead. Abbie had told many people our mom died. I wondered what she said when all of a sudden Mom reemerged from the sickroom. Zombie? Vampire? I think that, in a way, Abbie really wished it was true. She didn't want her any more."

"Did you ever wish that?"

"I never had time to wish it. I was busy doing everything at home. My father and Abbie had the luxury to hate; I didn't. That's what hurts the most. I was the only one who stayed, yet she hates me the most." I started to laugh. "Now that's what I call irony."

I noticed our time was up and I started to collect my belongings.

"Does it hurt enough?"

I raised myself from my chair. "What?"

"To get off the nail?" She looked serious.

"I guess so. Or to stick it in deeper and finish the job." I left the room.

I thought Liddy would stop me after that last comment and

insist on putting me in a padded room. She didn't. Perhaps she liked my honesty. Maybe she was earning my trust. And possibly, she didn't care that much. No one else did. I was a commodity, and if that were the case, she would want to keep me around to collect my fee. Fifty bucks, though, isn't much. Fifty times fifty-two was $2600. But the first five sessions were free. Only $2350—not much for a year. Then take into account the school year was not a full calendar year so it would be even less. Yeah, I probably wasn't worth the effort.

After my session, I wandered aimlessly around the campus. It was still hot out, and I swore under my breath since I had to wear long sleeves. I was told the scars wouldn't be too bad, but they were wrong. I really did bungle the job. Not only did I bungle the job, I left traces to advertise my failure. What was worse? Trying, or failing?

I needed air conditioning, so I headed back to my dorm room. I lay down on my bed, relishing some alone time. Minnie was still in class and Jenna and Karen were nowhere to be seen. Closing my eyes, I felt a wave of calm. Maybe I could get some sleep.

Insomnia became a part of my existence many years ago. I was lucky to get a few hours of sleep each night. Those who don't suffer from insomnia have no idea what it's like.

People say, "Oh, how awful."

No shit, asshole!

My body aches all of the time. I feel like I have a constant fever. My hands are perpetually clammy. I'm cranky. Every task feels like a chore. My brain sputters and stalls when I'm searching for the right word. Even simple words elude me. I get confused easily. These are my good days. My bad ... well you don't want to know. Trust me.

A knock on the door interrupted my quiet time. Should I ignore it? I needed rest. Common sense never was my strong suit. I climbed out of bed and forced my exhausted legs to carry my weight to the

Marionette

door. A young man stood on the other side—an extremely timid-looking boy. A Broncos hat sat atop his head, and from the looks of it, the hat rarely left his head. I wondered if he slept in it. He seemed the kind of deranged fan who might wear the hat even at his own wedding, but he had kind eyes and a sympathetic smile.

"Hi ... is A-Audrey here?" His voice, soft and pleasant, was surprising to me. A sensitive football fanatic? Did his football buddies make fun of him for not having a manly voice?

"Hello." I paused and considered inviting him in, but I think that would have pushed him over the edge. "M-Audrey's still in class. Can I help you with anything?" He probably thought I had a stutter. Maybe I should stop referring to Audrey as Minnie in my head.

"Uh ... no. Well, can you tell her that I stopped by?" He stepped side to side like a child who was desperate to use the toilet. I wasn't sure, but he seemed terrified of me. I wondered what Minnie had told her friends about me.

"Sure. What name shall I give?" I asked in an overly cheery voice. What the fuck? Was I turning into Minnie?

He smiled, and the muscles in his face relaxed. "Oh, that would probably help." He chuckled, and then stuck his hand out to shake. "Tom."

I shook his hand gently. "Nice to meet you, Tom. I'll be sure to tell her."

"Thanks."

"See ya, Tom." Again my cheery voice nauseated me. Did I have a goofy grin on my face as well?

He still held my hand. Color swarmed over his face, and he slowly let go of my hand. Turning, he then retreated down the hallway. As he walked, he stayed exactly in the middle of the hallway, and his head darted back and forth whenever he passed a door. Was he scared one of the doors would open and a girl would snatch him from this world entirely?

I shut the door, chuckling. When I turned around, I almost shit my pants. Karen stood there. One thing I was not prepared for about college life was the complete loss of privacy. I tried not to show my fear.

"I came in earlier, but it looked like you were asleep. Then, when I heard voices, I decided to come over." She had a way of dragging out a hello.

She walked into the main part of the room and plopped down on the beanbag, sighing a sigh that begged me to ask what was wrong.

"Rough day?" I inquired.

"Yeah. I got so lost finding my two o'clock lab. Then, when I walked in, the teacher made a point of telling everyone he would not excuse tardiness. I tried to explain that I got lost. He told me to shut up. He actually said, 'Shut it.' Then he said there was no excuse. I might have to drop the class. I think he hates me."

I laughed. *That* was her rough day.

"I guess it is kinda funny. How was your day?"

I shrugged. "Same shit, different day."

"Ha! I knew you wouldn't say much. I'm not going to give up, you know. You can try to brush me off, but we'll become friends, Paige. I insist on it."

Surprisingly, this didn't put me off. In fact, I was starting to find her funny—in an annoying way. She did and said what she wanted. Except, she farted a lot. I cringed, thinking how much she would fart later on in life. Even Minnie was put off by her farting. Jenna didn't care. In fact, the two of them had farting competitions. Jocks. Both had basketball scholarships.

"I wish you luck, Karen. Of course, I'm hoping that I win." I smiled.

She almost fell out of the beanbag, laughing. "You see, that's a start. You cracked a joke. There's hope for you yet, Paige Alexander."

I didn't expect that reaction. And how had she learned my last name?

Minnie walked into the room, and Karen seemed relieved. Sure, she wanted to conquer me, and make me talk, but I don't think she wanted to accomplish that all in one day.

"Hey, Audrey, how was your day?"

"Awesome," she chirped. "I love college. All of the people running around and having fun."

Awesome. A day of classes was "awesome." What qualified as "super dooper awesome," a trip to McDonald's?

"And don't forget all of the cute guys. There must be a million, and I'm determined to get a boyfriend this year." Karen had declared this intention the first night I met her.

She eyeballed me, expecting me to say something, but I just shrugged. What was I missing?

"And, speaking of boys, one stopped by to see you, Audrey." Karen raised her eyebrows at me.

"Oh!" I smacked my head. "Yes, a Tom stopped by." It had only been a few minutes, but I had completely forgotten. You see, my brain stalls! At least Karen was on her toes. But she was boy-crazy. It would take a lot for her to forget a boy stopping by our room. It was a momentous occasion.

I grabbed some clothes from my closet and entered the bathroom to change. I could hear them talking through the door. Karen was telling Minnie about her embarrassing day.

When I exited the bathroom, Minnie whistled. "Wow, you look nice."

I mumbled a thank you and tossed my dirty laundry onto a heap of clothes in the back of my closet. Sooner or later, I would have to venture to the basement to do my laundry. Or perhaps I should just buy new clothes. But wait, I had to pay for therapy.

"So do you have a hot date with a man tonight?" Karen teased.

"Nope. Do you?"

She stuck her tongue out at me. Karen has never had a boyfriend. I found this hard to believe. She was good-looking and funny. I thought a lot of guys would like to hang out with her. Maybe her farting turned people off. Did guys like a girl who farted more than them?

I snatched my car keys from my desk. "I'm heading out of town to see a friend. I'll be back later this weekend." I looked over my shoulder to spy Minnie and Karen exchange quizzical glances. I chuckled quietly after closing the door. They knew something was up, and it was killing them. I bet they would toss my room in search of answers. Go ahead, girls. You won't find anything. I've had years of experience at hiding.

CHAPTER EIGHT

THE DRIVE DOWN to Jess's was uneventful. I drove like a demon—fast. The roads weren't crowded though, so I didn't get a chance to weave in and out of traffic at breakneck speed. I loved that rush, almost clipping someone's bumper, cutting them off so I could get in front, using the emergency lane to pass stalled traffic. When other drivers flipped me the bird, I laughed. Like that was going to change my driving habits. Oooh—I'm scared! Screw off, jack off, and learn how not to drive like a grandma.

I arrived at the restaurant before Jess: typical Type A behavior. I was obsessed with time management. I didn't like people waiting for me. Worse, I hated waiting for others, but since I always arrived ridiculously early, I spent a lot of time waiting; hence, I always carried a book with me. I had developed the habit years ago. Reading always gave me comfort. It was a way to get away from me. Just another way to escape, to disappear.

"Wow, I thought I was early." Jess slid into the chair opposite.

"You are." I glanced at my watch. "Ten minutes." I noticed Jess wince when she saw the scar on my wrist, but she quickly plastered a smile on her face.

"I'm not sure I want to know how long you've been here." She gestured to my novel: *Rebecca*. "Hopefully, you didn't drive anyone off the road today trying to prove you're Mario Andretti's daughter instead of Mr. Alexander's."

"No reason to fret. Traffic was oh-so boring today. I didn't get to cut off one single person. Pretty much a straight shot, and no weaving in and out." I pouted.

"That's a relief to the rest of us, but I'm sure it drove you batty."

"Listen, smartass, it's nice to see you." I smiled.

"All right, truce. And it's nice to see you too, sweetheart."

Jess reached under the table and squeezed my hand. She was completely comfortable with showing affection in public; I wasn't. I didn't care what others thought. I cared whether or not they knew my parents. My mom once said that all homos needed a bullet in the head. And not as a joke. She didn't deal in jokes, only in "facts," like Mr. Gradgrind from Dickens's *Hard Times*.

Damn, why didn't I think of that last May! Instead of slitting my wrists, I could have said, "I'm gay!" and then just waited for the bullet. Of course it wouldn't be that simple. Not with her.

"Did you order yet?" Jess's voice brought me back to the present.

I shook my head. "I haven't lost all of my manners yet. Besides, isn't college supposed to refine me and not turn me into an uncouth slob?"

"Who knows, with you? You don't actually follow the rules do you? And slob is your middle name." She sipped her water in an exaggerated dignified manner—pinky finger out.

"You're feeling spicy tonight. I like it."

"I've had a good day. A very good day." Jess glowed.

MARIONETTE

"Are you two ready to order?" The waitress flipped open her notebook and tapped her foot, waiting for me.

"Sure, I'll have the fillet. Rare, please."

"Make sure the cow is still mooing." Jess teased. "I'll have the chicken Caesar salad."

The girl waddled off, and I turned my attention back to Jess. "So, are you going to share the juicy tidbits? Or do I have to force it out of you?"

"I got into the MBA program!" She could barely contain her excitement. She practically bounced in her chair.

"Congrats, Jessica." I squeezed her leg under the table.

Jess was older than me and had finished college early when I was still finishing high school. I know. Gross. But it never felt that way. I'd never felt at ease with kids my own age. They were immature and they cared too much about the little things in life. I'd learned long ago that the little things didn't matter. Surviving mattered.

We didn't have sex for quite some time when we first started dating, and I kept the relationship pretty quiet. I still do. Not one person at my high school knew about Jess. I didn't go to the prom or to any other dances. If I went to a football game or movies with friends, Jess stayed at home. Everyone teased me that I was a prude, but little did they know that I lived with Jess all through my senior year. My parents never cared to check on me. You have to care about someone to bother prying into their life. As long as I stayed out of my parents' way, and out of jail, they didn't bother keeping tabs on me. Oh, and I had to get good grades. That wasn't hard for me. I wasn't a rebel. For me, staying at Jess's apartment wasn't wrong. I wanted to be around someone who loved me, and it felt like a home to me. I don't remember that feeling during my childhood.

I gazed into Jess's emerald eyes. "So, you're one step closer to conquering the business world. What should we do to celebrate?"

"I was hoping you would ask. There's a Spanish movie I want to see at The Esquire."

My face must have showed my distaste.

"Don't start with me, missy," she said, waggling a finger at me. "You chose the last movie, and I didn't complain one bit."

"Come on, *Basic Instinct* will be a classic. How can you not love that movie?"

"I'm just not into Hollywood films. Too predictable." She pointed to my novel. "Now that book has suspense. And Mrs. Danvers is creepy."

Jess had bought the book last week and mailed it to me. *That* was her idea of a care package. Enrichment for the mind, she calls it.

"Predictable. The ending of *Basic Instinct* threw me completely. Did she? Didn't she?" I wiggled my head side to side for emphasis.

"That wasn't all that suspenseful. *Rear Window*—now *that's* a great thriller." She pointed her fork at my face.

"What?" I threw my hands up. "Do you only like black and white films or foreign films? Is tonight's Spanish flick a who-dunnit?"

"Nope. It's a love story."

"Love story!" Heads turned in our direction, and Jess giggled.

I whispered, "Oh, you're going to pay for this one, Jessica McCrae."

How did this amazing woman love me? She was going places in life. She had finished college in record speed, landed a great internship during her last year, and now she would be starting her MBA program next fall. She was educated, cultured, fun, witty, and intelligent. I looked down at my wrists.

"Uh-oh, you're getting that faraway look again." Jess snapped her fingers in my face and flashed me a confident smile. "You okay?"

Marionette

I brushed my thoughts aside. "Me? Okay? Of course." I let out a nervous chuckle. "Here comes our food. Now, time me." I glanced at my watch. "I bet I can scarf all of my meal down, have time for dessert, and still make it to your cheesy movie."

"You'll get a bellyache. And I know you'll get more sweets at the theater."

"You can't watch a movie without Junior Mints. It's the law, Jess." I tucked a napkin into my shirt. From the looks of the steak, it was bloody as hell.

"I don't remember studying that law in my business law class." She forked up a dainty portion of her salad.

"And they let you into an MBA program. What is the world coming to?" I joked, and started carving into my steak.

"Not to ruin your good mood, but how is therapy so far?"

I continued chewing an extremely large piece of steak. Ever since I was a kid, I had never consumed petite bites. It was all or nothing for me. While chewing, I tried to think of something clever to say. I wanted to tell her that I'd used her dog-on-a-nail story and that Liddy ate that shit up. The old Jess would have gotten a kick out of me using the story and having a therapist taking the bait. But the new Jess, the one after the bathtub incident, probably wouldn't find it funny.

Finally, when I couldn't come up with anything clever, I mumbled, "Its fine," with my mouth full of steak.

"Is that all you'll say?"

I swallowed too quickly, and then punched my chest with a fist to force a chunk of half-chewed steak down. After a sip of my iced tea, I added, "It won't be easy, Jess. But I'm going to give it the good ol' fashioned college try." I gave a Boy Scout salute.

"I hope you take more time in therapy than you do chewing

your food. Do they have any manners courses up there?"

I scanned her face. She was only half joking. "You're a funny lady."

"You know I support you, Paige."

"I know, Jess. I really do."

When I got back to my dorm room, the three stooges were there. Fortunately, after my marvelous weekend with Jess, I was in a decent mood. Minnie wasn't. She was crying, and Karen was patting her on the back. Jenna the jock looked distressed over Minnie showing her feelings. I was starting to like Jenna more and more.

"Hello," I whispered. I set my bag down and slipped quietly into the room.

"Hi," Karen replied.

I watched for a few seconds and then motioned to Minnie, whose head was buried in her arms, elbows on her desk.

"She had a blowup with her boyfriend on the phone." Karen filled me in.

"Oh ... I'm sorry to hear that." I didn't want to hear the details of the fight, though. Young lovers and their squabbles got on my nerves quickly.

"She wants to see him, but she doesn't have a car. Jenna's car broke down today, so she can't borrow it." Karen was full of information.

Jenna avoided all eye contact. I sincerely doubted that her car had happened to break down on the same day Minnie had asked to borrow it. My gut told me that Jenna didn't lend her car to anyone, probably not even her mom.

I walked up to Minnie and handed her my car keys. "You can take my car if you want. You might have to get gas, but don't feel like you have to fill it up all the way."

The three of them stared at me. I don't think any of them had expected that. Minnie wiped her eyes on her sleeve. "You really mean that?"

"Of course."

She jumped out of her chair and hugged me, and I noticed she needed a shower. When she went straight to the bathroom to get spruced up for Jeff, the boyfriend, I was relieved, although part of me wanted to remind her to comb her hair.

"You see, Paige, I'm starting to figure you out." Karen beamed.

The only way I could ever manage to hurt my parents was through their pocketbook. If Minnie wrecked my car, they would have to buy me a new one to keep up their image. It wouldn't do to have their darling daughter without a car—a nice car. It wasn't like I wanted Minnie to get killed or anything, but some serious damage to the car would be good. Lately, I had been looking for ways to make my parents suffer with little consequence for me.

"You think so, Karen?" I crossed my arms.

"Yep. You do have a heart."

That made me smile. Minnie emerged from the bathroom, and I told her which parking lot the car was in. The lot in front of our dorm was always packed, so usually I had to hike halfway across campus to retrieve my car.

She gave me another hug. "Thanks, Paige. I really appreciate this."

"Drive safe and take care of Junior Mint."

"Junior Mint?" inquired the grinning Karen.

"That's the name of my car. It's green, and I love Junior Mints."

"I'm blown away. I'm learning so much about you tonight. You, Paige, actually named your car. That's kinda cute."

Jess had named the car, actually. Watching Karen gloat about her new insight tempted me to tell her the truth, just so I could pull the rug right out from under her. Yet, I relished the thought that she believed she was "getting to know me," when in fact she knew nothing at all. Good!

Chapter Nine

AFTER THE FIRST week of classes, my nerves started to settle somewhat. I no longer dreaded going to lectures and seeing so many unfamiliar faces. In fact, I found that I liked being around so many people I didn't know and probably would never know. Those people never asked personal questions, so I wouldn't be forced to lie to them. It was a freeing feeling.

One part of my new life that I hadn't yet adjusted to was Liddy. Jess had made it damn clear I could not slouch on my promise. I was told—no, ordered—not to just go through the motions, but to try. To really try. She hadn't told me how to do that, though. People are good at giving advice, but not on giving a step-by-step, how-to guide. I wanted a procedure, something that would fix my problem. How did I repress the urge to kill myself? Step one …? Why can't there be a step-by-step program? Don't drunks have a program? I wanted a program.

The afternoon was beautiful. Puffy marshmallow clouds floated through the cerulean sky. Birds chirped. Squirrels scampered about, chattering at passersby. I felt a strong urge to jump in my car and head toward the canyon to hike.

Instead, I was sitting in Liddy's office, waiting. She walked in two minutes late—not bad, for her. I elected not to give her a hard time. After all, it had backfired before.

"How have you been since our last meeting?" Her words felt hollow to me.

"Fine."

She turned around and headed toward her desk. Her hair covered half of her face, but from the part I could see, she wasn't pleased with my reply. Liddy set her bag down and picked up the usual from her desk: pencil and notepad.

I was starting to loathe the pencil and notepad. What the fuck did she need them for?

She perched herself in the chair opposite and fussed with her blazer. I preferred her in jeans and a sweater, but I didn't think I really got a say.

Had she forgotten I was there? I opted to stay absolutely still.

As she adjusted her shirt, she asked, "What would you like to talk about today?"

Why couldn't she provide the blueprint for me? If I knew what was wrong with me, then I would fix it. I can be a rational person. Her question angered me, so I decided to be annoying. "The birds and the bees."

"Maybe next time, even though I think that would be an interesting discussion to have with you."

What in the hell did she mean by that? If I were braver, I would have asked. But I was logical, not brave. I didn't like people making assumptions about me, yet letting people make assumptions helped me stay hidden.

I inspected my shoes, making sure my laces hadn't magically

untied themselves. Just to be sure, I tightened the knots.

"You mentioned last week that you aren't close to your father."

"Correct."

"Would you like to elaborate?" She attempted a coaxing smile. Did another one of her suicidal patients attempt to kill themselves? Was that why she was in a crap mood?

"We lived in the same house—that was our only connection."

She tapped her pencil, but showed no emotion. "And that doesn't bother you."

I sighed. "You get used to it. I've had seventeen years to realize that he doesn't love me. He never wanted me. He's made that clear. Over the years, I've watched him torture my mother, me ... not sure how he feels about Abbie, though. I grew to hate him. Now ... I don't know. I don't like him, but hate ... I prefer to ignore the fact that he's my dad. I'm tired. Tired of hating. Now, I avoid. When I still lived at home, I could go for days and not see him once. I've turned avoiding my father into a game."

"And how do you know he feels this way about you?"

"Oh, he doesn't mince his words. And his actions—well, they don't lie either." I crossed my arms and slunk down further into my chair.

"How do you mean?"

I closed my eyes, trying to eradicate one particular image, but couldn't. I wished I had a delete button on my brain. I hated feeling normal and then—BAM!—a picture floating before my eyes taunted me, lured me back.

"A few years after the Lego incident, my mother had surgery. After surviving those years, I thought nothing could destroy her. I thought her surgery would transform her into a superhero. I put a lot of hope into that thought. I wanted my mom back.

"I blamed the Lego incident just as much as everyone else. My memories of her before were gone. All I remembered was the mean mom. In my head, I pictured a sweet, doting mother. The Lego had ruined it all. All of it." I jumped out of my chair. Being cradled in the arms of the chair felt like an abomination.

"I think wolves would have done a better job of raising me after the incident. My parents …"

Liddy followed my eyes up to the ceiling. Above us, people were going about their normal business, preparing for weekend frivolity. Down in the bowels of the building, clients like me were ripping their souls out, piece by piece. Hacking at them, hoping they might rejuvenate. But I had zero hope. All of this was pointless.

Fuck Jess for making me promise to do this.

"When my mom was in the hospital, my father wanted me to see her right after her surgery. The hospital had a policy that patients couldn't be seen so soon. Policies didn't apply to him; they never did. He wanted me to see. I hadn't told him that I'd believed she would evolve into a superhero, but maybe he suspected. Or maybe he's just an asshole."

I leaned against the far wall, still staring at the ceiling with dead eyes. The cracks in the paint blurred into one large hole. I wanted to climb through it. I wanted to plan for weekend merriment.

Liddy cleared her throat and I resumed the story. "I sat in the lobby of the hospital. I can't remember where Abbie was. Sometimes, I wondered if my sister actually existed. Was she a figment of my imagination? Was she me? Was I her? Or was she just too smart to let them fuck with her mind." I sucked in some air, but my lungs felt empty. Empty air.

"'No, I don't think you understand,' he said to the nurse. 'I want my child to see her.' He never said that she was my mom. He always said *her*. He demanded that the nurse wheel *her* out to the lobby since they wouldn't let me behind the locked doors.

"'Mr. Alexander, I don't think you understand—' the nurse started, but my father's eyes stopped her dead. She gathered her strength and whispered, 'This could be too traumatic …' she didn't finish the statement, but glanced in my direction."

I saw the hole in the ceiling spreading open for me. I breathed in more stagnant air.

"'I don't think *you* understand—you'll do as I say,' he said. I can still picture the odd, calm expression on his beet-red face. I'd often marveled over his dual emotions. His words commanded respect, as if he were a Marine drill sergeant.

"For all I know, he probably donated generously to the hospital. Not because he was kind. He was never kind. His tax guy probably suggested it. I think it was around the time he started setting up offshore accounts. If it made fiscal sense, then my father would do it. The word charity sent thunderbolts through his eyes. Ingrates stood with their palms out, begging for money. No one gave him a leg up. He had to toil for his bread. I often imagined that my father was Dickens's inspiration for Ebenezer Scrooge in a previous life."

I stopped talking, not wanting to continue. What was the point really? How was talking part of the step-by-step plan to stay alive? Shouldn't I focus on the good in life? Shouldn't I climb through the hole and announce, "I want to have fun with the rest of you! Fuck this slitting my wrists bullshit!"

"What happened?" Liddy's voice startled me. I was elsewhere, above, and I didn't want to come back down. Not to her office.

"The nurse left the lobby in a huff, but she followed orders. I tried hiding behind a potted plant, but that didn't last. I heard the buzzer on the door. The automatic doors creaked open. I heard a squeaking wheel and the pitter-patter of the nurse's footsteps. My eyes darted up, against my will. Slowly, a hideous creature emerged from the shadows.

"She sat slumped in her chair, spittle dribbling down her front. She was ghost-white. I reached for her hand, and it was frigid. I was sure the doctors had killed her. She was a corpse. Had to be a corpse."

I chuckled. "She was no Wonder Woman, I can tell you that. All of my hopes were dashed that day."

"Why did your father insist on it?"

"Oh, I don't know. I suspect he wanted to prove something to me. He had a life plan. Everything, for the most part, was going according to his plans. The things that didn't go exactly to plan, he could mold into a positive. Then the Lego piece sent his world swirling out of control. Everyone blamed me for it. He couldn't salvage what the Lego did."

"Your loyalty to your mother is impressive." Her expression told me she was egging me on. She was trying to uncover something.

I shrugged. "I just wanted to feel human again," I muttered.

"Did you feel the razor when you cut into your wrists?"

Her question left me speechless. I wasn't sure if I should feel indignant or answer the question.

Several seconds ticked by. "No."

"Where do you go when you don't feel?"

"Into the past."

"Your past?" She leaned forward in the chair, as if she were anticipating a big clue.

"Yes and no. It feels like my past, but I don't believe it either. I don't know what to believe anymore. Sometimes it feels like I'm watching a movie, and I don't know if I'm the star or in the audience."

Neither of us shattered the silence for several seconds.

MARIONETTE

"What are you thinking so hard about, Paige?"

"Oh, nothing much. Just trying to figure out an escape route from this office." I glanced at the ceiling, but the hole had snapped shut.

She laughed heartily. "There aren't any. Many clients have tried to find one." Then she added, "Besides, it's your past that you want to escape from."

I eyed her. "Oooh ... that was a good one." I gave a wan smile. "No wonder they say you're one of the best."

"It didn't sound as corny in my head." She shook her head, as if trying to knock the line out of her skull for good.

Again, there was a lull.

"It's difficult for you to open up, isn't it?" Her tone was kind.

"Jess always says I'm like an iceberg; I only share a tiny fraction of my life with people, just enough to skim the surface."

"Who is Jess?"

"The one I promised."

She looked at me as if to say, "Duh, you already told me that." Instead, she said, "Jess must be a special person."

"Yes."

"Not ready to share yet?"

"Something like that."

"I understand."

My brain snapped awake. What did she understand? I studied her eyes. There was no malice.

Possibly she did, then. Perhaps not. Did it matter? I was one of her batty patients. When she looked at me, she saw a loon. *Do crazy people emit a smell?* I wondered. *Or was it just a look in our eyes? Maybe I should conduct a study in the lobby here to see if I can determine who is mad and who is sane.*

I tried to picture people's reactions if I walked up to everyone and took a whiff and then clicked a pen to record something on a notepad. Would they say anything, or would they expect to find someone like me roaming the halls of the lunatic Mecca? What if I tried to lick them to see if I could isolate a taste? Squeeze them? Pinch them to hear them squeak? Would their pitch have a certain pattern? Was I missing a sense?

Liddy stood up and fetched a glass of water for me. I took a few sips and then went on my way. Weekend gaiety, here I come!

My cheerfulness revolved around escaping. Besides books, movies provided a way for me to escape. Jess did her best to take me to movies as much as possible, and I had a decent collection of videos on tape.

Since I actually had my room to myself, I decided to indulge. I put in my favorite movie, *The Silence of the Lambs*, made some microwave popcorn, and mixed Milk Duds into the steaming popcorn to make a delicious, gooey snack. I washed down the mess with Coke. I could feel the sugar coursing through my veins. I felt like a superhero.

The phone rang. I didn't answer since it was probably for Minnie. College students started to freak out by 4 p.m. on a Friday if they didn't have plans for the night. I was relishing my quiet time and the fact that I had the room to myself. Minnie was with her boyfriend and the duo next door had gone home to have their moms wash all of their laundry. I had thought about slipping my dirty clothes in, but didn't think it would go over that well.

The caller didn't leave a message.

Several seconds later, the phone trilled again. I still didn't answer, but I paused the movie. I had the urge to throw my popcorn bowl across the room. Instead, I got up to use the restroom and to splash cold water on my face. Minnie and her mystery caller were both starting to grate on my nerves.

Nestled back into the beanbag, I started the movie again. The fucking phone rang again.

I seized the receiver so hard that if it were human I would have snapped its neck. "What?"

"Nice greeting, Paige."

Shit. It wasn't for Minnie but for me.

"Hi, Mel. Sorry, I thought it was one of Minnie's friends."

"I really hope you don't act that way around her and her friends. Not very nice." She hesitated, but I didn't take the bait. "What are you doing inside on this beautiful afternoon?"

"I'm watching my favorite movie. Why aren't you outside, if it's so beautiful out?"

"I'm at work. Let me guess: *The Silence of the Lambs*. You need to stop watching such morbid films."

"It's a morbid world, Mel. Wait, this is my favorite part: Lecter is toying with everyone. What a fucking genius!"

"Most psychopaths are." Her words sounded flat.

"Are you saying I'm a genius? Thanks."

"Oh, I can tell what kind of mood you are in. Therapy didn't go so well today?"

Actually, I didn't really know how therapy had gone. I was baffled by the process. Each time I left, I felt crummy. Was that therapy? Had I signed up for a year of talking about difficult shit only to feel worse than I did before I started?

"Listen," Mel said, raising her voice so I would not blow her off. "I'm calling to remind you about tonight. You haven't forgotten, have you?"

"Of course I haven't forgotten, Mel."

What did I have planned?

"What time do you want us to pick you up?"

Realizing that I was supposed to have dinner with Mel and her asshole boyfriend, I made a gun with my fingers and pretended to blow my brains out. In a cheery voice, I said, "Ah, yes. Dinner with Wesley. I've been looking forward to it all week."

Wesley the Weasel. His name fit him well.

"Paige, knock it off. We'll pick you up at seven."

"Seriously, I can't wait to see Weasel. I suppose you want me to be on my best behavior."

"Like that's possible. I've never known you to try. Just try to be normal, and his name is Wes."

"Normal, huh. I may have to do some research on that. But the library is so far away, and I was only there earlier today doing research. I'll have to wing it tonight."

"What type of research?" Mel missed college and always wanted to know about my classes, even when I was taking college courses in high school.

I didn't want to tell her about my project so I said, "Nothing special. Just a paper on why no one likes weasels."

"Seriously, Paige. Behave." She hung up.

How rude! After I was doing my best to act "normal." And she was the one who interrupted my movie. Ingrate!

I grabbed a handful of gooey popcorn and shoved it into my mouth.

There was something odd about Weasel, but I couldn't put my finger on it. Jess had tried to be friends with him, but even she had backed off. When Jess was around him, she acted nice, but she was cool. I couldn't get her to tell me what the deal was, which was odd,

MARIONETTE

since Jess was so open about just about anything.

Some of you may be thinking, *Typical dyke—man hater.* But I don't treat all men this way. I don't hate men. I hate assholes. And Weasel was a bona fide asshole.

Mel had started dating him two years ago, at a low point in her life. After quitting college due to a lack of funds and horrible grades, she'd moved in with her parents and got a job at the local mall. Not an exciting life, but she was pulling things together. However, she felt like a disappointment. I'm pretty sure something happened at college to send her into a tailspin, but she won't talk about it. I've never pressed her on the issue. I'm not the type to force people into therapy.

Well, Weasel scurried in. His type preys on the vulnerable. He saw someone who'd be afraid to lose him and boy did he take advantage. He always borrows money. He blows her off to hang with the boys. Then he has the balls to call her late at night to pick him up since he's wasted and can't drive home. And he has affairs. I think he knocked up one girl. I'm not positive, but I'm fairly certain Mel paid for the abortion.

Every time, he comes crawling back saying how much he loves her and that it would be the last time. *Please!* All of us know how it will turn out—all of us except Mel. I keep hoping she'll wake up and smell the weasel in her bed.

Okay, he wasn't Hitler. But did that matter? He still treated my best friend like dirt. And she wasn't the same person anymore. I missed her. For months now, I'd been trying to overlook her aloofness because I couldn't face losing a friend at the moment. But the outlook doesn't look good. It doesn't help that when I'm around him I can't keep my own inner asshole in check. Mel always ends up in the middle.

The knock on my door arrived much sooner than I wanted it to.

Mel stood there alone, and my hopes started to soar. Weasel-free!

"Where's the weasel?" I didn't even try to stop the happiness from creeping into my tone.

"Hello, Paige. It's nice to see you." She gave me a quick hug and walked into the room. Mel never liked to answer questions about her beloved. I supposed it might have been my approach to the topic.

She fidgeted with some figurines on my desk, her mood reminding me of a child whose balloon had just flown off into the wild blue yonder. She looked completely crushed.

"Do you want to talk about it, Mel? Or is it none of my business?" I never liked to push people. After all, I was horrible at talking about my own feelings, let alone anyone else's. If Jess were there, she'd have whacked the back of my head for putting it so awkwardly.

Mel turned to me. "It's none of your business. Besides, I don't want to talk about it." She looked around my room, focusing on the messiness on Minnie's side. "Where are your roommates?"

"All of them are out of town for the weekend. Thank God."

"What, you don't get along with the masses?" she teased.

"They're okay. They are always sticking their noses into my business, though. So where is Wesley?" I figured if I used his actual name, I might get an answer.

"Oh, don't worry, he's here. He's waiting in the car."

Not the answer I'd been hoping for. "Always the gentleman, I see. I bet he's honking the horn right now."

She looked miffed, but also conceded that I was correct. "Are you ready then?"

"Of course. And on time, I might add." I wasn't about to let her tardiness slide. It was probably Weasel's fault. He was fastidious about his thinning hair. He actually curled it to add fullness. It didn't work and just made his hair look even worse, from all of the split ends. "What's the matter, did it take his curling iron too long to heat up tonight?"

Mel had shared this juicy tidbit with me when she'd first started dating him. She was really on the fence about hooking up with him on a permanent basis, so she had used this as one of the reasons why she didn't like him. Now, I was using it against her. There's something wrong with me. Obviously.

Her eyes bored into mine, warning me to back off.

"All I need are my keys." I cursed myself for being a jackass.

"On your desk, bottom right-hand corner. It's good to see you haven't changed much. You should glue your keys to your hand, since you are always looking for them." For the first time, she smiled.

"Maybe we can stop for some superglue. I can think of a few things I'd like to glue shut."

"So can I, Paige."

"Shall we go downstairs, where our chariot waits? All we need now is a gladiator. I think in Roman times men had curly hair."

She slapped the back of my head.

"Ouch! I was just stating a historical fact." I rubbed my head.

"If you don't watch it tonight, I'll glue your asshole shut."

As we walked down the hallway, I noticed how beautiful she looked. I towered over her five-foot-three frame. Weasel was over six feet. Her long golden hair flowed over her burgundy blazer. Her jeans revealed a body sculpted by hours in the gym. Her doe eyes glistened, so large in her face in contrast to her petite nose.

"You look nice tonight, Mel."

"Thanks. Don't say that in front of Wes, though. He'll think you're hitting on me."

I laughed. Simple minds couldn't believe that I didn't have the desire to hit on every girl I knew. Mel was my friend. I would never hit on her. Flirting was not a concept that I even understood, and anyway, I would never betray Jess.

Weasel, however, hit on every piece of ass he saw, no matter what the woman looked like. But *I* was the freak, the social outcast, the downfall of human society.

A chill surged into the hallway as I swung open the door that led to the parking lot, and I realized I'd forgotten my sweater. Knowing that Prince Charming wouldn't want to wait any longer, I forged on through the cold.

As I slid into the backseat, I saw Weasel adjust the mirror so it wouldn't show his reflection, only the road. He was still mussing his hair. I casually looked around to see if there was a curling iron in the car, but all I saw was a bottle of hairspray.

"Hello, Paige." His voice dripped with hatred.

"Hi, Wesley! How was the drive up?"

He hated driving, so I was trying to aggravate him in a non-confrontational way.

"It sucked."

He had so much personality.

"I'm sorry to hear that. I rather enjoy driving myself, getting out into the open and taking in all the scenery. Did you see any cows on the way up?"

Mel reached around the front seat and whacked my shin with a fist.

"Paige, where's the best restaurant in town?" asked Weasel.

I guessed I was picking up the check tonight. He never offered to pay, and I couldn't let Mel pay for it. She was on her feet eight hours a day, dealing with teenage brats at the mall.

But Weasel knew I was rich, and getting me to buy his meal was

MARIONETTE

probably the only reason he had agreed to come. He loved to screw me.

"Go back to the main road. You'll have your pick of restaurants for about a mile."

He started the car with a little trouble. Then we were off, the engine sputtering the whole way. I looked out the back window to see haze spewing out of the exhaust pipe. How was it that he never got a ticket?

We drove in silence—an awkward, angry quiet that sent chills down my spine. Eventually, he pulled in to the Olive Garden parking lot. Wise choice. On a Friday night, the wait would be over an hour, maybe longer since we had to wait for a table in the smoking section for Weasel. Mel never asked him to endure a meal without ruining his lungs, or ours. I despised smokers. Weak individuals. To me, people with addictions were worthless. Plus, smokers smelled like three-day-old ashtrays.

I placed our name on the waitlist and then suggested we sit in the bar. Weasel jumped at the chance, since he could smoke there. Before we had even spotted a tiny table in the back corner, he lit up. I glanced over at Mel and smiled. She avoided my eyes. I saw some families in the bar, and I cringed each time Weasel blew smoke in the direction of children.

"How are your classes?" Weasel's voice was high for a male. I thought smoking would have hardened it, but instead he always sounded like a dolphin chittering. Unfortunately, I understood what he was saying, but I think a conversation with a dolphin would have been more edifying. Whenever I heard his voice, I had to combat a strong urge to throw a fish in his face.

"Classes?" I smacked my head. "I knew I forgot something. Tell you what, I'll do my best to go to one next week, and I'll write you a letter and tell you all about it. I can do that each week if you'd like."

Weasel had never gone to college. I figured I was only trying to help the underprivileged.

"Don't worry. I'm sure your father can ensure you receive all A's no matter what. Nothing is impossible for a rich brat."

I was impressed that he had formed complete sentences, for the most part. I stared into his cold, steel-blue eyes. He might have been attractive if he'd had a semi-decent personality, and if he stopped curling his hair. It looked ridiculous. Before I could respond, I heard my name over the PA system.

"Wow, that was fast. Not too many smokers here tonight. Perhaps they didn't have the energy to lug in their oxygen tanks."

Mel's face showed her displeasure.

The hostess sat us down, and all three of us instantly hid behind our menus.

Mel set her menu down first. "How's Jess these days?"

"Fine." I didn't take my eyes off the choices on the menu. Dorm food was getting to me. I wondered how many meals I could polish off if I bought Weasel another pack of cigarettes.

Out of the corner of my eye, I noticed that Weasel bristled at the mention of Jess's name. He lit another cigarette, blowing the smoke into my face, and looked disheartened when I didn't keel over in my seat. Then he flicked his Zippo lighter and singed some of his napkin. Just great, I'm having dinner with an imbecilic pyromaniac.

The waitress took our order and I flinched when Weasel ordered the most expensive steak. I had to save money for therapy. Mel ordered a salad, and I settled on a cheap cheese ravioli. I would have to make more popcorn and Milk Duds to fill my belly tonight.

"So, Paige, how is Jess doing with her internship—does that job pay?" asked Weasel.

Marionette

I was shocked he even cared about it. And I was doubly shocked when I saw Mel kick him under the table. What was I missing?

I looked to Mel, who busied herself folding her napkin into a deformed swan.

"Ah, I think it pays. She doesn't seem to want for money," I mumbled.

"Ha! I bet she doesn't!" replied Weasel.

Again, Mel whacked him. Weasel turned his attention to the buxom blonde at the next table.

My eyes silently queried Mel, but she just shrugged. Was he insinuating that Jess was a kept woman? That I supported her?

"How's the used car racket, Wesley?"

The fact that Weasel was a used-car salesman tickled me pink. What a perfect job for Weasel. The salad and breadsticks arrived, and we spent the rest of the time listening to Weasel whine about low commissions, cheap customers, and a lousy economy. That he had actually used the word economy in context impressed me. He worked at one of those super-suspicious used-car lots in the bad part of town. You could find a hooker, get new wheels, and buy some crack all within one hundred feet of his day job. It was the type of place that would be perfect for a flick about degenerate gamblers who needed to sell their cars so they could hit the craps table again in hope of finally landing the big score. A real boulevard of losers.

Dinner didn't last long. Weasel inhaled his steak in four large bites. My cheese ravioli was nothing to rave about, and Mel's salad contained wilted lettuce doused with Caesar dressing. The meal sucked, but Weasel looked like he had just dined like a king. He dug into his rodent-like teeth with a toothpick while I settled the bill.

The drive home was in silence. Weasel slowed down just enough for me to jump out of the car without inflicting any permanent damage, and before leaping out, I said goodbye and whispered in Mel's ear that I would call her on Sunday for lunch.

Walking up the deserted stairwell to my dorm, I was just relieved to be alone. Back in my room, I saw the flickering light on my answering machine and, after hearing the message, I sighed. My night was only beginning.

It didn't take me long to locate my car in the far parking lot. Jess's message had said, "I want to see you tonight."

Sometimes, when Jess drinks, she gets somewhat insecure. I was hoping this wasn't one of those nights. Mind you, when she was in one of these moods, I tried to be as supportive as possible, but I probably didn't help her insecurities at all, since I was in the closet and she wasn't. She did her best to understand why I didn't tell anyone, and I tried to understand why she told everyone. I mean *everyone*: colleagues, friends, her pastor, the mailman, and even the clerks at the drug store. She didn't scream lesbo either. Not to stereotype, but Jess was extremely feminine and certainly not the type you'd see playing on a college softball team.

I hadn't even realized she was gay when I first met her. I should mention that I have terrible gaydar. Jess likes to put my skills to the test, but unless a guy is flaming or a girl is so butch that I feel like pissing my pants in fear, I invariably fail the test. I suppose that helps Jess feel more secure, since she knows I'm not attracted to really butch types. She teases me constantly. "I know you won't cheat on me, since you couldn't find a lesbian even if you tried."

I have zero attraction to men. I have no problem with bisexuals: I'm just not one.

Jess also has a fear of being abandoned. I'm no shrink, but I'm pretty sure it's because she's an orphan. She didn't grow up in foster care. She lived with an aunt during high school, an aunt who wasn't all that nice. Not an abuser, just overwhelmed by suddenly living with a sullen teenager who was trying to cope with the loss of her parents after a drunk-driving accident. The aunt was the type who had never wanted to settle down so was doing her best to travel the world by teaching English in faraway places. She didn't have any money, and she was suddenly thrust into supporting two people. It was too much for her. As soon as Jess had walked across the stage to receive her high school diploma, the aunt had hightailed it out of the States. Jess hasn't heard from her much since, except for the occasional random postcard from somewhere like Oman.

I'm not sure if I should be flattered or insulted that Jess thinks I won't cheat. Obviously, I found one lesbian.

Okay, I didn't. She found me—in a bookstore. There I was, in my local Barnes & Noble store, reading an excerpt from *Pride and Prejudice* when this stunning woman approached me and said, "Oh, that's a classic. If you don't buy it right now, I'll buy it for you and force you to read it."

Shyly, I had lowered the book and mumbled that I had to read it for class.

"Don't let that deter you. You'll love it. If you don't, I'll buy you twenty books of your choice."

Her smile was infectious. I didn't know what to do. I was used to men hitting on me, but not girls. But by then, I was sixteen and I knew I liked girls. Knowing that and acting on that were two different things. I don't want to think about how red my face must have gone on that day. Despite that, I had attempted to act cool. "Oh, really."

Jess had laughed. "What college do you go to?"

I knew it was too good to be true; she thought I was a college student. "Um, I'm not in college. I'm still in high school."

"Oh! I thought you were taking a class this summer." She continued smiling, undeterred.

I explained that we had been assigned some books to read over the summer.

Jess was wearing a long flowing skirt and a white tank top. I soon realized that she only wore skirts. She didn't own a pair of jeans, not one!

She spied a Sue Grafton novel in my stack of books.

"Is that on your list?" She gestured to the Grafton. "Have you ever read *The Maltese Falcon*? Sam Spade is one kick-ass detective."

We located a copy. Before I knew it, Jess had piled five books onto the stack I already held. I could barely peer over the top of them, but I was doing my best to steal glances at her whenever I thought she wasn't looking.

Then she shocked the hell out of me by asking if she could buy me a cup of coffee. I hadn't even liked coffee back then, but I'd started to that very day. It tasted bitter, but I drank three cups. And I paid for one of the rounds. I wasn't *that* clueless.

We talked for hours in the coffee shop inside the store. It was easy to talk to her, since she did most, if not all, the talking. She was in college and would be graduating early. She'd traveled to Europe earlier in the summer, spoke French and Spanish, and planned on learning German. She loved foreign films. I pretended that I enjoyed them as well, even though I had never seen one.

That was when she asked me on a date. I had never been asked on a date before. I didn't think anyone at my school suspected I was gay, but I didn't put out the vibe I was interested in dating anyone either. I had a few close friends but I mostly stayed well out of the high school scene. Books were my best friends.

Over the following two years, Jess introduced me to her favorite books, movies, restaurants, plays, musicals—she knew so much. I was probably the most well-read student in my school, even though I didn't let on. She had me read all of Austen's novels, the Bronte sisters, Dickens, Hardy, Hemingway, Steinbeck, Doyle, Faulkner, Twain, Camus, Thomas Mann—the list goes on and on. She read me *The Little Prince* in French to help me with my homework.

Jess knew all of the best restaurants in town; I don't mean the expensive ones my parents dragged me to, but the little holes in the wall with the best food. I didn't even know our town had Lebanese anything, let alone a restaurant.

We watched tons of foreign films and classic black-and-white films from Hollywood's heyday. Jess even had season tickets to the opera. It wasn't all intellectual pursuits either. She loved being outdoors: hiking, biking, and skiing. I had never met anyone like her before. There were times I felt like I was in a fairytale and had found my own princess.

I mentioned already that during my senior year, I practically lived with Jess. I would check in at home after school and then go around to her place. My family wasn't the kind that had sit-down meals together. After the Lego incident, we all got used to having separate lives. Even after Mom recovered, for the most part, we didn't resume being a family. None of us really liked each other. I got into the habit of going home after school to eat something and be seen by one of my parents, and then I would go upstairs to do homework. Jess always picked me up outside so my parents wouldn't notice my car was gone. Mom wasn't an early riser and Dad was in the office before the sun rose over the foothills. Abbie was never home either. I didn't have to worry about being discovered sneaking in before school in the mornings. I hadn't snuck out every night, only the majority.

Through it all, I marveled over Jess's energy levels. She never seemed tired and always had something planned for us. It wasn't always a night at the opera or fancy shit like that. There were nights when we stayed in and watched movies, or read books; rather, I read while Jess studied. She was finishing up a business degree and wanted to get into an MBA program. Jess had a thirst for life and for the finer things. She thought business was her yellow brick road. Ironic, huh? My girlfriend was desperate to experience all that life had to offer, and I wanted to kill myself.

Things started off slow in the sex department. I think my age was a huge stumbling block for Jess. We didn't even hold hands or kiss for the first six months. I started to think we were just good friends, and I was cool with that. More would have been nice, but having someone to talk to was great. I found her exciting. Just hearing her voice put me in a tizzy. And I started having fantastic dreams about her. Do girls have wet dreams? I didn't have anyone to ask. Abbie and I weren't close and asking my parents was out of the question. I didn't even have any cool high school teachers to confide in. And, I would never try to find out the information on my own. What if I got caught with a lesbian Kama Sutra or something? My parents would have killed me.

The night we kissed for the first time was one of the best nights of my life. I know—cheesy! Let me explain, though. When I first realized I was gay, I thought I would always be alone. After watching my parents and their fucked-up relationship, I wanted no part of that. My mom was a little like Miss Havisham from *Great Expectations*. She always told me that men would ruin my life and to stay away from them. Luckily, I agreed with her, and I did stay away. This doesn't mean I'm gay because I hate my father, and I hate people who make that assumption. It doesn't mean I was raped or anything either—

another idiotic way of thinking. If all of the women in this world who were raped turned to lesbianism, well, the human population would be much smaller. Think about it. I don't hate men. I'm just gay. I can't explain why. All I can say is that I don't feel any different. I don't bang my head on the wall and wish I were straight and plead with God to take away my sinful desires. Actually, God, if it's all the same to you, please don't take away my desires—they're fucking hot.

I realized I was gay while I was sitting in my homeroom class first thing one morning. The thought struck me like a lightning bolt. *I'm gay. I like girls.* That was it. It didn't bother me at all, but I had never planned to act on it either. Not until that day in the bookstore.

I'm in the closet out of fear, not societal pressures, which are sort of big in my hometown, but I can live with that. I fear my parents. They are bigwigs in town. If they found out, they would ship me off to one of those conversion places. It would be ruinous for their reputations to have a lesbo in the family. Maybe they'd even have me whacked. My father knows some shady characters. And my mom ... don't get me started.

Oddly enough, Jess has had death threats against her. She's in charge of a local gay group. With all of the Amendment 2 stuff going on right now, she's been in the public eye. The amendment is about gay rights in Colorado. One asshole—a fat, ugly motherfucker—threatened her. She can't prove it was him because he's smarter than he looks. You should see all of the hair on his neck, the way it just pokes out of his collar. You can't differentiate the hair on his chest from his long scraggly beard. Like I said, he's revolting. She received a letter that read: "Fucking die dike."

Yeah, he actually spelled it wrong! Jess laughed it off, but still reported it to the police. They didn't laugh about it. For weeks, the police followed Jess to and from work. After the dust settled, everything went back to normal. It never fazed Jess. She'd say, "Oh, don't worry, that guy knows he can't touch me."

At first, when I started letting Jess in somewhat, she laughed at the idea that my own parents might kill me or lock me up. The more she's come to know me, and the more she's seen of my family from afar, the less she's laughed. That doesn't mean that Jess is afraid of my parents—she isn't afraid of anything—but that she's tired of seeing me hurt. One of the reasons Jess wants to be super-successful is so we can run away together and never have to see my folks again.

I remember the first time she saw bruises on me. We weren't having sex back then, but we weren't completely innocent either. When she saw the marks on my ribcage (I might have had a broken rib), she immediately wanted to call the cops. "You can't call the cops on rich people," I told her. I didn't want to end up in a mental asylum: that's where they would have put me. My parents had threatened me on many occasions, not because they suspected I was gay, but simply because it was a power they had over me. I don't even know how they came up with the idea. Some parents send their kids to military schools, but mine wanted me to be declared loony.

In public, everyone thought my parents loved me. I was forced to attend many public functions. Perhaps some people suspected that things at home weren't so cheery, but most didn't. You always hear about people who say, "I didn't know he was such an asshole behind closed doors."

My thought was always: *Really? You didn't know? Did you never notice how, when you disagreed with him, anger flashed through his eyes like a rocket. You didn't know that, with that kind of rage, sometimes people get hurt. That he couldn't always control it? Or that at home, he didn't have to control it?*

Yeah, you didn't know.

MARIONETTE

Jess never attended these functions. Sometimes, she would see a picture in the paper and her blood would boil. Not about seeing me—she got a kick out of that—but she hated seeing my parents smiling and acting normal when she knew they were beasts. And Jess didn't even know the whole story. At college, I never worried that my roommates would see me in the paper. They weren't exactly newspaper-reading types. And if they did read the paper, they were too young to care about the society page. Society page—please, what a waste of space! Only the rich wanted to know what other affluent people were up to. Trust me, if I didn't need to be at a function, my parents wouldn't drag me along, and I never asked to go. I only went to the "must-be-seen-at" functions.

I'm not saying we were the Kennedys of the West, either, just that my parents are loaded.

What does my father do? Good question. I've never figured it out. I know the company he works for, and I can point out the building from the interstate. That's about it, though. When you don't give a crap about a person, why waste time finding out more about them?

Most people, when they hear my name, don't know anything about me, and I do my best to keep it that way. I've never wanted privileges; I know the price. I'm sure there are nice rich folks in the world. Not my folks, though.

When I walked into Jess's apartment, the lights were off, but I saw her outline on the couch and I could hear the clink of ice in her glass. Jess loved vodka tonics but rarely indulged.

I sat my bag down by the front door and flipped the light on.

"Don't!" She bolted off the couch and switched the light back off.

"Jess, what's going on?" I had to admit her behavior unnerved me, but then her giggle put me at ease.

"Oh, Paige, don't get your panties in a bunch. I'm just not in the mood for having the lights on, that's all." She sauntered back to the couch and resumed drinking.

"Okay."

We didn't often sit in the front room of her apartment with all of the lights off.

"Do you want me to light the fire? It's a little cold in here." I shivered to emphasize my point.

"Nah. Grab the comforter from my bed and we can snuggle out here."

After bumping through her dark apartment, I situated myself on the couch with Jess, both of us under the comforter.

"How was dinner with Mel and Wesley?"

Something about her tone sounded off to me. "Um, it was okay." I tried to stare into her eyes, but could only make out the outline of her face. "Are you okay?"

"Me? Yeah, why?"

"Well, you left a message on my machine saying you *had* to see me tonight and now we are sitting in the pitch dark. It seems a little odd."

"Oh, that. I just wanted to see you." She paused. "I had a hard day at the office today."

I wasn't positive, but I could have sworn she made quotation marks with her fingers when she said the word office. It reminded me of Weasel's comment about her internship.

"So, I think Weasel thinks you're a kept woman."

"What!"

Her alarm surprised me. "I think he thinks I pay all of your bills."

"Oh, really. Why do you say that?" I had her complete interest now.

"He asked if your internship was a paying gig. I said I didn't know, but I thought so since you never wanted for money, and he scoffed at that remark."

I felt Jess bristle and I patted her leg. "Don't worry about what Weasel says. He's a jerk, and a used-car salesman to boot."

Her body relaxed beside me. "Besides, wouldn't it be kinda cool to be a kept woman? You know that if I could I'd make sure you lived in the lap of luxury."

Jess leaned against my shoulder and I felt her tension melt away. "I do love your innocence, Paige. Please don't ever change."

The vodka tonics kicked in soon, and Jess was sound asleep. I, however, was wide awake. Slipping out of the apartment, I went for a drive. I hadn't seen the sunrise since I left for school, and I had a special place where I liked to watch it alone.

The first few times I had done this when staying at Jess's place, she flipped out. I have no idea what thoughts went through her mind when she woke up to find me missing. I didn't help the matter by not leaving a note. Jess hates feeling abandoned. I learned to leave a note and she learned that I wouldn't ever tell her where I went. She didn't like it, but she gave up asking.

When I crawled back into bed, Jess, half-awake, asked if I had taken one of my mysterious drives. I answered in the affirmative and kissed the back of her head. She nestled up close to me, and the warmth of her body eased me into sleep.

Chapter Ten

LIDDY APPEARED TENSE. She sat down and tapped her pencil on her notepad. I didn't say a word. I wanted to see what she was up to. Would she say that she couldn't help me? Would Jess buy that? Or would I have to find a new therapist?

Let's see, I counted on my fingers. This was my fifth session. So that meant I had forty more appointments to fulfill my promise since school isn't in session every week of the year.

"Paige ..." her voice cracked and she hesitated. "I'm wondering about your arms. How did you cut your wrists? Horizontal? Or vertical?" She made two separate cutting motions on her own wrist to demonstrate.

"Why?" I fidgeted in my chair. Was she going to mock my ineptitude?

"I want to know how serious you were at the time."

"You want to know if it was a cry for help." If I'd had anything in my hands, I probably would have thrown it against the wall.

"That's not what I'm saying. I just need to know."

"Okay." I unbuttoned my shirt cuffs and slowly rolled up each sleeve. The narrow, long jagged scars were getting fainter—no longer so red and inflamed. Sometimes, I didn't notice them, but I wondered if that was because I saw them in the shower every day.

Liddy casually looked, keeping her expression judgment-free. I think it surprised her that I had revealed my actual scars instead of just describing them. I had promised Jess I would do my best to open up more.

"Thank you." Liddy settled back into her chair. "I know that wasn't easy for you."

I looked away, wishing there was a window I could stare out. "This isn't my favorite part of the week."

"I know. At first, I didn't think you would let me in at all. You are so rigid when you sit there. This takes guts, and I want you to know it hasn't gone unnoticed." She made sure I was looking at her. "You are extremely brave, Paige."

Brave? Oh boy, she didn't know anything. Nothing! I was a coward. A chickenshit coward.

"Who found you?"

"Jess."

"Who's Jess?"

I shook my head, "Just Jess."

"Okay, we'll go with that for now. Why did you do it?"

I started to laugh. The "Why?" question again. If I knew any of the whys would I be in this chair? "I was having a bad day, I guess."

Her scrunched forehead told me that wasn't the right answer. "I don't think it was just one bad day. But let's take this slow."

Perking up in my chair, I started to devise a plan that would allow me to drop one piece of information over the next forty sessions. Maybe therapy wasn't so hard after all.

Liddy continued, "I don't expect you to have all of the answers, and I don't expect you to open up and tell me everything all at once. In fact, I never expected to see your scars."

The scars were easier to live with; I just had to wear long sleeves and *voil*à, I could forget about them. Mostly.

"Does that mean we can call it a day?" I quipped.

"Not exactly. But I do love your sense of humor." She looked down at her notepad. Was she intentionally avoiding eye contact? "Do your parents know?"

"No. I kept it quiet." I didn't add, *Or they would have locked me up and thrown away the key.*

"The first time I saw your name, I wondered if you were connected with the Alexanders who are in the paper from time to time."

"Yes." It was me who avoided eye contact now.

"I'm going to ask you once: do you think you need twenty-four-hour supervision?"

"Really? *Now* you're asking?" I scoffed. Five sessions in before she thinks of that question. University counselors are quacks. Good! Stupid people are easy to manage. I looked her in the eyes. "No. I don't."

"Good. We agree. My answer may have been different if I had seen you in the hospital right after the incident. But you have strength about you, Paige."

Why was she feeding my ego?

"I don't feel strong, but I promised"

"Your word is important to you, isn't it?"

"Yes." Why didn't she have a window in this office? I was suffocating.

"And you gave your word to Jess?"

I wanted to shout out: You can dance around Jess all you want, but I'm not going to spill the beans, Doc! But I didn't.

"Yes."

"Do you think your parents would lock you up?"

I didn't like her line of questioning. It was too close to the truth.

I sneered. "Shit no. My mom would just want me out of her hair—college seems to work fine for her. My dad wouldn't want the news to hit the papers. Besides, he'd call me a copycat."

She seized on that word, and I immediately regretted it. I had said too much! Again.

"Copycat? What do you mean? Has someone in your family committed suicide?"

I looked at her and sighed. Way to go, idiot. Did she know? No. She couldn't know. Only four people knew, and I was one of them. Abbie and my father didn't care, and the other person was dead. Liddy couldn't know. But I had let the cat out of the bag. Pull it together, Paige, or you *will* be locked up.

"Not successfully. My mom tried years ago."

"After the Lego incident."

I was starting to loathe the word incident. My life seemed to be made up of "incidents."

"No, after her second surgery. Before the first one, she thought everything would go back to normal, or at least close to normal; it didn't. Then she needed another surgery, and that one was even more painful and the recuperation took a lot longer. I actually don't think she recovered from the second one."

"What happened?"

"I was late. I was supposed to be home right after school, but I was running late." I removed my long-sleeved shirt. The air was stifling in here. Did they have the heat on? Did Liddy plot this so I would have to strip down to a T-shirt?

I let out a long, audible sigh. "I can remember it like it was yesterday. Why is it so much easier to remember the bad than the good?"

Liddy must have thought my question was rhetorical, or she flat-out refused the bait. Maybe she wasn't that much of a nitwit after all. So far, I was proving to be the bigger blockhead. Why had I let that comment slip out? Now I would have to explain because Jess had told me to answer all of Liddy's questions. I wondered if Jess had contacted Liddy to supply her with the correct subjects to explore. I wouldn't put it past her. Who could blame her really? She did find me in her tub, bleeding to death. A few more minutes and …

Liddy cleared her throat.

"Oh, sorry, I was wandering." I tapped my head. "I realized that I was really late and I knew I had to rush home to give my mom her next dose of pain meds. I don't know if this actually happened, but now I remember feeling that something was terribly wrong.

"When I got home, I slammed my body into the front door and hauled ass to the back of the house to her room. At first, I breathed a sigh of relief. She looked to be sleeping so peacefully, more peacefully than I had seen her sleep in some time. Usually, by that time of day, she'd be awake, barking at me for her pills.

"I crept to the bathroom to retrieve her pills. If I had kept them on the nightstand, she would have just kept taking them. The pain never truly went away, so she said. As I exited the bathroom, I smelled something: metal, rust, or—something."

I crinkled my nose. The smell still haunted me.

"The light in the room was always dimmed, so she could rest. Squinting my eyes I saw crimson tinged with black. All of her bedding was white. Mom didn't like colors. I knew right then. I was young, but I knew what she had done."

Needing a moment, I asked Liddy for a glass of water. My throat was parched.

She handed me a plastic cup filled with lukewarm water and settled back into her chair. "Did you call 9-1-1?"

Bobbing my head from side to side, I explained. "The blood had stained her nightgown. I panicked and reached for the phone on her bedside. My fingers were like lead weights and I fumbled the phone. When I leaned down to retrieve it, her hand knocked the receiver away. I saw the blood on her arm. The razor was on the ground by my foot. I tried to fathom how she managed to rifle through the bathroom to get it.

"She told me not to call—she wanted to die. Over and over she chanted, 'I'm already dead.' Over and over and over. All I wanted to do was run away from the room, from the house. I wanted nothing to do with any of it."

I took another drink of water. My eyes stared straight ahead, but I saw nothing in the room. Even with my eyes wide open, I still saw her. The blood. The razor. The dial tone of the phone droned in my head. And the disgusting smell—blood, sweat, and sickness, putrid death—was still in my nostrils.

I let out a mirthless laugh. "By the age of ten I was burned out. What could I do, though? I couldn't just stand there and watch her die. I had to conquer my fear."

Jesus. I couldn't believe I put Jess through the same torment. A tear rolled down my cheek. I prayed that Liddy thought it was for my mom. *Oh Jess. I'm so sorry.*

They say suicide is one of the most selfish acts a person can commit. It wasn't until that moment that I realized the extent of that statement. Why hadn't I remembered that before?

"What did you do?" Liddy's gravelly voice brought me out of

my head.

"I called 9-1-1. It was a struggle. She kept clutching at the phone, kept screaming for me to let her die. It was like I was trapped in a cheesy horror film and this old woman in a blood-covered nightgown was fighting me.

"The paramedics came. I didn't think of calling my father. By that time, he was just an entity in the house, not a person. But they called him. Or maybe the dispatch operator did, since he arrived before she was taken away. That was even worse. He pranced in and the first thing he did was slap me for being late. I was sitting in the hallway outside her room, covered in her blood, and he wrenched me off the ground and slapped me hard across the face. If we were alone, I think he might have killed me.

"But he straightened his suit jacket and strolled into the bedroom. My mother was still screaming, and from the sound of it, fighting off the medics. For someone who had been bedridden for years, she put up a mighty struggle."

Sitting in the chair, I suddenly didn't know what to do. Tears streamed down my face and my nose was dripping. I was never in the Girl Scouts, so I didn't pick up the habit of carrying tissues in my bag. I was never prepared.

Liddy handed me a box of Kleenex like a good Brown Owl—the name seemed fitting for sweet, innocent Liddy.

"I don't think my mother ever forgave me for not heeding her pleas. I know my father never forgave me. But I'm not sure if he was miffed that I was late or that I was not late enough. He's a tough man to read. That bastard counted on me to take care of everything at home, as if I wasn't his child, but a servant. I still have no clue where Abbie was that day. She was never accountable for anything. No chores. Nothing. Might as well call me Cinderella, except without mice and birds to help me out.

"My mom was away for a few months. How my father kept that quiet, I don't know. It was right after her surgery, so maybe people believed there were complications and she was in intensive care or something. My parents were popular, but they didn't have friends. No one asked if they could visit her. No one cared enough. I didn't see her once, not the entire time." I searched the ceiling for an answer. "In fact, I don't even know where he stashed her. Weird.

"And, if you want me to stick to this honesty thing that you like, I was glad she was gone. It was a relief to just be a kid for weeks. I didn't enjoy being alone with my father, and we never hung out. He was either at work or in his office at home. It was as if nothing happened. No one talked about it or anything."

I picked at the shirt in my lap, unsure whether I wanted to put it back on. "That's how it was all the time at home—nothing ever happened, everything was always on the up and up. If I disappeared to an institution like my mom, my father would put some fancy spin on it and no one would be the wiser. Fuck, he would probably forge a death certificate. He has a knack for sweeping shit under his magic rug so nothing stains his reputation."

Liddy's eyes showed interest. "Does your mom ever talk about it?"

"Nope. No one does. We're like automatons. When there is a camera on us, we smile and pretend to be a loving family. The rest of the time, we go through the motions and stay out of each other's way. Our house is huge. I can go days without seeing another living soul."

A thought crossed my mind. "I know there's a patient/doctor confidentiality deal, but does that apply here?" I glanced about the room, nervously.

"Yes, of course." She seemed puzzled. "Why do you ask?"

"I don't know. My dad has influence. I didn't know if there was a way he could find out about this … about me … and about what I say."

"You really do fear him?"

I didn't answer her.

"Paige, everything you tell me is confidential. None of this will get back to your father. You can trust me."

Oh, the famous last words: "You can trust me." Briefly, I considered what it would be like if all of my family's secrets were leaked to the press. Oh, that would be grand. I would love to watch my father try to wiggle out of it. Many might think there isn't a situation my father can't figure out, that he's like Indiana Jones. But I never saw him that way. I only saw him as he was: a despicable man who hated me from the start. Others could glorify him; I just wanted to escape him.

But what lengths did I have to go to just to be free? Death? There is a beauty about death. No one can bring you back. But fucking it up, that's just messy for all involved. I glanced at my arms. Without thinking, I turned my palms up and eyeballed my scars.

Did Liddy notice? Honestly, I didn't care right at that moment.

I walked into my dorm room with a strong sense of foreboding. I needed some time to myself. It was raining out, so I didn't go for my normal walk after therapy. Not good. My brain liked to spend that time processing the thoughts and emotions. Usually, it liked to percolate, and it didn't like sudden changes. I could be spontaneous, but that was rare. Jess was the spontaneous one. I was the one who tagged along. My rash acts were usually just to do with being lippy. Simply put: I could be an asshead.

Minnie and Karen sat on my bed, talking. That alone sent

flashes of anger coursing through my mind and body. Was I shaking?

"How was your day?" asked Karen.

"Just dandy. Yours?" My words were tinged with sarcasm, but she didn't seem to notice. More than likely, she didn't care. Karen never seemed to get rattled by me. She was determined to be my friend, and maybe in her book, friends ignored rudeness.

"Okay, nothing to write home about." Her voice sounded far off.

That meant she didn't meet any cute boys; hence, she wasn't any closer to getting a boyfriend. Her new goal was to have one by Christmas because she didn't want to spend another holiday alone. That made me snigger. She was eighteen. Save the drama, princess.

Minnie was holding my answering machine. Of course, we both used it, but I paid for it—just like I paid for the beanbag I could never sit in, the TV I didn't have any control over, the food that kept disappearing, the PC and printer that others felt free to use whenever they liked. Once, I had woken up at 3 a.m. to find Karen printing off an assignment. At three in the morning! Imagine waking up to the high-pitched screech of a printer.

"Are you praying that you'll get a message?" I gestured to the machine.

"Oh, no." Minnie sounded deadly serious. "We're trying to think of a funny message. I'm tired of the one on there. It's so bland."

"Bland, huh. Aren't all messages boring when you think of it? Their purpose is straightforward: to tell the caller you can't answer the phone right now. Not much more to it." I had recorded the original message. *Why isn't Jess here to help me concoct the perfect message that will leave everyone in stitches? Why can't she be around?*

Oh, that's right. That was my doing, not hers.

"Have you come up with anything?"

"Nope. Zip, nada, zilch." Minnie's face twisted up, as if a thought had hit her like a flash of lightning. "Hey! Can you think of something funny?" she squeaked.

Shaking my head, I said, "I doubt it. I'm the one who put the boring message on."

Minnie looked to Karen for help. Karen, though, was too enthralled with picking the polish off her fingernails.

Minnie grunted and then eyed me hopefully. "Sure you can. You can be funny sometimes."

I had to chuckle about that one. *Sometimes.* What a compliment? Usually, they found me funny when I wasn't trying to be. The other day, Karen had mentioned that she received the same math mod quiz she had failed a few days earlier. Math mods involved passing six quizzes before you could advance to the next level. There weren't any classes. Students waited in line to take the tests. If they passed, they could take the next level. If they failed, they had to keep taking it until they passed that level. I didn't entirely understand the system, as it revolved around luck, not learning. Fortunately, math came easy to me, so I had passed out of the entry-level math classes and would be taking calculus the following semester.

Karen remembered all of the answers to the test and had filled in the correct bubbles. She got one hundred percent. When she had gloated about it, I exclaimed, "But that's cheating!"

The three of them had burst into hysterics.

"That's the point, Paige. All of us share our tests so we can cheat. Who wants to learn math?" asked Karen.

I've been told I was born an old fuddy-duddy, and maybe I would have preferred a time when honor meant something. I don't see much honor in the world now.

I held up the answering machine. "Okay, let me think ..." I

MARIONETTE

cleared my throat, and started. "Hi! You've reached Audrey's and Paige's room. We can't come to the phone right now. Please leave your name, number, and physical description, and we'll call you back if we like what we hear. Mentioning your sex toys is a plus. Take care, and have an orgasmic day!"

Karen burst into laughter.

The frivolity was cut short by Minnie. "What if my parents or grandparents call, Paige?"

I rubbed my chin, pretending to think of an honest solution. "They don't have to leave a physical description. You know what they look like, and I'm pretty sure I'm not interested. Boom. Done. However, if they could mention their sex toys, that would be funny."

Minnie's face turned a vivid plum color. A vein in her forehead bulged, and I thought I could see it pulsing. Could a person's head literally explode from anger? Why was she getting so worked up?

"Oh, come on. Your parents have to know you're having sex. You borrowed my car last week and didn't come back until the next day. I figured out why: make-up sex." I crossed my arms and flashed her a bitchy smile.

"Don't make assumptions about my life. I try not to with yours."

I don't think Minnie meant to say the last bit, but I didn't want to push her on that. My best bet was to keep pushing her, to make her forget about that.

"You don't expect me to believe that when you spend the night at his place, nothing happens, do you?"

"Nothing does happen. We're waiting to get married."

Karen blurted, "Really! Nothing?"

Minnie looked disgusted by both of us. "Yes. I'm Catholic!"

"Oh come on, even the Pope has sex. They have for centuries. Ever hear of the Borgias and all of their kids? Only one way to get kids during that time period."

She looked aghast, and shattered. "Paige! I will not stand to have you ridicule my beliefs!"

I knew I should have stopped pushing her buttons then. That would have been honorable. Sadly, I'm not honorable.

"I'm not ridiculing your beliefs. I'm stating historical facts. Unless you believe in more than one Immaculate Conception, which I believe you would call blasphemy, your religion and its paragons do not hold up to scrutiny. Now, as to your own personal beliefs and adherence, I have a hard time believing that you and Jeff are not screwing. Or do you not count blow jobs and eating pussy?"

All of the color drained from Minnie's face. She tried to articulate a response, but nothing came out. Karen casually got off my bed and tiptoed out of the room. I maneuvered closer to Minnie, just in case she toppled over.

I had taken it too far, but I didn't know how to heal the gaping wound. Surely she had heard these phrases before. She went to public school for Christ's sake. It was a good thing I didn't blurt that out, however. Watching her face was like watching a grandmother react to porn—not that I've seen that personally, but the faces and sounds Minnie made brought that image to mind.

I picked up the answering machine and deleted my message. She snatched her purse and stormed out of the room. After she had slammed the door, I heard Karen's footsteps.

"Was it something I said?" I smiled meekly. I felt horrible. I was a wretched person.

Karen tittered, and then stopped abruptly and ran over to the door to peek out the eyehole. "Okay, I think she's gone."

"Oh wow, Karen." I slumped down onto my bed. "What in the hell do I do now? She's pissed. I mean she's more than pissed. I was just trying to be funny." I whistled. "I had no idea what a sensitive subject that was."

Karen shook her head. She was still laughing and her shoulders heaved up and down as she tried to control herself. "I think this issue has been the cause of some of their recent fights." Her look admonished me.

Oh shit! That wasn't good. If Minnie was being pressured into having sex and I said all of those things. Well, *that* folks, is why many people think I'm an asshole.

I leaned against the wall and groaned. "What do I do? I can't live another nine months with someone who hates me."

Karen ambled over to me and placed her hand on my shoulder. "You can always sleep on my floor. And let's be honest, you two weren't that close to begin with. Even Jenna knows about the boyfriend situation ... and she's like you, reserved and doesn't like to talk about emotions. You live with her, and you didn't know it at all."

"Thanks, buddy. Thanks for hitting me when I'm down."

"That's what I'm for. I like to keep it real." She slapped my arm. "They really don't have sex? How long have they been dating?"

"Three years."

"Oh boy. This is worse than I thought?"

"Yep. You stepped right in a steaming pile of dog shit."

I chortled. "Who knew you were so elegant, Karen. Screw psychology, consider poetry."

"Listen, I think you should stop throwing the word screw around."

I sat up straight on my bed. "Hey, do you know her favorite flower or something? Would it be weird if I gave her flowers to apologize?"

"Dude! Are you serious? She gets flowers all of the time from

Jeff. Look around, Paige. Daisies everywhere."

Sure enough, a gaudy vase on Minnie's desk was brimming with daisies.

All these weeks, I had thought I was the only one with issues. Did I mention that I'm a twit?

"Okay, flowers are out. Help me think of something else." I looked desperate.

"You're going to have to apologize."

"Like, in person." I bolted off the bed and dashed to open the window. "No, seriously, what can I buy her?"

"I am serious." Karen crossed her arms. "You have to say you're sorry. I don't think gifts will work with this one. Besides, you aren't dating. Friends talk things out."

Ah, shit. Everyone wants me to talk and to open up. What was the point of talking? I liked actions. Actions spoke louder than words, didn't they? I cringed at the thought of having a sit down with Minnie, having a heart-to-heart. She would probably use a phrase like, "In my heart of hearts ..." Gah. I hated that.

I knew Karen was right, but I didn't have it in me that night. I was supposed to go to some parties with the girls, but I got the feeling it would be best if I skedaddled for the weekend and let the dust settle. They would have more fun without me.

That's right. I was fleeing town. Getting out of Dodge. Running away. You name it, I was doing it. How's that for being spontaneous? Besides I knew Jess would know the right thing for me to do. She was like that Jeeves character: always reliable and prudent.

Fortunately for me, Jess was home when I walked into the apartment.

She skipped across the room, her skirt swishing around her, and threw her arms around me. "This is a nice surprise. I wasn't expecting you until tomorrow."

I kissed her passionately, and said, "I couldn't wait another second."

She stepped back, scrutinizing my face. "Out with it, Paige. What happened?"

"I don't know if I can talk about it yet." I limped over to the couch.

Jess pulled a chair over to face me. Taking both my hands, she said, "I think you'll feel better if you do."

I told her all about Minnie. She cringed a few times and then smacked my hand. "You ninny! I could have told you all that from what you've told me. Seriously, Paige. We need to work on your manners." She hesitated. "You're going to have to apologize."

What!

"Jess, I was really hoping you could come up with a different solution. Like a gift with some poetry or something …" my voice trailed off.

"That wouldn't work on me if my friend had said all that stuff."

I sighed and eyed the ceiling, searching for a different answer.

"Maybe I could go to church with her? Do a fake confessional thingy? I've always wondered what they look like inside."

"What, a church or a confessional booth?"

"Both I guess. I've never been to either."

"You've never been to church." She was flabbergasted.

"Nope."

"Are your parents atheists?"

"Not that I know of. I am, but I don't know what they believe."

Jess shook her head in disbelief. "Your family continues to shock the hell out of me."

"Really?"

She kissed my cheek. "Sometimes you are too sheltered."

"I don't feel innocent."

"You do know about 'eating pussy.'" The words made Jess blush. She hardly ever swore or used crude language. I'm not fucking kidding. To me, that was baffling.

"Oh, don't remind me about Minnie."

She teased, "I thought you liked it."

"Oh, you were actually referring to—" I blushed. "I thought you were bringing up Minnie, and that whole mess."

"Nope. I said what I had to say about that. Now, let's move on to more important matters. This situation will blow away sooner than you think. For someone who hates teenage drama, you're wallowing in it yourself today."

"Very funny, Jess."

"So, tell me, how do you know you're a true atheist if you haven't ever been to church? I think we need to start a new project with you: exploring different religions and beliefs. This weekend, a Buddhist temple!"

She seemed truly excited about the prospect.

"Is this my punishment?"

"Learning is not a punishment, Paige. For a rich girl, you don't know a lot about life. Maybe your parents shouldn't have sent you to private school."

"Trust me, rich people are damn stupid about the real world. I fit right in."

"Not good enough. I'm not backing down." The way she crossed her arms told me it was useless to protest.

"Oh, okay." I put my palms up to show my resignation.

"Now, what should we do?" Jess was giddy.

I leaned in to kiss her. She pushed me back against the sofa cushions.

"Hey! I'm not a cheap date. Since you're here, and I'm starving, let's have dinner first. What do you feel like for dinner?"

"You."

"Besides me … and haven't you learned that being crude hasn't paid off for you today?" She smiled, but I think she liked my answer.

We had been like Minnie and Jeff for some time: no sex allowed. When we had finally broken down that barrier, a whole new world opened up for me. Jess's thirst for experiences and knowledge was explored in all aspects of life, even in the bedroom.

She tapped the armrests of her chair, pushing me to answer her question.

This was a game we played often. Jess knew just about every restaurant in town and although I tried to stump her, so far I wasn't successful.

"Do you know a good place to have Peruvian?"

"Do I know a place?" Her eyes lit up. "Grab your keys. I'll give you directions in the car."

Really? She knew a Peruvian joint? I didn't even know what kind of food would be on the menu. How in the hell did she do it?

As we left the apartment, Jess casually mentioned that Mel had been looking for me and needed to talk to me. That didn't sound good. Hopefully, I could avoid sticking my foot in my mouth this time. I could always hope.

CHAPTER ELEVEN

I TELEPHONED MEL on Saturday morning and we agreed to meet at Julia's diner for lunch. Admittedly, I had been somewhat disappointed when I'd met the owner, Julia, and found out she wasn't French. True, her place didn't serve French cuisine, but I still thought there might be a chance. Jess had laughed when I'd told her that. Now, Julia's was a firm favorite.

I knew Jess would show up there later. Jess hated being alone, yet she was an orphan. Oh, how I wished I were an orphan. I would even change my name to Annie if I thought that would help my dream come true. Jess had never admitted to me that she hated being alone, but it wasn't hard to figure out. She was always searching for places with people—interesting people. Even when Jess read novels, she preferred to do it in public. And she liked a change of scenery. *Movement* describes Jess's personality. She was always moving on to new experiences. Jess didn't talk about her parents much, but she always seemed to have money for restaurants, movies, books, music, theater, sporting events—she never seemed to struggle with finances. I never felt comfortable enough to ask if she had an inheritance. Yes, she had an internship, but I assumed that was unpaid until after she graduated. She worked occasionally at a used bookshop, but I think she only did so because the owner was one of her good friends. If he needed a break or extra help around the holidays, he'd give her a ring. I'm pretty sure she didn't ask for a paycheck; that wasn't her style. Jess had honor, and I loved her for that. Instead of paying her, I think the owner allowed Jess to take whatever novels tickled her fancy. I loved that, because after Jess had devoured them within a day or two, she handed them off to me. Before I moved to college, I read three or four books a week. Now that I had a roommate, I couldn't lie in bed till the wee hours of the morning reading a book Jess had loved and passed onto me. It frustrated the hell out of me.

But, back to money. When we went out, I picked up our tabs. Jess never said anything. I think she knew I was waging a war on my parents: a war of pocketbooks. Aren't all wars about money? Petty? You bet. It made me feel good, though. And to spend their money on my girlfriend made me feel even better.

Julia's diner served the best pulled pork sandwiches. She had other choices on the menu, but you'd be a fool to order something else. Julia, a Midwestern gal in her fifties, had learned the secret family recipe from her Southern grandfather. Jess has begged her for the recipe many times, unsuccessfully. Ever since Jess wandered into Julia's last year, we've eaten there at least once a week. Julia has become part of Jess's family, and now mine.

When Mel walked into Julia's, I was sitting at a table by the window, stuffing my face with one of the famous sandwiches. Right before she approached the table, I took a humongous bite, splattering the sauce down onto the table, onto my hand, and all over my face. Secretly, I was upset that Mel had showed up right then. I didn't want to focus on her. I wanted to continue gorging.

She took a seat across from me and handed me a stack of napkins.

"Seriously, I thought Jess would have had you trained by now. She never makes a mess of herself."

"Yeah, but there's something odd about that, don't you think? Too perfect." I grabbed one of the napkins to begin the cleanup process, quickly realizing I would need more than one.

Mel wrinkled her nose. "Even Wes has more manners than you."

"He must have grown up in the cleanest barn ever then," I muttered.

One glimpse of her face told me I'd hit a sore spot. Mel didn't like that Wesley was poor.

"I'm sorry. Would you like one?" I gestured to the sandwich. "The food at school sucks, and I'm starving. I may even have another."

"Is that your first? Be honest." She leaned forward, resting her hands on the table.

"Yes, but it won't be the last today. Jess will be here later."

"How is she?" Her voice sounded cold. "Since you left for school, I barely see her."

"Uh, she's good. Just been busy, that's all." Was Jess avoiding Mel?

Mel caught Julia's eye and motioned that she wanted a sandwich. I waved frantically, too, but Julia didn't see me. Damn. I really wanted a second one.

"How are things?" I asked as I picked at some pork scraps on my plate.

"Good ... I mean, okay ..." Tears formed in her eyes.

"What's going on, Mel?"

Marionette

Her focus darted to a couple walking through the door. "I have to ask you for something, and I don't want to."

She wanted money. People get the same look when they need money, a look of desperation and anger.

I took a swig of my iced tea to wash down my feelings. "How much?"

"At least three hundred."

She continued to avoid eye contact.

"What's the max?" I forced down another swallow of iced tea.

"One thousand."

I clicked my tongue. "I can only get three hundred out of the ATM today. I can get more tomorrow, but I'm not sure about the whole amount." I looked away, wishing I hadn't agreed to give her any money.

The first thing that jumped into my head was *abortion*, but Mel was on the pill. That wasn't one hundred percent, though. One thousand bucks—that didn't add up.

"Before I get the money, can you tell me why you need it?"

"Because I need it."

It was a shady answer. And it hurt. We used to tell each other everything.

"Look." She squeezed my hand. "I would appreciate if you didn't ask. If I could tell you, I would."

Why couldn't she tell me? Before I could ask, Jess rushed in, all smiles. She took one look at Mel and her expression registered trouble.

"Oh, goodness, I know watching Paige stuff her face is awful, but I didn't think I'd find you crying. She doesn't mean to be such a brute, that's just how she is. It's one of the ways she rebels against her parents."

Rebels against my parents? I had to ponder that one. Messy eating as an act of rebellion?

Mel laughed, and I think she slightly meant it. Julia arrived with three sandwiches. Maybe she had sensed that Jess was near.

"What's going on here? Paige, what did you say to Mel?" Julia held my sandwich out of reach, waiting for me to explain myself.

I stared at Jess and then at Julia, speechless. Mel dabbed her eyes carefully so she wouldn't smudge her mascara.

"I ... I don't really know. I thought she already knew Santa Claus didn't exist." It was a feeble attempt.

Both of them took the hint. All of us suspected Wesley, I think. None of us liked him.

Julia sat down and wrapped Mel up in her arms. That was the straw that broke the proverbial camel's back.

"Oh, Julia." Mel burst into tears. I mean the whole waterworks. Tears poured out of her eyes, snot flowed freely like the Mississippi, and her shoulders heaved up and down like pistons on a steam engine.

If I weren't starving, I might have lost my appetite. Jess shot me such a nasty look when I picked up my sandwich for a bite, that I stuck my tongue out, but I didn't dare take a bite.

"There, there," whispered Julia, as she stroked Mel's back.

I hadn't mentioned the money to anyone. Causally, I excused myself from the table so I could hop across the street to grab the dough. By the time I returned with the wad of bills, Mel was picking at her food.

Thank God! I could eat.

When no one was looking, I slid the money into Mel's hand. The look in her eyes wrenched my heart. Picture someone who has lost all hope after crash-landing on a deserted island filled with crocodiles. Well, she looked worse than that. Her eyes reminded me of Alex's eyes in the days leading up to the rehab incident. I determined right then and there to be a better friend to Mel.

Julia and Jess did their best to cheer up Mel, and actually got her to laugh some, mostly at my expense. Jess told them all about my fight with Minnie. Jess is a great storyteller, even if she embellishes things. She has a knack for making me look even more like an ignoramus than I actually am. I'm not saying that's hard, but she manages it. At the end of her version of the story, everyone was in hysterics.

And all of them agreed that I had to apologize to Minnie in person.

"Seriously, I'm no good at it." I pouted.

"Don't do what you normally do," suggested Julia. Julia messed with her typical Midwestern hairstyle: short and grey like a football helmet. She tugged on her white apron, which was speckled with sauce, and flashed her best stern-mother look.

"Which is what?" I tried not to sound defensive.

"Get all nervous and start to ramble. Do it quick, like a Band-Aid. Say you're sorry, and that's all. Whatever you do, don't overdo it."

"I just have to say sorry?" That thought hadn't crossed my mind: no explanation, just utter the word.

All of them shouted, "Yes."

"None of you think I can actually do this, do you?"

All eyes suddenly darted away.

Jess started to giggle. "Remember when you accidentally broke my bowl I made in high school. You hid it and then took me to the zoo. While we were watching the otters, you blurted out, 'I'm so sorry—I broke your bowl!'"

"I thought the trip to the zoo would ease your loss. Otters are really cute."

Mel perked up in her chair. "Last year, Paige took me to the fanciest restaurant I've ever been to. During dessert, she said, 'I'm really sorry I said that shirt looked hideous on you.'"

"Didn't the dinner make the apology easier?" I squeaked.

"No. You didn't have to go to such lengths. You like to hide behind things instead of facing them head on." Jess held my chin and stared into my eyes. "Just say sorry. That's braver, and it's the polite thing to do."

Jess turned to the other two. "Don't you wish we could watch?"

All of them sniggered.

I shoved half of my sandwich into my mouth.

Mel didn't linger long with us. After she had finished her meal, she skedaddled.

I could still hear the tinkle of the bell on the door when Jess pounced. "How much money did you give her?"

The woman was like a hawk. Nothing got by her.

Julia chimed in. "Spill it. I saw the handoff as well, but I didn't want to say anything in front of Mel."

"I guess my future in the CIA is out. Three hundred—do you think it's for an abortion?"

Both looked troubled. Jess spoke first. "No, I wish it were that simple." She flushed. "Not that an abortion is simple, but I think Wesley is in serious trouble with some bad dudes."

I set my third sandwich down. "What do you mean, 'bad dudes'?"

"I heard he's gambling." Her voice sounded far away.

"Gambling! We don't live in Vegas. How does Weasel gamble?"

"For someone who has seen a lot in such a short life, I forget how naïve you actually are. If a person wants to gamble, there's a way.

I bet Wesley could figure out a way to gamble in heaven."

"If he gambles, would he go to heaven?"

Jess shot me a look that said, "Are you really that stupid?"

"So, I just paid off a bookie?"

"Something like that."

"She was in the restaurant last week, and I sensed she wanted to ask me something but couldn't. Be careful, Paige. I don't think this will be the last time she asks. We know you'd give the shirt off your back, but this is way over your head." Julia lifted her tired body and went back to work.

"I promised her another three hundred tomorrow." I whispered to Jess.

Jess patted my arm. "I know you mean well, but you can't fix all problems with money. Mel has to figure a way to leave the guy. He's no good."

"How do I say no if she asks for more money?"

"Tell her your parents are getting suspicious about all the money you've been spending and you need to save it for therapy." She whacked my leg. "Which you do by the way. One year."

Forty more sessions.

It might work, but I felt crummy about lying.

"It will be for the best. Tough love. If she doesn't leave this guy, she could get hurt."

Jess didn't say how, but images from gangster movies played in my head. *Gambling!* I never would have guessed that.

"Come on, sweetie. There's a foreign film I'm dying to see." She tugged on my arm.

I looked at the remnants of my sandwich. Finally, my appetite was shot.

"Fine, but then we're seeing one of my films."

"Deal. I could use a nap." She winked.

I slipped some money under my plate to pay for all of the sandwiches. Julia never gave me a bill, but I couldn't let her feed all three of us for free. Business was business. She'd complain the next time I saw her, but she never handed the money back. She just had a way of chewing me out. Instead of getting ruffled, it only made me smile. Julia would get flustered by this, and then she'd give me a hug.

CHAPTER TWELVE

WHEN I ENTERED the hallway to my dorm room on Sunday night, I felt queasy. I had lingered as long as I could at Jess's apartment, but she'd kicked me out around five so I could apologize to Minnie and start the week fresh. That's what she said, "You don't want to begin a new week with this hanging over your head. Start fresh."

Baffled, I protested that it would be nice to spend one more night with her, but Jess refused to budge. She was obstinate, and I felt as if she wanted some alone time.

Fine. I'll go say sorry and start fresh. Heaven forbid that Monday morning dawns before I say, "Minnie, I was an asshole."

Probably should say her real name, though. Even Jess was calling her Minnie now. It was only a matter of time before I slipped up.

No one was in the hallway so I marched to my room. Why was it so hard for me to apologize? It was simple really, just say, "I'm sorry." Or better yet, "Sorry." Boom. Done!

On the other side of the door, I heard two voices: Karen and Minnie. Minnie was crying, or I think she was. Shit! Was she still crying about the other day?

Leaning in, I tried to hear what they were saying. All I could make out were muffled sobs.

"Paige! What are you doing outside of your room? Are you eavesdropping on your roomie?"

I hadn't heard Jewels enter the hallway. Emily soon popped into view, too, with a cat-that-just-ate the canary grin on her face.

"Nope. I can't seem to locate my keys." I fumbled in my backpack, hoping she hadn't seen me drop my keys from my hand into the bottom of the bag. As I continued to fish around in the bag, I heard Minnie blow her nose.

"Oh, here they are." I raised them up for Jewels to see.

She wasn't buying it. She harrumphed, and crossed her arms. "Yeah, right. Can we go in now?"

I opened the door and stood back to let Jewels and Emily enter first. With all of the bodies in the room, there was no way I could apologize. Not in front of everyone. Shouldn't it be a private deal?

Avoiding eye contact with everyone, which was a challenge in a room that was twelve feet by nine feet, I busied myself emptying my backpack. There wasn't much in there, since I kept spare clothes and a toothbrush at Jess's. But I wanted to look like I had important things to do, like I was in a rush and didn't have time to stand outside the door and listen in on their conversation.

"So, I hope you two weren't talking about family secrets or anything. We found Paige eavesdropping." Jewels gave them a look of satisfied amusement. She apparently hadn't picked up on the fact that all of us were uncomfortable.

Emily put her arm around my shoulder. "Yeah, we're going to have to keep an eye on you, Tricky." She gave me a friendly squeeze.

Karen fidgeted on my bed. "Yeah, we heard you talking

outside." She was doing her best to act normal, which was never easy for her. I glanced at Minnie, noticing her swollen eyes and crimson nose. She must have been crying for some time.

"Audrey, have you been crying?" Jewels collapsed on the bed and enveloped Minnie in her arms. "What's wrong?"

No matter how hard I tried, I could not hate Jewels. She *was* the type of girl I hated, don't get me wrong. She fell in love with a new guy each day, even though she had a boyfriend back home. Sometimes, she played the ditsy blond, yet she was in the honors program and was valedictorian of her high school. Basically, she had two personalities, and that drove me nuts. However, she did it with such panache. Watching her switch from one persona into the other was like watching an Oscar-winning actress. She was our Meryl Streep.

And now I studied her third personality: caregiver. Minnie nestled her weary head on Jewel's shoulder and sobbed about her boyfriend. Jewels kept murmuring, "Poor Audrey," and patting her head. If I tried that, it would come across as insincere. Jewels looked like Pollyanna.

As it turned out, Minnie and Jeff had had a huge row that afternoon. She didn't go into details about the actual cause of the fight, but I remembered what Karen had told me on Friday night. Do I have to point out that I felt like the world's biggest heel right at that moment?

The three girls took turns saying things like, "What an asshole!" or "You're too good for him" or "I'm so sorry, Audrey." None of the phrases dripped with brilliance, yet they sounded heartfelt.

I sat on my desk chair, frozen. It wasn't like I didn't know what to say. Sentences kept invading my head, but when I tried to speak them, nothing came out. I knew the words would sound flat.

Unfeeling.

When a knock on the door interrupted the little pity party, everyone turned to me and I assumed it was my job to answer the door.

I regretted that decision instantly.

"Hey, Paige! Your troubles are over, the beer has arrived." Tom, Minnie's friend, held up a thirty pack of Keystone. Good thing it was a Sunday night, or he may have lugged in a keg.

He sauntered in, followed by two boys I hadn't met. Each gripped a beer in their hands. I glanced up and down the hallway to see if anyone had noticed. The rules were simple: no underage drinking.

Our hall adviser popped her head out the door and I said a friendly hello and slammed my door shut. Smooth. Real smooth. I held my breath until I heard her door close again.

Looking out the peephole, I realized she had disappeared back into her room. She didn't venture outside of her room much—fortunately.

Tom was introducing his buddy Ben and his roommate, Aaron.

Ben, the hippie, wore torn jeans and a smelly T-shirt. He sported a scraggly beard and continuously flashed a goofy but sincere smile.

Aaron surprised me. He resembled a Marine. His jeans looked starched, his polo was tucked in crisply, and his hair was cut short. Biceps bulged out of his shirt and his chest puffed out like he was on the parade ground. How often did he work out? Once again, I marveled at the university's roommate matchmaking skills. Not in a million years would I have placed Tom and Aaron in the same room. Tom, the sensitive NFL fan, and Aaron, the militaristic Neanderthal. Would Aaron knock Tom over the head with a club?

MARIONETTE

I looked over at Tom, whose blue eyes sparkled under his Broncos hat. He was wearing a John Elway T-shirt. Elway's horsey smile grinned broadly at me; it gave me the willies.

Jewels leaped off the bed and shook hands with Aaron. It didn't take a rocket scientist to realize that he would be her man for the night. Chuckling, I made eye contact with Minnie. She had stopped crying and it appeared she was also getting a kick out of Jewels fawning all over Aaron. When Jewels asked him to flex his biceps, he did. I have to say, even my eyes bulged out of my head. Jewels squealed. Aaron turned a brilliant red, but I could tell he loved it. I wondered if he could blush on command so he didn't come across as conceited.

"Where do you live, Aaron?" Jewels batted her eyelashes at him.

"G3."

"Really, you're right on top of me."

Aaron choked on his beer.

Having received the desired reaction, Jewels added, "I mean, I live on G2." She blinked foolishly again, and Aaron ate it up.

Tom cleared his throat. Was he jealous? "We thought we would watch the Broncos game with you ladies."

Ben, who had never been in my room before, flipped on the TV. None of the men noticed that Minnie had been crying, which I think was a good thing. She looked relieved to forget all about her troubles for the moment.

"Tom, there's some snacks in the cupboard by the fridge. Help yourself." Minnie gestured to *my* cupboard, which was filled with *my* snacks.

So that's why all my food kept disappearing: football parties.

Karen grabbed a beer and nestled into the beanbag. She gulped it like a drunken sailor—fast—and then swiped her mouth with the back of her hand.

I grabbed a Coke from my fridge. Beer was not my go-to drink. If I was in a pinch and that's all that was available, I'd drink it. But cheap beer, no way. I preferred fancy drinks. Jess always made fun of my umbrella drinks, but we hardly went to places that served them. Jess believed that dives always had the best food, and most dives only served beer, but usually not cheap beer like Keystone; that was only for broke college kids.

Everyone else had a beer except for Emily. When I offered her a Coke, she seemed relieved. I noticed that while everyone broke into cliques to chat and gossip, Emily sat on the outside of the group. I hadn't really thought of it before, but she was nothing like Jewels. Jewels could be nice when she wanted to be, but she could be the devil as well. Emily was sweet—the girl next door. She probably got good, not great grades, dated the same boy for years, and volunteered at her church.

For several months, Jess had been doing her best to train me to read people. At first, she would pick someone and then tell me her observations, such as that a couple hidden in the back of the restaurant were probably having an affair, or a girl who excused herself right after eating a massive dessert on a date was probably in the bathroom puking it up.

Jess felt that it was important for me to learn these things. She thought I was too isolated. I needed to learn some people smarts so I wouldn't get conned by someone, so she said.

I decided to fish for information, to see if I was right. "How are your classes going, Emily?"

She colored. I think she was used to fading into the background. It was typical Emily to make random comments and then disappear quickly. Around the girls, she looked more relaxed, but as soon as

MARIONETTE

Tom and his buddies arrived, she clammed up.

"Oh, they're okay. I have a test tomorrow so I'm a little nervous. We have a quiz each week. I got a B-minus last week. I'm hoping to do better tomorrow."

Yes! I got one right.

"Hey, there's nothing wrong with a B-minus." I gave her an encouraging smile. Then I probed again, "Have you been home lately to see your family and boyfriend?"

"I was there this weekend. I actually just got back when Jewels forced me to come here." Her face was scarlet, looking like it might burst into flames. "Not that I didn't want to see you and Audrey. It's just I wanted to study for that quiz."

"No worries. I understand. I have a French test tomorrow."

"French. I could never take another language course. Do you have to speak a lot in class?" She looked around nervously, as if a teacher might suddenly appear and demand that she speak to the group.

"Yeah." I hadn't thought of that when I had signed up for the course. I'd just thought it would impress Jess.

"How long have you and your boyfriend been together?" Was my probing too obvious?

Her face relaxed and she leaned up against the wall. "Oh, Brad and I started dating when we were freshmen in high school. We even went to elementary school together."

Her innocence told me that she and Brad were still virgins. Was I surrounded by them?

Now for the kicker. "Do you go to church?"

She cocked her head and stared into my eyes. Had she heard about the argument with Minnie?

I continued, "For one of my classes I need to do some volunteer work and I was thinking of finding a local church that would allow me to volunteer."

Once again, the tension melted from her face. "Oh, that's cool. I volunteer at my church back home, but I haven't had time to find one here yet." She pondered something for a couple of seconds and then said, "Maybe we could find one together, next Sunday."

Oh shit!

"Y-yeah," I stammered. Then I remembered that Jess wanted to drag me to different churches to broaden my horizons. "That sounds great." I'm sure I didn't sound that enthusiastic, but I hoped Emily hadn't detected that.

My church date dampened my mood. I was impressed that I had pegged Emily correctly, but now I had to pay a price. Jess would have been successful at sussing Emily out without getting stuck with a church date! I needed more practice.

"Hey, Paige! Where did you go this weekend?" Tom yelled across the room. I glanced in his direction. He was casually leaning against the heater by the wall with his arms crossed and his head cocked in a manly way, but his smile showed a softer side.

He was on his second beer, but the slight glaze in his eyes told me he had consumed others earlier that day.

"I went home to see some friends."

"Would any of these friends be of the male sex?" He seemed pleased with the question.

Karen and Minnie fixed me with their eyes. They wanted to know.

"There was one boy in the group."

"Is this boy cute?"

"Some might think so."

I was getting the feeling that Tom was asking for himself and that no one had put him up to it. Did Tom like me? At first, I wanted to laugh, but then a thought occurred to me.

"Not as cute as some." I winked at him.

I thought Minnie and Karen were about to explode. Would this work?

Tom smiled and turned his attention back to the game. It took several seconds for the group to resume their chit-chat, and the silence and the glares were unnerving me. When they did, Jewels raised her beer in my direction in a girl-type salute. Even Emily gave me a pat on the back. If only they knew.

Soon, Tom made his way over to where Emily and I stood and casually entered the conversation. Surprisingly, he didn't exclude Emily at all and even acted interested in what she had to say. If I *were* looking for a boy, Tom would be a great catch. He had a kind of sweetness to him that I bet most girls overlooked. Nice guys struggled in a post-James-Dean world. Girls from my generation wanted a rebel, wanted excitement, and they wanted the knowledge that their man could protect them.

But at that moment, I was looking for a sweetheart who would be too afraid to try to kiss me, since I didn't want to kiss at all. Tom fit the bill. He would be fun to hang out with and I could get the roommates off my back. Besides, he liked football and so did I.

Before the end of the night, I learned that he majored in international finance, his parents had season tickets to the Broncos, and he had four sisters. Oh, and he had never had a serious girlfriend. I was almost drooling at the opportunity he presented. If Jess wasn't so out of the closet, I think she would have been impressed by my plan. Part of me felt guilty for purposefully using Tom. But the bigger part of me felt that getting Karen, Minnie, and Jewels off my back was worth it. Maybe I could slip Tom into a conversation with Liddy and throw her off the scent as well.

Emboldened by my new project, I began to drop hints that I would like to go on a date. Unfortunately, I had no idea what I was doing. I had never asked someone on a date, and the only person who had ever asked me was Jess. And she had asked me to see a foreign flick. I knew that wouldn't be Tom's cup of tea.

I had to think of something, so I resorted to what I knew: sports. I turned our attention back to the game. To be honest, I was impressed that Tom the Broncos nut allowed himself to be distracted by a conversation with two girls. Of course, he was probably thinking he might get sex out of the deal, so I didn't want to give him too much credit.

"Uh-oh, Tom, the Broncs are down by ten." I placed a sympathetic hand on his shoulder.

Tom glanced at the screen. "Don't you worry, Paige. My boy, Elway"—he pointed to his shirt—"will take care of the Eagles."

"Care to make a friendly wager?" I smiled into my Coke can as I took a drink. This was too easy.

"Sure. Ten bucks!"

His excitement was cute. Ten dollars wasn't too rich for my blood, but I was aiming for something else. "How 'bout loser has to take the other to dinner."

Tom's eyes brightened. He was catching my meaning and he looked like a kid in a candy store. If only he knew.

He stuck his hand out and we shook on it. Did he notice my hand was clammy? Everyone in the room had heard our bet, and the focus of the room turned to the game. Karen and Minnie exchanged a few looks, but I was struggling to figure out what they meant.

Emily and I sat on the foot of my bed, watching the second half. Every time the Broncos made a mistake, Emily cheered. She was on my side. But I think she was the only one. Everyone else in that room was born and bred in Colorado. To make a bet against the Broncos was sacrilegious and I hadn't factored that into my plan. Aaron didn't say anything, but I could feel his loathing. Ben watched the game, although I'm not sure whether he was following any of it because his eyes had glazed over completely by the start of the fourth quarter. How much had the boys had to drink before they came over?

The girls didn't seem impressed by my bet either, but they were too busy trying to speak without words. Jewels kept studying me. Was she trying to determine whether I was serious about hooking up with Tom?

Tom couldn't contain his excitement. He really wanted the Broncs to win, but losing meant he got to pick the restaurant and take me on a date.

A date.

What had I done? Did this count as cheating? I wasn't attracted to Tom at all.

As the seconds ticked by on the game clock, I started to regret my scheme.

Aaron muttered, "Fucking faggots," and everyone else in the room became quiet.

What would Jess say? "Come on now, Aaron, don't be a sore loser. Some might consider you a fag—a baby, I mean," I said.

Jewels covered her mouth to stifle a laugh.

"Are you calling me a fag?" Aaron flexed his muscles and started to cross the room toward me. Was he going to hit me?

"She was just teasing, Aaron. Give it a rest." Tom rescued me.

Aaron continued to stare me down, menacingly. I wondered what thoughts he entertained. Torture?

After a few tense moments, Tom turned to me. "Well, little girl, it looks like I'm taking you to dinner." His grin stretched from ear to ear.

I paused, thinking of the best response. "Yeah," I whispered, shell-shocked. I had a date with a boy. I tried to convince myself that acting aloof was the right thing.

Tom looked crestfallen.

"So, what night do you want to go?" I acted more excited, which perked him up.

"Tomorrow."

"Oh, shucks, I have class tomorrow. How about Thursday?"

He nodded like a conquering hero. "Thursday works."

I had forgotten that Thursday was the beginning of the weekend in college. It was like going on a date on Friday—The Real McCoy date. It was like I was stating, "This is my man."

Everyone in the room took notice.

After lingering for a few minutes after the game, the group started to clear out. Aaron hoisted Ben onto his shoulder to carry him back to Ben's room. I couldn't tell if Tom was embarrassed that Aaron didn't need any help. It was obvious that Tom couldn't compete with Aaron in the muscle department. I hadn't seen him without a shirt on, but I was certain that Tom had never seen the inside of a gym.

Before I knew it, Minnie and I were alone. It was now or never. She sat at her desk and as I raised my head to say something, Minnie blurted out, "I'm really sorry for how I acted on Friday."

"Yeah, me too."

Minnie hopped off her chair and headed to the bathroom. I heard her turn the shower on. Really? That was it? I didn't even have to drag her to the zoo or to some fancy restaurant.

All in all, it was not a bad night. I got the Minnie thing off my chest, and I had a plan to get everyone to think I was straight. Now, if I could finagle a way for the parents to see a picture of Tom and me together, all would be perfect. I was not sure how to accomplish that one, but I was still feeling pretty good about myself. And I couldn't wait to share the news with Jess.

I dialed her number. She wasn't home. Where was she on a Sunday night after midnight? Maybe she just didn't hear the phone.

I was amped up on Coke, so I left a note for Minnie saying I went to the library to cram for my French test. Actually I had no intention to study, but I wanted to spend some time doing research. During the day, the microfiche machines were crowded. I learned early on that no one used the room late at night, even though it was open twenty-four hours.

The student who worked in the department nodded hello. He was used to seeing me scouring newspapers and magazine articles at odd hours. What I liked most was that he didn't partake in idle chitchat. A nod was the extent of his social skills, and mine for that matter. I assumed he was a grad student and preferred these hours because, besides me, no one ever showed up. As for me, I preferred the quiet. Having insomnia paid off sometimes; I was more productive at this time of night.

Chapter Thirteen

AS I WALKED up to Liddy's door, I noticed it was slightly ajar. Usually, it was wide open, inviting her clients to take a seat and wait for her. I peeked in and noticed her sitting in her chair, writing on her notepad. I stepped back to check the nameplate. I squinted and ran my fingers over the name.

"What are you doing?" she asked.

"I'm sorry. I must be in the wrong place. I could have sworn this was Dr. Elliot's office, but I guess not. Sorry to inconvenience you, but I'm off to find a dark and deserted office to sit in all by my lonesome." I turned and headed down the hallway.

"Very funny, Paige. Get back in here. You're not going to escape that easily, especially now that we are starting to make some progress." She darted out into the hall.

"Progress?" I held my hand up to my ear. "Did I hear that correctly?"

She crossed her arms. "Don't ruin it now." Her voice informed me that I wasn't in trouble.

"Why are you on time?"

"If you come into the office, I'll tell you." She pretended to dangle something in front of me.

"Not until you tell me." I planted my feet firmly on the ground.

Liddy stepped behind me and started to push me into her office. For a tiny thing, she was strong, and her jasmine perfume made me giddy.

"Oh, okay, you don't have to manhandle me."

"Manhandle!" She retreated to her chair. "My, aren't you in a good mood, today? What did you do, run over a small child on your way over?"

"Ha! Who knew you could be on time and funny all on the same day? You must be exhausted. We can call it a day if you want."

She lowered her head and her devilish smile turned me on. "Tell you what, it's gorgeous outside and you're obviously in a good mood, so why don't we grab a coffee or something and talk outside? A change of pace might do you some good."

Emerging from the bowels of the building with Liddy at my side gave me a sense of pride. Did she think I was fit for human society again? If only she knew the whole truth.

After stopping to buy two coffees, Liddy's treat, we headed out of the building. It was late September, and the sun blazed, not too hot but just perfect for a fall afternoon. We found a picnic table and sat across from each other. It didn't take long for the warmth to get to me, and the hot coffee didn't help.

As I rolled up my sleeves, I noticed Liddy peeking at my scars.

"I'm kinda glad you've seen them," I remarked.

"Why's that?"

"It makes it easier. It's bloody hot, and I'm tired of always hiding them." I noticed a dog that was frantically chasing down a tennis ball. "I guess I didn't think my plan through. The—"

"The what, Paige?" Liddy's sweet voice pressed me.

"I didn't think I would have to deal with … the aftermath, I guess." I scratched my head.

"How many people have seen the scars?"

"Less than a handful. My roommates tease me because I won't change my shirt in front of them. They're always getting undressed in front of me. I wish they wouldn't." I sipped my coffee. "I'm sure they think I'm the biggest prude."

"It must be hard to hide so much from them. What do you think they'd do if they saw the scars?"

"Oh, geez. Minnie would flip out. She's Catholic—and I found out recently that she's a virgin." I tapped the tabletop with my fingers.

"Are you?"

Shit! I hadn't been expecting that one. Logically, I should have seen it coming. I fidgeted with the zipper on my backpack. How could I get out of this one?

"I …"

She watched me closely.

"Can I pass on that question for now?"

"Of course." She placed her hand on my arm. "Paige, we can go as slow as you need."

Her touch soothed me. I tried to remember the last person who had touched me to reassure me, besides Jess. Alex. Shit. That was four years ago. Four years.

"Where did you go?" Liddy hunched her shoulders to make eye contact with me.

I colored. "Oh, sorry. I was thinking of a friend."

"What triggered the memory?"

"You, actually. When you touched my arm, I tried to remember the last person who had touched me in a friendly way." I laughed nervously. "I guess I'm not the type who puts out the 'I want a hug' vibe."

She smiled, but not in a mocking way; it was genuine. "I don't know about that. When I first saw you, my first instinct was to hug you."

"But you didn't." I raised my coffee cup in a victorious salute.

She chuckled. "True, but not for the reason you think."

I looked back at the dog, which was still playing fetch. "Why, then?"

"We have rules we are supposed to follow. No touching."

That made me burst into laughter. "But you just touched my arm."

"I'm not good at following rules." She smiled bashfully.

"Ah, so you're a rebel."

"Not sure about that, but I like to think for myself."

Liddy was saying all the right things to me today. Had she planned all of this? I smiled at the thought of her arranging for one of her friends to play fetch with his dog to distract me.

"What friend were you thinking of?"

"Alex."

"How odd that your friend is named Alex."

"Why, because my last name is Alexander? We were called the A-team at school." It wasn't so odd, actually.

"Yeah!" She smiled. "Tell me about her."

It was time to get down to business.

I bobbed my head and took a swig of coffee so I could get the words out. "She was my best friend."

"Was?" The question hung above Liddy's head like a cartoon bubble.

"Yeah. She died." I looked back at the dog.

"Was this recently?" Liddy's body language signaled that she was cautious not to press too hard, too fast.

I stared at the slats in the table. "Uh, no. It happened a few years ago."

"How did it happen?"

"It was an … accident. She was in the hospital and there was some type of mix-up." I looked away so Liddy wouldn't see I was lying. It wasn't an accident.

"What do you mean? Did they give her the wrong medicine?"

I could tell her concern was genuine.

"Oh, no. Nothing like that. She was in a treatment facility … for drugs … somehow another patient or someone gave her heroin and Alex overdosed." I reached into my backpack and fished out my water bottle.

Liddy sat back, taking this in.

"That must have been devastating. Was she being treated for a heroin addiction?"

"From what I know, she had never used heroin. Her drugs of choice were cocaine and alcohol. She used to joke that she'd drink gasoline if it got her drunk or high." I sighed, thinking about how quickly Alex became hopelessly hooked. The person who got her addicted to the junk was evil. Pure evil.

"How old was she?" queried Liddy.

"Thirteen."

Liddy whistled through her teeth. "You know I have to ask?"

I looked up from the table. "No, I don't use drugs. I never touched the stuff. Not even pot."

She nodded her head slowly, letting the information sink in. It looked like she was forming her next question but couldn't think of the right words.

"Alex and I knew each other since birth, pretty much. We were like s-sisters—" I couldn't finish the thought. Tears blurred my vision. I felt Liddy's hand on my arm again.

"My parents thought it would be too much for me to go to the funeral. At least that's what they said. I think my dad wanted to distance his name from the whole thing. Bad press—you know how it goes." I shrugged.

My last memory of Alex was the night the police had taken her away. I closed my eyes and saw her crazed face.

"After that, I didn't really let anyone in ... not until I met Jess. At school, I was friendly with some of the kids, but not close to anyone. I had casual friends to go to the movies with and such, but not a single true friend."

For some reason, Mel didn't enter into the conversation. I had met Mel around the same time that I met Jess. Jess started to ask about my friends, and I had been embarrassed that I didn't really have any, so I made sure to acquire one. Mel was there, and she fit the bill. When Mel and Jess hit it off, I thought everything had gone according to plan. Now, things were weird between the two of them. I couldn't put my finger on it yet, but something was wrong.

I scratched one of my scars. "Why do scars itch?"

Liddy contemplated my arm. "Did you hurt yourself because of Alex?"

Her question floored me.

I shrugged it off. "Maybe. I don't really remember much from that day." It was a lie. I remembered that day better than any other day.

"How did Jess react—after finding you?"

"Oh, geez. You should have heard all of the screaming." I smiled meekly. "It's not the best way to impress ... someone."

"At least not in the normal way." Liddy gave me a "Chin-up, Tiger" kind of smile.

"True. And now I get to do this." I motioned to her across the table.

"Next time, you might weigh your promises a little more carefully."

I cringed. "Tell me about it. But I did get a coffee out of the deal."

Sitting in the beanbag, I closed my eyes and tried to block out all of the hubbub going on around me. Minnie, Karen, and Jenna ran about getting ready for our night out at a party. I didn't give a damn what I looked like, so I refused to get dolled up.

Minnie had disappeared into the bathroom when I heard someone knock on the door. I groaned. If I could have, I would have stayed on my throne for the rest of the night. Instead, I heaved my body up and went to answer the door.

"Hey, Paige. What's up?" Tom strolled into the room.

"Not much. Come on in." He either didn't notice my sarcasm or chose to ignore it.

We'd had our "date" the night before. Surprisingly, it had gone well. All we'd done was talk sports. No awkwardness. When we'd said goodbye, Tom had given me a hug and that was all.

He lowered himself into the beanbag, grabbed the remote, and changed the channel to ESPN. Tom was feeling right at home, and I was responsible for that.

"Where are Ben and Aaron?"

"Oh." He waved the remote. "They should be here soon with the beer."

"That's good. I was worried we wouldn't have a drink before

ten."

"Never." He looked solemn, as if he were praying in church. It made me laugh.

He reached into his coat pocket. "Here, I got you this." He handed me a vodka shooter. "I know you don't like beer much." He winked at me.

I was touched. "Thanks, Tom. That was thoughtful." He focused on the TV again and I was relieved that he didn't expect a kiss in return. His cool demeanor was making it easy for me.

While I fixed up a Coke and vodka—I didn't have any tonic—Minnie appeared around the corner.

"Hey, Tom. I didn't hear you come in."

"I was hoping to see you naked so I snuck in."

Minnie looked aghast and both Tom and I broke into giggles.

"You two are wretched."

"Wretched," I mocked.

Tom shrugged and looked confused.

Karen sauntered in and threw open my closet. "Does anyone have a white scrunchie? I can't find mine." She was holding her red curls on top of her head with one hand.

"Why don't you go like that? It looks so darn cute."

"Very funny."

"Well, I don't have one." I motioned for her to shut my closet.

"Sorry." She put one palm in the air.

"Karen, look in my pink box. I'm certain I have one." Minnie pointed to the box with her curling iron.

Karen stuck her tongue out at me. "At least I can count on you, Audrey."

Another knock sounded on the door. Minnie opened the door one-handed, with the other hand in the air curling some of her hair.

Ben ducked under her arm, and Aaron looked puzzled that she had opened the door in such a state. Not very military-like, was my guess.

"Uh, I have the beer," said the muscle man.

"Dude, in here," commanded Tom.

Aaron sidled in along the wall, avoiding contact with Minnie and her deadly curling iron.

"Is Jewels coming?" He tried to regain some of his maleness.

"Nope." Minnie seized another chunk of hair and wrapped it around the device.

Aaron shuddered. Tom and I made eye contact and sniggered behind his back. He mouthed, "Only child."

Ben looked on, but I'm pretty sure he was stoned out of his mind. I wondered if he would make it through the year without getting kicked out.

Hours later, I dropped the entourage off in front of the frat house, and went to park my car in the back. Jenna followed me in her own car. I let her take the first available spot while I located another vacant spot at the back of the lot.

When I walked past Jenna's car, another car drove by, kicking up dirt. I waved the particles away and spat some from my mouth. Jenna had already gone inside. I threw my arms up in the air. I had let her have the parking spot, she could have at least waited for me.

Several groups of people gathered in front of the house. As I made my way to the door, I felt their eyes on me. Frat parties gave me the willies, but it was all part of my cover.

I tripped down onto the dance floor and collided with a huge dude.

"Careful, the first step is killer," he shouted, and held me up so I could recover my footing.

Marionette

"Thank you."

I squinted, trying to adjust to the darkness. Every few seconds, a strobe light eradicated it, but the fleeting light disconcerted me even more. Music pounded my eardrums. All I could make out was a massive, moving herd of dancers, making it nearly impossible to pick out an individual.

"Paige, what the fuck are you doing here?"

I turned to the voice. "Jewels, is that you?"

"Yup." She didn't stop dancing to answer. "I didn't think you did the whole party thing. What are you doing?"

"Drowning in beer."

She misunderstood, and raised her beer. "Me too."

I had been referring to all of the beer on the floor.

"Oh, Aaron is looking for you," I said.

"What?" She looked around nervously. "Is he here? What a bore!"

"Another failed romance?"

"You could say that." She motioned over her shoulder. "But I got a good feeling about this one." I couldn't see her all that well, but I'm sure she winked at me.

I patted her on the shoulder. "Good luck. Do me a favor, if you see my roomies, tell them I'm looking for them."

"Righty-o." She waved her beer and vanished into the dancing herd.

Why had I agreed to come to this party? I wasn't fond of crappy beer. I hated dancing. And silliness—not a fan. Yet here I was, meandering from one absurd situation to another.

Working my way through the maze of blackness and stinky bodies, I happened upon a group that was too drunk to dance. They all leaned on each other in a way that gave new meaning to the song,

Lean on Me.

"What do you mean the keg's dry?" demanded the first drunk.

"That's ex-exactly what I mean. It's dry. Gone. N-no more," hiccupped the next one.

"There's no more beer!" stated the third.

It has always amazed me that for some reason drunks think the beer is never-ending, especially free beer. It's always comical to watch their reactions when they find out that's not true.

"But … I'mmmmm nnnnnotttt done!"

"You are if you stay here."

Knowing this conversation would take hours, I moved on in search of my friends.

"The only pussy my boyfriend gets is mine." The voice came from someone I faintly recognized, and from what I heard about the boyfriend, he got pussy anytime he wanted.

"Isn't that right, honey? The only pussy you get is from me," said the sweet talker.

There was no reply from her lover.

"You better not be fucking anyone else, you sonofabitch." Her voice lost her sweetness. "Because I'll cut your dick off."

Still no response.

"You asshole … you *are* fucking around." She staggered back to take a swing, but before she could raise her arm, the drunks had fallen on top of each other. Only half of them realized what had happened. The other half complained about swimming in a pool of beer and undesirable liquids on the floor.

I sighed. Finally, I located an empty tree stump outside and slumped down on it. What would Jess say if she found out about Tom? The girl inside the party took things to a whole level Jess wouldn't fathom, but still, it wasn't nice what I was doing. But what

MARIONETTE

could I do? I had to pretend to be straight. I didn't want to end up like Alex, locked up in a treatment facility. She hadn't survived that, and we'd been two peas in the same pod. Who was to say I would survive if I got locked up? I knew damn sure my parents wouldn't care if I didn't. "Dating" Tom was a must: survival of the fittest and all of that hoopla.

I wanted to cry. If I could just get through college quickly, I would be free of my parents forever. Then I could get a job, move away with Jess, and let my family rot in hell for all I cared. I scanned the backyard and studied the partygoers. What did they have to worry about? Grades? Probably not. Money? Maybe, but most were spoiled brats. Sex? That was about all that mattered here. Not life and death situations. Well, not unless they got AIDS—then that would be life and death. But what was the likelihood of that at an isolated school in this town? Besides this college and the one main street, there wasn't much to the area. That's why I had chosen it: anonymity. This place was insulated from the real world.

"Paige! How the fuck are you?" Karen fell on top of me, spilling my water.

I brushed the water droplets off.

"Where have you been? We've been looking for you for hours." Minnie stared at me with one eye. Why was her left eye closed? Minnie the pirate.

"I was inside, looking for you three."

"Why, we've been out here the whole time." Minnie waved her beer.

It was obvious that the three mouseketeers had hit the keg before it tapped out.

"Oh, don't worry, I've been conversing with our school's elite this evening." I smiled ruefully.

"Sounds so boring, and speaking of boring, this party is dead. The beer's gone. Do you know where we can go?" Jenna looked hopeful as she swatted at an imaginary gnat. *Obviously, she won't be able to drive the guys home*, I thought. Where were they? I looked around, but couldn't see hide nor hair of them. I shrugged. They had a better chance of finding a ride home unmolested.

"Yeah … this partay has had it." Karen threw in her two cents.

"Yeah!" clarified Minnie.

I scratched my chin, mulling over an idea. "Actually, I do know of a place we can go."

"Great! Letzzzz go!" Karen marched off before I'd even finished getting all the words out.

They filed into a line and headed toward the fence. We always entered a frat party via the front door, but we always left by hopping over the fence, in case the coppers were outside waiting to pounce. I didn't understand this logic. Wouldn't the cops be smart enough to wait in the back? But who was I to ruin a tradition? Besides, watching drunk people jump a fence was entertaining. I did my best to shove all three of them over before gracefully swinging over myself. Occasionally, one of them got hurt, but they never knew it until the next morning, and by then I could lie about how they'd sprained their ankle. Another tradition for the sober driver, I'm assuming.

I smooshed all of them into the back seat, since I didn't trust their drunk asses not to mess with all the shiny buttons in the front.

Before they knew what was going on, I had parked the car, whisked them back to the dorm, and opened the door to my room.

"Hey, wait a minute, this is your room. There's no party here. I should know; I live next door." Karen put her hands on her hips.

Minnie waggled her finger in my face. "This is a nasty trick."

"You're all so smart. I can't put anything past you."

Marionette

"You mean this is a joke," asked Karen.

"Nope. I mean goodnight." I shoved my way past them and fell onto my bed, not bothering to change out of my clothes.

The three stooges jibber-jabbered at the door for a minute and then admitted defeat. Slowly, they dispersed. I heard Karen and Jenna crash through the bathroom on their way to their own room.

I hoped Tom and the boys had made it home safe. While Minnie was in the bathroom, I tried calling Jess. She didn't answer. Then I dialed Tom's number. Again, no answer. Where was everyone?

"Where are you going?" asked a lethargic voice.

"Heading home for the weekend. I'm sorry I woke you." I patted Minnie's arm. She was still in bed. Most people were, at four in the morning.

"What time is it?" Minnie tried to sit up, but ended up grabbing her head and falling back down onto the pillow.

"Early. Too early to talk. I'll see you Sunday night or Monday morning."

She grunted a goodbye as I slung my backpack over my shoulder.

When I had woken up a few minutes ago and dialed Jess's number, she still wasn't home. I had a bad feeling.

The highway was deserted, so I made good time to the apartment. I pulled into the parking lot and spied her car. That was a relief. Now what, though? Should I barge in and wake her up, or should I head to Denny's and have breakfast and wait? What if I was super quiet and crawled into bed with her? She might like that surprise. Smiling, I let myself into the apartment.

Jess stood in the kitchen, pouring a beer. I looked at my watch. Was I mistaken about the time? Six. I tapped my watch.

"Hey, what are you doing here?" She slapped the glass down on the counter and rushed over to me.

Her hug seemed genuine. Everything was normal, except that it was dawn and she had apparently just returned from her evening exploits.

"Are you just getting home?" I asked.

She reeked of smoke.

"And have you been smoking?"

Jess pushed me away, teasingly. "Are you checking up on me, Paige?" She tapped her foot, waiting for my answer.

"Yes. I tried calling you last night when I got home and then I called this morning when I woke up. I was worried. Where have you been?"

"At work. You wouldn't believe the mess my boss, Richard, got us into. He signed this client, and Tim, Sally, and I had to work all night to get a presentation together for first thing Monday."

I thought about that for a minute. "Why couldn't you work on it over the weekend?" I wasn't trying to accuse her of anything, I just found her explanation odd.

"Oh, I wish. No, Richard was flying out this morning to New York to meet with the client, so we had to have it done before his flight." She glanced at her watch. "Which he should be boarding in another hour or so. I had to drive the presentation to the airport. Trust me, Paige, they don't pay me enough." She marched back into the kitchen and took a swig of her beer.

I followed meekly. It all sounded believable, but something was gnawing at me.

Jess scrutinized my face. "Are you hungry? I'm famished. Let's head to Denny's. My treat."

I wasn't going to turn down a hot meal. Denny's wasn't a five-

MARIONETTE

star restaurant, but it was heads above dorm food.

"You're on. I can't wait to tell you about this party I went to last night."

She leaned in and gave me a peck on the cheek. "Even if you were checking up on me, I'm glad to see you."

"I wasn't spying. I was worried." I defended.

She patted my arm. "I know. That's what I love about you."

After the zombie of a hostess seated us, I scanned the menu. Just looking at the laminated pictures of French toast, ham, bacon, pancakes, and hash browns made me salivate.

"Do they feed you up there?" Jess peered over her menu. "You look like you're about to devour your menu."

"The food is shit there, and my roommates keep invading my emergency stash. I never feel full anymore." I continued to scrutinize the menu.

Jess pulled out a wad of twenties. "Well, you can eat until you can't eat any more."

"What'd you do, rob a 7-Eleven on the way home from the airport?" I gawked at the rolled-up notes.

"Yes." She looked deadly serious.

I fidgeted in my chair.

"Paige, I'm just kidding." She whacked me on the head with her menu. "Richard gave me a bonus for working all night."

I thought she said she didn't get paid enough by them.

Our waitress approached. "What'll you want?" she asked rudely, glancing at her watch. I wondered how much longer until her shift was over.

Jess ordered a Tex Mex omelet and I started with their biggest breakfast: eggs, bacon, ham, pancakes, and hash browns. I also asked for a chocolate malt.

"Will that be enough for you? Nice touch with the malt." Jess winked at me.

"Hey man, I don't like to waste opportunities." I gestured to the cash in her purse.

"So tell me about the party. I miss college." She got a faraway look in her eye. "The working world is no fun."

"Really? So far, I'm not seeing why people say it's the best time of your life. All people do is drink and make fools of themselves."

Jess laughed heartily. "That's the fun part, Paige. Trust me, when you finish and join the rat race, you'll miss those days. Gosh, you are such a fuddy-duddy."

"I am not! I just don't understand it. Take Karen, she's determined to bag a boyfriend by the end of the semester. Why?"

"Is she cute?" Jess sipped her water.

"Yeah, I guess."

Jess threw her straw at me. "You better behave while you're up there."

I knew she was only joking, but I decided then that she could never find out about Tom.

"So, if Karen's cute, why can't she find a boy?"

The waitress set my chocolate malt in front of me. Before I had a chance to dig in, Jess jabbed her finger into the whipped cream and licked her finger. I almost forgot what I was saying.

"Oh, I think it's because she farts a lot. And she's a jock. She and Jenna are on the basketball team. She's girlie, but also masculine, if you get my meaning."

Jess nodded. Our food arrived; that was an advantage to getting to Denny's so early in the morning: you didn't have to wait long.

I reached for the maple syrup and started to douse my pancakes, bacon, and ham. Jess poured Tabasco on her omelet.

"How can you stomach that much Tabasco?"

"I like to live on the edge." She shook a few more drops out.

We ate in silence because I was too busy shoveling food in. After several minutes, Jess mentioned that Mel called for me.

"Do you think she wants more money?"

A look of concern marred her lovely face. "Yes. You can count on that."

I leaned back from the table. "Sometimes I feel as if Mel treats me like I'm her personal ATM. Like I owe her somehow."

"She's going through a lot right now ... and ..."

"And, what?"

"Oh, it's nothing."

I could tell it was something.

"Come on, Jess. What?" I set my fork down and braced for the news.

"She feels guilty."

"Guilty? About what, taking my money?"

Jess stirred her food around on her plate, not looking at me. "I'm sure she feels bad about that too, but she feels guilty about ..." She motioned to my arm.

"That I tried to kill myself?" I fished.

"Sorta."

"Jess, you're killing me. What did she tell you?"

The waitress stopped by to ask how the food was. I didn't respond, but Jess said everything was wonderful and ordered another coffee.

I lowered my head and asked quietly, "What did Mel say?"

I knew I wasn't going to like what I heard. Why else would Jess take so long getting it out? That wasn't like her. Quick, like a Band-

Aid, was her usual method.

"She thinks we should tell your parents."

"What?" I shouted. The only other people in the restaurant turned and stared.

Jess put a finger to her lips to shush me. "I knew I shouldn't have told you."

"Why in the hell does she think she should tell them, of all people?" I threw my arms up in the air.

Jess waved her fork in the air. "Oh, you know how close Mel is with her parents. She still lives with them. She thinks if your parents knew about"—she motioned to my scars again—"they would be nicer to you."

"What kind of logic is that?"

"Mel logic," Jess confessed sheepishly.

"She …" my voice quavered.

Jess looked startled. "Oh, no. She hasn't said anything to them. And she won't, Paige. I talked to her and she won't say anything."

"How can you be so certain?"

Jess reached across the table and rubbed my scar where it emerged a little from my shirt. "Paige, you have to trust me on this. Besides, what can you do about it? It's not like you can hire some dude named Guido to teach her a lesson."

I shivered.

"I want to go home."

Jess reached into her purse and walked up to the register to pay the bill. While she did, I went to the car and sat in the passenger side. Usually, I drove, but I didn't have the energy. I leaned my head against the cool window. Condensation trickled onto my forehead.

Jess slid into the driver's seat without any protest. When we got back to the apartment, I took a shower—a long, hot shower. My shoulders were tense and I wanted to wash all the filth off me. I hadn't showered after the party, and all of a sudden I felt like I was drowning in shit.

By the time I was done, my body was parboiled. I didn't bother getting dressed, just walked out to the front room in a towel. Jess looked deflated.

"Paige, everything is going to be okay. I won't let anything happen to you."

I didn't speak, just sat on the couch, utterly drained. Jess didn't know the full truth. No one did.

"Listen, I worked all night, and I'm betting you didn't get much sleep. Let's go to bed and get some rest."

I nodded.

As I closed my eyes, I heard thunder off in the distance and then a streak of lightning lit up the room. My mind flashed back to that night. Alex screaming like a madwoman. I didn't want to become like that. What would I do if the police came to take me away to one of my father's hidden gems? Actually, he would probably be more subtle and have someone snatch me from the street, like those kids you see on the back of milk cartons. Boom. Done! And no one would be the wiser. Oh, Jess would look for me, but there's no way in hell my father would leave a trail of any type. Then my mother would get involved. She was the real threat.

The fucking rich—they can do anything.

I rolled over and hid my face in Jess's arm. She felt warm. Alive. Even after working all night, I felt the vitality that always emanated from her. She could go for days without sleeping and not be any worse for it. I longed to be more like her. Confident. Brave. Assured. Happy to be alive. She was like Elie Wiesel.

When she said she wouldn't let anything happen to me, she

meant it. But even Jess didn't know what she was up against when it came to my parents.

My mom flashed before my mind: her manic laugh, the shake of her fist. "Watch yourself, Paige, or I'll do it to you too."

I buried my head further into Jess's and she held me tighter.

Not even Jess could save me.

Alex, I know you tried to warn me. If I had only listened that night. We should have run away. We should have left.

It had been raining that night as well. I'd seen Alex shouting through the deluge, "Let's go, Paige. We have to get away from them!" She had pulled on my arm frantically. She'd been so hysterical, and Alex was always the calm one. The smart one. Level-headed, even.

I had just thought she was having a bad trip and that in the morning everything would be okay.

I was wrong.

Alex was dead.

And I would be next if I wasn't careful.

The pitter-patter of rain on the skylight made me cringe. I had to fight the urge to jump out of bed and leave. To keep moving. To never come back. I knew it was harder to hit a moving target.

Jess snored gently next to me. She was all I had. Mel was out of touch with reality—why did she want to tell my parents? After everything I'd told her. Minnie and all of them, I really didn't give two shits about. There was Julia, but she wasn't enough to keep me in town.

But Jess.

I loved and trusted her implicitly. I couldn't leave.

I had to pretend for three and a half years. I could get through school, and Jess could finish her MBA, and then we would get the fuck out of Dodge.

Marionette

New York City maybe? Or London.

Shit, Jess spoke three languages and soon-to-be four. We could live anywhere.

I just needed to hold on for three and a half years.

After our much-needed nap, Jess and I wandered into Julia's for lunch. I hadn't eaten much of my breakfast and by this point, I was famished. No one made a crack when I ordered two sandwiches, fries, and baked beans. If my metabolism ever slows down, I'll be screwed.

Before I had demolished my first sandwich, Mel walked in. Jess's entire body tensed, but Julia hopped up and gave her a "mom" hug. Mel avoided looking in Jess's direction and sat down right across from me. I felt Jess's eyes on me; they said, "Don't say anything. Be cool."

How could I not say anything? I wanted to tell her to go to hell, that what she contemplated was idiotic. Did she want me dead? Then buy me a gun so I could do it—on my terms, not on theirs. No more strings.

My parents would never see the light and realize how awful they've been to me. I didn't matter to them. All they wanted was a servant. Now that I was out of the house, my usefulness was expended. Yes, my father still had to pay for my school, but I bet he kept a running tab of all of the money I'd cost him since the day I was born. I half expect to see a bill once I "make" it. He probably knows just how many boxes of diapers I went through, and how many rolls of toilet paper I've used to wipe my ass.

Money. Plain and simple. My folks spoke in terms of money. Will this make me money? Will this cost me money? I was a cost—an expensive liability. And in business, that meant I needed to be cut.

Jess kicked me under the table and I did my best to erase any trace of loathing from my face.

"What's up, Mel?" I tried to sound normal.

Jess gave me a nod of approval.

Mel looked away. "Not much. How's school?"

"Oh, it's going well. I'm starting to make some *new* friends."

Jess's swift kick under the table made my knee smack into the table and upset my water glass.

"Paige! I'm so sorry that old knee injury is acting up, huh." Jess grabbed some napkins from the holder and began to wipe up the water.

Julia eyed me out of the corner of her eye, and then searched Jess's face.

"How's work going, Mel?" Jess asked as she set the sopping napkins off to the side.

Mel didn't answer right away. She was seething; I could tell. What did she have to be upset about? Had Jess told her she was a ninny? If so: good. At least one person in my life had some sense and was looking out for me.

I flashed Jess a loving smile and she winked at me. I could feel her tension melting away, and mine with it.

"Are you getting geared up for the Christmas season?" I put out there as a peace offering.

"Not yet, thank goodness. Last season nearly killed me." Mel still avoided looking at Jess, which wasn't that hard since they sat on the same side of the table. However, I noticed that Mel kept her body pivoted to avoid any chance of seeing Jess, even out of the corner of her eye.

"Well, if you need help with anything outside of work, let me know. I'm always willing to help. And Paige tells me I can whip up a fabulous meal in seconds."

MARIONETTE

Jess was trying. Really trying. Why?

"By whip up, she means she calls me and orders home-cooked meals." Julia laughed.

"Julia! That was a secret!"

I chuckled. "If you want to keep it secret, you should throw out the wrappers that say 'Julia's Kitchen.'"

"Now you tell me!" Jess slapped her forehead.

The three of us laughed, but Mel just looked miserable. I got the feeling she wanted to talk to me in private, but I wasn't going to let that happen. My bank account was dangerously low, and my father wouldn't put any more money in until the first of the month. It was only the twenty-fifth.

Jess kept chattering away and Julia, who I don't think knew the true story, did her best to keep things cheerful. I continued eating my lunch while Mel sulked in her chair. Every time she attempted to catch my eye, I focused my attention on Jess.

When I stood up to use the toilet, Jess bounced out of her seat to join me. Her panic made me want to laugh so hard I nearly peed my pants. Did she think Mel would lock me in the can until I handed over my wallet? The image made me smile because there was no money in my wallet anyway. Thank goodness Jess had paid for breakfast, and I knew Julia wouldn't give me a bill. I would catch up with her the next time I was in town.

The charade didn't last much longer. Mel gave up and left, empty-handed. At one point, I thought she was going to ask for money right in front of Jess and Julia, but then she saw my scars and looked away quickly.

"Do you mind telling me what that was about?" demanded Julia.

"Beats me." I said as honestly as possible.

"I don't want Mel asking Paige for any more money," proffered

Jess, which was partly true. She also didn't want me blowing through my cash. She feared that Mel would turn against me and run to my parents to get even.

"How much money have you given her, Paige?" Julia's concern showed on her face.

"Over six hundred this month alone."

She whistled threw her teeth. "I had no idea. Okay, next time I'll do my best so Paige won't be alone with her either. I love Mel to bits, but this Wesley is bad news. She needs to learn that."

Jess gave Julia a squeeze. "I knew we could count on you." She looked more relieved than I did, which puzzled me. Usually, Jess was calm and collected. But ever since she had told me about Mel, she was frazzled. It made me wonder whether Jess secretly felt she didn't have Mel under control and she was doing her best to reel Mel in fast.

I admired her dedication to me.

As Julia cleared our dishes, I turned to Jess and asked, "What foreign flick can I take you to today?" I wanted to repay her for her devotion.

"Actually, there's a new exhibit at the Denver Art Museum. Van Gogh."

Ugh. Museums gave me the creeps, but I didn't let on. "Cool. He's the dude who cut off his ear. Maybe he's my long-lost soul mate." I flashed my wrists.

She leaned across the table to kiss me. "Don't even start with me, missy."

Jess had me. I was putty in her hands. And she knew it.

Chapter Fourteen

WEARING A GREY suit and blood-red blouse, Liddy rushed into the room five minutes late. Her expression said, "Don't give me shit today."

I wondered what it would be like to work with clients like me every day. Let's face it, I tried to off myself, so I couldn't be that much fun to hang out with. And suicidal ideation seemed to be her specialty. Why? Had someone she loved committed suicide? Had she made a promise to herself to help others? Or did she love being around self-absorbed assholes like me? I shuddered at the thought of having her job.

"What was that for? Are you cold?" She eased into her chair and retrieved her pencil and notepad from the desk.

I motioned to the notepad. "What do you write down?"

"Little things, really. Like, you mentioned once I should have pursued a bike accident you had when you were little, so I have a note to explore that further."

"Is that what you want me to talk about today?"

"Do you want to talk about it?"

"Not particularly."

"What would you like to talk about then?" She smiled, knowing what my answer would be.

"Well, that seems to be the issue, Doc. I don't like to talk about things."

"No, really?"

I was starting to like her. Maybe this therapy thing wasn't so bad. I thought she would demand to know every secret I had and would push and push until I revealed all, but she wasn't like that. Maybe her sweetness was just a way to dupe me into talking. And it helped that she was drop-dead gorgeous. Pardon the pun.

"Why don't you tell me about your sister—Abbie. We haven't talked about her yet." Her eyes looked hopeful.

"There's not much to tell about Abbie. I don't really know her. I know this may sound odd, since we are fraternal twins, but we're like strangers. She's a lot like my mom."

"How so?"

"She's not very nice to me. She isn't outright mean like my mother, but she has a way of making it clear that she never wanted me for a sister. And she drinks, just like my mom. Abbie, though, has taken it one step further: she likes drugs."

Liddy scribbled something down on her paper.

"What did you write?" I leaned forward. Surprisingly, Liddy showed me, but I couldn't decipher her chicken scratch. "You write worse than my father."

"My girlfriend tells me that all the time."

Girlfriend? Like lover or friend? I tried not to react to the word, but I know I did. Was Liddy baiting me? Part of me wanted to confess, because keeping Jess a secret was difficult. Having three separate lives meant having to remember to put the correct hat on in each place.

MARIONETTE

Sometimes, I would get befuddled about where I was.

"Jess says the same thing about my writing," I said, squinting at Liddy's words to no avail.

"Can you decode it?" I asked.

"Of course. There seems to be a common theme to your childhood. Your mother, sister, and Alex all had issues with alcohol and drugs. I think that's something we should explore."

I expected her to demand to know what I thought about that connection, but she didn't. Instead, she asked, "How do you know Abbie uses drugs?"

"How do you know the moon exists?"

"I'm sorry, what?" She tapped her pencil gently on her leg.

"I've seen it ... I mean, I've seen her use them."

"Even though you are twins, you weren't close growing up?"

"Not one bit—it was almost like we weren't sisters at all. We always had separate friends, different activities. We never had the same teachers. I loved sports and Abbie is a musician. I love to read. Abbie can't sit still for more than a minute." I folded my hands together and rested my chin on them. "We never wore each other's clothes, never had heartfelt discussions, and we never plotted against our parents. Our rooms were on opposite sides of the house. We all live in different wings of the house."

Liddy looked up from her notepad. "Even your parents."

"Yes, even them. You've seen our photos in the paper. You probably wouldn't have guessed that the four of us hated each other." I stopped to mull something over. "Actually, I don't think Abbie and I hate each other. There's something else, but I've never been able to put my finger on it. We just don't know each other."

"When did she start using drugs?"

"Early on in high school. She has a lot of friends who are in bands. I know its cliché, but I think Abbie went down that path since she wants to be a musician. Music is her passion. I've never known her to date anyone seriously. Oh, she had a date for the prom and such, but never a boyfriend."

"What about a girlfriend?"

I almost smiled at that one. Liddy was trying to make it seem normal for me.

"Nah. She's not gay." I unfolded my hands and gripped the armrests of my chair. "It's like she can't share herself with a person. Music—music speaks to her. A couple of months ago, she tried to share her passion with me. At first, I was touched, but it ended up being a horrible experience."

"Why?" Liddy's voice was low, soft and coaxing.

"Well, it was right after"—I motioned to my scars—"the stitches were gone, but the marks were still quite visible, all red and puffy. She took me to Red Rocks to see one of her favorite bands. I can't even remember their name. It was like walking into a hippie commune in the sixties.

"Everyone talked with their heads tilted to the side, their eyes half open, their speech was slow and painful, and they all stank. You know when people use natural deodorant? That stuff doesn't work, especially on humid days. It had rained earlier in the day. By the afternoon, it was muggy and stifling. For some reason, all of them wanted me to play Frisbee. I was afraid my shirt would slip up and reveal my wrists, so I sat out during the reindeer games."

I stirred in my seat. "I think Abbie was embarrassed by me. They were her friends and I was snubbing them. That wasn't my intention, but I just couldn't relate to them. That's when it became clear just how different we were. While I had retreated into my own world filled with books, she had retreated into this one, filled with peace-loving hippies. It's comical really. If my mother knew, she would rip the heads off all of Abbie's cohorts. I can kinda picture her shouting, 'Off with their heads.'

"Abbie's last attempt at bonding with me that evening was to teach me how to smoke pot. She said that I was leaving for college soon and I would need to know how to fit in."

I closed my eyes and pictured Abbie sitting in her car, teaching me the finer art of trimming marijuana leaves.

"She said, 'The secret to good pot is in how you cut the leaves,' as she meticulously cut the leaves with her Eddie Bauer knife our mom had given her the previous Christmas. Closing one eye and sticking out her tongue, she cut the leaves into tiny pieces of art. Her precision amazed me. We were alone, and I think she felt closer to me and had started letting me in a little.

"She continued, 'You don't know it yet, but college is going to be the best time of your life. Fuck Mom and fuck Dad. In college, we'll really start to flourish.'

"She took pride in showing me how to roll a joint." I laughed, even though I found it pathetic. "Abbie's one thing she wanted to teach me was how to roll a joint, and I didn't even smoke pot."

Again, I shut my eyes on the room and put myself back in Abbie's car.

"Abbie handed me a slip of paper. Tapped the leaves onto it and then licked the ends."

I opened my eyes, and squashed the memory like a bug. "When she took her first hit, she was a whole new person: relaxed and kind. I hadn't known her to be kind before. She talked about the classes she wanted to take in addition to her pre-med courses. Even though she wants to be a musician, our mother wants Abbie to become a doctor. Abbie doesn't have the courage to tell her to go to hell. I felt sorry for her that day."

"Does your mom know Abbie doesn't want to study medicine?" Liddy's cheerless tone indicated that she knew the answer but felt compelled to ask for clarification.

"Of course. But what Mother wants, Mother gets. She thinks that since she suffered so much, she is owed everything now. Thinks that my sister and I should just kowtow to her and not complain. She's suffered, and we can never make it up to her completely."

"What happened after Abbie rolled the joint?" Liddy gestured for me to continue the story.

"That's when things started to get interesting. Her calmness didn't last long. She started to flick her lighter. From an early age, Abbie had been fascinated with fire. She loved putting out candles with her fingertips or holding her hand above the flame, lowering her hand closer and closer until she couldn't stand the pain."

The thought made me uncomfortable and I wriggled in my chair. "I've always been terrified of fire. Alex used to tease me about it. She said that in a former life I was a witch who was burned at the stake. Just lighting a match freaks me out. To this day, I've never lit a grill.

"Abbie knew about my fear of fire, but she started flicking the lighter closer and closer to me. At first, I laughed it off and shoved her hand away. A few minutes earlier she had been in such a good mood, so I didn't think anything of it. Then she singed some of my hair."

I rubbed my head. "That pissed me off. I reached for the lighter, rolled down the window, and chucked it out. When I did, my shirtsleeve raised a tad, enough to show Abbie what I had done.

"She stopped and stared. I didn't know what to do, so I did nothing. I was frozen. Then she said, 'Jesus, Paige.' She reached out and felt my scars, running her finger along one. 'You weren't messing around when you did this.'"

I bolted up out of my chair and walked to the water cooler. When I depressed the button, I heard the glugging of the water as it dripped into my cup. My hands were shaking so much that as I lifted it to my lips, I spilled some on my chin. I felt too tired to wipe the droplets away.

"It was like she was proud of me. That I hadn't half-assed the attempt—that I really dug in with the razor."

"And that upset you?" Liddy probed.

"Yeah, it did. She's my sister. Shouldn't she be a tiny bit concerned that I tried to kill myself? Instead, she was impressed. I wondered how impressed she might have been if Jess hadn't found me in time. Would she have gushed at my funeral?" I took a sip of my water. "Sometimes I feel like no one loves me. And maybe that's my fault. I haven't really tried to let people in. Jess, well sh—"

I froze. Liddy didn't show any sign of recognizing that I had almost come out.

Does it count if it wasn't intentional?

Glancing at her notepad, I noticed she hadn't jotted anything down, not that she would need a reminder. What did I think she'd write down, "Ask Paige if she is a dyke"?

"Go back to Abbie. What happened next in the car?"

"I sucked in some air and my lungs burned. Abbie started laughing and said, 'Make sure Mom doesn't see those. She'll kill you.' Then she laughed hysterically and said, 'Or maybe you should, since you failed.'"

Rubbing my eyes, I left my hands in front of my face. As I stared at my fingers I said, "One moment she was proud of my attempt, and the next she was mocking my ineptitude. I didn't say anything and

Abbie stared out of the windshield. Then she said we should hike to the top, to the amphitheater, so we wouldn't miss the show.

"That was it. The rest of the night, she didn't mention my wrists. In fact, we didn't talk. Abbie was in her element, dancing and singing. She kept offering me hits, but I bluffed my way out of it.

"The next day we bumped into each other in the kitchen and neither of us said a word to each other. That night, in her car, was the last conversation we had before we both left for college."

Thoughts pounded in my head. Who did I have in my life? I couldn't face the weekend in my dorm room, pretending. I didn't want to fake liking Tom. I didn't want to act normal. What I wanted was to curl up in a ball and cry, kick, scream. I couldn't do that at school. At school, I wore my frivolous college girl hat.

I grabbed my bag and started to throw in some clothes and a couple of books when Minnie walked in.

Giving me a wide berth, in case I accidentally heaved her into my bag, she assessed the situation quickly and asked, "Are you going out of town?"

I wanted to say, "What the fuck do you think?" Instead, I mumbled, "Yes."

"Is everything okay?" She looked nervous.

"Yeah, I'm just running late."

"Oh." Minnie's relief spread throughout her body.

I was amazed by how quickly she could relax.

"I'm not sure when I'll be back," I said.

"Okay. I'm heading home as well. I'm sure Karen and Jenna will hold down the fort for us." She smiled, apparently not noticing my look of derision. She was such a simpleton.

The drive to Jess's wasn't fun at all. Not once did I cut someone off, which angered me. I wanted to weave in and out of traffic. I needed the excitement to make me feel alive, to get my heart pumping.

When I walked into Jess's apartment, she was taking a nap on the couch. Groggily, she lifted her head up and smiled. "I wasn't expecting you this evening." Her voice was thick with sleep, as if she'd been asleep for hours.

"I'm sorry that I woke you."

She motioned for me to come to her. "Don't be silly. This is the best way to wake up."

I sat down heavily on the couch.

"What's wrong, Paige?" She popped up next to me and wrapped me in her arms.

"Nothing."

Casually, she wiped my tears off my cheeks. "Ah, sweetie. I don't think it's nothing. But if you don't want to talk, that's okay."

I nestled my head into the crook of her neck. "I'm just so tired, Jess. I'm so tired." My eyelids felt like steel traps, forcing themselves shut. Before I knew it, I was drifting off to sleep.

When I snapped my eyes open, it was dark outside and Jess still held me in her arms. At first, I thought I had been asleep for just a few minutes, but the clock informed me otherwise. Two hours had passed.

Jess felt me stirring, kissed my forehead, and asked, "Are you hungry, baby?"

I realized I was ravenous. "Yes."

"Good! I discovered this Mexican place recently and I've been dying to take you there. Let me shower and we'll go. Would you like to hop in?"

The thought of warm water oozing over me enlivened me. I

used to love baths, but now the thought of lying in a tub disgusted me. I briefly remembered the bloody water, and trembled.

After showering, we walked to the restaurant. It was only a fifteen-minute walk and the chill in the air helped wake us both.

"Are you feeling okay?" I asked.

Jess looked at me askance. "Yeah, why?"

"When I came in, it looked like you'd been sleeping for some time. Did you call out sick today?"

She waved her hand. "Oh, that. I worked another all-nighter, so Richard let me leave early today."

I whistled. "Man, they have been working you to death lately."

Not the best word choice, but we both let it slide.

When we entered the restaurant, I relaxed completely. The place was a hole in the wall. It had enough room for a small stage, and a mariachi band was in full swing. As soon as the waitress sat us at a table, Jess tugged on my arm, dragging me onto the dance floor. I wasn't the dancing type, but Jess knew how to persuade me. As she writhed around the dance floor I did my best to wiggle my butt some in a pathetic attempt to keep up. Several other people were dancing, and one of them was just as bad as me. We chuckled together and stood to the side. Jess paired up with a bulky man to show us amateurs how it was done. After they had finished, the entire restaurant broke into a cheer and, laughing, Jess led me back to our table.

"How in the world did you learn to dance like that?"

"Like what?"

"Oh, like you know what you're doing." I couldn't think of the right words and felt silly.

"I just let the music tell me what to do, Paige. You can't think, you just feel." Her face glowed with perspiration and she placed her hand on my heart.

The waitress came by to take our orders and it was obvious that she knew Jess and knew what Jess would order. I hadn't had a chance to look at the menu, so I just said ditto.

Soon, two tamale platters and two Coronas arrived. It was hot in the restaurant, and the enticing lime in the neck of the bottle lured me in. Before I knew it, I'd had another one. After the third, the hefty man tried to teach me how to dance. I was utterly hopeless, but he didn't give up on me. By the end of the night, I could manage a half-decent spin without making a complete fool of myself. To celebrate my victory, all of the remaining patrons partook in tequila shots. It was my first time, and Jess had me lick the salt off her chest, which got a rise out of everyone—which called for more dancing. Jess and the man paired up again and I leaned against the wall. The room started to spin, but I didn't care. The music soothed me.

On the way home, Jess had to hold me up. She was giddy and it had started to drizzle, but I didn't bother putting my jacket on. The drops felt like electrified bee stings, only pleasurable. I peeled off my long-sleeved shirt and raised my arms, soaking my scars. Jess giggled and peeled her shirt off too. By the time we reached her apartment, Jess was down to her bra and skirt. We stepped outside, onto her balcony, and I stripped from the waist up. The rain, the cold air, and the alcohol made me feel alive. I hadn't felt that alive in years.

Gazing into Jess's eyes, I started to cry. I never wanted the moment to end. I wanted to stand naked in the rain with a radiant-looking Jess forever. I slipped off my jeans and threw them over the railing. Jess did the same with her skirt. Then I rushed inside Jess's apartment, grabbed the shirt I had been wearing, and ran back outside to heave it as far as I could. Tugging off my panties, I then threw them even further.

Both of us stood there, stark naked. Flashes of moonlight broke through the passing clouds, revealing her body to me like an Impressionist painting. I could no longer resist. We hadn't made love since that day in the bathtub. Jess had felt that I was too vulnerable. Now, I stood before her, naked, crying, and in control. Powerful. Alive. Jess must have sensed it, because she led me inside, into her bedroom.

Three hours later, Jess lay next to me, sound asleep. We had kicked the covers from the bed, and although sunlight was starting to peep in through the window, the apartment was cold and autumn was in full swing. Birds were fussing about outside. After placing the comforter back over Jess, I left the bedroom and walked to the front room. The place was spic and span, as usual, apart from a stack of business books on the kitchen table. Jess was already preparing for her MBA program. Her classes didn't start for months, but she had already started cramming.

I flipped through the books. Honestly, I didn't understand why she loved business so much. The topics seemed boring: marketing, management, finance, and strategic operations. I shuddered. I wondered if Abbie's medical coursework gave her the same feeling.

On the coffee table, I spied a copy of *The Stand*. That appealed to me more than her schoolbooks. I curled up under an afghan and cracked the book to the first page. I felt free: lying on my girlfriend's couch, completely naked, reading a Stephen King novel. If my parents saw me, there would be blood on the walls. The thought made me smile. When I was with Jess, they couldn't touch me. She was my refuge.

I nodded off after a few pages, and the smell of sizzling bacon woke me to a flood of sunlight pouring in through the window.

Marionette

Wrapping the afghan around me, I wandered into the kitchen.

"Morning, sunshine!" Jess stood at the stove, flipping bacon strips over in a hot pan. I stood back from the spatter.

"M-morning," I mumbled.

"There's a fresh pot of coffee." She gestured to the coffee pot.

Without speaking, I poured myself a cup and then added an abundance of sugar.

"How did you sleep?" I slurped a mouthful of coffee.

"Splendid. I see you got restless." She eyed me. "I was relieved to find you on the couch and not on one of your drives."

I waved the words away. "My head hurts."

"Ha! I wondered if you'd be hungover today." Jess placed some aspirin in my hand.

"How are you not?" I rubbed my head.

"I've had more practice than you." She winked. "I'm glad you liked the place. You and Santi hit it off."

"Who's Santi?"

That got a rise out of her. "You don't remember last night?"

"I wasn't that drunk. Was he the guy I was dancing with?"

"Yes. He owns the place. The best tamales in town."

I nodded. They were damn good. "Not sure if tequila is my drink, though."

"Oh, I don't know. It brought out a whole different side to you, one I haven't seen before." She scooped the crisp bacon onto a plate. "Greasy food is one of the best cures for a hangover." Jess opened the oven door and pulled out a plate heaped with hash browns and scrambled eggs.

Like Pavlov's dog, my mouth started to water.

"Go put some clothes on so we can eat."

"I threw my jeans over the railing, and I only packed shirts to change into."

She laughed. "That's right. Grab a pair of my sweats. I take it we'll have to go shopping for new jeans for you. Or you can wear one of my skirts."

"I think I'd rather buy a new pair of jeans. Hopefully, we won't run into anyone we know at the mall while I'm wearing your sweats."

I disappeared into the bedroom and reappeared quickly in a T-shirt and pink sweats. Jess was back at the oven, pouring pancake batter into a pan.

"Good lord, you're cooking enough food for an army."

"Are you complaining?"

"Never." I grabbed a strip of bacon and chomped down on it. It was extra crispy—just the way I like it.

We sat at the table and said nothing. Jess didn't cook a lot, but she could cook a mean breakfast and I didn't want to waste any time.

"Don't worry, Paige," she said as she watched me eat. "There's no time limit. Take your time eating." She slapped my thigh.

"Oh, sorry." I set my fork down and fiddled with my napkin. "Thanks, Jess."

"You're welcome. I love cooking for you."

I looked out the window at a hopeful bird that was perched on the railing. "That's not what I meant. Thanks for last night."

"I hope you aren't referring to our bedroom activities." She teased.

I felt color rise in my cheeks. She could still embarrass me, even after everything. "No—I mean that was great—but I was talking about taking me out last night. Yesterday was difficult, and you knew exactly what I needed."

Jess played with her scrambled eggs. "I know therapy isn't easy on you. I'm always here when you need me."

"That means the world to me, Jess." I felt tears forming in my eyes. "I feel like you are the only person I can count on these days."

Her eyes darted towards the stove. "Oh, damn, I think I left the burner on."

As she got up, I wiped my eyes and then began shoveling food into my mouth again. The grease was making my stomach feel better, and the aspirin was taking the edge off the jackhammer in my head.

She sauntered back to the table, carrying an extra-crunchy slice of bacon. "Have a piece of charcoal?"

I looked at it skeptically, but still ate it. "Not too bad."

"The food up there must be awful if you think that's good." She sat back down and put her napkin in her lap. Even at home, her manners were impeccable.

The mere mention of school and my life up there depressed me. This was where I wanted to be, not up there with Minnie, Tom, Liddy. Only Jess made me feel safe. Loved.

I wanted to get to The Gap as quickly as possible. Jess would not let me wear her pink sweats out in public, so I rushed through the parking lot in one of her long, flowing skirts. The fabric rustled around me, and I felt like I was drowning. How did she wear these?

The Gap was at the south-east entrance, and if I was quick enough, I could get in, grab a pair of jeans, and head straight for the dressing rooms before being seen. All of my jeans were from this store. I knew my size and the cut like the back of my hand.

Of course, today had to be the day when I couldn't find my size and cut. I frantically rummaged through a stack of jeans when I heard a familiar voice.

"Paige, is that you?"

Turning, I saw Mel and Weasel standing there.

"Are you wearing a skirt?" Weasel reached for my skirt, but I slapped his hand away as if he were a mosquito. He was lucky I didn't squash him.

"Easy there," Weasel said with a smirk. "That's not very ladylike."

Mel's face prompted me to answer. "I had a mishap last night with my jeans and Jess wouldn't let me go out in sweats."

"Pink sweats, I might add." Jess sidled up next to me and grabbed my hand protectively. "I don't have a wide selection of casual wear."

Jess and Weasel locked eyes. Flaming daggers shot out of his. Jess's eyes didn't show any hatred, just a steadfast "stay the fuck away from us" look.

Mel stepped closer to me. "Let's find you a pair of jeans before you faint away from embarrassment."

Mel and I sorted through the stacks of jeans while Jess and Weasel kept their eye battle going. I had to hand it to Weasel, he didn't back down.

"Ah, here you go, Paige." Mel stood up victoriously and handed me the jeans. "Now, scoot." She shoved me in the direction of the dressing rooms. To my surprise, she didn't follow me in. Glancing over my shoulder, I watched Mel and Weasel surround Jess. I had thought for sure that Mel would take advantage of the opportunity to corner me in the dressing room, knowing full well I couldn't leave half-dressed.

By the time I had my new jeans on, Jess and Weasel were going at it. Their voices were hushed, so I couldn't catch anything that was said, but from their body language, there was no going back. A war had been declared, but over what, I had no idea. Mel stood to the side, looking dejected. When she saw me, she gestured for me to stay put.

Marionette

I'm not sure why, but I did. I knew Jess could handle herself.

A few seconds later, Weasel grabbed Mel by the hand and yanked her out of the store. His limp curls bounced pathetically as he left. Jess's face was a vibrant crimson and I thought she might need to sit down.

"What in the world was that about?" I asked as I approached, fearful that Weasel might jump out of a rack of clothes.

Jess inspected my jeans. "Oh, nothing. He's such a charmer." She motioned for me to turn around. "I do like those. Look at your cute butt." She pinched my butt cheek. By the time I turned around to face her, her coloring was back to normal and she was in complete control of her emotions. Maybe what I had witnessed wasn't that big a deal.

"Would you mind if we looked for some shirts while we're here? I need some more long sleeves." I tried hard not to touch my wrists, but the scars always demanded my attention.

Jess nodded dejectedly. I secretly watched her eyes wander over the scars and her expression became despondent. I wondered if she envisioned me in the tub every time she caught a glimpse of them. I know that whenever I saw her eyes taking them in like that, all I could hear were her screams from that day.

Jess, however, seemed determined not to dwell on the past. "Now, be a good girl and let me dress you up today. I saw some adorable tops on my way in." She whisked me off to the front of the store and started holding up shirts for me to try.

By the time we finished, I had two pairs of jeans, four shirts, and two sweaters. I felt like a whole new woman when we headed to Julia's for a bite to eat. Jess was ecstatic to see me in a pink sweater, and I consoled myself that at least it wasn't yellow. A pink sweater was okay in public, apparently, but not pink sweats. Jess made it clear that I should wear more colors, not just white, black, and navy with my jeans.

"Have you ever seen a rainbow? Those colors aren't in it," she said.

I don't remember seeing pink either, but I refrained from pointing that out.

Julia's place was hopping, so Jess and I squeezed in at the counter. It was stifling so close to the kitchen, and I pushed up my sleeves. Julia grimaced when she saw my arms. Too embarrassed to pull them back down, I left them that way.

When Julia went to wait on a table, Jess fingered the scars on my right wrist.

"Have you ever considered getting tattoos?"

She sounded serious.

"You've got to be joking. My parents would flip out if I got tattoos on my wrists."

"Think about it, Paige. How will they react if they see the scars? Besides, more than likely they'll never see your wrists. Usually, you are pretty careful not to reveal them."

Of course, I was hypervigilant about everything when it came to my parents.

"Besides, tattoos would be badass."

"As opposed to pathetic," I teased.

"You know I'm not saying that." She squeezed my arm. "But you can't go around wearing long sleeves buttoned tight for the rest of your life. Wouldn't you like to wear short sleeves and have people admiring your tats instead of gawking at your scars?"

I shrugged. "I guess. But won't it hurt?"

She started to say something and then stopped.

I had a good idea what she wanted to say.

"Don't worry about that. I'll get you loaded on tequila," she said instead.

"What do you propose, matching rainbows?" I was still tempted to mention that pink was not really in the rainbow. I liked the sweater for its feel—it was cashmere—not because of the color. Jess had insisted on buying me something nice, and the three-hundred-dollar price tag hadn't deterred her.

"No! I said cool, not asinine." She thought for a minute. "Let me chat with my friend who's a tattoo artist and see what he suggests. He'll cut us a deal, and his work is fantastic."

"You have a friend who's a tattoo artist? How many people do you actually know in this town?" I didn't wait for an answer, because I knew it would never come. Jess didn't share too much about how she met people. Knowing Jess, she had wanted to find out about tattoos and had wandered into a parlor to ask questions. I knew she didn't have any tattoos herself.

"Maybe he can squeeze you in tomorrow."

The thought made me squirm. Needles were not my friends.

I felt a tap on my shoulder, and even before I turned around, I had a good hunch who it would be.

"Hi, Mel. Care to join us?" I gestured to the stool next to me.

"I see you bought more than jeans this morning. Nice sweater." Her words dripped with scorn.

"Thanks. Jess bought it for me—an early Christmas gift." I tried to sound confident, but it was a pathetic attempt.

"Mel, can I buy you a beer?" Jess chipped in to rescue me.

"Yes," Mel said, but her look said, *Only so I can throw it in your face.*

Jess either didn't notice or pretended that everything was kosher—just three friends out for a few drinks together.

A table opened up, and Julia ushered us over before someone else nabbed it. A few moments later, Julia brought three beers to the table and collapsed next to Mel.

"Whew, what a lunch rush!" She fanned herself with a menu.

"I see that review paid off." Jess smiled broadly.

"I don't know if I should thank you or throttle you." Julia dabbed the back of her neck with a napkin.

"What are you talking about?" I turned to Jess.

"Oh, I had one of my newspaper buddies write a review of Julia's to drum up more business."

"It worked. We've been slammed every day since it appeared. Now I need to hire some help."

"Jess, I know you like helping out at the bookstore, but what about picking up some shifts here?" Mel looked triumphant as she tried to corner Jess into a waitressing job.

Jess, however, looked thrilled with the idea. "Do I get to keep the tips?"

"Of course!" Julia perked up in her seat. "But don't expect high rollers here."

"Oh, if there are high rollers, I bet Jess would spot them a mile away," quipped Mel.

Briefly, I saw a flash of anger in Jess's eyes, but it just as quickly disappeared. "For one of my classes, I have to design a business model. I wonder if working here would help with my project."

I chuckled. "That's so you: picking up an extra job to get a better grade in school. And you haven't even started the program yet!"

"What about you, Paige?" Julia arched her eyebrows.

"What do you mean? Work here?" My voice squeaked.

"Yes, on the weekends. You can work on your people skills."

"I thought you were trying to drum up business, not kill it," I retorted.

"You've never had a job. It's time you started building up your resume." Julia gave me a look that said, *Don't argue.*

"How do you feel about tattoos, Julia? Paige is thinking of getting some on her arms." Jess didn't mention that they were to cover up my scars, but I'm sure Julia and Mel figured that out on their own.

"I've got no issue with that. Next Saturday, Paige; that'll be your first day." With those words she leaped out of her seat and went back to work.

"Is she serious?" I queried Mel's face. She had tried to screw Jess and somehow she had screwed me instead.

"I think she is. It'll be fun. We'll work together. And it will help our fund to get away from here and start a whole new life away from your folks." Jess sounded thrilled at the idea and it did appeal to me more, when she put it that way.

Mel looked pensive. Would she miss me, or my money? Again, I saw her scrutinize Jess, but the anger had vanished. I couldn't put my finger on the new emotion. It looked like a new idea was dawning on her, one that she'd never contemplated before.

"Maybe she'll hire me. I could use the extra dough." Mel's shoulders relaxed, and she guzzled her beer.

"Oh, this is going to be so much fun." Jess darted for Julia to give her the news. I had a feeling she wasn't asking for permission, but rather informing Julia that all three of us would begin working there next Saturday.

"How's school going, Paige?"

"All right. It's hard being away from here, though." I picked at the label on my beer.

"I bet. Jess has a way of calming you down." Mel's eyes clouded over.

Jess banged both hands down on the table. "It's all set, ladies!" She raised her beer and clinked bottles with both of us.

Chapter Fifteen

ON MONDAY MORNING, Jess woke me before the sun had considered rising for the day.

"Sorry, sweetie, but you have French class, and I have to get to work."

I grunted in reply. Jess handed me a cup of coffee and sat down next to me. After pulling myself into an upright position, I took a swig.

"Mornings should be illegal."

She brushed some hair off my cheek. "Some of us enjoy them."

"That's because you're sick and demented." I glanced at the clock, which alerted me that I didn't have much time. Slamming down half of my coffee, I then crawled out of bed and hauled my exhausted body to the shower. The mirror was fogged over from Jess's shower, preventing me from seeing how bad I looked.

Before I left the apartment, Jess handed me a travel mug of coffee and a breakfast bar. How in the world was she so organized all of the time?

Traffic was light at that time of day, and fortunately there was a parking spot right in front of my dorm room. I ran upstairs to grab my French notebook. Minnie was nowhere to be seen, but Karen was asleep in my bed. Did Jenna have company?

I didn't have time to ask, and Karen never stirred.

By two in the afternoon, I was spent. Skipping my afternoon walk to settle my mind, I went straight to my dorm room.

Karen, Tom, Jenna, and Minnie were in a deep discussion. Before I had even set my backpack down, Karen asked, "Paige, what do you think?"

It didn't take much effort to see that Minnie felt like she was being attacked.

"Um, about what?" I really didn't want to get involved.

"Amendment 2." Karen swiveled her head to stare me down.

I knew something about it because Jess was so involved in her gay group. Basically, it denied gays and lesbians the right to be recognized as a protected class, which opened the door for lawful discrimination, but I wasn't sure what angle I should take.

"What about it?" I stalled.

Karen whipped around to face Minnie. "Audrey, here, thinks that gays shouldn't have any rights whatsoever." She waved her finger in Minnie's face.

This was not a conversation I wanted to have with any of them. It hit way too close to home for me. Yet, I also knew I couldn't side with Minnie. Going on fake dates with Tom was one thing, but condemning gay people altogether was another.

"I don't see what the fuss is all about really," I croaked.

Karen scrutinized me. Tom and Jenna stared at their feet.

"What do you mean?" asked Minnie, hopefully.

"So what if people are gay." I waved a hand nonchalantly through the air. "It doesn't bother me one bit. None of my business really." I looked Minnie in the eyes. "And none of yours."

"You see, even Paige is with us." Karen looked triumphant.

All three of them were against Minnie, which surprised me somewhat. Tom was a nice guy, but I figured a good ol' boy would be homophobic. I wasn't surprised by Karen and Jenna. They were on the basketball team, and half of their teammates were probably dykes. You couldn't be a female jock and be homophobic in our part of the world.

"It's just wrong," stated Minnie. "According to my church, homosexuality is a sin."

"Come on, Audrey. Times have changed. The Bible can't be taken literally. Why, it even tells people not to eat lobsters." Tom tried to lighten the mood.

"Wow, you mean I'm doing something right? I hate lobster," I declared.

Tom gave me a sly smile.

Karen put her hand up to silence me. Humor was not allowed for the moment. "It's not funny. My brother is gay, and he tried to kill himself—" She bolted out of the room in tears.

The four of us studied each other. From the expressions on everyone's faces, none of them had known about that; I sure in hell didn't.

"I didn't know," Minnie whispered as she slid onto her chair.

"I knew she had a brother," offered Jenna.

"One of us should talk to her." I stated the obvious. None of us knew who was the best emissary to send. "I'm sorry, Audrey. I know you are better at this, but I think you should hang back for now."

She nodded numbly.

"I'm her roommate," said Jenna, but she stood immobile.

"I'll go." Tom started for the bathroom.

"I'll go with you." I followed hesitantly.

We found Karen on her bed with a pillow over her head. I sat down on the bed next to her and rubbed her back. Jess did that when I cried. Tom pulled up a chair and sat down next to her. Tenderly, he took her hand and held it.

No one spoke for several seconds.

Karen pulled the pillow from her face and seemed taken aback to see Tom and me sitting there. She smiled meekly. "I didn't mean to break down like that." She sat up on her bed, wiped her eyes with her sleeve, and then hugged her pillow tightly.

"It's okay." I adjusted my position on the bed so I could face her. "I'm sorry, Karen. I had no idea; otherwise I wouldn't have joked about the situation."

She waved my words away and stifled a sob. "Oh, I wasn't upset about that. I just get so worked up about this."

Tom started to say something, and then stopped.

"All of these protests for Amendment 2 are driving me insane. So many people don't know how painful it can be for gay people or for their families."

"How's your brother, Karen?" Tom finally found the words he had been searching for.

"Oh, he's doing much better these days. In fact, he speaks to high school students about his experiences. He's the bravest person I know."

I nodded.

Karen continued. "He … did it many years ago. He's a few years older than me—I was an afterthought." She attempted to giggle, but it stayed in her throat. "Jake was always so protective of me, and brave. When he …" She burst into sobs again.

Before I knew what to do, Karen leaned against me for a hug. I wrapped my arms around her, and Tom moved to the side of the bed to get closer.

In between sobs, she revealed more of the story. "He t-took a b-bottle of pills, and the doctors p-pumped his stomach." She paused to take a deep breath. "My p-parents found him in his room."

I heard noises and looked up to see Minnie and Jenna standing by the door, clearly unsure of what to do.

Karen continued. "The doctors said my parents found him in the nick of time." She wiped her eyes and pulled away from me, locking eyes on Minnie.

"Karen, I'm so sorry," babbled Minnie, rushing over to hug her.

Jenna followed suit, reluctantly, and Tom and I retreated to the opposite side of the room to give them some space.

He looked at me with eyes that seemed troubled with the burden of Karen's account. "Can I take you to dinner tonight?" His words were barely audible.

I almost burst into laughter. What a time to ask me on a second date. Then I realized he was trying to be supportive. I leaned up against him and he kissed the back of my head.

"Sure. Let's wait to make sure everything will be okay."

"Of course. They can come if they want."

His gesture touched me—and made me feel like a shit for playing with the emotions of such a sweet soul. As it turned out, Karen and Jenna had a team meeting that night, and Minnie had a study group to attend, so Tom and I headed out alone. We didn't talk much, and I was relieved when he suggested a movie afterwards. I needed some quiet time before heading back to my dorm room to deal with everything. Of all the roomies the university could have placed me with, I was stuck with a girl whose brother tried to off himself. Now that the cat was out of the bag, I thought Karen might want to talk about it, and to educate the homophobe, Minnie. I groaned at the thought. I wasn't in the mood for homosexual education.

People's reactions when they find out someone is gay annoy the hell out of me. They usually say something stupid or offensive. I've defined three categories. Category one: ignorant, but well meaning. People from this level might say something like, "My cousin who lives in Hawaii is gay. Do you know him?"

No dumbass, I live thousands of miles away from Hawaii. But you have to be polite to these people, who just don't know what to say but are trying to be nice.

Category two: ignorant and insulting. An example is: "How do you know which one of you should take out the trash?"

Please, are you so stupid that you stick to strict gender roles in your own life? It's the twentieth century asshole; wake up and smell the equality.

Category three is the most dangerous. Men often fall into this category. One of their statements follows this logic: "How do you survive without having sex with a man? Don't you like dick?"

First, I don't like dick or dicks of any type. Second, your poor wife or girlfriend. Imagine being stuck with an ass who only assumes the missionary position to satisfy himself and no one else. Monotonous and unimaginative. Sex should be fun for both partners, not just the males. Dick or no dick.

I don't go into details with people who ask me that question. I figure they would never understand, because they don't want to. My orgasms are plentiful and usually multiple. And I never have to fake it. Never. It's amazing how much joy you can receive when the male ego is not involved.

I've heard Jess handle this question on many occasions. She kills me. She loves to respond with, "Well, I can see in your eyes that *you* like dick. Be proud."

One guy was so stupid that he didn't get her meaning. When he said, "Hell yeah! Dick pride!" I almost choked to death on my drink. Most guys get defensive and say, "Fuck off, you dyke."

One guy even threatened her, but Jess knew the owner of the bar and he got 86'd permanently.

I never have witty comebacks when jerks confront us when we are out. Once, while driving, someone cut me off in traffic. I went to flip him the bird, but instead I gave him a thumbs up. Jess laughed hysterically and said, "You sure showed him!"

She's never been bothered that I'm not overtly confrontational. People can think what they want; I don't give a crap. Jess tries to educate people, which took some getting used to for me, but everyone is different. I'm learning to accept that.

I'll have to remember that lesson when Karen starts her crusade to turn Minnie into a gay-loving Catholic.

Now, religious people, I don't get them at all. I can never remember a day when I thought God existed. At times it would be nice—easier maybe—but I consider that I'm responsible for me. There's no predestination. No afterlife. This is my one shot, which kinda puts that whole suicide thing into perspective. Maybe if I were more logical, I would have something brilliant to say on the subject. I'm not. I just don't get religion.

Chapter Sixteen

THE BANDAGES ON my wrists itched. As I made my way to Liddy's office, I worried about what she'd say. Would she give me time to explain, or would she throw me into a padded room instantly and duct tape my mouth shut so I couldn't talk my way out of it? It was hard enough hiding the bandages from my roomies.

Liddy wasn't in her office, so I sat in the chair, with my backpack on my lap and held it with both arms to hide the bandages. Earlier in the semester, the room had been stifling, but now it was freezing. Didn't they have any air conditioning or heat in this basement?

Liddy rushed in, full of apologies.

After she sat down and issued her third apology, I mumbled, "Don't worry about it."

She shivered. "Aren't you cold?"

I was trying to stop my teeth from chattering. "Oh, it's not that bad in here."

"What? It's as cold as the North Pole. Didn't you wear a jacket today?"

I shook my head. The arctic front had taken me by surprise.

MARIONETTE

Yesterday had been pleasant enough, but today I thought my fingers would freeze and fall off.

"I didn't check the weather on the news." I shrugged.

"You poor thing. Your cheeks are still red from the wind." She stood up and grabbed her jacket. "Here, put this on."

I didn't know how to refuse, and I was freezing. Carefully, I stood to yank her jacket on without revealing the bandages.

"Paige!"

I wasn't successful.

"It's not what you think!" I rushed out of arm's length, in case she tried to grab me.

"Why didn't you call me? You can call me twenty-four hours a day, seven days a week. You have all of my numbers." She moved closer to me and gingerly took my right arm.

I had to laugh. Liddy was being so sweet and supportive.

"Don't laugh. This is serious."

"I know. Permanent."

That caused her to step back. "Permanent? What?"

"I got tattoos last night to hide my scars. I'm tired of always wearing long sleeves or freaking out that my roommate will see my arms while I'm asleep."

Liddy started laughing hysterically. "Oh, thank God." She moved back to her chair, still laughing. "By the way, does Jess know to call me if anything does happen?"

"Trust me, Jess will send a helicopter or jet to get you there." I wrapped Liddy's jacket more tightly around me, and settled back into my chair.

"I think I would like this Jess."

I hesitated, unsure how to proceed. "I think you would."

"What's she like?"

And there it was; she didn't even give me an option. Of course, I could lie, but both of us would know I was lying.

"How long have you known?"

"Flags go up for me when one of my clients plays the pronoun game."

"The pronoun game?"

"When you talk about Jess, you never use any words to suggest Jess's sex. Jess said this. Jess thinks that. People don't talk like that unless they are hiding something."

"But you are the first one to call me out on it." I defended myself.

"Not many people are looking for clues like that. Don't worry. I doubt that your roommates know. I have a feeling you are good at hiding things." She gestured to my wrists. "How do they look?"

I touched one of my arms. "Right now, red and gross. Jess—my girlfriend—says they'll heal and they should look normal in a few weeks. Is that better?"

"A little. Still not natural." She winked at me. "What are they?"

I reddened. "Japanese symbols. Jess found some proverbs about strength and the markings of the letters hide my scars completely."

Before we had gone to get the tattoos done, Jess had handed me a list of proverbs. The only one that struck me was: Even monkeys fall from trees. It left me in fits of laughter. I let Jess choose the other one: Seven times down, eight times up. I still don't get it, but not many people can decipher my tattoos, so I can make up shit.

Liddy looked contemplative. "How many people know?"

"About my tattoos? I've only told you. Jess was with me when I got them. And the tattoo artist."

"Very funny, wise guy. I mean about you being gay." She leaned one elbow on the arm of the chair and adjusted her shirt.

MARIONETTE

"I'm pretty sure Jess has figured it out."

"I should hope so, if she's as smart as I think she is, but you're hedging." She waggled her pencil at me.

I sighed. "My friends, Mel and Julia."

"Are Mel and Julia dating?"

I chuckled over that. "No! Julia is in her fifties, and Mel is only a few years older than me."

"And you haven't told your parents, I'm guessing?"

"Correct."

"What would they say?"

"Say?" I scoffed. "They won't say anything." My bitter tone sliced through the air.

"What do you mean by that?" Her quizzical expression annoyed me.

"They would have me locked up."

"You can't lock people up for being gay."

"Uh-huh. You don't know my father."

"Trust me, Paige. I wouldn't let that happen." She flashed me a stern look.

I crossed my arms. "You don't know my father."

"Is that why you tried to kill yourself?"

I laughed angrily. "No. I wouldn't try to kill myself for *that*. Don't be ridiculous." I remembered Karen's brother and wanted to kick myself. It would have been the perfect explanation, and I hadn't even thought of that before answering Liddy. Damn!

She laughed heartily. "Well, I'm glad to hear that. Of course, I would like to learn why you did try to kill yourself." She sounded hopeful, as if she actually expected me to blurt it out. I had finally confessed I was gay, so why not share all?

"So would Jess, but I haven't told her either."

Liddy studied me intently. "I think you'll find I have a lot of patience, Paige. And I'm persistent."

"Liddy,"—using her first name seemed appropriate—"I wouldn't even know where to begin. I'm still trying to piece together all that shit." I tore a string of cotton off my shirt; it had been bugging me all day.

"Why don't you start at the beginning, and I can help you piece it together."

"That's the problem. I don't know the beginning. I don't know *who* I am. I don't know when it all started. Why? Who the fuck knows? My entire life has been filled with secrets. What happened, and why—it all baffles me. I just don't know. And I don't know how to figure it out."

Liddy stood and then kneeled down next to me. At first, I didn't know why, and then I realized I was crying. No, I was sobbing—complete and total floodworks. Snot gushed from my nose. Tears poured out of my eyes as if from a pipe that had no stopper.

I tried to speak. "I-I-I … s-s-s-o tired of lies!"

Liddy held me tight. Maybe it was a victory for her: to get me to break down, finally. It's a cynical thought, I know, but that's me. Fortunately, Liddy didn't try to force me to talk. It was useless for me to try anyway. After several minutes, we walked to the café and ordered coffees. The warmth of the liquid as it cascaded down my throat was almost orgasmic. I've always hated being cold. Liddy seemed perfectly content to sit in silence and let me gather myself. Besides, she knew that I had promised Jess. I would be back in her office next week, no matter what. Is there a cure for cynicism?

Later that night, I stood outside a frat house freezing my ass off because I couldn't stand the scene inside. So many drunks. Images of

Alex danced in front of my eyes, taunting me to end it all. Why hadn't I listened to her that night? If I had, she'd still be alive.

"Paige, have you seen Karen?"

I turned just in time to catch Minnie, who had tripped over a tree root and was about to knock us both to the ground. After righting her, I asked, "No, why?"

"I want to go home." She swayed. Maybe the tree root hadn't tripped her after all. Her eyes resembled a field of wet poppies: red, droopy, and glistening.

"Are you okay?"

"Yeah ... I just don't want to be here anymore."

Her breath was foul, causing me to turn away.

"Okay. I'll go find her." I sat her down on a tree stump. When I turned around, I noticed Karen stroll out with some dude who was in one of my classes. She was just as inebriated as Minnie, if not more. I could see the muscles straining in the guy's arm and shoulder as he supported her.

"There you are. Audrey and I are ready to go."

Karen nodded.

"So come on," I motioned with my hand for her to follow me.

She didn't budge.

"Come on!" I gestured again and gave an encouraging smile, as if I were calling a puppy.

"But it's early, I don't want to go." She moved her left arm up and squinted one eye to see her watch, in the process whacking the guy in the face and spilling his beer all over him, which caused her to go into paroxysms of laughter.

I hated drunken laughter. It sounded fake.

"Karen, I know it's early, but both of us are tired." I gestured to Minnie, so Karen would understand that she was upset. "Come on, now. Let's go."

"I can take her home," said the guy dripping in beer.

"And which home are you referring to?" I asked coldly.

Karen tilted her head to hear his response.

"Karen, come on, let's go." Minnie sounded firm, and desperate. She tugged on Karen's arm ineffectually, since she was still sitting on the stump.

"But—"

The guy cut Karen off. "Paige, I promise, I'll take her home."

Feeling helpless, I looked at Minnie. She wasn't going to last much longer before the waterworks hit. Some people are sad drunks.

"Okay, but if you can't bring her home, call me." I stared at Karen. "Call me if you need a ride. Okay?" I ensured she made eye contact with me. She nodded, but nothing was getting through to her. I reached into my pocket and pulled out a pen, wishing it were a permanent marker. Then I grabbed his hand and wrote down my number. I wrote it on Karen's too. She kept giggling and said it tickled. It took a lot, but I managed not to throttle her right then and there for being a dumbass—a drunk dumbass.

They sauntered back into the drunken den. Minnie looked apprehensive. "How can we leave her?"

I didn't have a good feeling about it, I had to admit, nor did I have the strength to drag her back to the dorm room.

"I know the guy. He's decent." My words sounded hollow and I could tell they didn't convince either one of us.

Minnie stood and made her way to the fence. After two failed attempts, I managed to hoist her over with the help of some friendly strangers.

We drove home in silence. When we arrived at our room, Minnie grabbed the phone and headed into Karen's room, to call her boyfriend, I assumed—the cause of her tears. I didn't bother waiting up, as I had a feeling the phone call would not be quick nor pretty. It was a private matter, and I didn't want to intrude. Besides, I had to get up early for my first shift at Julia's. I was not looking forward to joining the rat race. I fell onto my bed.

The ringing phone interrupted my slumber. I reached for it groggily and toppled out of bed onto the beanbag. "Hello," I slurred into the wrong end of the receiver. Realizing my mistake, I turned the phone around and heard: "Is this Audrey?"

"No, this is Paige. Audrey can't come to the phone right now." I was about to hang up, when a frantic voice shouted, "Wait!"

"Yeah."

"Do you know Karen?" The voice was male. One I didn't recognize.

"Yes. Why?" All of my sleepiness lifted.

"Um, she's at my house, and she needs a ride home. She asked me to call."

"Is she okay?"

"To be honest, she's real fucked-up."

"What do you mean?" I shouted.

Minnie popped her head over her bunk bed. "Is everything okay?"

I waved at her to be silent. "What's wrong with Karen?" I said to the man on the phone.

"Oh, not what you think. She's just really drunk."

I rubbed my forehead, exasperated. "Where do you live?"

He gave me the details and I got up to get dressed.

"Is everything okay?" Minnie sat up in bed and leaned against the wall. I wondered if she felt the room spinning.

"Yeah. That guy didn't drive Karen home. I'm going to get her."

"Do you want me to go?"

I didn't. I envisioned her puking all over my car. "That's fine. Why don't you get some rest?"

I bolted out of the room and ran smack into Tom.

"Hey, Paige!" He staggered back and propped himself up against the far wall.

I glanced at my watch. It was 3:30 a.m. "Hi, Tom. What brings you here?"

"Is *Cheers* on?" He looked hopeful

"Don't think so, and I don't mean to be rude, but I have to go pick up Karen." I started to move.

"Wait, I'll go with you."

Seriously, I wanted to scream. When I turned to look at him, he looked so sweet, trying to act brave. Where did he think we were going? To rescue her from bandits? Maybe it would help to have a guy to lure Karen with.

The house wasn't far away. As I pulled up to the curb, I saw a couple walking to a car across the street. Upon further inspection, I realized it was Karen. Darting out of the car, I yelled, "Karen, what in the hell is going on?"

She didn't answer. Her eyes were so far gone I was surprised she was still on her feet. Then she ripped a fart. The guy with her and I studied each other, neither of us in the mood to laugh. I was seething. It was the guy who had promised to drive her home.

"Paige, let me explain. About an hour ago, I was ready to leave, but when I looked for Karen, I couldn't find her. I assumed you'd come and got her."

Karen let out another massive fart. Drunken farts—is that really a condition?

"I was in the bathroom," Karen mumbled.

Drunk shits? Really? No wonder she couldn't get a boyfriend.

"Then I heard she was still here, so I rushed back."

"Good, but I'm here now and we live in the same place, so I'll take her home." Karen farted again. Jesus, I was tempted just to let the guy drive her home, but he handed her over quickly. The thought of being trapped in the car, even for a short ride, with the fartster made me want to vomit.

After loading her into the backseat, I asked Tom to roll down his window. He looked at me, confused, until another of Karen's farts announced why. He waved a hand in front of his face and quickly rolled his window down with his free hand.

"Jesus!" Tom sputtered.

Karen passed out in the backseat. I groaned. Great. Now I would have to carry her upstairs.

"Apparently, Karen gets the farts and the shits when she's really drunk." I shrugged.

Tom peered over his headrest to get a good look at Karen. "That's disgusting." He wrinkled his nose.

I pulled my shirt up over my nose and drove home, fast. I parked in the loading zone so we could get her out of my car quickly and up to her own room. How did Jenna live with her?

Several minutes later, Tom and I stood in my room. He was still quite drunk and I felt bad sending him away after he had helped me carry Karen up three flights of stairs. I told him to stay put so I could park my car.

After twenty minutes, and a fucking cold walk from the other side of campus, I arrived back in my room to find Tom sound asleep in my bed. Too tired to argue, I crawled in next to him—not that he noticed. He snored away, and I shook my head. How had I ended up surrounded by a homophobe, a chronic farter, and now a boy? Not exactly how I imagined my life in college.

The next morning, I awoke early. Tom was still in bed with me and I was surprised to find that he was holding me. I wasn't the cuddling type in bed. His wasn't a "lover" type embrace; it felt friendly or maybe brotherly, not that I had a brother. It felt safe and comforting rather than exciting.

However, I didn't have time to ponder what it meant. I hopped out of bed and went straight to the shower. An eight-hour shift awaited me and I would be on my feet the entire time. Why Jess and Julia thought this was a good idea bewildered me. Didn't they know I had recently tried to slash my wrists? I was delicate. And I wasn't the chitchat type. Waitressing? Really? Did they even know me?

I left the room, closing the door on Minnie's and Tom's sonorous snores. How in the world had I slept through that racket?

I didn't drive straight to Jess's. Instead, I made a quick detour to my spot to watch the sunrise. Living so far away limited my chances to go, so I seized the opportunity. Sitting on the cold, wet grass, I studied the changing colors of the sky as the sun peeked over the horizon. Here, I never felt alone.

When I walked into Jess's apartment, she was busy making breakfast. She danced around the kitchen, flipping bacon, scrambling eggs, whisking pancake batter, and she didn't look the least overwhelmed. It was like watching a ballet.

Dread overwhelmed me. *Is this how everyone feels the first day on the job?* I picked at my scrambled eggs and poured too much syrup on my pancakes, rendering them inedible.

"Boy, you are not looking forward to this at all, are you?" Jess smiled sheepishly.

"Not really." I pouted.

Marionette

"It will be good for you."

Can I take a moment to say that I hate it when people say that. *Good* for me? How was feeling stressed out and nauseous *good* for me? And what was the big deal about getting a job? My parents would hardly be jumping up and down to discover I had a job as a waitress. A waitress! Being bossed around by strangers serving greasy food. I loved eating at Julia's diner, but I was not loving the idea of working there. I fiddled with the car keys in my pocket. If I left now, I could still make breakfast in the dorms, see what the gang was up to for the day.

"Hey, Paige, it'll be okay. I'll be there the entire time. You need to break out of your bubble and join the real world. You can't just read about it. You have to experience it." She looked sincere. And stern.

I tugged on my keys again. Then I remembered that Karen would probably fart all day. Minnie, the homophobic religious nut, would probably drive home to be with her sex-crazed boyfriend. And Tom ... well he was Tom. I'm not sure what he did besides watch football and *Cheers*.

Maybe being surrounded by strangers *was* better, and Julia said I could eat all I wanted. I planned on making good on that promise.

Hours later, I was finding my job to be pretty easy. The restaurant was slammed from the get-go. As soon as Julia flipped over the sign announcing that we were open, customers poured in like lava from a volcano. I ran around like mad, taking orders, bringing food and drinks, and collecting money. The beauty of it was that I didn't have any time to think. Not once did a vision of my mother or Alex flash before my eyes. I worked, and that's all.

Before I knew it, I was done. The new shift came in to relieve us, and Jess, Mel, and I sat down at a table for dinner. Not only was I satisfied with the day, I was seventy-five dollars richer.

"How much moolah did you get?" Jess whipped out her share as she asked.

"Seventy-five," I said proudly.

"Ninety," said Mel.

"That's great, girls. We rocked today, didn't we?" Jess beamed.

"Wait, how much did you make? Your wad looks bigger than mine and Mel's put together."

I reached over to snatch the bills, but Jess swatted my hand away. "Don't be grabby."

"How much, Jess?" whined Mel.

"Over a hundred."

I eyed Mel, who nodded. Mel made a move for the money, and Jess tried to swat her away while I grabbed the pile.

"One hundred and twenty-five! How? We had the same amount of tables?" I was astonished.

"What can I say, people like me?" Jess blushed.

"Or they're afraid of you."

I looked up and saw Weasel.

"Of *moi*, who would be afraid of me?" Jess winked at him.

"People with secrets." Weasel scowled down at her.

Mel gave him a swift kick to the shins under the table.

Jess just smiled sweetly at him as Mel pulled his arm to get him to sit. Weasel did so reluctantly.

"Hi Wesley, long time no see." Julia strolled over with sandwiches and beers, and did her best to sound genuine.

"Hi, Julia. Business is booming." Weasel waved his arms at all the customers.

"Yes, thanks to Jess." Julia patted the top of Jess's head.

Weasel didn't say anything; instead, he grabbed one of the

sandwiches and chomped half of it off. Bits of pulled pork dangled out of his mouth, painting his chin with sauce. He slurped up the meat with a sound that made my stomach turn. Then he wiped his mouth on his sweatshirt. Watching him eat was grotesque.

"Oh, finally, someone who eats just as bad as Paige." Jess squeezed my leg under the table.

I wanted to shout, "I do not look like that!" Then I thought that maybe I did. I had never watched myself eat in front of a mirror. I picked up my sandwich and took a dainty bite, and then carefully dabbed my mouth with a napkin. I never wanted to be compared to Weasel again. Never!

"Oh my goodness, it knows how to use a napkin," exclaimed Julia.

Seriously, did I eat like Weasel? The thought horrified me. I took another careful nibble and dabbed my mouth again.

"It's a miracle!" shouted Jess. Then she whispered in my ear, "You aren't as bad as him, but close. Darn close."

Lesson learned. I would no longer inhale food and wipe my mouth on my sleeve. Yes, I loved pissing my parents off, but looking like the Weasel, well that was too much, even for me. Life was too short to be a Weasel.

Weasel raised his beer and tipped the bottle until half of it was gone in one gulp. I couldn't help but stare. Before, whenever we ate together, I usually stared down at my plate and took little notice of him. Now, it was like watching an animal documentary. He ate like a wild beast that had traveled across a desert without food or water for days, maybe months. He was revolting.

Chapter Seventeen

MY MONDAY MORNING didn't start off well. Streetlights peeking through the blinds woke me to a strange weight on my bed. Karen was sitting next to me, intent on gaining my complete attention.

"Paige, are you awake?"

"I am now. What's wrong?" I rubbed the sleep from my eyes and yawned.

"Nothing. I wanted to say sorry for keeping you up late the other night, and thank you for rescuing me." She looked like a child who just been busted for breaking into the sweets jar.

I laughed bitterly. "You woke me up to apologize for keeping me up the other night."

Her girlish giggle told me my bitterness had no effect. "I guess I did. Ironic, huh?"

Staring blankly at her, I didn't respond.

"Well, thanks. You're a good friend, Paige, even though you try hard not to show that you are." She leaned down and gave me a hug.

"Next time, can you brush your teeth before you give me a hug?"

She swatted my arm. "You don't smell that great either."

MARIONETTE

I sniffed my armpit. "Yuck!" I smelled like sweat, pulled pork sandwiches, and stale beer. After my shift last night at Julia's, I'd hopped in the car and rushed back to my dorm. Jess had plans with friends and I was beat from my first working weekend.

"You want to grab some grub before class?"

I was surprised that Karen had asked. Usually, she and Jenna ate with their teammates in an effort to stay "as one" to improve their play; it wasn't working. Their team had the worst record in the division, not that Karen cared. Jenna, though, was quite unhappy. I don't think she'd lost a game before coming here. Her high school team won state and she was the star of her entire school. Losing was not the norm for Jenna, and it was completely unacceptable.

"Meet you down there in ten minutes. I want to shower and change my clothes first."

Karen nodded and waddled off to her own room.

Minnie didn't budge in her bed. I wondered whether she was purposely ignoring us or whether she was still dead to the world. She wasn't a morning person and all of her classes started after 11 a.m.

When I reached the cafeteria, Karen already had a plate stacked with bacon, eggs, and toast.

"Do you always have three glasses of milk with your meals?" I gestured to her hoard.

"I love milk. Anything with milk. I could never live without milk." To prove her point, she gulped the entire glass and then wiped her milk moustache on her shirtsleeve.

I had never been a fan of milk, maybe because I wasn't breastfed. I don't know. I found the stuff thick and revolting. I could handle cheese, but plain milk—no way.

"How was your weekend?" Karen stabbed some eggs with her fork.

"Not bad. Started a new job. Yours?"

"You got a job?" She looked baffled.

"Yeah, why?"

"I thought you were rich."

Taken aback by her bluntness, I said, "Not really. What made you think that?"

"You're an Alexander. My parents showed me one of your pictures in the paper." She guzzled another glass of milk.

"Oh, that." I sipped my orange juice. "So much for being incognito." I shrugged.

"Don't worry, I haven't shared that with anyone. I didn't think you'd appreciate it." She winked at me.

I leaned back in my seat, studying her. This was a side of Karen I had never seen.

"Thanks for that. It's weird when people know."

"I can imagine. Your dad has quite the reputation in this state." She buttered her toast.

She had no idea.

"So, what did you do this weekend?" I changed the subject.

Karen's frown told me she knew I was purposefully diverting her away. "Oh, not much. I felt like shit on Saturday and my coach chewed me out. Apparently it was my fault that we lost. Again." She waved the idea away.

I loved that nothing bothered her. "How did Jenna take it?"

"She's not talking to me."

"Really? It bugs her that much to lose?"

"I'm learning that. Notice how she doesn't hang out with us much. Most of the time, she doesn't talk to anyone. She's a sore loser."

I finished my Cheerios and said goodbye. My first class started in five minutes. I was regretting taking French so early in the morning. The teacher had a way of saying *bonjour* in such a cheery way it made my bones rattle. Morning people sucked.

By 2 p.m., I was spent and sitting in the student center. When I spied Liddy, I waved to her nonchalantly, enough that I wouldn't be considered rude, but not so much that people would think I had a connection with a headshrinker. Not that many people actually knew she was one, I guessed.

She took my wave as an invitation. I groaned as she approached, but I still cleared the seat next to me so she could sit down.

"Hi, Paige."

"Hello, ma'am."

The ma'am made her smile. "My, aren't we formal today?"

I fidgeted with my pen. "How was your weekend?"

"Fine. Whatcha doing? Homework?" She motioned to my notebooks and papers.

"Yeah." Carefully I slid my photocopies under my books. I wasn't in the mood to deflect questions about them.

"I won't keep you from it. You look good, Paige. See you Friday."

Seconds later, Tom sidled up next to me and wrapped his arm over my shoulder. At first, I thought he was going to give me a kiss. Instead, he gave a friendly squeeze.

"How 'bout having lunch with me, Paige?" He slipped into the seat across from me.

Out of the corner of my eye, I saw Liddy take notice. Great!

"Where do you have in mind?" I asked my faux boyfriend.

"Fancy Mexican?" His eyes shimmered.

My stomach grumbled and color rushed to my face.

"Goodness, we better get going." Tom flashed a sweet smile.

I had hardly finished packing my bag and had made to sling it over my shoulder when Tom took it from me.

Again, Liddy took notice. She watched intently from across the room.

I gave her a wave and rushed out. Did she notice how red I was? Would she know what I was up to?

One reason I had wanted to go this school was that it was small, but not *too* small. Not everyone knew each other. However, I hadn't factored in one thing: a small place meant most people knew each other. It was not the best planning on my part if I truly wanted to keep my life private.

Chapter Eighteen

FRIDAY ARRIVED AND I prepared myself for a deluge of questions from Liddy. Who was the boy? Why was he carrying my bag? Had Jess and I broken up? What happened to being a lesbo?

I wasn't expecting Liddy to ignore it altogether, but she did.

"How was your week, Paige?"

"Just dandy, and yours?"

Liddy locked her eyes on mine. "I have no complaints."

Really? Because I have tons. I wondered what her daily life consisted of. Listening to clients bitch and complain all day—how fucking annoying. Shrinks should figure out who can be helped and then kill the rest. Boom! Done!

"What are you thinking so hard about?" Liddy's question brought me back to the room.

"Uh, can I pass on that one?" I tapped my fingers on the arm of my chair.

"Maybe. Why don't we go back to last week's session?"

I interrupted, "If I answer your question, can we not go back?" I smiled to cajole her.

It didn't work.

"I don't think so, Paige." She moved her head from side to side.

I wasn't buying the act. "But you aren't positive. I was thinking that people who are depressed are downers to be around and that you and your colleagues should start selecting the hopeless cases and picking them off. Why bother?"

"So you consider yourself hopeless?"

I wasn't sure how to respond. If I said yes, would she put me in an institution? Images from *One Flew over the Cuckoo's Nest* flashed before my eyes.

"Can you stop asking me questions?" I rubbed my face with both hands. "All questions. Even, 'How do you like your coffee?'"

"I already know the answer to that one."

I looked up confused. "What?"

"With lots of sugar."

I smiled meekly. "What is it like?"

"What do you mean, Paige? I have a feeling you aren't talking about drinking coffee."

I chuckled, but it sounded more like a cat hacking up a hairball. "Correct. What's it like dealing with people like me?"

"You mean hopeless cases?" Her raised eyebrow suggested that she didn't subscribe to that belief.

"Yeah."

"I don't see you that way. I don't see any of my clients that way."

"Really? Come on. Could you have helped Hitler?"

She laughed. "Thankfully, he was never one of my clients. Now what's going on? You can stall all you want, but we will address the issue you are so desperately trying to dance around."

I sighed heavily. "It started five years ago."

Liddy looked like she wanted to pat me on the back and say, "I knew you could do it." Instead, she nodded her head for me to continue.

"Alex tried to tell me—to warn me—but I was too stupid to heed it."

"What do you mean? What did she warn you about?"

"That's just it, she just kept telling me that we had to get out. We had to leave before they found out. Before they acted."

"Who? What?" Liddy wriggled in her chair, clearly eager for me to spit it out.

"My parents. She warned me about my parents."

"What did she say?"

"That we needed to leave."

"Leave? Leave for where? From what?"

"Home. We had to leave home."

"Why?"

"She wouldn't tell me. She just kept saying we had to leave. That if they found out we knew, we were done for."

I stood up and paced the tiny room. The walls seemed to move closer and closer, and I frantically tried to escape by striding back and forth.

"Paige, tell me everything she said."

"I wish I could. I don't remember much." I tugged on my collar, trying to get air. "All I remember was that she kept saying we had to leave. No matter what, we had to leave."

"Did you?"

"No." I stopped dead in my tracks. "No, I didn't. At the time, Alex was always hopped up on coke. I thought she was having a bad episode, and I ignored her."

"What did she say?"

"I didn't understand much. She was panicking. I wanted to run away with her. I meant to. But I didn't."

"Did she?"

"No. And her death is my fault."

"Paige, I'm sure that's not true."

"It is. If I had listened to her, she would still be alive. But I didn't. I didn't listen. I should have tried harder to escape." I fell heavily back into my seat and placed my head in my hands. Rocking back and forth in my chair, I repeated, "I'm sorry."

"Paige, listen to me. Alex's death was not your fault."

"But you don't understand. If I had listened and if we had left like she said we should, then she would be alive."

"How old were you when this happened?" Liddy leaned back in her chair.

"Uh, thirteen"

"How were two kids supposed to leave home? Where did she suggest you go?"

"She didn't say, but anywhere would have been better."

"I don't want to sound insincere, and I'm trying my best to understand." Liddy lowered her head so I could see her face. "Can you help me understand?"

"The next day, Alex was sent to rehab. That was the last time I saw her. She died in rehab, of an overdose."

"Did you ever find out what she was talking about?"

"Yes. But it was too late. She tried to warn me, but I didn't listen that night."

"You can't be blamed for her addiction. How were you supposed to know she would have access to drugs in rehab?"

"If I had listened to her warning, she wouldn't have been in rehab," I shouted.

"Rehab didn't kill her, Paige. The drugs killed her."

"No they didn't. *She* killed her."

Liddy looked over her shoulder. "Who?"

"I'm trying to explain. It all started that night—when Alex tried to warn me. I was too stupid to listen. Because I didn't, she's dead. She wouldn't leave without me. If she had left, she wouldn't be dead. Plain and simple."

Liddy cupped her hands under her chin and scrutinized my face. Slowly, her frustration melted away and she asked calmly, "How do you know she wouldn't leave without you?"

"She told me—she told me that night she wouldn't go unless I went. Maybe she thought I was placating her, and that I didn't take her seriously. But she said she would drag me away if she had to. Instead, they dragged her away, kicking and screaming." I rubbed my eyes. "God, it was an awful scene. The cops. The flashing lights from their cars. And Alex. She stood in the middle of the street in a ripped T-shirt and jeans screaming for me. Her eyes—they pierced right through me."

"What was she screaming?"

"My name. She kept repeating my name and saying she wouldn't let them take me."

"Take you, not her?"

"Yeah. I didn't understand at the time. My mom barricaded me in the house. No matter how hard I tried, I couldn't get to Alex."

"But you understand now." Liddy coaxed.

"Yes. I understand. That's why it's hopeless."

"Paige, I need you to know: you are not hopeless."

Oh, but I am, Liddy. I am. I raised my eyes slowly to hers. "I should have listened to her."

It must have been obvious that I was too worked up to continue for the day, because Liddy asked, "What are your plans for this weekend? Will you be with Jess?"

I stifled a sigh. Jess. My promise to Jess. If only Jess knew all of it, she would understand. She wouldn't hold me to it. If only she knew. This farce was for her.

Nodding my head feebly, I gathered my backpack and jacket.

Liddy placed her hand on my arm. "Wait." She opened a desk drawer and pulled out her business card. Flipping it over, she then scribbled something on the back. I noticed Japanese writing and smiled. It was the same as my monkey tattoo.

"Take this. It has all of my emergency numbers on it. If you need it, don't hesitate to call."

Again I nodded, unconvincingly. I didn't have the energy to speak. Placing the card into the back pocket of my jeans, I left the room.

Outside, the cold air invaded my lungs. The burning in my chest and throat made me gasp. I couldn't remember a colder winter. As soon as November had hit, the temperatures plummeted. Snowflakes fluttered around my head, but it was too cold for serious accumulation. If I hadn't seen the flakes with my own eyes, I wouldn't have believed they existed. The ground was dry as the desert.

Halfway to my dorm, I stopped. My car was parked on the opposite side of campus, but if I left now, I would be at Jess's when she got off work. Being around Minnie, Tom, and Karen seemed overwhelming. I wasn't deserving of friends.

It's hopeless. This whole fucking situation is hopeless. Why had she waited so long to finish the job she started five years ago? Why?

Turning around in my tracks, I trudged over the frozen ground to my car. The inside of my car didn't offer me any relief from the cold. The steering wheel wouldn't budge, and the gear shift felt like Excalibur, set in the stone. I had to sit and wait for the heat to kick in, and I didn't have the energy to shut the vents off. I sat there for I don't know how long with arctic air blasting directly on me.

Staring at the field ahead of me, I wondered how long it would take to walk to the horizon. *Is that where Alex wants us to go? Head west until we reach the ocean?*

Would the ocean have stopped her? Knowing her, no obstacle would have stopped her. She was strong. Courageous. Not frail like me. I stared at my tattoos. She wouldn't have needed them. I wiped a tear off my arm.

"Come now, don't be weak."

I felt warm air against my face. The heat was finally working. I tested the steering wheel; miraculously, it worked. I turned my car onto the highway and aimed for the horizon. The road disappeared under my wheels, but no matter how far or how fast I drove, it kept coming. I felt like Ms. Packman eating white dots. On and on it came, faster and faster. A smile spread across my face.

"Alex, I'm listening now."

Hours later, I found myself outside of Jess's apartment. I jiggled the key in the lock, trying to force the icy knob to accept the key. Out of the corner of my eye, I saw a figure lurking in the shadows. Frozen, I didn't move. Was my mom making her move finally?

"Hello."

I turned to face the man and quickly determined that he was no killer. His angelic face matched his innocent voice.

"I didn't mean to startle you." He put his palms up.

"Oh, I just didn't see you there."

"Are you friends with Jess? I was hoping to see her." He looked around nervously, as though he expected someone to jump out of the shadows and attack him.

"I don't think she's home yet." It was freezing out, so I added, "Do you want to wait inside?"

He smiled, and his entire face transformed into a confident and deadly warrior. "That's very kind of you, Paige. But I have to meet another friend."

Paige? I didn't remember saying my name. Maybe Jess had told him. Or maybe this guy was fucking with me. My blood went cold. Was this my mother's game? Torture me slowly? Make it look like I was actually going cuckoo?

"Can I say who stopped by?"

"Tell her Davie wanted to say hi." The sweet voice returned, but his eyes looked like a wolf on the hunt. Was I the prey?

"Okay, Davie." I tried to hold my ground, but my voice faltered.

He placed a hand on my shoulder. "I'm sure I'll see you again. Now, you better get inside before you freeze to death."

I nodded.

"Adios, Paige."

I nodded again. Why did he keep saying my name? And why did he say it like that? Like he owned me.

When he reached the bottom of the staircase, I watched from the front window of Jess's apartment to see which car he got into. However, he didn't saunter to a car. Instead, he skulked through the parking lot and ducked behind another apartment building. Who was he? Did he stalk all of his prey on foot?

After several minutes, I determined that Davie wasn't making his way back. I made sure the front door was locked and then headed for the shower. My entire body was frozen. When Jess and I ditched this town and my parents, I hoped we ended up on a tropical island. There wasn't a single thing I liked about winter. For those who think snow is pretty, how do you feel about it when you slip on it and crack your ass? Or when you can't feel your fingers and toes?

An hour later, I was curled up in front of the fireplace, reading an Agatha Christie novel.

Jess bounded in the front door. "Goodness, Paige. It's like breaking into Fort Knox." She gestured to the front door before leaning down and kissing the top of my head.

"Sorry, some dude gave me the creeps when I got here."

"Oh, do you mean Jimmy? He's harmless," she said, heading for the kitchen.

Jimmy was her next-door neighbor who never left his apartment. He just stood furtively behind his window and leered at everyone within sight. I don't think Jimmy was his actual name, but Jess called him that after Jimmy Stewart in *Rear Window*.

"No, it wasn't Jimmy." I didn't like Jimmy, but I had grown accustomed to him. Besides, he had a calming effect. If he was staring out the window, I knew he would know if something wasn't right. I thought back and wondered if he had noticed my conversation with Davie.

Jess returned to the front room with a beer. Plopping down on the couch next to me, she said, "Are you going to tell me who this mystery person was?"

"He said he's a friend of yours. Davie."

Jess sipped her beer slowly and looked out the window.

"Do you know him?"

There was no response.

"Seriously, Jess. Tell me!" I poked her ribcage with my finger.

"Ouch!" Jess laughed. "Okay, I was just messing with you. I think you've been reading too much Agatha Christie. Of course I know Davie. Don't get your panties in a bunch." She pushed my shoulder. "Maybe we should have you read some more Austen or something, so your imagination doesn't go wild."

"Who is he?"

"Oh, he's just a guy I know. He's …" She stopped. Usually, Jess wasn't speechless.

"He's what?"

"He's just odd. I think something bad happened to him, and he doesn't know how to talk to people. But don't worry about Davie." She patted my leg like I was a child.

She was holding something back, and I was determined to find out what. But I knew she wouldn't budge at the moment.

She held the beer bottle against her cheek. "It's bloody hot in here, Paige." Her pale face started to color.

"It's bloody cold out there. Let's move some place tropical." I closed my eyes and imagined sitting on a beach.

"Speaking of tropical, how would you like to go to the Denver Art Museum tonight?"

"Tonight! It's fucking cold out."

"Oh, don't be a pansy. I have tickets to an exhibition on Matisse's life. It will spur your desire to move to an island and become a painter."

Her eyes bewitched me.

I groaned, knowing I wouldn't be able to say no. I never could. Jess's magnetism was more powerful than that of any snake charmer—not that I knew any, but my money was still on Jess.

"Will there at least be naked ladies for me to gawk at?"

"Only in the paintings, and I'm not sure they'll be your type."

"What, this isn't performance art? Such a shame." I feigned disappointment.

"Go on, put on some decent clothes, not my pink sweats."

"Don't blame me for your lack of style. I didn't pack any clothes for the weekend, so I only have what I wore; hopefully, that will pass muster."

She eyed me. "Was it that bad today?"

"Running into Davie, the creep. Yes!"

"Why don't you ever talk about therapy with me?"

"I do!"

Jess threw her scarf at me. "All right, I'll drop it. As for your clothes, we'll add some accessories and make you look decent."

I wrapped her scarf around me. "This is a good start. Do you have any long underwear?"

"It's not *that* cold out."

"It's below zero, and that's without the wind chill!"

"Always so dramatic." She threw her arm up and pretended to faint. "Maybe Austen isn't good for you either. You and your imagination are starting to act like Catherine Morland."

"Whatever. I'm hungry."

"Good. I found this wonderful new Italian place."

Two hours later, I found myself wandering through the first floor of the art museum and staring not at the paintings but at all of the people. I kept expecting to see Davie burst out from behind a pillar or something. Why had he shaken me up so much? Jess had said he was a friend of hers. She wouldn't lie about that, would she?

"Have you even looked at one display?" Jess tugged my arm to get my attention.

"Of course," I lied.

"What's been your favorite so far?"

I described a watercolor of a peacock.

"You are hopeless. That's the poster hanging in the women's restroom, inside the stalls. You have no choice but to look at it while peeing."

I looked up to apologize, but stopped before any words came out. Jess followed my eyes to see what I was gaping at.

"That gay couple isn't on display either, Paige."

"Gay couple?" I could barely get the words out.

"If they aren't on a date, I'll eat my shoe."

I looked at the couple and then down at her shoe. It was Tom … with some dude.

"I go to school with that guy."

"Really?"

I shouldn't have said anything. Jess pulled me all the way across the room and then practically threw me at Tom.

"Hi, I'm Jess."

Tom looked at me, and then gingerly took Jess's offered hand and shook it. "Hello, Jess." He casually glanced at me. "Hi, Paige. Didn't think I'd see you here."

I could tell he wasn't thrilled to see me, but I wasn't either. And I certainly didn't expect him to be on a date—a date with a boy. Not a boy, actually. The dude looked to be a few years older than Tom.

"Paige has told me so much about you." Jess looked eagerly to his date, hoping for an introduction.

Both Tom and I looked like we wanted to crawl under a large rock. Too bad this museum didn't have a mummy section; we could have hidden in a coffin.

Tom's date flashed him a knowing smile. "Hi, I'm Nick." He shook Jess's hand and then mine.

"Would you two like to grab a drink? A friend of mine owns a bar down the street, so there won't be any issues." Jess nodded at Tom and me—the underage drinkers.

"That would be great. I've seen enough of Matisse for one night. Is that okay?" said Nick as he squeezed Tom's hand.

Marionette

Tom and I locked eyes. Busted.

I couldn't contain a giggle. Jess looked at me puzzled, and then kissed my cheek. Busted.

Tom started to laugh. Jess and Nick eyed each other, and comprehension flashed across their faces. Little did they know that both of us had used the other for straight cover. I wasn't sure about Tom, but I didn't plan on telling Jess that part.

We arrived at the bar, and while Jess and Nick went to get drinks, Tom and I sat uncomfortably at a booth.

"Okay, how do we handle this one?" I asked.

Tom sighed. "I'm not sure, but I don't want to tell Nick about our 'dates' if that's all right with you."

"Duh! That's a given. I meant at school." I slapped his hand.

"Now that we both know, I think we can really mess with everyone's heads. It might be fun." He flashed a devilish smile.

"Oh, it would drive Min—I mean Audrey—mad!"

"What were you going to call her?"

His curiosity made me smile. It was nice to let someone in on one of my secrets.

"Minnie—for Minnie Mouse."

"That's perfect!" He clapped his hands gleefully.

How had I not noticed he was gay?

Our dates returned with the beers.

"So have you two recovered from your shock?" Jess fixed me with a look.

"What do you mean, Tom and I already knew." I tried to sound confident.

"Of course!" Tom's falsetto voice didn't help much.

Nick and Jess said at once, "Sure you did."

"Whatever. Believe what you want. We found out when Karen

told us about her brother."

Tom picked up my cue. "That's right. One of Paige's roommates has a brother who's gay, and he tried to kill himself because of it. Paige and I had dinner together the night we learned about it and had a heart-to-heart."

"You didn't tell me that, Paige." Jess's sincere face made me feel slightly ashamed.

Nick put his hand on Tom's thigh. "That's horrible."

Tom tapped my foot under the table. I imagined it was his way of giving me a high five. Yes, I felt guilty about lying, but did Jess have to be right about everything? From the looks of it, Nick was a lot like Jess. If Tom and I wanted to survive the evening, we had to join forces. And I'll admit it felt good to pull the wool over her eyes.

"Do you guys come to town much?" Jess looked to Nick for an answer. Maybe she wasn't buying our act completely.

"Not often. Tom and I go to school in different states. Fortunately, we're only a five-hour drive away from each other."

Jess gave her "that-must-be-tough" look. "We should plan a date in your town, Nick. What school do you go to?"

"I'm in vet school in Kansas."

"Large or small?"

I wondered why Jess was asking about the size of the school.

"Small animals. I'm not too fond of sticking my hand up a cow's butt for pregnancy tests."

The thought made me cringe. Tom's face turned a sickly gray. Only Jess was intrigued. "I bet ranch vets make a killing, though."

While Jess and Nick discussed the pros and cons of veterinary medicine, I glanced around the dive. We had never been to this bar before. Jess had mentioned knowing the owner. It was more of a biker bar than a gay bar. I looked behind the counter but couldn't quite determine who was the owner. Maybe the burly, tattooed guy who barked at all of the customers instead of saying hi.

"Hi, Jess. I was hoping you'd pop in tonight."

The voice made me jump.

I looked up and saw Davie.

"Good, you're in tonight. I heard you stopped by my apartment. If you three don't mind, I need to talk to Davie for a moment." Jess leaped up like a cat after a mouse.

Davie motioned her into a back room. When they shut the door, I felt uneasy. What in the hell did they have to talk about in private?

Embarrassed, I looked to Nick and Tom and shrugged.

"She seems like a bundle of energy," said Nick.

"You haven't even seen the half of it. Sometimes, she makes me feel jittery, like I'm hopped up on caffeine or something. And she always knows someone at the perfect restaurant or bar."

Nick stood. "Would you like another beer, Paige?"

I nodded. "Yeah. Thanks, Nick."

Jess darted out of the back room before Nick made it to the bar. She pranced up to him and starting chatting nonchalantly. Nothing about her mood had changed. She was still happy-go-lucky Jess. I kept one eye on the door, but I never saw Davie emerge, so I couldn't determine his mood. Jess and Nick returned to the table, laughing at something the burly bartender had said. I didn't peg him as a jokester, but maybe I should stop judging a book by its cover.

Was my gut wrong about Davie? I had thought he was a nice guy at first. Could my second impression be off—is there such a thing? But there had been something in his eyes when he'd said my name. Something was off about him. Jess always tried to look for the good in people; I was living proof of that. Could Davie be using Jess to get closer to me? If so, why? Images of Alex and my mother flashed before my eyes.

I tapped my foot anxiously under the table while Jess and Nick chitchatted. Idle talk wasn't Tom's cup of tea. Besides, there was a college football game on the TV above the bar and Tom was watching it. I pretended to watch, but I kept a close eye on Davie's door. After an hour, he appeared looking relaxed. He whispered something in the bartender's ear and then disappeared behind the door again. The bartender approached us with four beers and told us it was on the house.

Okay, maybe I *was* completely wrong about the creep.

"Do you get this treatment wherever you go?" asked Nick, somewhat baffled. I guessed that two gay guys in a biker bar didn't normally receive beers on the house. Hassled, yes. Free beer—no fucking way.

"Yes. If you need anything in this town, start with Jess. She'll make it happen." I clinked glasses with Jess, who basked in my praise.

"Can you make my calculus teacher take it easy on me?" queried Tom.

"What's his name?" Jess smiled as if she could actually make that happen.

"Dr. Maxwell." Tom looked hopeful.

"I'll see what I can do, Tom." She raised her glass and I could tell her brain was already working on the problem. Surely she couldn't know Tom's calculus professor?

The next day, Jess and I arrived at the restaurant at 9 a.m. to get ready for the early lunch crowd. Mel had to work at the mall, so her shift wasn't starting until the evening. Surprisingly, working together had helped the three of us bridge that uncomfortable gap. Jess was right: showing Mel how well I was adjusting had seemed to make her more apprehensive about telling my parents about the incident. Getting the scars covered with tattoos actually helped too. Now, Mel and Julia smiled when they saw them, instead of looking ashamed. Why they felt shame, I didn't know. Perhaps they felt guilty for looking, akin to leering at a car accident on the highway. We all know it's impolite to stare, but seriously, how can you not search for gore? It's human nature. The tattoos helped hide the fact that I'm pathetic. Some may not be keen about having black ink on their arms, but trust me, it was better than red-ribbon scars that shouted, "Look at me! I'm a failure!"

By 5 p.m., I was ready to sit down and devour a few sandwiches. Ever since the review in the paper, Julia's business had been growing like a chunk of snow that was careening down a mountain. Oddly, most of the clientele was male. Jess thought it was a good way for me to work on my flirting skills, which baffled me. Why would I want to flirt with men?

"Trust me, Paige. You'll have to flirt in all aspects of life, not to just get a date."

It seemed pointless, at first. Then I gave it a go and my tips increased dramatically. Each dollar helped me toward my goal of escaping home and the parents. After a few attempts, I had the flirting game down. Of course, I paled in comparison to Jess, who always made twice as much in tips—at least. But that was still advantageous to me, because all of the money we earned went into a checking account in Jess's name, so my parents wouldn't learn about it. Jess had balked at my idea of keeping the money in a red Folger's coffee can in her kitchen. Apparently, that's the first place she would look if she were robbing someone.

Soon, Mel strolled in the front door, looking ragged and with Weasel right behind her looking, well, weasely.

"Good lord, this place is packed." Mel took a seat next to me at the counter.

"I don't envy you, Mel. You already look exhausted, and the customers keep on coming."

Mel's downcast demeanor told the whole story—she needed money. I eyed Weasel and wondered why he didn't get a second job. If Jess was right, their money troubles were his fault, so why wasn't he working his tail off? Oh, that's right, he's a weasel, sucking the life out of his prey.

I watched Mel heave her tired bones off her seat and head into the back to get ready for her shift. Weasel stayed put and ordered a sandwich, which I'm sure was on the house.

Before I could comment, Jess occupied the seat Mel had just vacated.

"Tom and Nick are joining us for dinner tonight." She glanced at Weasel, gave him a quick nod of acknowledgement, and then continued. "I'm so happy to meet some of your friends." She shook my shoulders.

"Did you have to pay them, Jess?" Weasel sniggered.

Jess patted his leg. "No, I only have to pay off your friends."

The hair on his neck stood on end. Was he ready to pounce, or was he scared?

The bell on the front door jingled and I felt a chill from the outside.

"Ah, Wesley. I heard you might be here."

I turned and saw Davie. "And Paige. We keep running into each other this weekend." He spoke my name as if he were devouring each letter. It made my blood run cold.

"Yes, a table just opened up!" Jess pulled my arm. "Let's grab it. The boys are meeting us here."

Weasel looked betrayed that we had left him alone with Davie, but the glint in Davie's eye told me to stay out of that conversation. To be honest, I enjoyed watching Weasel squirm as Davie spoke to him. We weren't that far away, but Davie's hushed voice didn't carry beyond Weasel-range. Was Davie the bookie I had paid off? Was Jess helping Weasel with his debt? I know she's kindhearted, but that was too much. Besides, she had told me not to get involved. So, why was she?

"Hey, how many sandwiches have you eaten?" Jess snapped her fingers in my face to get my attention. "We're having dinner soon." She grabbed a napkin from the holder and wiped my cheek.

"Seriously, you're worried I won't be able to eat again." I tried looking around her head to watch the action at the counter, but she bobbed her head playfully.

I did get a glimpse of Davie patting Weasel on the shoulder as he sat down next to him. Soon, they were drinking beers together but still not talking. Shit! I just couldn't put my finger on what was going on. Each time I thought Davie was a creep, he turned out to be friendly. Next time, I planned on flirting with him to coax information out of him—if there was a next time. Part of me hoped there wouldn't be.

As Nick and Tom walked into Julia's, Davie headed out. Weasel sat at the counter. More than likely he would stay during Mel's entire shift, just to get free beers. What an ass!

"Does that guy own this place as well?" Nick eased into the booth and Tom sat down next to him.

"Nope, I do." Julia approached. "Jess told me you're friends with Paige. Everything is on the house. What can I get you, boys?"

Nick chuckled and Tom looked impressed.

"What do you suggest?" Nick asked.

Julia winked. "I think I know what you'll like."

Off she went like a mother hen and quickly returned with beers and four pulled-pork sandwiches, all of them dripping with extra sauce.

"I make the sauce myself. Word on the street is that it's like crack: once you try it, you can't get enough." Julia set the tray down and ambled off to greet incoming guests.

"Trust me, this stuff will make you hate the dorm slop they try to pass off as real food." I handed Tom a sandwich.

He took a bite, and his eyes rolled into the back of his head.

Jess clapped her hands. "I think that counts as a triumph."

Tom blushed, but didn't stop eating. By the end of the night, he had eaten four sandwiches. I had three, but Nick only ate two and Jess managed to nibble on just one. It didn't take much to fuel her ninety-pound frame. She had plenty of beer, though. Whenever I tried to get her to drink less and eat more, she prattled on about how America was founded by a bunch of dudes drunk on beer, and how they got it right. It was hard to argue with her logic, since there wasn't any. They had drunk beer because the water wasn't safe and there was no choice. She had a choice, and she chose beer. You can't argue crazy without sounding crazy. She should have been a lawyer, but then again, business was a decent calling. Jess could out-talk, out-smart, and out-work most of her competition. And clients loved her spunk.

Chapter Nineteen

SUNDAY MORNING ARRIVED, and I sat at Jess's kitchen table, my hand propping up my chin. I was nursing yet another hangover. Jess, on the other hand, showed no signs of a hangover as she flitted around on tiptoe, conjuring up several varieties of greasy food for me.

"How is it that you never get drunk or hungover?" I asked. My head felt ready to pop off.

She gazed at me over her shoulder. "Like I've said: practice."

"You aren't that much older, Jess."

"No, but I started drinking years ago." She turned back to the stove and I couldn't see her face. It was the first time I had heard this.

"When did you start?" I was curious, and Jess laughed and then flipped some bacon over in the pan.

"You make it sound like I have a problem," she said. "You're the one looking like crap."

"Thanks." I slurped my coffee angrily. "But when did you take your first drink?"

"Let's see." She paused and stirred the spluttering hash browns. "I think when I was nine. But I would just sip drinks."

"When did you start consuming your own?"

"Really, Paige! What's with all of the questions this morning?" She sauntered over to the table and set a plate in front of me. The bacon, hash browns, and scrambled eggs made my mouth water.

"You aren't having any?" I motioned to the food.

"I thought we'd share. But eat up, I'm not that hungry." She grabbed her coffee but didn't taste it. Instead, she held it against her cheek, contemplating something.

"Are you going to answer my question?" I said, and scooped a pile of eggs into my mouth. "These are good," I mumbled with my mouth full. "What did you put in them?"

"A secret ingredient." She set her cup down and took a bite of the eggs. "How come you never told me about Tom?"

"What do you mean? That he's gay?" I avoided her eyes and nibbled on a crispy piece of bacon.

"Oh, shit!" Jess bolted out of her seat and opened the Belgium waffle maker. "Whew!—it isn't burned."

She placed the waffle and a jug of maple syrup in front of me.

"There isn't much to tell about Tom." I doused my waffle in syrup and Jess crinkled her nose. She hated sweets.

"You didn't know he was gay, and he didn't know you were. Nick is a nice guy, but not the brightest." She grinned triumphantly.

I sighed and stared into her bright green eyes.

"You two talked like you're super close, and I saw the way you guys communicated without speaking. Tell me the truth, Paige."

"This isn't fair. You won't tell me about your drinking or anything about Davie, and yet you're interrogating me about my friendship with Tom."

She must have known I wasn't all that upset, since I continued eating, mixing some bacon with waffle before shoving it in my mouth.

"I don't know why or when I started drinking. I just love the taste of beer. It doesn't give me a buzz or get me drunk. I just like the taste. End of story."

"You never feel buzzed."

"No." Her flat voice indicated she was about to get testy. If I pushed the issue we were heading for a fight.

"Tom is a nice guy who my roommates think I'm dating." I lifted my orange juice glass to my face to hide behind it in case that information angered her.

She slammed the table with her hand. "I knew it! Only you would target a gay guy as cover."

"Well, he targeted me as well for cover." It was a meek attempt.

"Sometimes I forget how young you are." Sadness clouded her eyes.

"Why was Davie looking for Weasel? Is he the bookie?"

"Davie!" She flicked some strands of hair off her face. "No, Davie is one of Weasel's customers. It seems that Wesley sold him a stinker, and Davie wanted to talk to him about it."

That explained why he didn't have a car the first day I met him. "Why didn't he go to the lot?" I asked.

"Oh, Wesley hasn't shown up there for the past few days."

"You're kidding me. Mel works two jobs and he fucking quit his!" I threw my fork down on the table in disgust.

"Not that I like the guy much, but I think he's working at a different car lot now—a more respectable one." Jess looked as surprised as I felt.

"They had a couple of beers together last night. Maybe they worked it out."

"I'm sure they did. And seriously, Paige, do you think I'd have a bookie hanging outside my apartment? Look at me." She motioned to her purple nightie, matching robe, and penguin slippers.

"He gave me the willies." I tried justifying my accusation.

"He wouldn't hurt a fly. I think he was trying to act tough because he's a tiny guy and Wesley is over six feet. And no man likes to be made a fool off, especially when it comes to buying a car. It's like an extension of the penis."

I picked up my fork and started work on the hash browns. "There's something off about him."

"You have trust issues, Paige." Jess stabbed a piece of bacon with a fork and thrust it into her mouth, chewing it slowly but decisively.

Chapter Twenty

BY THE TIME my next appointment with Liddy arrived, I couldn't stop fixating on Davie. Why did Jess trust him? Why didn't I?

Liddy arrived one minute late—not bad for her. At least she didn't start the clock until she sat down in her chair, ready with her pencil and notepad.

"Good afternoon, Paige. How are you today?"

"I have a problem."

Liddy examined my face. Was she trying to determine whether I was conning to avoid a repeat of last's week's discussion?

"Would you like to talk about it?"

Uh, yeah. Why else would I bring it up?

"Yes."

She looked at me expectantly and nodded. "Why don't you tell me what it is?"

"I think Jess is in trouble."

Liddy crossed her legs and balanced her notepad on her knee, her pencil at the ready. "How so?"

"She's friends with a bad man."

"What do you mean *bad* man?" Liddy looked worried.

"Oh, no. It's nothing like that. He didn't molest me, if that's what you're thinking. Last Friday, he was waiting outside Jess's apartment when I arrived. At first, I thought he was nice. But then something changed. I can't explain it, but something changed." I slumped back in my chair.

"Did he say something that upset you?"

I shook my head and fiddled with the chair. "No, it wasn't that. It was how he spoke. He says words like he's devouring all of the letters of the word. I got the impression he was about to lose it."

"Did you tell Jess this?"

"Not about the devouring letters thing. I told her that he stopped by. We ended up running into him two other times over the weekend; she lives in a small town. Jess talked to him privately for two minutes and didn't seem fazed by it. She says Mel's boyfriend sold him a lemon and he just wanted his money back. But it ain't right. There's something else going on."

"Do you think Jess is trying to protect you?"

"What do you mean?" I leaned forward in my chair.

Liddy coughed nervously and then pointed at my wrists.

It dawned on me. "Shit! I didn't think of that. That would be something she would do. Even though she weighs less than a hundred pounds, she has fighting spirit in her, like a mama bear with her cubs."

"Under a hundred pounds." Concern spread across Liddy's face.

"Oh! She's not anorexic or anything. She's only five feet tall."

Liddy laughed. "How tall are you? You must tower over her."

I smiled. "Yeah, I'm almost a foot taller. I feel like an NBA star."

"Tell me, what do you think the real problem is?"

"Me."

Liddy flinched like she'd been struck in the face. "Please explain."

"I don't know how to explain it to you without sounding paranoid."

"Paige, you're going to have to trust me." She tapped her pencil on the notepad. "I've known you for several months now, and I don't think you are the paranoid type."

Trust. I was getting tired of that word.

"Can I show you something?"

Liddy motioned for me to continue.

I pulled a folder out of my backpack. "Since Alex's death I've been doing some research. The night before she was hauled away by the cops, she said she'd spoken to a reporter named Neil Michaels on a few occasions."

Liddy narrowed her eyes, lost in thought. "That name rings a bell."

"I'll get to that. At first, I didn't understand why a reporter was talking to Alex. She was just a kid. My first thought was that he was doing a story on kids who were addicted to drugs."

I opened the folder and pulled out photocopies of the library's microfiche. The same ones I had hidden from Liddy when I ran into her at the student union. "Then I started reading his articles. He's a business reporter, or was a business reporter."

Liddy clicked her pencil. "That's right. He's the reporter who was burned alive in his car. The circumstances of the accident seemed fishy, but the cops never found anything—they assumed electrical problems."

"Yes! That's him."

"But how does this relate to Alex and that night?"

"Alex didn't tell me. She was so amped that night that I thought she was high. As it turned out, she was just terrified out of her wits. That's why her behavior was so erratic. Alex was scared for her life, and for mine."

"Because a business reporter talked to her." She looked skeptical.

"Not just any business reporter. Mr. Michaels had it in for my father." I handed her the stack of articles. "All of these articles hint about deceit, corruption, and cover-ups."

Liddy flicked through them. "Okay, but I still don't get it."

"I didn't either for quite some time. A lot of people don't like my dad. And this isn't the first time I've encountered bad press about him or about my family. But this guy was different. He didn't let up. It's like he was on a crusade."

"But why target Alex? She was your best friend. Why not go to you?"

She was catching on.

"Odd, huh?" I gestured to the stack of articles and Liddy relinquished them to me. Thumbing through them, I found the one I needed. "In this article, he changed tack. He started to write about the family. My dad's children."

"You and Abbie."

"If you read the article closely, it hints that there were more."

Liddy sucked in some air. "Okay, but a lot of powerful men have affairs. Illegitimate children have occurred throughout history—why would this cause such a ruckus?"

"You don't know my father. Mr. Perfect. He likes to control everything, even people's thoughts. Have you read *Nineteen Eighty-Four* by Orwell?"

Liddy nodded.

"Remember the scene when O'Brien tortures Winston to get him to believe that when O'Brien held up four fingers he was actually holding up five?"

Liddy nodded again.

"My father thinks he has that type of control over everyone. That power."

Understanding spread across Liddy's face. "Are you saying that Alex was your sister?"

"Yes." I was surprised Liddy had caught on so quickly; I hadn't.

"And that's why she was killed?"

"Yes, but there's more to it."

Liddy took the stack of articles back. "How so?"

"From the articles I got the sense that Michaels was close to solving the mystery or he had, but didn't reveal all yet. That's why he contacted Alex."

"Then he died." Liddy looked aghast and dubious at the same time.

"I know. It's hard to believe." I put my palms up in the air.

"So you think your father—"

I interrupted. "No, my mother."

"Your mother? But I thought your father was like O'Brien from *Nineteen Eighty-Four*."

"He is. She's worse. My father probably hired the killer, though."

Liddy slumped back in her chair. "I'm sorry, Paige. This is a lot to take in."

I sat silently while she flicked through the pages in her lap. "How did you start putting all of this together?"

"I had help."

"Alex?"

"Yes, in a way. But Alex only left clues. When she was ranting and raving that Michaels was afraid. He thought someone was following him. To be honest, at the time, I didn't think Michaels existed. I thought her performance was coke-induced. And I couldn't fathom why a reporter told Alex to get away. She said we had to leave. He found out the truth and he was worried about her safety, and his. He said the Alexanders would 'take care' of the problem."

I jumped out of my seat and paced the room.

"Followed. Who was followed? Michaels or Alex?"

"Michaels."

"By whom?"

"I'm assuming Alex's killer or the killer's people."

She stared blankly. "Go back to that night. What else did Alex say?"

"I go back to that night all the time!" I sighed. "Sorry." I made my way back to my seat. "Alex freaked out when she learned that Michaels had died in a suspicious accident. That's why she decided to finally tell me, I'm guessing.

"I have to admit, when she started rambling about a reporter who had been killed and that we were next, I really thought she had lost it. Gone crazy. I didn't tell her that of course, but that's what I thought." I paused. "I will have to live with that mistake for the rest of my life."

"How did Michaels figure out the mystery?"

I shook my head. "Don't know. In his articles, he repeatedly mentions that in order to solve most crimes all one has to do is follow the money. I'm only guessing, but Alex's parents—or her mother— more than likely blackmailed my father. I always wondered how they survived financially. Her parents owned several frozen yogurt places that went belly up years ago, yet they still had fancy cars, a house with an indoor heated swimming pool, and extended trips all over the world. They claimed to have 'family money.' My guess: it's my family's money."

"Why would your father pay all those years?"

"Alex's birthday is just three days after mine. Back then, my father wasn't as rich and powerful. He was well on his way, but he wasn't there yet. Now, everyone fears him. Back then, everyone kept a watchful eye on his rise. Otherwise, I think he would have taken care of the Alex situation long before."

"So he was covering up the affair?"

"Yep. And the idiot messed around with a woman who lived right across the street. My dad must have gone ape-shit when he learned that the baby was named Alexandra. I have to give it to the woman—what a great way to keep the threat alive."

"Who do you think killed Alex?"

"My mother."

Liddy's desk phone rang, and I nearly had a heart attack.

She motioned for me to stay seated while she got up to turn it off. "I'm sorry, I didn't think the ringer was on." After she took her seat again, she said, "Paige, you're going to have to explain this to me."

"I'll try. I still don't have all of the answers, and I doubt I ever will."

"Do you really think your mother killed Alex?"

"Yes."

"Why?"

"She told me." I closed my eyes and saw my mom gloating about it, heard her cackling.

"She told you! She just admitted it?" Liddy sounded doubtful.

"Yes, but she was drunk at the time—drunker than normal." I

looked away. "I'm pretty sure she remembers telling me, though." And her threat. *Watch yourself, Paige, or I'll do it to you too.*

"How?"

"Paying someone to slip Alex drugs laced with something—a lethal dose."

"Who?"

"A friend of Alex's—a druggie."

"A friend?" She sounded skeptical.

"Money is a powerful motivator. But this friend ended up dying last year anyway, from a drug overdose." I tapped my fingers on the armrests of my chair.

"Do you think your mom did that?"

I sucked in my breath. "Hard to prove. Guilt is just as deadly. Maybe the friend couldn't live with what he had done."

"Davie?" A hint of understanding flashed across Liddy's face.

"Mom worked through Alex's friends. Why wouldn't she find someone who could get close to me too?" I remembered something else. "Actually, she told me she was the one who got Alex hooked on drugs too. She asked someone to introduce Alex to the stuff. I don't know if she planned it all from the beginning, but she was thrilled with the results."

"How did you find out Alex was your sister? Did Alex tell you?"

"No, not Alex. That night, when my mom bragged about taking care of Alex. She said my charming father would go into her room when she was bedridden and boast about his exploits to torture her. One night, he was either really drunk or extremely cocky, and he told her all about Alex. How I was best friends with my half-sister and neither of us knew. Even Alex's father didn't know.

"No wonder my mother hated me. Alex and I looked almost identical, even more so than Abbie and I. The sight of me must have made her sick. My mom blamed me for the Lego incident and then this. When she looks at me, her eyes scream bloody murder. I never understood until that day."

"Oh, Paige. I don't know what to believe."

"Probably that I'm paranoid." I crossed my arms.

"No, not that. But all of it is ... far-fetched."

"I know. It's still hard for me to fathom, and I've spent months tracking down as many clues as possible."

"When did your mom tell you about Alex?"

I looked down at my wrists.

"You aren't worried that your parents, or your mom, will lock you up because you're gay. You're worried that's the excuse they'll use to silence you."

"Exactly. And my parents hate scandals. They believe everyone thinks they are perfect. Having a lesbian in the family would be catastrophic. And I am one of the remaining connections to Alex. They have no issues taking people out who are connected to us."

"Are you worried about Jess's safety?"

I nodded.

"It's only a matter of time until my mom stumbles upon the fact that I'm gay. I worry about that constantly."

"How much does Jess know?"

"Nothing."

"Nothing?"

"I've never shared this with a soul. I keep those articles locked away so no one will discover them."

"Can I keep them to read over the weekend?" She set the stack aside, not giving me a chance to refuse the request.

"Yes."

Liddy made no move to end the session. Did she think it was

safer to keep me in her office? Did she believe me? Trust me? Or did she think I was a loon—a paranoid loon?

After my session with Liddy, I wasn't in the mood to head straight to my dorm room. Instead, I barged into the student center. Sometimes, the best way for me to feel alone, at least since moving to college, was to get lost in a crowd. I grabbed a ham and cheese sandwich and a large Dr. Pepper, and then found a seat in the back of the dining room.

Tom moseyed by, but didn't see me. He looked downcast, like he needed a friend. I hesitated before I called out to him. Turning, he smiled and then made his way to my table.

Tom slid his tray of food down on the table. He had a ham and cheese sandwich and a large Dr. Pepper too. Maybe it was a gay thing.

"Do you normally eat this late?" he asked.

I shook my head. "No. In fact, this is my second lunch today. How about you?"

"I stopped by your room earlier to say hi. Karen was there with her brother."

I started to speak, but he waved my words away.

"Yes, that one. I got suckered into hanging out with them while her brother tried to convince Audrey and the gang that being gay is just dandy. Afterwards, Aaron kept making fun of him. I couldn't handle it, so I came here to get away."

"I'm a little disappointed that I missed Karen and her performance. Probably a good thing." I squeezed his hand. "Sorry about Aaron."

"Oh, he can be such an ass. And with all of the Amendment 2 shit earlier this semester, to be honest, I'm fed up with him. I'm trying to talk to the people in charge of room assignments to get a new roommate next semester."

"I'm so sorry, Tom. I didn't know it was that bad."

"Aaron is okay, I guess. But his military bravado and crap gets old real fast." He fiddled with the straw in his drink. "Every day, he makes a crack that I haven't brought any girls back to the room. He's laid off a little since you and I started 'dating.'" He chuckled and made quote marks in the air.

"Tell me about it. It was a relief not to have to explain where I spend my weekends."

"To make matters worse, Nick and I broke up."

"Oh Tom, I'm so sorry."

He seemed relieved that I didn't ask why. I had a feeling, and I felt guilty about it.

An idea struck me. "Hey, why don't you come to Jess's this weekend? Jess and I have to work tomorrow, but you can hang out at Julia's or borrow my car while we work. It looks like you need a break. And we can tell our roommates you're going home with me to meet the parents!" I slammed my hand down on the table victoriously.

Tom straightened up in his chair. "Are you sure? I won't be in the way?"

"Nonsense. Jess would love to have you there. Of course, she may grill you about our dates—she figured it out." I looked shyly down at my sandwich before taking a huge bite.

I still felt guilty about Nick.

Tom slurped his soda as if he were forcing the thought of Nick down into a hidden reservoir inside. A few moments passed before he said, "Seriously, you wouldn't mind? I would love it! I hate going to frat parties every weekend."

"Come on, some of the guys are cute." I winked at him.

"What about the girls? They're all dolled up to get free drinks."

He pushed his sleeves up, and then hoisted the sandwich to his mouth. One bite and a third of it was gone.

"That doesn't do it for me. I hate all the fakeness. It seems like everyone here is lying or hiding something. I can't stand that."

Tom chortled. "That includes us!"

"Right, I didn't think of it that way," I said sheepishly.

His face grew serious. "But I know what you mean. There's a lot of hate towards gays boiling under the surface here. Something bad is going to happen."

The two of us hammered down our sandwiches and made plans to meet in my room so Karen would see us leave for the weekend together.

It didn't take me long to pack. I had a supply of toiletries at Jess's, so all I needed was a change of clothes. Karen wandered into the room.

"There you are. I was looking for you earlier. My brother came up for lunch." She beamed.

"Yeah, Tom told me. I'm sorry I missed him."

"Are you going away again?" She gestured to my bag.

Before I could answer, there was a knock at the door. Karen answered it. I rolled my eyes.

Tom came in all smiles, strolled up to me, and planted a kiss on my forehead. "Are you ready?"

Karen got a jealous look in her eyes. "Are you two going away for the weekend? Together?"

I laughed. The plan was working beautifully. "Yep. Tom is coming home with me for the weekend."

"Really?" Karen couldn't control her excitement.

Minnie sauntered in and looked about quizzically.

"Paige is introducing Tom to her family!" Karen exclaimed.

Marionette

Minnie dropped her bag to the floor, looked at Tom with his arm around me and then looked back at Karen. "Really?"

It wasn't until that moment that I realized Tom wasn't wearing his Broncos hat. He looked respectable. Combed hair. Clean shirt. And khaki trousers. He looked like he was actually meeting my parents.

I patted his cheek "Really," I said. "Tom, dear, we better go. We have dinner plans." I tapped my watch.

Tom scooped up both of our bags and held my hand as we exited the room. When we reached the stairwell, we both exploded into laughter.

"Did you see the look on Minnie's face?" asked Tom as he gasped for air.

"Ha! You said Minnie." I leaned against the wall and cackled till my sides burned.

Minutes later, we approached my car and Tom dropped the bags by the trunk. "Whoa! Minnie said you had a nice car, but are you serious?" He stood back from my car. "This is legit—a Jaguar XJS—how old is it?"

"Less than a year. Got it for graduation." Embarrassed about my car, I pulled the keys out of my pocket. "Care to drive?"

"Seriously?" His falsetto voice informed me I had just made his day.

What's with men and cars? Even gay men go gaga over them.

By the time we reached Jess's apartment, she had finished work. I didn't bother calling her to tell her Tom was coming. I knew I didn't have to. As soon as Tom walked in, Jess threw her arms around him and welcomed him to her place. Actually, she said *our* place.

Over a beer, we explained how our plan worked with Minnie and Karen.

Jess laughed. "I bet they are still talking about it."

"Those two won't stop talking about it until we return from our trip." I smiled at Jess.

Jess turned to Tom. "What kind of food are you in the mood for, Tom?"

"Can we go to Julia's? That's the best sandwich I've ever had."

Since it wasn't that cold out and all of us hoped to drink, we walked to Julia's.

The restaurant was slow for a change, so Julia sat with us at a booth. While Tom was in the bathroom, I explained his situation with Aaron, and told them about Nick. Both Jess's and Julia's nurturing impulse kicked in.

When Tom returned to the table, Julia asked him what he was doing the next day while Jess and I worked.

Tom shrugged. "Don't know. Maybe just hang out."

Julia waved her hand. "Fiddlesticks. How 'bout I teach you how to make my secret sauce? What do you think? Would you like a job?"

Tom's eyes grew big with excitement. "Cool!"

Jess turned to me. "We should get a bigger apartment so Tom can have his own room. He'll need a place to stay so he can work."

And that was it: Tom was included in the inner circle—like family. The thought of moving to a new place was appealing. Now if I could only convince Jess not to tell anyone the address, not even Mel. Then maybe I wouldn't have to worry so much about Davie or others lurking out there. How many were there?

Chapter Twenty-One

WEEKS LATER, THE phone in my dorm room rang. Karen answered it, and then tried to hand the receiver to me.

"Who is it?" I asked, refusing to grab it.

"Don't know. Some dude."

I was annoyed. I had a French final the next day, and I didn't want any interruptions.

Karen waved the phone in my face. "Paige, don't be rude."

I muttered, "Hello," into the receiver and tried to mask my annoyance.

"Don't say anything, just hang up and come to my room. Now." Tom sounded scared.

"Uh, he must have hung up." Casually, I replaced the receiver and stretched. "I think I'll head to the library to study. Fewer interruptions."

Karen shrugged. She was sitting at my desk, cramming for her chemistry final.

Taking the back stairs, I ran most of the way to Tom's.

Before I had a chance to knock on the door, he yanked it open.

"Get in here."

"Tom, what's going on?"

"It's awful. Just awful." He was almost in tears.

"What happened?"

"Yeah. Something happened, Paige. Something bad."

I sat on his bed. "Tom, you're freaking me out. What's going on?"

"The police came and took Aaron."

"Aaron! Why?" Even to me, my voice sounded like it was coming from across the room.

"There was an … incident."

He was trying to protect me. But from what?

"Why don't you start at the beginning?"

Tom walked to his mini fridge and grabbed a Keystone Light. He popped the top and poured a generous amount into his mouth. Then he removed his Broncos hat and frantically rubbed the top of his head. His hair was matted down with sweat.

"I knew he was a douche, but this?" Tom's eyes bored into mine.

"What did he do?" I sensed I wasn't going to like the news.

"He and a couple of his buddies beat up this guy."

Tom took another swig of beer.

"Who? Why?

"It … he … was a gay guy."

"What?" I blinked several times trying to erase the image from my mind.

"They ambushed him outside of the student union."

"Why?"

Tom's glare told me the reason.

"Just because he was gay?" I clarified.

Tom nodded once and then finished off his beer. He went back to the fridge and grabbed another, and one for me.

At first, I was numb. I barely even registered I was holding the beer. Seconds later, I set the beer down, unopened. "I don't want to be here. Let's get away."

"Where?" Tom stared into his beer can, searching for answers.

"Jess. She'll know what to do, what to say. Tom, you can't stay here. Not with Aar ... Him." I couldn't utter his name. I tried, but the name died in the back of my throat.

We sat silently for several minutes. When Tom went to the bathroom, I looked over at Aaron's desk. He had photos of his family and friends. Smiling. Full of life. Young. How could someone hate another person for such a stupid reason?

Holding his jacket and backpack, Tom walked back into the room. "Do you need to go back to your room for anything?"

I shook my head. Tom threw a few beers into his bag. "I'm ready."

The drive to Jess's felt like hours. Neither of us spoke. Not once did I break the speed limit, swerve into a different lane, or tailgate. Tom was drinking, and the thought of us getting arrested steadied my foot on the gas pedal and made me control my impulses.

Finally, I asked, "How bad was it?"

"Bad."

"Hospital bad or dead bad?" I peeked out of the corner of my eye to see his reaction.

"Hospital. The guy will never be the same again, though." Tom didn't flinch. Didn't react. He was robot-like.

I sighed and gripped the steering wheel tighter. I needed something firm to hold onto, something I could understand.

Tom leaned forward in his seat and clutched his knees. "Attempted murder. That's what he was arrested for—and he was the ringleader."

The words hit me hard. My chest constricted. I was able to choke out, "My God," as I stared absently at the road in front of me.

Jess didn't speak when we walked in. She just got up and gave Tom a hug—no, not a hug, an embrace. She held onto him and Tom broke down. Despite the heavy sobs escaping from him, he made no sound, and Jess's petite frame didn't give way. Slowly, she maneuvered Tom to the couch and sat down next to him.

I stood awkwardly, watching Tom as he hid his face in both hands.

"It was on the news," Jess told me. She motioned to the TV, and for the first time I noticed that it was on.

I hit the off button to silence the clamor, but they had already moved on to another story anyway. A sixth grader had won the local spelling bee. Zip-a-Dee-Doo-Dah.

Motioning to Jess to meet me in the kitchen, I slipped out of the room. She joined me and gave me a hug. "It's worse than you think," I said, nestling my head on her shoulder.

She pulled away to study my face.

"Tom's roommate was one of the guys arrested."

Jess glanced towards the room where Tom was sitting.

"Shit!" She turned to me. "He can't go back. Even if his roommate isn't there, he can't go back."

"I know. But what can he say? He won't want to admit anything. Not now. How will he explain that he needs a new room? A new roommate? They already turned him down last week."

"What do you mean?" She pinned me with a stare.

"Tom tried getting his own room. They got along, but Aar—" I still couldn't say it. "Well, let's just say that he would make comments that made Tom uncomfortable. The administration said no. They don't have any rooms for him or for anybody."

"Bullshit. They probably think they're helping him build character." I could tell she was angry. Swearing was not her thing normally.

Slogans from the posters hanging in the dorm hallways suddenly popped into my mind:

"We are all one."

"Once a terrier, always a terrier."

"Minds and friends connecting forever."

Yeah. Only if we were just like everyone else. I swallowed, and it felt like I was forcing a pill down my throat.

"Let me think about this. But we should go back out there." Jess gestured for me to go first.

Tom looked up when we entered the room. "I'm sorry."

Jess flitted over to him. "Don't be sorry. I'm glad you're here." She nestled on the couch next to him and pulled his head down onto her shoulder. "And thanks for bringing Paige to me. I was worried about her."

For some reason, this statement brought tears to my eyes. Jess noticed and flashed me a sad, fleeting smile.

"Have you two had dinner?"

We shook our heads.

"I know you probably don't want to eat, but I have an idea. Santi's is having an all-you-can-eat tamale night for a charity, and Tom, you look like you need some tequila. I will warn you, the last time I took Paige there, she lost her clothes before the night was over." Jess brushed my arm lovingly.

Tom let out a snort that was half laughter, half blubber. He wiped his nose on his sleeve. "Sure, why not? But, Paige, I would appreciate it if you kept your clothes on tonight."

I marveled at Jess's ability to calm him. And me.

As soon as we entered the restaurant, the smell of tamales and mole sauce hit my nostrils. When Jess had proposed coming here, I'd been certain I wouldn't have an appetite. Now, I couldn't wait to pile tamale upon tamale on my plate. Tom eyed me guiltily, and I knew he felt the same way.

"Grab that table over there, Paige." Jess motioned to a table in the back. "I'm going to say hi to Santi."

I nodded. Like dancers, Tom and I wove through the buffet line to take the last available table. Santi sure knew how to pack in a crowd. It wasn't even five in the afternoon, yet people were lined up for food. The rest were half-sloshed on tequila and wiggling their butts on the dance floor, even though there was no mariachi band playing this time.

Jess appeared a few minutes later with plates for all three of us. "All paid up. Now, I'm counting on you two to get our money's worth." She winked at me and led us to the buffet line.

Tom and I didn't want to disappoint her, so we overloaded our plates.

Santi chuckled when he saw how many tamales I had on my plate. "Señorita, if you finish all of those, I'll give you as much tequila as you can handle."

"It's a deal." I tried shaking his hand to seal the deal, but almost upset my entire plate.

As Santi steadied the plate, he said, "Hurry up if you want more. The buffet line closes at six." He playfully patted my back, not in the least concerned that he'd lose the bet.

"If she goes back for more, Santi, I'll buy you all the tequila you can drink," said Jess.

"Careful, Jess. I can drink a lot." Santi patted his belly and grinned.

"Oh, I know."

I wondered how often Jess and Santi had gotten drunk and danced together.

"Paige, how much food can you actually eat?" Mel said, as she walked up to us, her nose wrinkling in disgust.

Before I could respond, Jess asked, "Santi, can you add another plate to my tab?"

"Sure thing." He gave a half wave and waddled off to greet other customers. Even from the other side of the room, I could hear Santi's booming laugh, which matched his imposing presence.

"I wasn't expecting to see you, Mel. Did you leave work early just for this?" I asked, sitting down and following my question with my first bite. Exquisite. I rubbed my belly and then dug in. "Jesus, these are good."

Tom nodded, but he was too busy shoveling in bite after bite to speak.

Mel looked at me and then at Tom and shuddered. "Jess, we may need to get separate tables." She crinkled her face in disgust as she watched us eat. Then she finally answered my question with, "I had the day off, and Jess was kind enough to invite me."

"Wow, I can't remember the last time you took a day off," I mumbled through a mouthful of tamale.

Mel caught Jess's attention and they both joined the tamale queue.

As Tom and I continued eating, I watched Mel's expression as she spoke to Jess. She was animated, and Jess was doing her best to quiet her. What in the world where they talking about now? Finally, Mel stood still—completely still—and listened to every word Jess said. I couldn't hear the conversation, but it looked serious. Mel glanced over her shoulder at me and then turned away quickly. Jess continued to talk rapidly. Once Mel had finished gathering a measly four tamales, they returned to the table.

"Four, that's all? I ate four while you were in line."

"Not sure you should be bragging about that, Paige." Jess smiled and turned to Tom. "I had a feeling you'd find your appetite here." She nudged his arm.

Tom remained silent. He took his tamale-eating seriously. He never stopped chewing or shoving more in, and I sensed that as long as he focused on eating, Aaron and everything else was pushed from his mind.

"Paige, Jess was filling me in on your day." Mel set her fork down. "I'm really sorry." She peeked in Tom's direction.

He glanced up from his plate and then looked away, resuming his eating.

Mel and Jess exchanged a look, the meaning of which completely escaped me until I saw Mel quickly glance at my wrists. Were they worried I would try to off myself again? Would that fear ever dissipate, or would everyone panic every time I had to deal with life?

"Where's Weasel?" I steered the conversation away.

"Working. He's been working nights lately." She laughed. "And I have to admit, it's been wonderful having him gone while I'm home. How long are you in town?"

"Just the night, I think. I have a French final tomorrow." I caught Jess's eye to see if she had any solutions for Tom's situation yet.

She looked away.

Nope.

"Can't you postpone the test, considering?" Mel offered.

MARIONETTE

"Doubt it. My French teacher doesn't mess around when it comes to following the rules. No wonder so many people hate the French." I tried to joke, but it fell flat.

Tom continued eating, but I felt his unease. He didn't want to go back either, not to his room. Not to school. He needed a break.

"You can always drive back after your test," Jess chimed in.

"Of course." I looked at Tom. "You can stay here. I don't have any exams on Wednesday, so we can stay for a few days. Jess, you won't mind, right?"

"Not one bit. In fact, I might be a little insulted if you didn't stay longer."

Tom looked slightly relieved. Mel motioned for the waiter and ordered four beers.

No one spoke. That's when I heard it.

"Paige! What the fuck are you doing here?"

I looked up and saw Karen with some guy. How in the world had she managed to run into me here?

"Uh, I'm eating tamales," I responded glibly.

"I can see that. And I see Tom's with you. How come you didn't invite me?" She sounded hurt.

"Y-you were studying for your chemistry test." I tried to sound convincing.

"And you were studying for your French test," she accused.

The guy she was with held out his hand. "Hi, I'm Karen's brother, Jake." I shook his hand, and Tom and Jake nodded at each other.

"Would you two like to join us?" Jess was amazed that another one of my school friends had magically appeared.

"Sure, I'm starving." Karen plopped down on a chair that Jake had pulled over for her.

"You better hurry, then," I said. "The buffet stops at six." I motioned to the line, which grew with each passing second.

Karen sprang out of her seat like a hundred-meter sprinter and pulled on her brother's arm.

Tom looked at me and said, "Shit!" under his breath.

"Hold on, you two. She doesn't know anything. Tell her I'm your cousin." Jess flashed a supportive smile.

The thought repulsed me. It was okay to "date" Tom at school, but this was my territory with Jess. Lying seemed reprehensible here.

Tom shook his head. "That would probably work with Karen, but not with Jake. Besides …" His voice drifted off.

Jess nodded in agreement and Tom's eyes welled up as he said, "Not today."

When Karen and Jake sat back down, Mel scrutinized Karen, which made me grin. Was she afraid Karen was her replacement?

I started to laugh uncontrollably.

"What's so funny?" asked Karen.

I continued laughing. "This." I gestured to the table.

"What, eating tamales?" Karen looked baffled.

Tom howled along with me.

"N-no!" was all I could get out.

"We came here to get away from all of you, and here you are." Tom choked the words out.

Karen frowned slightly, suggesting she was hurt.

"I didn't mean it that way," said Tom. "It's just that this has been a difficult day." His laughter halted.

"Why, did you two fight?" inquired the clueless Karen.

Jess placed her hand on my arm to stifle my laughter at Karen's expense.

Jake broke into the conversation with, "Karen, I think they are referring to the beating on campus."

"Oh, you heard about it." I could tell she was ready to gossip about it.

"Tom told me what happened," I replied.

"How did you find out, Tom? Jake called me and told me. I didn't feel like staying the night there. Who could do such a thing?"

I dropped my fork onto my plate. It clattered, and everyone stared at me. "You don't know, do you?"

"What? I don't know the guy, but I feel bad about it." She searched my face for an answer.

Tom cleared his throat. "Aaron was one of the …"

"One of the what?" asked Karen.

Jess sat up straighter. "Karen, Tom's roommate was one of the guys who beat up that student."

Karen's face went ashen. Then she shook her head and said, "No. I know him. That can't be … How? Why?" The words came out so fast that it seemed as if she was chasing away the answers before they had time to take root in her mind.

Jake shifted in his seat. "You okay, Tom?" His voice said it all. He knew Tom and I weren't dating.

Karen looked to Jake, and then to Tom, and then her eyes finally settled on my face. Slowly, her gaze made its way down to Jess's hand, which now rested on mine.

"Shit, I feel like an ass," was all she said.

"Oh, please, Karen, don't feel that way," Jess reassured her. "Tom and Paige have tried to keep it quiet from everyone. Not just you."

Karen sucked in her breath. "And you didn't mind? You didn't mind that they pretended to date?" Honest Karen couldn't wrap her brain around the deception.

"She didn't tell me, actually. We ran into Tom and his boyfriend, ex-boyfriend now, at an art show. I'll admit that it rattled me some." Jess turned to me. "But at least Paige picked out a gay guy for her fake boyfriend—and she didn't even know it." She patted my cheek tenderly.

Karen fixed Jess with a defiant stare. "What do you mean, didn't know it? Didn't they plan it together?" Her tone was accusatory.

Mel laughed; this was the first time she had heard the full story. "Oh, that's perfect! Paige has always been clueless."

I feigned being hurt.

"You mean that Paige and Tom both thought the other was straight and used the other for cover?" Karen burst into laughter.

Jake joined in, chuckling, but all the while his eyes stayed on Tom.

Jess nodded. "Yes! You should have seen the look on Paige's face when she found out. I thought for sure she was going to have a heart attack, or faint."

Tom stabbed the air with his fork. "Now, hold on, I suspected it about Paige all along."

I waved that idea away. "Liar!" I accused.

His face crinkled into a heart-rending grin as he skewered a tamale.

Jess patted my thigh. It was good to hear everyone laugh, even if it was at my expense.

"Uh-oh, Paige, are you slowing down?" Santi waddled over and pointed at my plate.

I looked down at it. I still had more than ten tamales to go. "I got sidetracked." I defended my pathetic attempt.

"You only have one half hour to finish or no tequila for you." He waggled his finger in my face.

Marionette

"Hey, you didn't tell me there was a time limit." I straightened up in my chair, prepared to take the challenge more seriously.

He shrugged. "Only seems fair."

Karen looked to Santi, then to Jake and said, "Tequila? I've never tried it. I want some."

Santi put his palms in his air. "Tell you what, if Paige finishes that plate and Jess's plate, since I know Jess won't"—he winked at her—"all of you can have tequila shots for free."

My eyes glazed over. Jess still had five left on her plate. I had already eaten twelve of my own. Granted, they were small, but fifteen more seemed overwhelming.

But I didn't want to let my friends down. I sighed heavily. "You're on, Santi."

He rubbed his hands together. "*Muy bien*. I'll be back." His words sounded encouraging, and sinister.

"Shall I call an ambulance now or later," teased Jess.

"Oh, so funny." I looked at her plate, and she gleefully dumped her tamales onto mine.

I'm not sure how, but my stomach felt like it had immediately shrunk.

"Santi told me about the bet." Davie walked up. How was it that he was always around? "My money is on you, little lady." He walked behind Jess and leaned down. "Want to make it interesting, Jess?"

She turned to look him square in the face. "Not sure Santi would appreciate betting for anything but tequila in his restaurant."

Davie stepped back, chuckling. "You're probably right, just thought I'd ask." He turned to me. "Paige, give it hell, I know you can do it." Then he sauntered off, disappearing in the crowd like a ghost in the night.

"Come on, Paige. I've seen you eat more at Julia's," Tom

pleaded.

"No one can eat fifty eggs," said Jake.

Tom's head snapped up and he met Jake's stare. "I love that movie."

"*Cool Hand Luke.* It's a classic." Jake shrugged shyly.

Karen nudged her brother and nodded toward Tom, at which Jake turned three shades of scarlet.

Tom stared down at his plate.

Jess and I shared a look, and I wondered if the hamster in her head had already been set in motion. Mel couldn't help but laugh.

"Smooth, Karen," I said.

"What?" she tried to act innocent. Then she stood up. "These tamales are good. I'm going back for more."

Her brother, still embarrassed, decided to dish back some humiliation. "Stay away from the beans. I don't want you farting all night."

Instead of blushing, Karen looked proud of her flatulence. If we were at school, I was certain she would have melted into the floor from embarrassment. Here, now that she was part of the inner circle, she felt no shame. She felt included. Or at least that's what I wanted to think. That's how I felt: included. Not on the outside or afraid, but protected by friends.

Jake pointed to my pile of tamales. "Paige, you better get busy. I want free shots."

"Yeah," echoed Mel, who flashed an encouraging smile.

Tom looked at his plate and then at mine. I didn't want to let Tom down. Not that day or any day. Somehow, I felt connected to everyone at the table. Everyone had scattered to deal with the tragedy, and yet somehow, we had all found each other at Santi's.

I plunged my fork into one of the tamales, and Jess cringed as I shoved it all in my mouth. Seconds later, I was cramming more in. My stomach constricted, but I pushed the thought out of my mind.

Karen returned to the table with a pile of tamales larger than my own. I thought my eyes would burst out of my head.

"I wanted to offer my support the only way I know how," she said. "To jump in."

The thought touched me, but I didn't have time to speak, and my mouth was full anyway. I didn't think she'd appreciate me spraying her with tamale as I said thank you, so I nodded. She dug in. Together, we could do this.

Minutes ticked by. Then more.

"Holy shit," Jake said. "I think you two are actually going to do it."

Our plates were nearly empty. Santi returned with a tray bearing an entire bottle of tequila, six shot glasses, slices of lime, and a salt shaker.

"I wanted to show you what's at stake." His papa bear smile encouraged me.

As I plunged the last bit of tamale into my mouth, I had to force down the urge to puke. Karen gestured to the little that was left on her plate, "Feel free."

I shook my head. At that moment, I never wanted to eat another tamale.

Tom leaned over the table and speared Karen's tamale with his fork. "Thanks!"

"Next time I have a tamale fundraiser, Paige, you are not invited." Santi set the tray down and removed my plate. "I can't afford you."

I smiled weakly. I was victorious. Yet I felt like crap.

"No worries. I'm not sure I can ever eat another one."

He put on a hurt face. "*Mi dios*! Don't ever say such a thing to me." He waved his finger in my face. Then he turned, chuckling, and wandered away from the table.

Karen grabbed the bottle and poured out hefty shots. "What charity is this for?"

Jake answered. "I saw an ad in the school paper. It's for a young woman whose parents cut her off because she's gay. She needs to raise money to stay in school."

"Jake runs the gay group on his campus." Karen beamed proudly.

"Jake Cooper!" All of us turned to Jess. "We've exchanged a few emails," she explained. "I used to run the gay group at my school. Jessica McCrae."

"Oh, that's right. We never found a time to meet in person."

Karen steered the conversation back to the fundraiser. "So all of these people are helping." She looked impressed.

Jess wiggled in her chair. "I need to pee."

I noticed Mel trying to catch her eye, but Jess kept her eyes averted.

"Yes and no. Let's be honest, these are good tamales," said Jake.

"What are the odds that this was planned on the same day we found out about Aaron?" All of us had been avoiding the topic.

Jess returned to the table, all smiles.

"Okay, Karen. It's time for your first tequila shot."

Everyone prepared the lime and salt.

"Bottoms up!" Jake shouted.

Karen's face was priceless: all scrunched up and with tears forcing their way out of her clenched eyes. "Mah Gawd!"

"Not a fan?" asked Tom, licking his lips.

"Yes! Gimme some more." She snatched the bottle and poured

another shot for everyone.

I wasn't expecting that reaction, given her scrunched face. I tried to picture what she must look like in the midst of an orgasm. Then I remembered that Karen was still a virgin.

Two hours later, the bottle was nearly gone. Everyone, including Tom and Jake, took turns dancing with Santi, who was patient and strong enough to hold up any inebriated dancing partner. The only one of us who wasn't drunk, was Jess. She did her fair share of shots, but not one seemed to faze her.

Later that night, we settled Tom in on the couch and headed for bed.

I lay on my back, one arm under my head.

"You okay, Paige?" Jess flicked some hair off my cheek.

"I guess so. I just feel so …" I wasn't sure how to confess.

"What, honey?" she said sweetly, urging me to continue.

"I feel so guilty," I blurted out.

"For having a good time tonight?" Jess probed.

"No, not that. For turning Aaron into a monster." I finally uttered his name.

She cocked her head. "What are you talking about?"

I sighed. "Months ago, Aaron made a crack that the Broncos played like faggots and that's why they lost a game." I turned my head to face her. "I insinuated that gay bashers were actually fags."

Jess let out a long breath.

"You should have seen how mad he got. He started asking if I was accusing him of being a faggot. All of us laughed it off, but now …" I couldn't continue.

"Now you think it's your fault? That if you hadn't antagonized and embarrassed him in front of everyone, this wouldn't have happened?"

"Yeah."

"Paige, this isn't your fault. Aaron obviously has issues. And yes, you could be right; he might be gay. Studies prove that the likelihood is high. But don't for one second think this is your fault. Aaron and his friends made their decisions. They acted on them. This has nothing to do with you." She took my face in her hand and peered into my eyes. "This is not your fault."

I nodded, and hoped to God she was right.

"Now, you better get some rest. You have that French final in the morning."

I groaned. I had completely forgotten about the whole thing.

The next morning, I woke up early. Jess was already up making me an egg bagel for the drive. Tom was still sound asleep on the couch. I whispered a goodbye and left. Jess mouthed, "*Bonne chance.*"

When I arrived back at Jess's apartment that afternoon, Tom was still asleep and I was surprised to find Jess in the bedroom, curled up with a book. I glanced at the cover: *Don Quixote*.

"What, you aren't reading that in Spanish?"

"I couldn't find a copy in Spanish."

I sat on the bed and took my shoes off. "How come you aren't at work?"

She set the book aside and patted the spot next to her, gesturing for me to lie down. "Oh, I thought Tom could use a friend today. How did the test go?"

I shrugged. "Not sure, really. I always think I did horribly, and then when I get it back, I'm surprised that I got an A."

"You are always so hard on yourself." She ran her fingers along my arm, briefly stopping on one of my tattoos. "So, shall we try to set Jake up with Tom?"

I sat up. "Don't lie to me. I saw you talking with Jake last night when the rest of us were dancing. You already have a plan in motion, don't you?" I waved a finger in her face accusingly.

She put her palms up. "Maybe."

"And that's why you stayed home today."

"Maybe."

"No one has a chance, with you."

"Paige, I'm not sure what you mean." She placed a hand on her chest, as if she'd been struck by an arrow.

"Don't act innocent. You are always conniving."

"Conniving!"

I put my fingers to my mouth to shush her.

"I am not conniving, or devious, or anything." She defended herself.

I waved her away. "What's the plan?"

"Lunch and a movie later this afternoon."

"Will Karen be there?"

"Yes. Jake says she's pretty shaken up about the whole Aaron thing."

"Oh, that reminds me." I leaned over to grab a newspaper out of my backpack and tossed it onto Jess's lap.

An article about the attack had mentioned that a gay rights rally was planned on campus the following night.

"Are you going?" Jess asked.

"I haven't decided yet. Would you like to go?"

Jess bolted upright. "You mean I can invade your space?"

I laughed. "Might as well. Keeping you hidden hasn't worked out that well. But I probably won't introduce you to Minnie, if that's all right? Tom and Karen are one thing; she's a whole different ballgame."

"Oh my God! This is huge!" Jess waltzed to the bathroom and jumped in the shower while I picked up the novel and turned to page one. It wasn't unusual for us to read the same book at the same time. Of course, Jess always beat me. As I read, I heard her singing in the shower.

A knock on the door woke me, and I blinked a few times to figure out where I was. Then I remembered. Rubbing the sleep from my eyes, and wiping some drool off my face, I got up to see who was at the door.

Tom sat on the couch with a cup of coffee. The news was on—footage of Aaron's arraignment hearing. The sound was muted.

"Who's here?"

Tom shrugged. "Don't know, Jess answered it and then stepped outside." He turned his attention back to the TV, but the story was over, replaced by the weather report. Snow was predicted.

I casually walked to the window to peek outside. Davie—I just knew it! He had a knack for just showing up.

Davie was doing most of the talking. Occasionally, Jess nodded. When I sensed their conversation was winding down, I hurried to the kitchen so I wouldn't get caught snooping. When Jess walked in, I was pouring a cup of coffee.

"Who was at the door?" I felt horrible questioning her in front of Tom, but I needed to know if she would answer honestly.

"Davie. How was your nap?"

Tom studied me, an odd look on his face.

I dropped the Davie subject. "Fine. I guess I was more tired than I thought."

"Doesn't say much for *Don Quixote*."

"You were reading *Don Quixote*? I thought that book was out of print!" exclaimed Tom.

Jess whipped her head around, scowling.

I laughed and shook my head. "Oh, you're in for it now, Tom." I felt bad for the guy.

"What do you mean?" asked Tom, a little afraid.

"Just wait." I motioned with my head toward Jess.

The wait wasn't long. "What's the last book you read?"

Before he could answer, Jess added, "Not for school!" She crossed her arms.

"Uh …" Tom looked at me imploringly.

I nodded. "Yes, she's serious."

"Uh, I don't know." His voice was a whisper, and I barely heard the last word.

"Okay, before lunch at Julia's, we're taking Tom to the bookstore." Jess put up one palm and neither of us argued. Tom hung his head in shame.

"Now, Tom, I bet one of Julia's greasy sandwiches will perk you right up and cure that hangover. What do you say, Paige, are you ready?" She winked at me.

Chapter Twenty-Two

THE NIGHT OF the rally was crisp. People stamped their feet to stay warm, and Tom's nose was so bright red that Jake was already calling him Rudolph. I rubbed my hands together, and then blew into them, but the warmth was fleeting, so I repeated the process. I was already fed up with freezing my ass off, and it was only December.

Tom leaned in and whispered, "Don't look to your right, but Minnie is walking towards us."

I mumbled, "Thanks." Tugging on Jess's jacket, I motioned with my head to the other side of the quad.

"Hi, Jake," I heard Minnie say, and I was surprised that she had acknowledged him. However, I didn't stay to find out more, just lowered my chin into my jacket as Jess and I made our way to the student center. I was dying for a hot chocolate.

"I gather that was Minnie." Jess pulled my arm so she could stop briefly and glance back.

"Yes ... and Jenna's with her."

"Really? The tall blonde?"

I nodded.

MARIONETTE

"She's an Amazon." Jess sounded impressed.

"Yep. Come on, I'm freezing."

"Okay, you baby, it's not even that cold out." Jess rubbed my arms in an attempt to warm me up.

Turning around, I bumped into someone and without looking up, muttered, "I'm sorry."

"Paige?"

I froze.

"I wasn't expecting to see you here."

I stared into Liddy's face, speechless.

Jess stuck out her hand. "Hi, I'm Jess."

Liddy shook her hand, grinning like a fool.

I still hadn't moved. I'm not sure I had even taken a breath.

Liddy said her name and Jess knew immediately who she was.

"Oh!" Jess looked to me and then to Liddy. "Would you like a hot chocolate? We were heading in for one."

If I could have moved, I would have given Jess the "you can't be serious" look. But I was still pretending to be invisible, or a statue, and my brain wasn't functioning enough to decide what course to take.

"Thanks for the offer, but my friend is speaking next." Liddy said her goodbyes and patted my shoulder as she left.

Several seconds later, Jess said, "You can move now. Nice job imitating a statue, by the way. I don't think she knew you were there."

I moved my eyes slowly to the side but I couldn't see any trace of Liddy.

"Paige," squeaked Minnie. I looked to Jess, who was again doing her impression of a kid in a candy store. All of these people she had wanted to meet were now flocking to us like moths to a flame. Why had I thought inviting her was a good idea?

I turned around and Minnie gave me a hug. Then, not knowing what to do, I stood there, solid as an oak tree.

Minnie introduced herself.

"Hi, Audrey. I've heard so much about you. I'm Paige's best friend from back home."

I let out a silent sigh of relief.

Minnie made pleasant chitchat with Jess before she got down to business. "Paige, how is Tom doing? I still can't believe this." She waved a hand in the direction of the crowd.

I wasn't sure what Minnie meant by her statement.

"I guess he's okay, but it's not every day you discover you're living with a murderer." I corrected myself, "Or attempted murderer."

"To think Aaron is capable of such a …" she looked up at the stars, as if searching for the right word. "Atrocious act." She sounded completely disgusted. "To beat up someone just because he's gay … really, who does such a thing?" She shook her head fervently.

I wanted to remind her that she thought gays were repugnant. The words were about to leave my mouth when Jess piped up, "You never know what people are capable of." She tapped my foot to shut me up. "Audrey, would you like some hot chocolate?"

"Thanks, Jess, but I'm meeting some classmates here. One of my teachers is offering extra credit for anyone who came tonight. I need to check in."

I wanted to shout, "I knew it!"

"Oh, that's nice. Good luck finding them." Jess yanked my arm to get me away fast. When we were far enough away, she whispered, "At least she came. It's a step. Don't discourage her."

Jess was right, but I wasn't willing to admit it. Instead, I marched up to the counter and ordered two hot chocolates. Jess corrected me, and ordered five. Turning around I saw Jake, Tom, and Karen. I settled the bill and stood to the side, waiting for the next frozen dyke to place her order.

"I tried to stop her," Karen blurted.

"What?" I wiggled my toes to get feeling back into them.

"I tried to stop Audrey, so she wouldn't—" Karen didn't know what to say, so she pointed to Jess.

"Oh, thanks. Jess told her we were just friends. I think she still believes I'm dating Tom." The hot chocolates started to appear on the counter. No one said anything. Everyone ripped off the covers and breathed in the steam. "It's fucking cold out."

"I heard someone say it's minus twelve." Tom sipped his drink and gasped when he burned his tongue.

"Seriously, you thought it was ready to drink?" Karen shook her head. "Don't you see the steam?" She swirled her cup in front of his face.

Jess placed a hand on Tom's shoulder. "You okay?"

"Yeah." He stuck his burnt tongue out at Karen.

Karen turned to me and asked, "Who was the woman you were talking to before Audrey?"

Again, I turned into a statue.

"She's a friend of mine." Jess saved me.

"Oh, I wondered why you didn't speak, Paige. It looked like an awkward situation." Karen turned to her brother and said something, but I was too busy controlling my heart rate to pay attention. Tom eyed me, and I wondered if he remembered seeing me with Liddy. Thankfully, he didn't ask. I wasn't sure how many more shocks I could handle.

The five of us made our way back outside just as the news crews started to arrive. At first, I didn't see them, but when a reporter stuck a microphone in Karen's face, I ducked away. Shit! If my parents saw me at this rally, I was done for. Screwed! Sayonara!

Jess screened me from the camera and the four of us left Karen to her fifteen minutes of fame. I was sure she was talking about Jake and his suicide attempt, and I wondered how he felt about that. Tom placed his arm on Jake's back. I speculated that Tom was wondering the same thing.

When Karen rejoined the group, Jess asked, "Shall we head back?"

Everyone nodded, except for Karen. "I'm going to stay here tonight. I have a test tomorrow."

Tom didn't mention any of his finals, but surely he had some; it was finals week after all. I had one tomorrow evening. Neither Jess nor I quizzed him about it.

Later that night, I finally settled into bed after a piping hot shower. Even though I had blasted the heat in the car all the way home, I still couldn't feel my toes.

Jess came in and sat on the bed next to me. "So, Liddy is quite beautiful."

I was not expecting that comment.

"And I'm betting you haven't guessed she's gay."

My head snapped up. "What?" I did remember Liddy once referring to a girlfriend, but I thought she just meant a friend, like older women, who often called their female friends girlfriends.

"Think about it, Paige. She noticed you were playing the pronoun game and then one of her 'friends' was speaking at the rally. Yep, she's gay."

"But she doesn't look like a dyke."

Jess whacked me on the shoulder. "Neither do I, and I assure you that I'm gay."

MARIONETTE

"It seems like everyone I know is turning out to be gay."

"Maybe your school has gay water." Jess joked. "I wasn't expecting Minnie to be so, well, pretty."

I sat up. "You think Minnie's pretty? Now, come on, I agree Liddy's pretty, but Minnie looks like a mouse. Hence the name, Minnie Mouse. And what about her hair?" I waved her preposterous idea aside.

"That does make me feel somewhat better."

"What do you mean?" I examined her face.

"Well, I found out that not only is your roommate hot, but so is your therapist." Jess looked away.

"You're serious. You are actually jealous." I couldn't help but laugh.

"Stop laughing. It's hard being down here and knowing you're up there living it up."

"Living it up! I'm taking six classes so I can graduate early. Usually, I'm too busy studying, writing papers, or taking exams to live it up." I crossed my arms. "Besides, you're down here living it up." I paused, but then decided to dive in headfirst. "What did Davie want yesterday?" For the past day I had wanted to ask the question, but wanted us to be alone. It was now or never.

She stood up and headed to the bathroom. "He heard about Santi's fundraiser and wanted to learn how to throw one of his own." Jess disappeared into the bathroom, and I heard her turn the shower on.

Her response didn't sit well with me. I didn't have proof she was lying, but I felt it. Why? What was she keeping from me? Was she trying to protect me? Or was I being completely irrational? Not everyone was out to hurt me. Not everyone was controlled by my mother.

271

Chapter Twenty-Three

I LEFT TOM at Jess's on Friday morning. Friday was one of my busier days, with three finals and then therapy. Tom was curled up on the couch, engrossed in an Agatha Christie novel. Turns out he can't get enough of mysteries. Jess hooked him up at the used bookstore, and while I had been commuting back and forth, Tom had read two novels. Now, he was glued to *And Then There Were None*.

When it was time for my therapy appointment, I was greatly relieved. All of my finals were done, and I had a few weeks of breathing space until spring semester. Taking so many classes had its pluses and minuses.

Liddy was already sitting in the office when I rushed in. I wasn't late; she was early. Blowing on my hands to warm them up, I asked her if everything was all right.

"I know, I'm early today. Can you believe it?" She smiled mischievously.

"No, I can't. Are you sure I'm not late?"

Instead of answering, she gestured to a cup. "I picked up some hot chocolate. I can't believe how cold it's been this week. I nearly

Marionette

froze at the rally."

The mere reference to the rally stilled my heart.

Liddy continued casually, "Jess is a lovely woman."

I picked up the hot chocolate and cupped it with both hands, refusing to speak.

"I'll be honest, Paige, I wasn't expecting to see you there with Jess. That was bold and I'm proud of you."

"It's a little more complicated than that. I wasn't proclaiming anything. I was supporting some friends."

She watched me curiously. "How so?"

I explained about Tom, Aaron, Karen and her brother. "As long as we're being honest, I wasn't expecting to see you there, either. I thought I would be perfectly safe bringing Jess. I didn't expect to run into you, or my homophobic roommate."

She laughed. "I wish I could have seen your face when your roommate showed up. I know how you reacted to me."

"Didn't your mom teach you not to laugh at people? Or don't they teach that in shrink school?" I tried to sound defensive.

"I'm not laughing at you, but with you. How's Tom? Is he the guy I saw you with at the student center weeks ago?"

"Yes. I wondered if you'd noticed. Why didn't you ask before now?" I sipped the hot chocolate, which burned pleasantly all the way down until I felt the cold dissipating from my fingertips. "Thanks for this." I raised the cup.

"You're welcome. I felt bad about rushing off the other night."

"Does that mean you lied about your friend speaking?" I saw a ray of light. Maybe Jess was wrong. I was tired of her being right all of the time.

"She spoke, but I would have preferred going someplace warm. However, I didn't want you to go into cardiac arrest." She winked.

"And you didn't know Tom was gay?"

I threw my arms up in the air, nearly spilling my hot chocolate. "Am I the only one who didn't know? I didn't know you were gay either!" As soon as the words slipped out, I sucked in air hoping to retrieve them, which only made Liddy laugh.

She pulled her notepad out from under her leg.

"Time to get down to business?" I said.

"Not unless you want to talk about me being gay, but I was hoping to talk about your sister Abbie." Her eyes sparkled.

"Abbie? Why? We aren't that close. Besides, didn't we cover that already?" I fidgeted in my chair.

"I'm curious. Do you think she ever had an inkling about Alex?"

I thought for a moment. "Huh, I guess I never thought about it. Now that I know, it seems so obvious. All three of us look so much alike. And we all resemble our father more than our mothers."

"You don't think your mom ever slipped up around her?"

"As much as my mom hates me, I don't think she's that much closer to Abbie. I don't know how to explain it." I leaned forward and placed my palms together, as if in prayer. "No one in our home likes any other person. There's no alliance, no friendship, no camaraderie. It's all-out war. As much as I despise my father, I hate my mother more."

"For what she did to Alex?"

"Yes! And to me."

"Can you explain that?" Her face urged me to say it out loud, not just drop hints.

"A Lego incident ruined my life. When my mom stepped on that damn piece, my life became a virtual hell. She not only held it against me and turned me into a slave, but she convinced me that I was a worthless piece of shit that didn't matter to anyone."

"Did you hate Abbie for not coming forward?"

"Damn right I did!"

Liddy winced some. I had said the words much louder than I'd planned on. "Good," she responded finally.

"Good?" I stood up and leaned against the wall, my arms crossed. "What's good about it? How Abbie could watch me suffer everyday for something I didn't do still baffles me. To be so unfeeling. So selfish. So ... I don't even know the right words for it. God, what a fucking cunt!"

Liddy started to speak, but I cut her off. "Don't say *good* again. I don't care if you think it's good that I'm getting in touch with my feelings."

She nodded once and gestured for me to continue.

I slumped back down in my chair. "And for my mother to seize on something to torture me, just to get back at my dad, what a monster. Not that he even noticed. For years, I was the pariah in the family. Still am, but now I know why. I was the only one who didn't do anything wrong. Abbie lied. My father lied. My mother—she's the worst of the bunch. She lies, manipulates—kills. I'm sure, though, she has my father's help."

"Does that make it easier? Finally knowing the truth?"

"No." My voice came out in a whisper—puny, ineffectual. I rubbed my forehead. "I wish I had it back."

"What?"

"My childhood. I wish I had it back."

Liddy looked stunned, but remained silent.

"I wish I knew what it was like ... to be loved. Oh, I have Jess and that feels good, but I'll never have parents who love me. I'll never know what that feels like. Every milestone in my life will be celebrated as if I'm an orphan. It's worse, though, having a family that just doesn't give a damn, that just wished I'd go away or die for that matter. The entire time I've been at school, I haven't called them or seen them. And I'm willing to bet they're just fine with that arrangement. They think that as long as they pay my college tuition, that's all I need. I didn't even hear from them on my birthday. Maybe they think I'm dead. They've hoped for it for so long. And who knows, they could be plotting my death right now."

"What was Alex's life like?"

I grunted out of disgust. "Worse in some ways. Her father kicked the shit out of her a lot. Thinking back on it, I wonder if he'd found out that Alex was the product of an affair. He had to know his wife was magically getting money from somewhere." I stopped to think. "I'm surprised my father had the balls to live right across the street from his bastard. Maybe he relished it when everyone said that Alex and I looked so much alike, maybe he felt more like a man. A conqueror. He loves to control things. And that's what we were: things. Not children." I picked up my cup and took a drink; the hot chocolate had grown cold and chunky.

"From an early age, we daydreamed about leaving. Alex loved *The Adventures of Huckleberry Finn* and wanted to float away on a raft." I stopped and smiled somberly. Closing my eyes, I envisioned Alex smoking a corncob pipe and steering a raft down the Mississippi River in search of freedom.

Liddy shifted in her chair.

I snapped back to reality. "Of course, my father probably loved living across the street from his mistress. It was another way to drive my mother insane. You can't take anything for granted when it comes to him. Everything is Machiavellian. Everything! If he asked me to pass the salt during dinner, I would spend the rest of the meal wondering what he really meant. Did he only want salt, or was he

MARIONETTE

hinting that he knew something? Or was he threatening to send me away to a salt mine, or whatnot? I know it sounds insane, but that's how I've felt my entire life. Nothing was ever as it seemed. No one was ever as they seemed. There were hidden messages in everything. Codes. Nuances."

"It's hard to live your life, thinking like that."

"Trust me, it drives people I'm close to insane. Jess tries to be patient, but it's not easy living with someone who has so many demons." Davie's face flashed into my mind. Was this an instance of letting my past cloud my judgment? Was he just a nice guy? One of Jess's friends, maybe? Why couldn't I let it go? Why couldn't I trust her and move on, and not ruin the relationship with my doubts?

"Are you okay?" Liddy lowered her head and made eye contact.

I roused myself from my thoughts, realizing that several seconds had ticked away without either of us speaking. "Uh, yeah. You know, I'm sorry. This week really has taken it out of me. Do you mind if we call it a day?"

Before she could answer, I was preparing to take flight. Liddy jumped out of her chair, but instead of reading me the riot act, she wrapped her arms around me. "Take care, Paige." Then she handed me one of her cards. "Give this to Tom. I'm sure I can talk to his teachers discreetly. And if he wants to talk, I'm here."

I thanked her and then ran down the hallway, up the flight of stairs, and crashed through the back door. Not even five minutes had passed and I was already in my car, heading to Jess's.

I wanted to apologize to Jess for questioning Davie. My craziness had to be controlled. Losing Jess would be catastrophic, especially over something so inane. If I pushed her away, it would be another victory for my father. And for my mother. I couldn't let it happen. I would *not*. All of these years I had let them have power over me, and it was time to take back the control.

In the apartment, Jess and Tom sat at the kitchen table, drinking tea and plunging shortbread into their teacups. Jess's smile radiated happiness when she saw me.

Why would I want to push her away?

"Hey, we weren't expecting you for another hour or so." She jumped out of her seat, gave me a peck on the cheek, and then busied herself making me a cup of tea.

I flicked Liddy's card towards Tom. "Give her a call. She'll get all of your absences excused for you."

Jess peered over Tom's shoulder and gave me a quizzical look.

"You found a shrink to help me out?" Tom looked touched.

"Don't give me too much credit. She offered to help." I eased into a seat across from him.

"How did she find out about me?"

"I talked about you … in today's session." I mumbled the last words and avoided his eyes.

Jess nearly dropped the kettle onto the floor.

Tom nodded.

"She also said if you want to talk, make an appointment."

"Is she any good?" His words came out slowly, and I felt as though I could see every letter forming in a bubble over his head.

Jess still stood at the counter, the kettle dangling in her hand. I could tell she was hanging on every word.

"Yeah. It took me some getting used to, but yeah, she's good."

Tom scrutinized the card, noticing the Japanese writing on the back. He looked up at me, questioning it.

"It's a Japanese proverb: Even monkeys fall from trees."

Tom cocked his head, not following.

I shrugged. "It just means everyone can make a mistake. No

one's perfect." I was tempted to raise my sleeve to show my tattoo, but I held back.

He tucked the card into his wallet. Jess collected herself and finished pouring my tea. When she sat down next to me, she patted my hand, but didn't dwell on the subject. That wasn't her style. Jess simply acknowledged, and then moved on to the next subject.

"Do you feel like helping out at Julia's tonight? She's hosting a fundraiser for Davie."

"For Davie? What's that about?" I controlled my tone so I didn't sound either displeased or suspicious.

"His son has leukemia. He's raising money for hospital bills." Jess sipped her tea and stared blankly across the room.

Instantaneously, I felt like the biggest schmuck in the entire world. That was why Jess always talked to him in private. She was helping him! Jess would never share anyone's secrets unless the person didn't mind. Privacy mattered. Loyalty mattered. Friendship mattered. And I had questioned her friendship and her loyalty. God, I was an ass—a complete and total asshole.

"I would love to. When does it start?" I dipped the shortbread into my tea and then relished the wet, gooey concoction as I slipped it into my mouth.

"Six. But we might want to get there early to have dinner. I have a feeling we'll need our strength. I've heard it will be a packed house tonight. Can Tom borrow your car?"

I didn't expect the question and looked in his direction. "You aren't working tonight?"

Julia had let him pick up some shifts during the week so he wouldn't go completely stir crazy. Since he worked in the kitchen, he didn't have to talk to people and he could keep his mind occupied.

Tom shook his head, embarrassed.

"He has a date with Jake tonight." Jess beamed.

Tom fidgeted with his napkin.

Jess always had her fingers in so many pies that it was hard for me to keep up. Fixing up Tom. Helping Davie raise money. Taking care of me. And all of the other junk I didn't even know about. Once more, I marveled at her energy and desire to help others. How could I have suspected her or Davie? It made me feel queasy. Here was a father coping with his son's illness, and I had envisioned him working for my mother and biding his time to bump me off. Despicable.

Later that night, when all of the customers had left, Mel, Jess, Julia, Davie, and I all sat around a table and devoured the leftover sandwiches.

"Thank you." Davie made eye contact with each of us and raised his beer each time. "Thank you. Because of all of you, I feel … for the first time … a … a sense of relief. Thank you." He placed his hand on his heart and sat back down, wiping his eyes, too emotional to say more.

After a few minutes, Julia told him that after all of the credit card slips were accounted for, Jess would deliver the money to him. He left the restaurant with a huge grin on his face.

"I have no idea how the man deals with all the stress," said Julia, as she got up and went into the back of the kitchen.

Right at that moment, Tom and Jake rushed in.

"Paige, we have to go." Tom's face was flushed and he motioned for me to get up pronto.

"What's going on?" I asked as I stood.

"Karen's in the hospital," replied Jake.

Having heard the commotion, Julia rushed in, her hand on her chest. "What happened?"

Marionette

"They don't know. Mom said they're running some tests."

Tom started to pull me to the door. "Wait." Looking over my shoulder, I asked Jess, "Aren't you coming?"

Julia and Mel exchanged a nod, and Jess hopped out of her seat, trying not to show too much glee at being invited to invade my space again. Karen was sick, after all.

Jenna and Minnie sat in the waiting room. When Jenna stood to shake Jess's hand, I almost fell to the ground in hysterics. She was well over a foot taller than Jess and was dressed in track pants and a hoodie. Jess wore a skirt and sweater. It was like watching a giant say hello to the town princess.

Minnie stood and gave me a hug. Twice in one week. "Isn't this awful, Paige?"

"Yes, what happened?"

"No clue," Jenna said. "I came home from practice pissed because Karen had skipped it. Then I found her on her bed, writhing in pain holding her stomach." Jenna didn't show much concern. She seemed more upset about Karen skipping practice just for a bellyache.

"You should have seen Jenna, Paige. She picked Karen up, threw her over her shoulder, and carried her all the way to the parking lot." Minnie glanced at Jenna, obviously admiring her strength.

I bet she could have picked up Jess with her pinky finger.

Jake and Tom went to talk to the front desk nurse to see Karen and the rest of us sat silently on the uncomfortable plastic chairs.

"Do you think that machine works? I'm thirsty." Minnie eventually broke the silence.

I followed her gaze to a soda vending machine that bore a huge sign stating: Out of Order.

"Give it a go."

Jenna contained a smirk. Minnie hopped up, pulled out a crisp dollar bill and put it in the slot. When the machine ate her dollar, she clapped her hands and hit the Dr. Pepper button. Nothing happened. She hit the Pepsi button. Still nothing.

She turned around and glowered at me.

"What? Didn't you see the sign?"

Jenna couldn't contain her laughter any more.

"Come on, Audrey." Jess stood. "I'll help you find a different machine." As they turned the corner, Jess shot me a nasty look.

"Why is this my fault?" I threw my arms up in the air.

Jenna shrugged and turned to the TV. SportsCenter was on.

The two new best friends returned with sodas for everyone and enough candy bars to feed an army.

"Who knows how long we'll be here," said Jess.

I selected a Snickers and a Pepsi. Jess gave the rest of the goods away and then headed for the chair next to Jenna. "So, what are we watching?" She popped the top of her Mountain Dew and took a slurp.

Jenna turned to her, looking at Jess as if she had bats flying around her head, and grumbled, "SportsCenter."

"Paige tells me you play basketball."

"Yeah."

I continued watching, wondering if Jess would go down in flames for the first time.

"Tough luck last week. If it weren't for that bad call, you guys would have won—at least that's what the paper said." Jess casually took a sip of her soda and gave me a smirk.

Jess's comment perked Jenna right up. "It was a *horrible* call. The NFL has instant replay, why can't we?" She went on to give Jess the play-by-play of the whole game.

Marionette

I had to give Jess credit: she looked plausible as a basketball fan. I knew for a fact that she had never watched a game—or at least not a college game. But she read every newspaper cover to cover, even the classifieds and obituaries. One of her hobbies was to read the obituaries and to average the age. I found it odd.

Tom returned, and I motioned to our stash of soda and candy bars. After making his selection, he sat down next to me.

"How is she?" asked Minnie.

Tom chuckled. "Rolling about on the bed in agony. I've never seen someone put on such a show."

"Tom!" Minnie yelled.

He shut up, but we shared a smile when Minnie wasn't looking. Jenna was still telling Jess about the last game.

Tom nodded to them, and I shrugged. "The bad call in last week's game."

Tom nodded again. I wasn't positive, but I think he muttered, "Bullshit," under his breath. Every week there was a "bad call" or Jenna's teammates let her down. It was never Jenna. She never failed. Others failed her.

Jake approached, all smiles. "I take it Karen's okay?" I asked.

"Oh, she's still suffering." Jake tried to stop smiling and put on a serious face.

"What's the joke?" asked Tom.

"Well, you know how she's always farting?" Jake rubbed his hands together, looking for the words.

All of us nodded, even Jess who had only recently met Karen.

"Turns out she's lactose intolerant."

Minnie put her hand to her mouth and muttered, "Oh no. We had cheese enchiladas for dinner."

"And she drank four glasses of milk," added Jenna.

"Four glasses?" Normally, Jess wasn't fazed by things, but this shocked her.

"In her defense, they are small juice glasses," I offered, thinking of the tiny glasses in the dorm room.

Minnie shook her head. "No, they were tall glasses. We went out for dinner."

"So, what, she has the shits?" asked Tom.

"And the farts." Jake lost it and buckled over in laughter.

Even Minnie couldn't help but join in.

"That does explain a lot," I said. I caught Jess's eye and beckoned for her to separate from the group.

"I want to leave," I whispered in her ear. I hated hospitals. Now that I knew it wasn't serious, it was time to skedaddle.

"What about Tom?"

Before I answered, Jess walked up to him and they talked quietly. Then she said her goodbyes and told Jenna she had faith they would win their next game. Jenna nodded gravely.

"So, what about Tom?" I asked.

"He's staying with Jake."

"Another success story for you," I teased. "Do you ever fail, Jess?"

She looked away. "I don't feel like going home just yet."

"Where do you want to go? It's three in the morning."

As we took our seats in the car, she said, "Let's just drive."

"Can I take you somewhere? Don't worry, it'll take some time to get there, so you'll get your drive." I squeezed her leg.

She took her sweater off, bundled it up like a pillow, and placed it against the car window. "I'm all yours. Take me wherever you want."

It felt good to hit the highway. The last week had involved a lot of driving, but I was always rushing from point A to point B with no time to enjoy the thrill of driving. The road was completely empty. I headed east. Soon the sun would start to rise over the road before us. I always loved seeing the rays peeking over the horizon, offering hope. The black purple sky just before dawn was my favorite time of day. I still felt protected by the darkness of night, but comforted by the thought that light would soon follow. Transition. I loved transitions, no matter how fleeting.

Jess fiddled with the radio and settled on classical music. Of course she had flown right by the channel playing U2, my favorite. But I didn't mind too much. The style fit the mood. Haunting—there was no other way to describe it.

We arrived much earlier than I had planned. The sky was still pitch black and the place was closed. I parked the car, and as soon as Jess felt the vehicle stop, she opened her eyes.

"We're here," I said.

She peered out through the windshield and then looked at me in disbelief. In a voice still thick with sleep, she said, "You brought me to a cemetery?"

"Yes."

"Okay." She pulled her sweater on. "Where to?"

"Follow me." I led her to the gate, which had been broken for years. The funding was dire and it seemed they only mowed a quarter of the place at a time, not being able to afford to take care of the entire property. They did their best. Personally, I liked the overgrown look, as if the natural world were reclaiming the lost souls. It was an old cemetery and each headstone was different. Some featured angels, others broken columns signifying a life cut short. It had character and a quiet beauty.

The grave I was heading for didn't have any significant marker.

In the old days, it would have resembled a pauper's grave, but in today's world, it was a grave designed to hide the dead. To be forgotten. Not to be visited. I had combed the cemetery for weeks until I'd stumbled on it—literally. The night I had discovered Alex, it was because a small marker had poked out of the ground and tripped me.

Happenstance.

Since that night, I had visited as often as I could, usually at this time of day. It was the time of day when Alex and I were supposed to run away together. It comforted me to visit her at sunrise. To let her know that I had not forgotten. That I would never forget her. No matter how hard everyone wanted me to.

Jess stood there staring at the ground, shivering. I took my jacket off and wrapped it around her shoulders. Normally, the cold didn't affect her.

"Paige, you'll freeze," she protested through clattering teeth.

I waved her words away. Out of the corner of my eye, I spied something white behind the minuscule marker. When I leaned down, I saw it was one white tulip. Looking around, I tried to make sense of it.

"What's wrong, you look like you've seen a gh—" Jess bowed her head. "I'm sorry."

"No worries." I gathered my strength. "Jess, I'd like you to meet Alex." I gestured to the ground.

"Your best friend?"

"Yes, and my sister."

Her eyes darted to mine, searching for the punch line.

There was none.

"But I—"

"Alex is my half-sister."

Marionette

"How come you never told me? Why the secret?"

"Why indeed?" I looked towards the horizon, watching a faint purple color make an appearance near the horizon. "I love it here at this time of day."

"I always wondered where you went on your drives in the middle of the night." She took my hand. "It's beautiful."

"Yes, it is." I stood stock still, watching the mauve sky turn darker and then start to fade, giving way to a soft pink hue. "There's a diner around the corner, if you would like to grab some breakfast. I'm sure you have tons of questions."

Jess squeezed my hand. "Thank you, Paige."

I glanced at her, puzzled. "What for?"

"For finally letting me in completely." She rested her head on my chest and put her arm around my waist. "Give me a moment here before we go."

"You're the only person I trust completely."

Her grip around my waist tightened. "I hope that never changes."

"I don't see how it could."

She pulled away. "I could use a hot cup of coffee."

"Sure. I think you'll like this dive."

Two hours later, I was polishing off a second round of pancakes and bacon.

"I can't believe it." Jess shook her head in shock.

"It shocked the hell out of me, too."

"Poor Abbie," said Jess.

I set my coffee cup down heavily. "How so?"

"She's suffered a loss as well, Paige." Jess stirred more sugar into her fourth cup of coffee. "And she's all alone at school."

"I doubt she even knows. Besides, she's good at keeping her own secrets."

"Paige, that was years ago. She was just a child—"

"It doesn't change the fact that she's never come forward."

Jess put her palms up. "I understand, I do. It's just a darn shame, all this stuff your father and mother have put everyone through."

I laughed. "A darn shame? Careful, Jess, you came close to swearing."

She playfully slapped my hand. "I think we should pick up more shifts at Julia's. Knowing this," she faltered, "we might have to make a quick getaway if something gets leaked. I'm amazed they kept it this quiet this long. It's only a matter of time."

I sighed deeply. "I'm not so sure. They seem like Teflon. All of the shit slides off them and the rest of us have to muck it up."

Chapter Twenty-Four

WE HAD THE apartment to ourselves. As I lay on the couch with my head on Jess's lap, I kept thinking, *It's so quiet.* Tom was out with Jake. Karen wasn't here. No Julia. No Mel. And thank God, no Weasel. It was just the two of us.

Jess ran her hand through my hair. "What are you thinking?"

"How wonderful it is to have some alone time."

"It is nice, isn't it?" Jess looked around, appreciating not seeing anyone. No one invading our time.

The quiet didn't last long. Within minutes, someone knocked on the door.

I pressed against Jess in the hope that she wouldn't get up to answer the door. She pushed me away, laughing. "Stop that. It might be important."

"What you mean is, it might be a way for you to butt into someone's life and fix everything."

Jess whipped her head around and smiled when she saw that I was teasing. Then she opened the door, or tried to.

The person on the other side shoved the door right into her, crushing her against the wall. I jumped off the couch.

"Where is it?" Davie waved a knife in Jess's face.

For a moment, I didn't react.

Jess moved away from the door and positioned herself in front of me.

"Where is it? Answer me!" Davie brandished the knife, waving it in her face. I could see his hand shaking violently from fear. His eyes bulged. His breathing was erratic. He was barely in control.

"You know where it is, Davie," Jess said calmly.

I tried to look around her, to search her face. How did she know what he was talking about? Why was he threatening her with a knife? What in the fuck was going on?

Perhaps Jess sensed my impulse to rush Davie, because she shoved me further behind her.

"How could you? I thought we were friends … How could you? My son. You stole from my son!" He tapped his chest with the knife. His words oscillated from barely audible to high pitched.

"Listen, Davie, this isn't a good time. Why don't we talk about it tomorrow? I'm sure Richard and I will be willing to sit down with you and work this out."

Richard? Her boss. How was he involved?

Davie laughed manically. "Yeah, sure, Jess. I'm sure Richard would love to hear my side."

"Davie, can you put the knife away? I can't talk to you like this." Jess motioned with both hands for him to set it down on the table.

"*You* can't talk like this. Like I give a fuck." Davie moved forward, as if about to strike.

Jess jumped back, and I closed my eyes. Nothing happened.

That's when it hit me: I had to do something.

I sidestepped around Jess, straight for Davie.

MARIONETTE

"Paige, don't." Jess's voice was calm but her eyes betrayed her panic.

I turned to Davie. "I'm sorry, I don't know what's going on, but I like you, Davie. How can I help?" I put my palms up, showing I wasn't going to make a move for the knife.

"You can get my money back."

"What money?" I nodded sympathetically, keeping my voice soothing.

"The money I raised for my son." He darted towards Jess and then stopped abruptly. "The money she stole!"

I eyed him for a second and then slowly turned to look into Jess's eyes. I couldn't comprehend what I saw.

"I didn't steal it, Davie. You owed it," she stated bluntly. "What did you expect me to do? I didn't take it all, just what you owed." She planted her feet firmly, bracing for whatever might happen next.

"Wh—?" I couldn't get the question out. Things were starting to crystallize in my head.

"That money was for my son."

"You should have paid your debt, then." Jess crossed her arms defiantly.

"I was working on that. If I don't pay the hospital, they won't continue treating my son."

"Davie, that's why I want you to sit down with Richard. Explain it to him."

My gaze darted back and forth between the two, as if I were watching a demented game of ping pong.

"How would you feel, losing someone you love?" Davie stared at Jess, demanding an answer.

Jess didn't respond, just took a deep breath. Maybe she knew what would happen next, but I didn't.

In a fluid movement, Davie grabbed me and held the knife to my throat.

I was too shell-shocked to react.

"How does *that* make you feel, Jess?" He pressed the knife to my skin and I felt a twinge of pain.

"This isn't helping your situation. You know what will happen." Jess's hard voice stunned me.

He backed away toward the door, dragging me with him.

"All right, stop!" Jess shouted. Finally, I saw her resolve cracking, but it didn't make me feel any better.

He kept dragging me to the door, the knife still scraping my neck.

"I'll give you the money!"

"Where is it?" he demanded.

"In the back room."

All of my breath left my body. Part of me still believed that she had nothing to do with this.

"Go get it, or I swear I'll—"

I felt the knife dig in, but didn't feel any pain. How was Jess involved in this?

Jess dashed from the room and returned faster than I would have thought possible. She set down a wad that was wrapped in pink paper with a string tied around it. Very girly. It was not the first time I had seen a package like that.

"Open it up!" he shouted.

Jess complied and I saw a flash of green.

I could feel my eyes bulging from my head and I realized at that moment that the pressure from the knife and his arm was cutting off my air. I pulled at his arms frantically.

"Let her go, Davie." Each word was said with force.

MARIONETTE

He relaxed his grip and pushed me to the side, but as I started to move away, he said, "Just so you know who you're dealing with."

I saw him jump at me with the knife and I put my hands up to protect myself, feeling a stinging sensation on my right wrist. Jess rushed forward and landed a few punches, but so many arms and legs were flailing about, I couldn't determine if it was Jess hitting me or Davie.

Davie grabbed the money from the table and bolted out the front door.

A warm sensation oozed down my arm, into my hand.

Jess didn't move towards me. "Are you hurt?"

I continued to stare at the table, where the wad of cash used to be.

"Paige, are you hurt?" She inched closer. Was she afraid?

I slowly lifted my head. I felt as if everything was being played in slow motion.

I felt Jess reach for my arm and apply pressure.

"Shit!" she shouted, but the word was barely audible. She pulled her shirt off and wrapped it around my arm, told me to hold it in place, and then rushed into the kitchen. I heard her on the phone, but didn't bother to listen. The words were so far away.

"Help is on the way," she said, reappearing around the kitchen wall. "Why don't you sit down?" She disappeared behind the wall again. I think she made another phone call. Slowly, I turned my wrist so I could see it. A brownish stain was seeping through the shirt.

Why was everything happening so slowly? Why couldn't I hear anything?

I glimpsed Jess moving toward me, but she was moving so slowly I didn't think she'd ever actually reach me. Maybe I was drifting away from her. Then I felt her arms on my shoulders guiding me to the couch. Her lips moved. I craned my neck to catch her words, as if they were falling out of the sky into my ears.

Then I heard a snap.

My cheek burned. Jess had slapped me.

"Jesus, I wish he would hurry up. You're in shock." She reached for the afghan on the back of the couch and wrapped me up in it.

I wondered who *he* was, but didn't ask.

It seemed like hours later that a man carrying a black bag walked into the room. He unraveled the cloth around my wrist and I saw a gash where my monkey tattoo used to be. The blood smeared all over my arm reminded me of a painting Jess and I had recently seen at the art exhibition. What was the name of the artist?

Another man entered, and he and Jess stood in the corner, whispering to each other. Then that man left abruptly and Jess was at my side again, talking sweetly. I couldn't hear her words.

When I saw the needle, I realized this was the same guy who had stitched me up once before. But this time, I hadn't cut myself. Davie. Davie had cut me.

Why?

I couldn't remember.

I stared into Jess's eyes, which were filled with tears. One large tear plopped onto my jeans and I watched it spread and melt into the denim. What painting did that remind me of?

Jess said something, but not to me, and the man nodded. Then I saw him plunge the needle into a vial of clear liquid. Before I could react, the needle pricked my skin and entered my vein.

Almost immediately, I let out a long sigh and leaned back on the couch, letting them fiddle with my arm. Their fingers poked and prodded my arm and along my neck. I shut my eyes on the whole thing. I felt like I was drifting off. A smile crept onto my face and I

MARIONETTE

thought, "It's over. The pain, it's over."

I had always wondered how I would die. Now I knew. And I wasn't scared. I was relieved.

Chapter Twenty-Five

WHAT WAS THAT racket? Cautiously, I pried my eyes open and looked around the room. My head hurt. My neck itched and burned. There was pain. Where was the pain?

I heard a scuffle outside the window and ducked under the blanket, fearful. Then I heard a cry. *Not human*, I thought. I lifted the duvet off my head and peeked out the window. Two cats fought briefly and then the loser scurried away. The victor licked one of its front paws.

Why did I hurt?

I started to pat my body to localize the pain. Slowly, events started to flood my mind. Reaching for my wrist, I winced.

"The cut isn't too bad."

Jess leaned against the doorframe, her head resting on the wood. She looked beat. I couldn't remember the last time I had seen her tired. A blanket wrapped her petite body and she looked tiny. Frail.

I wanted to rush to her, hold her, make it better, but something held me back.

Davie. Jess. The pink money package.

MARIONETTE

I rubbed my eyes, trying to banish the thoughts. "Why?" I croaked.

She didn't bother pretending. "It's a long story, Paige." Her words sounded flat and lifeless.

"Why can't I think straight?" I couldn't move either, I noticed.

"Steve gave you something so you could sleep."

"Can I have more?"

Jess straightened up. A pitcher of water stood on the nightstand along with a bottle of pills. Cracking the lid off the bottle, she dexterously separated one pill and handed it to me. I eyed it suspiciously, but I didn't want to face anything at the moment. Jess handed me a glass of water. After I had swallowed the pill, she started to get up.

"Don't go."

She sat down hesitantly, not saying anything.

"I don't want to be alone."

She held my hand as I felt the medicine slowly kicking in. "What happened to Davie?"

"I don't know." She turned her face away from me. "It's out of my hands." Her voice seemed full of sadness. "This isn't how I wanted it to end."

I wanted to ask if she meant Davie, or us, but sleep overcame me.

The next time I awoke, it was dark out. The clock displayed 7:00, but I couldn't make out if it was morning or night. Jess wasn't in the room, and I smelled bacon cooking. My stomach rumbled. I tried to remember when I had last eaten.

When I walked into the kitchen, Jess had her back to me and was busily flipping pancakes, bacon, and hash browns. She looked so innocent in her violet robe and penguin slippers. How did all of this happen?

I cleared my throat and she turned abruptly, armed with her spatula. My palms darted into the air. "Jesus, it's just me!"

She lowered her weapon. "Sorry. I haven't slept much, and I'm a little jumpy."

The black circles around her eyes made it hard to see her eyeballs. Lines creased her forehead, and I noticed she hadn't showered lately. Then again, neither had I. All of a sudden, I had a fierce urge to be clean.

"Do you mind if I hop in the shower?"

She nodded that it was fine, but when I went to leave the room, she said, "Wait."

I turned back to her.

"Don't get your bandage wet."

I nodded, disappointed. Things felt awkward, but how could they not? Jess usually set things right, but she was more out of sorts than me. I undressed carefully as I waited for the water to warm up. Once I had removed my shirt and bra, I looked in the mirror. My neck had dozens of microscopic scrape marks, which weren't all that noticeable unless you really looked for them, more resembling pimples, or a rash. However, they itched like hell and burned when I scratched them. A bruise was forming on my neck as well.

Sighing, I removed my jeans and stepped into the shower. I couldn't get my right arm wet, so I did the best I could shampooing my hair with one arm. I didn't even bother with conditioner. Then I lathered soap all over and rinsed off. The shower took less than three minutes.

When I stepped out, Jess was waiting for me with a bathrobe and a towel.

MARIONETTE

"I thought you might need help."

Neither of us spoke as she dried me off and wrapped the bathrobe around me.

"Why don't you sit down so I can change your bandage?" She gestured to the toilet and I sat down heavily on the lid.

The sight of the gash made my stomach turn. If Davie had been around the day I'd tried to kill myself, I would have been successful. Not much time would have been needed.

"Do you think he can fix it?" I asked.

Jess looked up at me, tears brimming in her eyes. "What?"

"My tattoo. Why couldn't Davie have sliced the saying you chose?"

She laughed half-heartedly. "I'm pretty sure Raul can fix it."

"Good." I thought for a moment. "Of course, this is more fitting."

She cocked her head. "How so?"

"Well, another monkey fell out of a tree."

She squeezed my hand. "You ready to eat?"

I thought for sure she would ask me what I meant, but maybe she was scared to.

"I'll get the food ready," I insisted. "Why don't you shower?"

Silencing her protest, I shut the bathroom door and stayed there until I heard the shower stream. My mind was racing. I briefly considered walking out of the front door and never coming back. Before, only Jess would look for me if I disappeared, but now, even she might not. She might think I didn't want to be found, especially by her. This was the perfect moment for me to do it. I would never see my parents, sister, or Jess again. A clean break.

Placing my ear to the door, I tried to tell whether she was still in the shower. Then I heard her singing, one of her sad Irish ballads. Her voice, full of melancholy and tenderness floated in the air. For a moment, I thought I had lost my mind, which seemed to search the air above me to find the right one of her words to take with me.

Then I heard Jess twist the shower nozzle off. I wasn't sad to have missed my opportunity. Scurrying into the kitchen, I grabbed a couple of plates and cutlery to set the table.

Jess appeared within seconds, wearing her bathrobe and with a towel wrapped around her head. Somehow, she had been able to wash the black circles from her eyes. She looked much more refreshed than I felt after my shower.

We sat down and I hesitated at first, and then rushed in. "How did it start?"

She nibbled on a piece of toast and peered directly into my eyes. "My internship."

I scoffed. "Bookies don't have interns."

Jess sighed and poured me a glass of orange juice. "Are you going to listen?"

I nodded and gulped the OJ.

"Good. Richard, my boss when I first started as an intern, introduced me to his brother because he said I had a way with people and numbers. They needed someone to talk to their clients—someone who wouldn't raise red flags when he or she popped into an office for an appointment. Secretaries don't notice me. If you send in a guy named Guido with arms bursting through a shirt, heads turn. Me, I go in, I work out terms, and then I leave. Sometimes, I collect payments, but mostly I crunch the numbers."

"Crunch the numbers?"

"Work out payment plans. Many of the guys owed small amounts, lost too much at poker the night before, but didn't have the cash on them. Some didn't want to withdraw too much at a time or their wives would notice. I helped work out terms that were agreeable for both sides."

"So, no baseball bats or crushing fingers?"

"Of course not. You can't do that shit in this town."

Her tone didn't set me at ease, and I think she noticed that. "Seriously, Paige, this was small-time stuff. A few hundred bucks here and there. Richard and his brother are reasonable."

"What happened with Davie? How did that go so wrong if they're so reasonable?"

A dark shadow seemed to loom over Jess as she walked over to the coffeemaker to refill her cup. "Davie began to cause problems. He started gambling in the hope he'd win enough to pay for his son's medical bills. At first, it worked brilliantly."

She leaned against the counter and took a long swallow of coffee.

"But his luck ran out."

"You could say that, but the bastard thought it would come back. He started hitting the tables day and night. All of us tried to convince him to stop. Even Wesley."

"Wesley?"

"Wesley learned about my ... job. And he made me introduce him to some of the guys. He had this notion that he was a high roller."

I rolled my eyes. "Does Mel know?"

She nodded.

"All those times when Mel was whispering to you, it wasn't because she felt guilty about not telling my parents ... it was about Weasel."

She nodded again.

"It must be hard to keep all of it straight," I said bitterly.

Jess fixed me with a look, but didn't respond.

I motioned with my hand. "Go on. Tell me the rest."

"Wesley and Davie kept getting in over their heads. I bailed Wes out a few times and then had him cut off. No matter how hard we tried, we could not keep Davie away. That's when Davie came up with an idea."

"What?" I demanded.

"A strike. Do you remember when you ran into him the first time? Here?"

I nodded.

"He was trying to get hold of Wesley to convince him not to pay his debt. He wanted everyone not to pay their debts. He wanted"—she looked around—"Better payment terms."

"The Norma Rae of gambling? You've got to be kidding!"

"Yes! Ridiculous!" She refilled her cup again, and I started to wonder when she had last slept. "I really tried to talk to Davie. I knew about his son, and I wanted to help. He didn't know it, but I had paid off some of his debt so Richard would back down a little. But when Davie tried getting everyone to refuse to pay, he had to be dealt with."

"The fundraiser you set up, that was a scam?" I crossed my arms.

"No. Well, yes. I knew he would raise more than he owed. He raised a lot more than he owed, but I had to take a cut. There was talk that …"

She looked away.

"The friendly bookies were going to call in Guido," I stated bluntly.

"Yes. Davie has a wife, two daughters, and his son. I couldn't just turn my back and let it happen. So I took half of what he owed and I paid the rest with my money. The morning he came here, his debt was paid. Nothing was going to happen to him. When I answered the door, I thought it would be Richard, who wanted the money right away. He was tired of dealing with the fuck."

The word shocked me. I had never heard Jess use it.

"That guy who came here, when Dr. Steve was …" I motioned to my wrist. "That was Guido?"

She shook her head. "No. Richard. He came to check on me and to see if you were all right. I know you think otherwise, but he's a nice guy."

"Yet he's sending Guido after Davie."

Jess fidgeted and repositioned her legs. "No. They decided to let it go."

"How did you convince them to do that?" I looked at her, stunned.

"Leverage."

I groaned. "Do I want to know?"

"I wish you wouldn't ask," she confessed, as she stared at her penguin slippers.

I lowered my head and glared into her eyes.

"I told Richard that you would inform your father about his 'business.'"

"And that stopped him?"

"Paige, everyone knows your dad. Everyone is scared shitless of him." She set her cup down and crossed her arms. "Besides, I gave them the rest of the money. As far as everyone is concerned, the debt is paid, and every dealer in town knows not to let Davie sit at one of their tables."

I picked at my bandage, deep in thought. "And you?"

"Oh, and me?" She reached into her purse and pulled out a cigarette. After lighting it and inhaling deeply, she said, "I'm unemployed. I knew when I used my card that I was done. Let's just say I tendered my resignation, effective immediately."

"When did you start smoking?"

She rummaged in the cabinet above her fridge and pulled out an ashtray. "I quit when we started dating. Lately, however, I've been craving one." She sucked again, and then slowly blew out the smoke. "Damn, I've missed it."

"Can I have one?"

She looked at her feet, and then shrugged. "Sure, why not?"

I pulled a cigarette from her silver case and she flicked open her Zippo. "Take a deep breath. Good, now exhale."

I had expected to cough, but surprisingly, it felt good. Some of the tension in my shoulders released. I took another drag.

She set the case and ashtray down in front of me. The initials on the case were hers. "A gift," she said, in answer to my unspoken question.

"There's a lot I don't know about you, isn't there?"

Jess opened her mouth, but swallowed her words.

"I guess you could say the same about me." I finished her thought.

"I've learned a lot in the past few months, Paige." She stubbed out her cigarette and lit another.

"Really, what's that?"

"Circumstances. All of us try to live with the life we are dealt. You, Alex, Abbie, and your parents. Me being an orphan. We all try to get by the best we can."

For several minutes we sat silently at the table, smoking.

"What's next?" I broke the silence.

"I spoke to Julia last week. She wants to open a second restaurant and have me run it. I wasn't going to take her up on it, but

Marionette

I think I might, at least until I can save enough money to pay for grad school."

"That's good." I looked down at my hand holding the cigarette. The smoke swirled towards Jess. I waved it out of her face.

"That wasn't what you were talking about, was it?"

I shook my head.

"I don't know what's next with us." She exhaled, smoke billowing around her.

I took another drag of my cigarette and then stubbed it out clumsily. Pushing my chair back, I cringed at the sound it made on the linoleum. "I need to lie down."

When I passed her, she lowered her head.

"When's the last time you slept?" I asked.

"Don't know, really. Can't shut my mind off." She went to grab another cigarette, but I stopped her.

"Take one of my pills. You won't be able to stay awake."

I climbed under the covers and nestled down into the cold sheets. Jess followed minutes later and settled on the other side, careful not to invade my space. I wasn't sure it would be possible for either of us to breach the chasm.

"You may not want to hear this, but I did it for you, Paige. For us."

I stared out the window. "I know, Jess. I know."

The pill I took before getting into bed started to kick in, silencing my racing thoughts.

Chapter Twenty-Six

BIRDS SANG OUTSIDE the window, and a ray of light fell on my face. I sat up, holding my wrist to appease the ache. Jess was still snoring. Several minutes passed before I realized what my next move should be. I crept to the kitchen and fished a business card from my wallet.

Dialing the number, I leaned around the wall to ensure Jess was still sound asleep.

"Hello."

I whispered, "May I speak to Liddy?"

"Speaking." Her voice sounded heavy with sleep.

"I'm sorry I woke you, but I need to talk to you."

"Paige, is that you?"

"Yes."

"Are you okay?"

"It's not what you think." Then I looked at my wrist. How was I going to explain that? "I … just need to talk."

"Okay. Where can I meet you? The office is closed today."

"Can I come there?"

Liddy hesitated. Then she agreed and gave me her address. I

Marionette

hung up the phone, grabbed my wallet, and then saw Jess's cigarettes. After taking a couple from the case, I left the apartment.

The drive to Liddy's didn't take long—or maybe it did; my mind was in a fog, probably the pills for my wrist.

Liddy opened the door, took one look at my wrist, and then gasped. "Oh my God, are you all right?"

I started to cry. Liddy wrapped an arm around me and led me inside. After sitting me down on the couch, she left me for a couple of minutes and then returned with two cups of tea. I took one of the mugs gratefully and held it close to my chest.

"Please tell me what happened to your wrist." Her tone was commanding but polite.

"Davie."

"Davie? Jess's friend." She sat on the chair next to the couch.

I looked up to see if she had a notepad and pencil, but she only held her teacup. "Where to begin?"

"You know me, Paige, I like to start at the beginning." She smiled.

I told her all of it. Jess. Davie. Richard. By the time I finished, I had polished off three cups of tea and a turkey sandwich.

When I stopped talking, Liddy sucked in air but didn't speak. Then the doorbell rang. She looked scared, and I wondered if she expected Guido to crash into her home with an Uzi.

Liddy stood up to get the door, and I stayed put on the couch. I could hear muffled voices, but couldn't make out who was talking or what was being said. Then I saw Jess walk into the room. The directions! I had left the directions I'd written down on the kitchen counter. Once I wrote something down on paper, I had it memorized.

"Hi," was all I could muster.

Liddy followed Jess into the room. "Why don't I make some

more tea?" She disappeared around the wall.

Jess didn't stay with me. She followed Liddy into the kitchen. Was she defending herself?

Both of them soon reappeared looking nervous as hell.

"What happened? Is Davie okay?" I demanded from Jess.

Liddy answered, "That's not why she's here."

I turned to Liddy. "What's going on? Something happened?"

"Paige—" Jess stopped abruptly.

Liddy looked down at the carpet. "Paige, I don't know how to tell you this."

"What?" I screamed.

"Your parents—"

I whirled around to look behind me, expecting to see them there with hulking men in white coats to haul me away.

"No," Liddy said. "They aren't here."

"What, then! Tell me!"

Jess sat down next to me and took my hand in hers. "Honey, they're dead."

Everything went black.

CHAPTER TWENTY-SEVEN

I OPENED MY eyes to find Jess and Liddy leaning over me.

Jess smiled. "Hey there."

Liddy sat down next to me, and Jess sat on the other side.

I rubbed my eyes, wincing when my chin brushed against my wrist.

"Do you need something for the pain?" asked Liddy.

"No. It only hurts if I nudge it."

"How about your neck? The bruise is really starting to show."

I ran my fingers over it gently and felt the scratch marks. "No, it's fine."

I turned to Jess. "Tell me, please. Wh-what happened?"

"It appears that Abbie—"

I cut her off. "Abbie? Is she okay?"

"She's in the hospital."

"What happened? A car accident?" Had Abbie come home early for Christmas?

"No, Paige. This isn't going to be easy to hear, so let me tell you all that I know."

I braced for the news. Jess took a deep breath and then let out a torrent of words. "Abbie is in the hospital. She's been shot. It seems that your father shot her."

Jess paused and locked her eyes on mine. "He was defending himself … Abbie had a gun."

I turned to Liddy, who just nodded.

Jess continued, "Abbie shot your parents, Paige. She confessed to the cops when they arrived. It's all over the news."

I looked to the blank TV in the hope I would find my answer, but I didn't. "Why?"

"*That* I don't know."

"What next?" my voice croaked.

Both of them shook their heads in unison.

"Is she going to be okay?"

"She's in intensive care," said Liddy.

"I want to see her."

Jess fidgeted. "She's surrounded by police. I don't know if they'll let you in."

Liddy stood up. "Let me make a few calls, Paige. I know the chief of staff at the hospital."

I nodded my thanks.

Jess and I sat on the couch and I rested my head on her shoulder. "This has been the weirdest few days."

She ran her fingers through my hair. Liddy came back into the room and announced, "It's all set, and the police would like to talk to you."

The news didn't shock me at all. "Okay."

"I think you should go to the station first. I'll go with you," said Liddy.

Jess hopped off the couch. "Me too."

Marionette

I turned to Jess. "What if they ask where I've been? I don't think you should be there."

"Don't be ridiculous, Paige. They don't suspect you, and I'm your alibi anyhow."

Jess being around the police made me nervous, but the look on her face made me acquiesce.

As it turned out, I had no reason to worry. The police only asked me about Abbie. Her frame of mind? When I had last heard from her? How close we were? So many people believe in the twin connection. I think they expected me to confess that I had felt it when she snapped, and did nothing to prevent it. It became apparent that they didn't like my father. I was too stunned to show much emotion either way.

Jess and Liddy were waiting for me in the hallway when I finished. Before I knew it, we were leaving the police station. A pack of reporters was waiting outside. The constant camera flashes blinded me. If my father had still been alive, this media circus would have been averted. The thought almost made me smile. Instead, I tucked my head down, pulled my collar up, and slid into the backseat of Liddy's car.

The chief of staff arranged for us to arrive via the hospital employee entrance, so we avoided the police and reporters outside. A nurse led me into Abbie's room, where a police officer sat in the corner reading a newspaper. Abbie lay in the hospital bed, hooked up to several machines. The cop must have recognized me, because he picked up his coffee and stepped out into the hallway. I pulled his chair over and sat next to Abbie. I took her hand. She didn't respond. A nurse came in, checked her chart, glanced in my direction, and then left.

I sat with Abbie for hours, hoping she would wake. She never did.

Chapter Twenty-Eight

THE NEXT WEEK passed like a bad dream. Each day, I visited Abbie. Each day, I found her in the same condition. The same cop would get up and leave. The same nurse would come in and check on her. Jess stayed with me in town, but Liddy had other clients to take care of. Each night, I called Liddy to check in. She said it was so she could say hi, but I knew she wanted to know that I was still breathing.

Abbie's medical team approached me on the sixth day and asked about a DNR: Do Not Resuscitate. The entire time she'd been in the hospital, not once had she opened her eyes. Not once had she breathed on her own. The machines did it all. They wanted to know if I was ready to let her die. I didn't want to make that decision, but I was the only one left.

The only survivor of the once-great Alexander family.

My father's lawyer showed up at the hospital. I was to inherit fifteen million dollars. I told him I didn't want it. He looked at me like I was insane, and then said something about me being in shock and that he would talk to me later.

I hated that money. It was dirty money—every cent of it. My

father cheated to get it. Then he used it to control all of us. That money was the cause of all this suffering. And too many deaths.

However, the doctors wouldn't go away like my father's lawyer. Abbie was never going to wake up, they said. I knew that even if she did, she would be tried and convicted for murdering our parents. They didn't say that, but it was implied. What choice did I have?

I signed the DNR, and then I didn't leave Abbie's side until she was gone.

It was Christmas Eve.

After all of the funerals and the media frenzy, Jess and I boarded a plane to pack up Abbie's apartment on the East Coast. Abbie had chosen a small school, just like I had. However, hers had been even farther away from home. *Had she hated everyone knowing that she was an Alexander?* I wondered. Of course, it would be hard for people to forget her now. The rich heiress who went berserk and murdered her parents. How long until a made-for-TV movie aired?

My picture was plastered over every newspaper too, with the headline: ALEXANDER SURVIVOR TO INHERIT MILLIONS!

Survivor. I wasn't even at the house when it all happened, but that detail was usually left out of the articles. Instead, millions of people thought I was there for the horrific event. When people looked at me, their eyes were filled with pity. But some looked at me accusingly, as if I had been in on it with Abbie and had left her to take the fall.

I wasn't prepared for Abbie's dorm room. Newspaper and magazine articles were strewn about. The same stories I had tracked down over the past few months. Not once had I thought that Abbie might have been going through the same hell as me. All I had been able to focus on was Alex. Alex's death. My mother's threat. Abbie never entered my mind. I had forgotten or ignored the sister who was still alive. My twin.

We boxed everything up and took it to the condo we rented for a week. All of her clothes and furniture we donated to a battered women's shelter. All that I kept were her papers. That first night, I read her diary. She had begun it when she was approached by the wife of the reporter who had been mysteriously killed. She was also a reporter, and was following up on her husband's lead about my father. Both reporters knew that I had taken care of my mother during my childhood and neither had approached me.

Abbie had hired a private investigator. Even though I had been living in fear of my parents, part of me had hoped that my mom's drunken confession was fictional. The P.I. didn't find concrete proof, but he made the same connections as the reporter and they matched what I had concluded. And he tracked down the sister of Alex's friend—the one who had given Alex the heroin when she was in rehab. He had left a suicide note explaining what he had done, how much he'd been paid to slip Alex the tainted drug. The friend had thought he was being followed, and he had ended it. The family never came forward, and they'd burned the note out of fear of my father.

Abbie's diary read like a thriller. Each entry revealed a new piece to the puzzle. Most importantly, it revealed how guilty she had felt all of her life about the Lego incident. Abbie may not have slit her wrists like I had, but she was much worse off than me, I soon realized. All of her life, she had been jealous over my friendship with Alex. I had never realized how alone Abbie was in the world. Being an Alexander cut her off from everyone. She had no one to turn to. She hated Alex. She hated me. Then when she found out what our father had done, and what our mother had done … The manipulation had driven her mad. Abbie couldn't live with it.

In the last entry of the diary, Abbie stated she was going to correct the wrongs that had been done. Retribution. I set the diary aside and thought of the white tulip I had seen at Alex's grave. Had Abbie gone there asking for forgiveness?

Later that night, while Jess slept, I fed each page of Abbie's diary into the fire. Then I burned all of the evidence. By the time I went to bed, nothing remained. All I kept was a necklace with a locket. Opening it, I was surprised to find that it was empty. No matter, I put the necklace on and lay down next to Jess, deciding what my next move should be. Then it hit me.

Time to disappear.

Epilogue

I WAS SITTING at the table, a book in one hand and a pulled pork sandwich in another, when I heard the bell on the front door tinkle.

"Paige!" Karen shouted, and darted towards me. Following her, Tom and Jake strolled over and each gave me a bear hug, lifting me off the ground.

"How was the drive?" I asked.

"Long!" Karen sank down into a chair as if she had just completed a marathon.

I laughed and turned to the boys. "I see she still has a penchant for drama."

"Oh, you know Karen." Jake mussed the hair on top of her head.

"Sit down, you two. You must be famished. Let me get you something to eat." Before I entered the swinging doors to the kitchen, I heard Tom shout for some beers.

When I returned with the tray, Karen asked, "How do you like owning your own restaurant?"

I gazed around at my small place. "You know, it's not how I envisioned my life, but now, I wouldn't have it any other way."

Marionette

"And Louisiana? You like it here?" Tom pinned me with a look.

"It gets hot and humid in the summer, but people leave me alone for the most part. At first, when I opened this place"— I spread my arms out—"they thought I was mad. An outsider opening a BBQ joint just outside of New Orleans—many were outright insulted. My first week, I didn't charge customers a cent. Then, word spread. And now they come in droves. You just missed the lunch rush. The madder they think you are, the more you fit in around here."

"Is it just you here?" Karen looked about the deserted restaurant to confirm her suspicions.

"Yeah. We close down after the lunch rush. Not too much traffic in these parts around dinnertime. The rest of my staff went home already. I like this time of day. It's so quiet. Almost every afternoon you can find me here, reading a book."

Waiting.

"So that's your truck in the lot." Tom pointed to my beat-up '74 Ford.

"Yep."

Karen looked over her shoulder. "That jalopy? It's probably older than you."

"Nah, we're the same age." I looked at Tom's Jag next to my beater. "How you liking the car, Tom?"

He smiled guiltily. "It's a little nicer than your new old vehicle."

"Trust me, they would run me out of town if I drove around in a Jaguar."

Jake pulled a photo album from his bag. "We thought you might like to see some of the kids."

Mr. Alexander's lawyer was right: I had ended up wanting my inheritance—just not for myself.

With Liddy's help, I had opened a home for runaway and

abused kids. Jake finished his degree last year and has taken over the day-to-day operations. Liddy sits on the board, along with my lawyer and Jake, and Tom works as an intern there. When he graduates, he'll join the board and help run the place. The first year, we had three kids. Now we had more than a dozen. And I wanted to help more. No child should feel as if they have no one to turn to.

I fingered Abbie's locket, which now contained photos of both my sisters.

I flipped through some of the pages, stopping when I saw a photo of Liddy.

Two years. I had disappeared two years ago.

Liddy had her arm around a young man who couldn't have been much older than fifteen. Both of them were smiling, and both wore Santa hats.

The next photo was of Mel and a young girl. Weasel stood off to the side, looking awkward and annoyed. When Mel had dumped him, he'd decided to clean up his act, attending Gamblers Anonymous meetings. From what I hear, he is turning out to be a semi-respectable person, but I still think of him as a weasel.

I stared at the boys sitting across from me, who had become men during my absence. Even Karen, with her curly mop of hair, looked a little older, a little wiser.

"You coming home for Audrey's wedding?" asked Karen.

I shook my head. "I don't think that would be wise. I can't believe it: Minnie dumping her boyfriend and then marrying a bloke she's only dated for four months. She's not pregnant, is she?" I joked.

Karen guffawed. "Nope. Still a virgin."

"Good for her. I hear the guy's nice."

"A male Pollyanna if I ever met one," stated Tom. "They're perfect for each other."

Marionette

None of us ever brought up Aaron. He was in prison for what I hoped would be a very long time. To be honest, I'd never had the heart to follow the trial. By that time, I was through with drama.

Jenna had transferred to a different school and was finally a member of a winning team. Unfortunately, she sat on the bench most of the time, and I'm sure she bitched about that every day.

The sound of a truck brought me back to the here and now. It was the one I had been waiting for, the one I waited for each day around this time. I swallowed some beer as the tires came to a screeching halt, kicking up gravel from the lot. The door opened with a horrendous creak. Then I heard the kick. Every day, she kicked that old truck door shut; otherwise it wouldn't close all the way. Her tiny footprint was permanently embedded in the door. She never bothered locking it; neither of us locked our trucks. Our insurance policy was worth more than the actual vehicles.

I watched as she opened the door with one hand, balancing a stack of books in the other. My three guests jumped up to greet her, and after the ceremonious hugging and exchange of greetings, she slid onto the seat next to me, grabbed my beer and took a generous swig.

She wore her favorite Tulane shirt, proudly stating she was an MBA nerd.

"How was school, sweetheart?" I gave her a peck on the cheek.

Jess smiled. "Thrilling."

I rolled my eyes and looked to our friends. "She's the only person I know who gets excited when she sees a spreadsheet."

Everyone laughed, except Jess, who feigned being hurt.

"To friends," Karen said, raising her glass.

We all clinked our glasses. "To friends."

I stared at the sign over the bar. *To absent friends.* Silently, I toasted my sisters. No one ever asked why I had named the place The Two Sisters. Those who knew me, understood. Those who didn't, assumed Jess and I were sisters.

We lived off the money we made from the restaurant, and everything we had was ours. I didn't owe anyone. It felt good to be an Average Joe in the world. No society pages. No reporters. No one gave a fuck about me—except for Jess and my friends.

I wasn't rich, but I was happy. I had done it. I had escaped. Had disappeared. Finally, I could live my life on my terms

Jess squeezed my leg, bringing my attention back to our guests.

"Who's up for hitting the town? Tom you won't believe this, but you can walk around the French Quarter with an open beer." I stood to clear the dishes.

Jess lit a cigarette. "I bet we can track down some Cuban cigars for you boys this weekend."

Jake looked pleased, but Tom started to turn green.

On my way back from the kitchen, I said, "And, Karen, southern men are charmers. Maybe we can finally track down a boyfriend for you."

Jess swatted my arm. "Play nice, Paige."

"Besides, I already have one." Karen stuck out her tongue.

I fell into my chair, dumbstruck. "What's going to happen next?" I asked.

And for the first time, the thought didn't scare me.

Author's Note

Thank you for reading *Marionette*. If you enjoyed the novel, please consider leaving a review on Goodreads or Amazon. No matter how long or short, I would very much appreciate your feedback. You can follow me, T. B. Markinson, on twitter at @50YearProject or email me at tbmarkinson@gmail.com. I would love to know your thoughts.

Acknowledgments

I would like to thank my editor, Karin Cox. I am extremely grateful for all the hours she spent hunting for all of my mistakes and for her wonderful suggestions on how to improve the final product. Thank you to my beta readers who assisted me in the early stages. Two of my blog buddies hunted down typos with gusto and their commitment is much appreciated. Lastly, my sincerest thanks goes to my partner. Without her support and encouragement this novel would not exist.

About the Author

T. B. Markinson is an American writer living in England. When she isn't writing, she's traveling the world, watching sports on the telly, visiting pubs, or taking the dog for a walk. Not necessarily in that order.

Printed by Amazon Italia Logistica S.r.l.
Torrazza Piemonte (TO), Italy